Time Will Tell

Time Will Tell

by
Donald Greig

THAMES RIVER PRESS

Time Will Tell

THAMES RIVER PRESS
An imprint of Wimbledon Publishing Company Limited (WPC)
Another imprint of WPC is Anthem Press (www.anthempress.com)

First published in the United Kingdom in 2012 by

THAMES RIVER PRESS
75-76 Blackfriars Road
London SE1 8HA

www.thamesriverpress.com

All the characters and events described in this book are imaginary
and any similarity with real people or events is purely coincidental.

A CIP record for this book is available from the British Library.

ISBN 978-0-85728-624-6

History is the witness that testifies to the passing of time; it illumines reality, vitalizes memory, provides guidance in daily life, and brings us tidings of antiquity.

Marcus Tullius Cicero, *Pro Publio Sestio*, II, 36

And if the whole world's singing your songs
[...]
Just remember what was yours is everyone's from now on

Wilco, *What Light*

For Tessa, of course...

CHAPTER 1

The Memoirs of Geoffroy Chiron: Prologue *ed. Francis Porter*[1]

Frevier 6, 1524

Josquin was a prick. Everybody thought so.

'When I die,' Jehan once said, 'they'll probably ask him to write a lament for me. And he'll do it, the hypocrite. He's never said anything good about anyone his whole life.'

For Jehan to call anyone a hypocrite was strong language indeed. I liked Ockeghem; he was my friend, though I wasn't the only one who was encouraged to call him by his first name: it was always Johannes, or Jehan, never Ockeghem.

'No one can spell Ockeghem,' he once told me, 'so I've given up trying to correct them.'

And, of course, when Jehan died it was Desprez who wrote that beautiful lament. Even then, having written an apparently heartfelt and undoubtedly beautiful testament, Desprez's sarcasm and contempt for others was never far away.

It was written to be sung by five of us: me – Geoffroy Chiron – his friend; Loyset Compère, the composer whom Josquin rated above all others, and everyone else

---

Translator's note. In the interests of maintaining the flow of Geoffroy Chiron's account, I have chosen to avoid the use of footnotes and render his (very) occasional obscenities in forthright Anglo-Saxon equivalents. Chiron's background as a singer is nowhere more evident than in his quotations from the Psalms, which I have transcribed as they appear in his text, then adding my own punctuation and translations from the Rheims-Douay Bible. All other translations are my own. In many cases, Chiron's fading memory proves unreliable. Where dates of significant events can be corroborated I have provided them in square parentheses. As with all academic endeavour, I can claim copyright only on errors. To paraphrase Chiron, they are mine and mine alone. © 2012 Francis Porter *thought merely good; Pierre Perchon, known as De La Rue by the Northerners; Antoine Brumel, the pederast who soon would be in charge of the Notre Dame choirboys (a post that suited him down to the ground); and Josquin Desprez himself, the greatest of all the new composers and the biggest arsehole you could ever hope to meet.*

All of us were accomplished singers with the obvious exception of Compère. In his early years he'd been able to get away with it, but he could never sing fast notes and often ended up on the slow cantus firmus lines, despite reading music as if it were his native language. Burying his voice in the middle of the texture was one way to mask the rough tone; when we looked at the draft Desprez had prepared, it was obvious who would sing which part.

Desprez bustled into the schola cantorum *[song school] where we had agreed to meet, late as usual, and threw the copy onto the stand, shouting out instructions with nary a hello or an embrace. Then he counted us in and off we went. It was, inevitably, stunning, even at the first attempt. We were all touched that he'd covered up Loyset's inadequacies by giving him that simple tenor line with the requiem text itself. The rest of us sang the familiar words of Jehan Molinet's poem (we'd all agreed that it should be that text and no other) and Loyset blended as well as he could. The black notation Josquin had used, the seriousness of the occasion, and the beautiful balance he had created distracted us from looking too closely at what others were doing. That's why we didn't see what was coming.*

The final section that named the four great composers gave Loyset time off before the final Requiescant in pace *and* Amen, *yet, despite this contrived recovery period, he began to look worried. I soon realised why. Over the years Loyset's range had shrunk to one hexachord, which had been all that was required of him until now. Unaccountably his part leapt up an octave at the very moment when we were to invoke peace for the departed and sing our Amen in descending phrases, trailing away to nothing. Poor old Loyset had to sing a note he'd scarcely been able to get before his balls had dropped and which he now could probably have reached only if His Holiness himself had ordered them to be cut off. It was a terrible noise and brought to mind that ditty in which Loyset's voice was compared to the sound of a cat up a tree. I think it was Brumel who first giggled, a stifled, high-pitched squeak. Perchon snorted his derision, accompanied by a gob of snot that splattered onto the manuscript, by which time I'd also stopped singing and Loyset, scared as he was of Desprez, decided that laughter was his best defence.*

And so the piece fell apart, leaving Desprez singing on his own, his small, angry, dark eyes even sterner than usual. He cursed, pulled the manuscript from the stand, wiped the snot off with his sleeve, and stormed out. And that was why we ended up singing a three-part Mass at Jehan's memorial in the church of St Martin of Tours, and why it was Jehan Molinet himself who read the poem as a tribute, rather than us singing that sweet musical setting.

The rumour went round soon thereafter that, as with many of Desprez's pieces, he was insecure about it and didn't want it performed in the first place: that what he was really doing was finding an excuse to pull out of the commission by staging a scene. I didn't really believe that and I'm not the only one who thinks the main reason he wrote it that way was to humiliate Loyset. Certainly I don't think there was anything wrong with the first draft we sang and, although I can't swear to it, I think it was exactly the same as the one printed by the Italian, Petrucci, some years later [1508].

Deus qui das vindictas mihi et congregas populos sub me qui servas me ab inimicis meis. Et a resistentibus mihi elevas me a viro iniquo libera me. Propterea confitebor tibi in gentibus Domine et nomini tuo cantabo

[O God, who avengest me, and subduest the people under me, my deliverer from my enraged enemies. And thou wilt lift me up above them that rise up against me: from the unjust man thou wilt deliver me. Therefore will I give glory to thee, O Lord, among the nations, and I will sing a psalm to thy name.]

I'm sorry. I shouldn't have begun like that, but I had to unburden myself. Time is no longer my friend. Just this morning the doctor came to bleed my legs and, judging by his manner, I may not have long to live.

Desprez was as talented as he was troubled and if only he could have trusted in the abilities that the Lord God gave him, all of us – and I include Desprez himself – might have had a more enjoyable life.

Many things have changed: the King and his court no longer reside here in Tours but in Paris; Loyset Compère and Josquin Desprez are both dead. A new era beckons and it is time to pay homage to the old one. So forgive my outburst and let me begin again, more calmly and appropriately to my subject: the life of Jehan Ockeghem, my mentor and patron in music and civil law, and the man whom I and many others have come to think of as our bon père, *the man who composed the grandest of all motets, his* Miserere mei.

CHAPTER 2

The line of passengers up ahead in the Coach cabin stuttered and then stopped, and Andrew Eiger found himself in the First Class section, standing between two businessmen who were sipping on sparkling wine and chatting across the aisle. It was a relaxed, communal atmosphere here, where shared assumptions of warranted self-importance spawned easy, casual friendships. No wonder they called it 'Club Class' in Europe, thought Andrew, as he passed through the curtains towards his seat: 20C. His travel agent had assured him he would be in the emergency exit row, but the frantic late check-in meant he'd lost his preferred seat and had to settle for second best. He hoped there would be no one reclining too far into his personal space, preventing him from working.

The plane looked to be quite empty. All the children were aboard, seated mainly to the front of the cabin where their crying would not disturb him. It reminded him of the trip to Karen's mother in Florida when he'd held John on take-off. The poor boy, already suffering from a cold, was fractious and fidgety, and the ascent and subsequent decompression had hurt his ears. As usual he seemed to find his father little comfort; yet Andrew was determined that, on this occasion at least, he would offer the same kind of meaningless assurances as the boy's mother might. When the fourth passenger had turned around and glared, however, he had given in to the inevitable and passed John into Karen's welcoming arms.

His itinerary for the next twenty-four hours was considerably more exhausting than it had been on that occasion. Ahead lay flights from Columbus to New York, then the red-eye to London's Heathrow, followed by a third short flight to Paris and finally a train to Tours. As if that wasn't enough, once he'd arrived he was to deliver a lecture, attend a concert in the evening by the early music group Beyond Compère, and then meet with them afterwards to discuss what he'd cryptically (and he hoped enticingly) described as 'an exciting collaboration'.

The lecture he could cope with – all he had to do was read it out loud – and the only demand of the evening's entertainment was to stay awake, jetlagged and sleep-deprived as he would be. The meeting after the concert, though, would require his full concentration, being more important than any job interview. He had to convince Emma Mitchell and the singers of Beyond Compère to commit themselves to the first modern-day performance of a piece that he'd discovered. Upon it depended his imagined new life, the fantasy of which he'd refined over the past six months since the moment he'd discovered the manuscript stuffed into the spine of the leather-bound book in the archives of Amiens Cathedral.

An elderly woman was sitting in his seat.

'Er, I think I might be sitting there.' He held out his boarding stub for her to see. 'Perhaps you're in another?'

She looked up sharply, avoiding his gaze and seeking the seat numbers overhead.

'20C.' Andrew pointed at the numbers printed next to the "Fasten Seatbelt" sign. '20C,' he repeated, showing her the stub once more. The woman glanced down at her lap, unclasped the catch on her handbag, and began to search inside.

'Is everything all right, madam?' asked the stewardess.

Immediately Andrew offered his defence, peeved by the assumption that the occupant of his seat was correct and that it was he who was mistaken.

'The, um, the lady here is in my seat. 20C. So I was just letting her know. I need to work. That's why I got the aisle.'

'Of course, sir. I'm sure we can resolve this,' said the stewardess with a fixed, ingratiating smile that softened considerably as she leaned towards the old woman.

'It's here somewhere,' said the old woman, raking through tissues, powder compacts, and sweet wrappers. 'I had it earlier.'

Andrew leaned into the emergency exit seat as someone brushed past, and nonchalantly held his boarding slip directly in the stewardess's line of sight. *Here's the documentary evidence*, he wanted to say; *this is what you need to consider, not the woman's unreliable memory*. If the airline had made a mistake and double-booked them in the same seat, then he would insist on an aisle seat somewhere else. In First, if necessary. He couldn't possibly work in the window seat; he'd be too cramped. And he *had* to work. Although he'd written the lecture for tomorrow, he needed to tidy up the text and add something that had come up that very day in his 'Medieval and Renaissance Music' class.

'Here it is,' cried the old woman, triumphantly holding up her boarding pass.

'There you go.' The stewardess scanned it quickly. 'Ah, 28C.'

Despite there being no acknowledgement of his innocence, Andrew was relieved that he would not have to take the matter any further.

'Your seat is further back, but I'm sure the gentleman wouldn't mind switching, seeing as how you're settled and all.' The stewardess turned to him and smiled, a little too sweetly for his liking.

'Well, um, actually, I did choose this particular seat. For good reason. I wanted to be in a seat where the one in front couldn't recline too far and stop me from working. I've got to work, you see. I have to give a lecture. In Tours. France. Tomorrow. Well, less

than tomorrow really. Less than twenty-four hours from now, anyway. So, you see…'
He shrugged in a way that he hoped expressed mutual agreement but, judging by the
two women's reactions, he'd failed to convince them.

'Well, if that's the way you feel…' The stewardess kept the final part of her sentence
to herself.

'Yes,' added the old woman, in an aggressive endorsement of the stewardess's
unspoken criticism. Grabbing the back of the chair on which he was leaning, she
heaved herself up unsteadily – and, in Andrew's opinion, over-dramatically. His field of
vision was filled momentarily with a cloud of grey hair, and he jerked back just in time,
narrowly avoiding a head butt from the old woman. Caught off-balance, he grabbed
the open locker overhead and the tines of the lock bit deeply into his palm, drawing
blood. He cried out in pain and the stewardess, who was leading the old woman to the
back of the plane, turned around.

'There's no need for melodrama, sir,' she said tartly. 'You've got your seat. And I
don't think it would have been too much trouble for you to sit somewhere else. I'll bring
you a form if you want to make a complaint.' She turned on her heel and wrapped a
consoling arm around the woman who was shaking her head and muttering.

Andrew examined his palm: two puncture wounds from the metal lock, as if an
animal had sunk its fangs into his right hand. He was sucking the wound to staunch
the bleeding when he became aware of a younger woman standing close to him, peering
hopefully at the number above his seat.

'I'm…' she said, indicating the window seat. He let her through and then took his
own seat. It was still warm from the previous occupant and he reached up with his
damaged hand to shut off the narrow jet of accusatory air pointed at his face. The
incident had left him feeling unfairly treated. Should he complain? Or, perhaps better
than that, he could get his wife to write a letter for him. Early in their relationship,
Karen had entrusted him to deal with everyday bureaucratic mismanagements. Thus
problems were his to solve, and compensation for him to pursue – but he'd proved
himself inadequate at both tasks. He always seemed to rub people up the wrong
way, his tone pitched uncertainly between exaggerated grievance and obsequious
inadequacy, whereas his wife, trained in psychology, possessed some magical insight
into human behaviour as well as reserves of feminine empathy which endeared her
to most service industry workers and assured willing reparation. Nowadays, with his
wife acting as nominal head of the family, they received due apology together with
the occasional upgrade and Andrew found himself wanting mistakes to be made
so Karen could apply herself and corrective forces be summoned. His role in such
situations was to stand haplessly behind her, not so much a silent supporter as a
symbol of her misfortune, a role that required no effort at all, his vacant inadequacy
apparent to all.

He'd hoped things might change when his son, John, was born. Holding the baby in his arms for the first time, tenderly, carefully, he was distracted first by the tiny, wrinkled feet. 'John,' he said. They'd known it would be a boy and had agreed on the name – coincidentally the name of Karen's paternal grandfather, and Johannes Ockeghem – but Andrew saw no likeness to either, only the eyes tightly closed against a world wherein it was his responsibility to provide safety. He knew immediately that he would protect John, would shield him from the taunting and bullying that he himself had suffered silently as a child. He felt an emotion he'd never experienced before and for which he had no name: a thick bubble of anxious love that burst inside him. And then he'd dropped the baby. He'd heard the story countless times since, first recounted by Karen to his in-laws at Thanksgiving. She'd told it with evident fondness and, for a moment, he had thought himself forgiven. He might have been, but later that evening the anecdote was picked up and circulated amongst neighbours and friends, along with crackers and onion dip ('Made with a tin of real Campbell's soup') until Andrew had almost begun to believe that the story was about somebody else. When a friend of the family had related the episode, unaware that he was telling it to the subject himself, Andrew had realised that, from this single incident, an enduring myth had been created: his childcare skills were not to be trusted. What had been lost in the re-telling was the fact that no harm had come to his son. Blinking away his misty vision, Andrew reacted as he never had in softball or football games where he was always the last to be picked – he'd caught the falling baby, who had neither murmured nor complained.

With boarding nearly complete, he was relieved that the spare seat next to him was still empty so he could spread out his papers. He felt vindicated for standing his ground.

'Howdee,' said a voice. 'Well, things are gonna get a little bit snugger now!' A heavy belly was thrust into Andrew's face as a large figure stretched up to deposit his bag in the overhead locker. The face leered down at him and a ham-like hand was proffered. Andrew offered his in return but, rather than the expected handshake, he was hoisted onto his feet, his injured palm screaming in protest.

'Sorry, fella, but I'm in there.' The red-faced man indicated the middle seat and then waggled his fingers at the woman by the window. She smiled back and retreated into her magazine. The huge man squeezed his body into the narrow confines with some difficulty and the woman turned away to accommodate the huge bulk.

'Looks like she won't be joining in the conversation then.' The man gave Andrew a conspiratorial wink. Andrew had no intention of conducting any such exchange with his new neighbour. But politeness needed to be observed, and might well be his best strategy. The space he'd momentarily envisaged had shrunk considerably and working on his laptop would be impossible; the man's broad shoulders were simply too wide for the airline seat and, with the armrest swamped by the spill of his waist and his fleshy forearms, it was impossible for Andrew to avoid physical contact. He could feel the damp warmth of the man's body gusting through his shirt, and a vague reek of socks and cheap deodorant made him wish that he'd left the air vent fully open.

'Foster. Earl Foster. But you can call me Earl,' said the man, trotting out his well-polished introduction.

'Andrew Eiger. I have a lot of work to do, so I probably won't be talking much.'

'What kind of work?' said Earl, ignoring the hint. 'I'm in sales. Extruded plastic. This kind of stuff.' With a meaty forefinger, he tapped the seat-tray and then the plastic housing for the overhead lights and air vents.

'And this stuff,' he added, tapping his head. 'Both solid. Both my business.' He chuckled at his own patter. 'You?'

'Er, musicology. The study of music, that is. Music history and music theory.' Andrew hoped for once that it sounded duller than it was, and that his career afforded his neighbour no conversational comeback.

'Hey, buddy. That used to be my thing too. Well, not the musicology bit. That was boring. To me, that is,' Earl added quickly. 'I was a music major. Trombone.'

If Earl was involved in music in any way at all, then he had to be a brass player, thought Andrew – one of the clowns of the orchestra given to drinking games and horseplay. They were the ones who offered nothing in music history classes other than the occasional supposedly witty one-liner; they were the people who laughed at early music, and medieval music in particular, the ones who thought music began when the trumpet got valves. An oaf, in other words; one who laughed at historians and theorists.

'Oh. Trombone?' Andrew tried desperately to think of some way of closing down the conversation. 'Do you still play?' he asked, hoping the answer was no.

'Sure. If you've got the money,' said Earl, laughing loudly. He slapped his broad thighs and then Andrew's knee. Andrew, who never paid much attention to the safety demonstration, found himself fervently wishing for it to begin, if only to quieten down the garrulous salesman. He reached under the seat in front and pulled out his briefcase to signal his intention to work, flicked through his papers and withdrew the conference proceedings, a copy of his lecture and the familiar blue folder.

'Please stow your briefcase right under the seat in front of you, sir.' It was the stewardess again.

'I was only…' he began. But she had swept away to the front of the cabin, closing the overhead lockers as she went.

'She got ya!' said Earl, chuckling. 'She got ya, didn't she?'

'Well, it was a bit unnecessary,' remonstrated Andrew. 'I was just about to put it away.'

The flight attendants had begun their routine, holding up seat belts and showing how to lock and unlock them. Andrew gave them his full attention, frowning in a display of exaggerated concentration, hoping it would stop his neighbour talking.

Earl shrugged his enormous shoulders making Andrew's body lurch into the aisle, then he dropped his head back on the seat and closed his eyes. By the time the safety demonstration was over and the plane had pushed back from its stand, he was snoring loudly, his mouth dropped open like the drawer of a Coke-dispenser.

From the various papers on his lap, Andrew pulled out the printed copy of his lecture. '"Ockeghem's *Katholika*: obscurity, calculation and reception" © Andrew Eiger.' The previous night he'd delivered it to a post-graduate seminar and, as he'd fully expected, it was received coolly. The title alluded to the composer's preference for musical and notational games, features which had come to define the composer's genius; it added nothing new to Ockeghem studies, nor was it going to set the conference alight, not least because, yet again, his audience was being presented with a rehash of old material from his Ph.D. It was getting to the stage where there was virtually nothing left of it, the flesh having been stripped from the bones to provide material for lectures and academic articles on so many occasions – yet still he hoped his thesis might be published as a book. His pursuit had not been helped by the appearance of what had been hailed as *the* definitive book on Ockeghem by Francis Porter, a scholar three years his junior whom Andrew viewed, with more than a trace of hopeful envy, as his chief rival. Porter had received his D.Mus. from Oxford, having graduated *summa cum laude* from Yale. His area of expertise was the same as Andrew's, in the relatively new field of reception theory, but where Andrew's thesis was a dully pedestrian, essentially chronological account, Porter's book was ground-breaking, strongly influenced by fashionable French revisionist theory, yet lucid and accessible. Entitled *Framing Music History*, it was everything that Andrew's Ph.D. was not – witty, light, insightful and graceful; it had been picked up immediately by Yale University Press and was now in its third reprint in only five years.

Andrew scanned his lecture. It began with the definition of a canon provided by Tinctoris, a musical theorist of the time, which was 'a rule showing the purpose of the composer behind a certain obscurity'. It was this opposition between design and uncertainty, between the overt and the hidden, that still divided people today, most obviously the students in his Med/Ren class. It didn't help that most of them had signed up merely because they had once heard or sung a madrigal in High School. Rather than an extended encounter with frolicking nymphs and randy shepherds singing 'Hey nonny no' and 'fa la la', they found themselves grappling with arcane subjects like isorhythms, modes, and *formes fixes*. If he'd had his way he would have avoided the madrigal entirely. To him, it was the lowest common denominator, a cheap entertainment whose musical sophistication was best compared to today's popular music, which he held in equal contempt. Behind the pastoral image lay equally ignorant assumptions of medieval music as plainchant sung by po-faced monks or simplistic folk tunes designed to entertain smelly peasants with maybe a thudding drum to liven up proceedings. Such beliefs were reinforced by terms like The Dark Ages which suggested the absence of knowledge, whereas the medieval period was rich in literature and philosophy, and peopled with multi-talented individuals like Andrew's hero, Ockeghem – composer, Treasurer of St Martin at Tours, *premier chapelain* of the royal chapel, and Baron of Châteauneuf – who should properly have been described as a Renaissance man, had the term not been hijacked for later history.

That very morning, one of his more troublesome students, Peter Giacometti, a boy who thought himself cool and who always sat at the back, had banged another nail in Ockeghem's coffin: 'I reckon this dude's problem was that he thought too much. He should have just got on with it like Josquin did.' The other students had laughed. It was the kind of line Giacometti often came up with: derisory yet, annoyingly for Andrew, a distillation of the prevailing view and, in its way, astute.

Though not a quote from a contemporary observer like Tinctoris, it echoed the common themes of Ockeghemian reception that his lecture would address – calculation and musical pleasure – and Andrew transcribed the student's comment at the top of his paper. He'd begin his talk with it, offering it as a friendly *ad lib*, a suitable antidote to his sterile delivery. And maybe, if the mood took him, he would tell his audience about how difficult it was sometimes to excite his students with Ockeghem's music: proof that Ockeghem was only for those of more refined sensibilities.

When he'd begun to teach the course four years ago, he'd started by playing a recording of *Nymphes des bois*, the lament on Ockeghem's death by the composer's own pupil, the great Josquin Desprez. The idea was, through the personal testament of the younger generation of composers, to introduce students to Ockeghem. It had backfired. The students loved the lament itself rather than its subject, and thereafter all they wanted to talk about was Josquin. He'd tried to rescue the situation by playing more Ockeghem, but with each new piece of music, accompanied by an explanation of the complex musical design, he'd only bolstered their initial reaction. He felt like a shopkeeper trying to sell vegetables to six-year-olds; however much he proclaimed the health benefits, all they wanted was candy.

These days he had stopped playing the music entirely, instead presenting a handout of *Nymphes des bois* in the original black notation, a fitting garb for Ockeghem's memorial. Thus presented, the lament yielded none of its moving sensuousness to his classes and they were forced to take as fact his assertion that Ockeghem was the greatest composer of them all. At least in Tours, surrounded by academics who had devoted a considerable portion of their academic lives to the study of the fifteenth century, he would be in the company of like-minded enthusiasts. He wouldn't have to sell Ockeghem there.

✦ ✦ ✦

February 5th, 1997: Beecham Concert Hall, Newcastle-upon-Tyne, England

As Andrew Eiger fretted over Ockeghem's place in the pantheon of medieval composers, 3,700 miles away Emma Mitchell was offstage contemplating the very piece that Andrew refused to play in his music class: Josquin Desprez's *Nymphes des bois*. Earlier, when they'd rehearsed in the unappreciative acoustic, the members of Beyond Compère had agreed that an encore wouldn't be needed: the acoustic would kill it off. Unlike large churches or cathedrals where the sound of clapping rolled in the vaulted space, rewarding the audience's appreciation with echoing encouragement, dry concert halls like this one muffled sound and gave each concertgoer the impression that he or she had been the only one who'd really enjoyed the performance, leaving all but the wilfully arrogant doubting their judgement. But now the applause showed no sign of stopping.

In the wings Emma turned to the singers to issue her instructions. Released from the concentration of performance, they were trading excited apologies for minor mistakes and observations of audience reactions, acknowledgements of a job well done.

'We'll have to do it,' said Emma over the hubbub. '*Nymphes des bois*. I'm sorry it doesn't involve everyone, but it'll make a good ending.'

Even after coming offstage having twice delivered their bows, they could still hear the audience cheering and the occasional wolf whistle.

'We're going to have to do it,' she repeated. '*Nymphes des bois*. Just the five singers. The rest come on for a final bow.'

The group split into two. The five required for the encore lined up in voice-order and walked confidently onto the stage, smiling at the audience; Emma followed, carrying the bouquet with which she'd been presented.

'Thank you,' she said loudly, as the applause died away and the audience re-took their seats. 'Thank you so much for that lovely reception. I'd love to say that we have a new piece by Ockeghem to round off the concert, but he hasn't written much recently.' The audience laughed, obviously pleased that an encore was going to be forthcoming. 'As you know,' continued Emma, 'Beyond Compère consists of eight singers – and me – yet there are only five singers here.' She gestured upstage to the smaller group.

'It's our policy when we do an encore to include everyone, but it's a special occasion. Tomorrow marks the five-hundredth anniversary of the death of Johannes Ockeghem, an event that we will commemorate in a concert tomorrow in the very place where he lived most of his life: Tours, the old capital of France. We thought it appropriate, then, to break with our usual tradition and sing a piece dedicated to the great composer: Josquin Desprez's beautiful lament on the death of Ockeghem, *Nymphes des bois*.'

Someone whistled encouragement from the audience.

'Well, I see that somebody knows it,' said Emma, prompting further laughter. 'I'll let the music speak for itself – it really is lovely – but I'll just draw your attention to the fact that the song references the four composers who may well have sung it: Josquin himself; Loyset Compère, after whom our group is named; Pierre De La Rue; and Antoine Brumel. No one knows who the fifth singer was.'

The audience applauded and Emma walked offstage to join her colleagues in the wings.

'Nice one, Em,' hissed Charlie, one of the tenors, giving her the thumbs-up. She smiled back and they turned to watch the performance. It was already underway, the music being greeted with hushed respect, and finally she allowed herself to relax, closing her eyes and tipping back her head to ease the tension from her neck. The decision to perform Josquin's lament made a lot of sense both theatrically and musically, as an intimate portrait of Ockeghem. But it had also been forced on them by circumstance; there simply wasn't another obvious piece with which to close the concert. Ideally they would have ended with something on a symphonic scale, but such pieces weren't written in the fifteenth century. Or they could even have concluded with something unknown but, as the conference tomorrow would prove, there was nothing new in Ockeghem studies.

The singers had reached the point where the composers were named, a moment that never failed to send shivers down her spine:

Acoutrés vous d'abis de dœul,
Josquin, Perchon, Brumel, Compère,
[Wear garments of mourning,
Josquin, De La Rue, Brumel, Compère,]

Emma loved this section. The top voice and the bass moved in parallel, a limpid sweep towards a high note that fell back on itself like a sob of grief. It was rare for Josquin to marry musical expression so intimately with graphic description, and she was convinced that this descending phrase deliberately mimicked the falling tears demanded by the poet. Ockeghem's children were called upon by the poet not just to mourn their 'good father', but to cry *heavy* tears, a poetic and musical hyperbole that argued nothing less would suffice:

Et plourés grosses larmes d'oeil;
Perdu avés vostre bon père.
[And cry heavy tears;
You have lost your good father.]

Emma wanted the audience to feel what she did, a communion with the past that perhaps only those who sang the lines could fully appreciate. She envied the singers that direct contact, and much more. Her voice was too weak to shape and mould the lines as they did with that even yet muscular tone. One American commentator had likened it to high-speed jet formation-flying: they could power through a straight, he said, and then veer off at any angle with effortless precision.

The lament was nearing its conclusion where all the voices would sing '*Requiescant in pace*', and Ollie, her boyfriend and the group's baritone, cast a discreet glance towards her. He had to swap parts at that point with Marco, the tenor, Ollie's line rising over an octave for no apparent reason, making it almost impossible to sing, and the slight smile he exchanged with Emma referenced their agreed solution to the strange problem.

The piece ended and the silence was interrupted by a few murmurs of satisfaction before the applause began. Allie, the bass, led Emma and the group back onto the stage for the final bow and then they were all in the wings again, congratulating each other. As the applause died away the short evening and early morning ahead became the group's new focus.

'Six-thirty: taxis,' said Emma.

'Ouch,' said Charlie, the other tenor, speaking for them all.

'I know, I know, but we can't miss the flight and that's cutting it fine as it is,' she explained. 'The champagne's on me tomorrow night. In Tours.'

The announcement was greeted by a muted cheer, grudging acknowledgement of the tough schedule ahead and due recognition of Emma's thoughtfulness in promising a quiet celebration at the end of a tough day.

'What are you up to?' she asked Ollie, as the others drifted away to the dressing room.

'Thought I'd go off with the boys. Are you going to come?'

It was a familiar routine. Emma's duties as the leader of the group required her to schmooze with management, fans and other concert promoters, while Ollie, as one of the singers, had no further responsibilities. Their relationship, they'd agreed after several well-meaning attempts to accommodate each other, only suffered from manufactured compromises and sometimes it was easier if they went their own ways. The conversation they were having now was merely residual politeness, a conversational ritual whose practice, if overheard by anyone else, suggested the pursuit of a normal relationship in the face of an abnormal career. Spending the remains of the evening with her lover was tempting, but the reality was that Ollie would become fractious and she would feel pressured. Instead she would have a quick drink in the bar with the two sopranos, Susan and Claire, and one of the altos, Peter, who formed the self-christened 'Wet Set' because of their tendency to look after themselves, in contrast to most of the men in the group who liked to burn the candle at both ends.

'I really need to get some sleep,' she said. 'Where are you going?'

'Don't know. Allie's got an idea.'

'That sounds dangerous.'

Allie's 'ideas' generally involved alcohol, usually to excess. There was no such thing as a quick drink, unless it was a quick drink followed by another quick drink. And another.

Ollie smiled. 'Don't worry. I won't let you down. Shall I ring you and let you know where we are?'

'No. I'll be fine. You go off and I'll see you in the morning.'

Ollie kissed her briefly on the lips and scurried after Allie, who had already changed and was making his way to the exit.

In her dressing room, Emma placed the flowers in the sink. They were too cumbersome to carry to Tours tomorrow and she would leave them here for the cleaner. In the meantime at least they added some colour and life to the featureless room. The usual venues for the group were churches or cathedrals where they would all change in the same room, and she missed the camaraderie. Down the hall the onstage incidents and accidents were having their first tentative outings, one-liners punctuating conversations fuelled by residual adrenalin. She liked being there when the stories began to form, like crystals created in experiments at school with a string hanging in a solution of blue liquid. At least tomorrow, with the concert in the Cathedral of St Gatien, they would all be together, an event that Emma had looked forward to since the concert had first been suggested by the conference organiser. Despite her interest in Ockeghem and his circle, she'd never been to Tours. The past three years had been hectic, and Ollie's idea of a holiday was not a cultural visit to the birthplace of the music they sang. Even though St Martin, the church of which Ockeghem was Treasurer and at which he'd sung, no longer existed, she looked forward to being in the city, to soaking up something of its atmosphere and letting her imagination wander.

A leather-bound book lay on the coffee table: the concert hall's guest book. It was open at the page she was expected to sign, the details of the concert penned in cursive italics: *"Ockeghem and his Contemporaries" by* Beyond Compère *directed by Emma Mitchell.* She could never resist looking at the earlier entries, names of famous conductors and groups in whose company she felt like a naïve but enthusiastic student once more. Flicking through the pages she came across the names of Simon Rattle, The Pat Metheny Group, The Kings' Singers, each with a non-committal, bland yet polite message which made her feel less fraudulent about her own contribution: 'A wonderful hall with beautiful acoustics, matched by a beautiful audience and a warm welcome.'

As her pen scratched on the paper she was struck by the silence, incongruous after eighty minutes of intense music. She removed her all-black concert clothes and slipped into jeans and sweatshirt, then turned up the loudspeaker in the hope of hearing the sounds of the audience making their way out of the hall, but the auditorium was quiet, as if the concert itself had never happened. She looked in the mirror and flicked back her short hair. Her stage make-up had smoothed away any expression of concern or relief and exaggerated the darkness of her eyes. It was a suitable mask for her final public performance of the evening, that of meeting the audience at the stage door. One final effort, and then her time would be her own once more.

'Ubera et dentes,' she said: cod Latin for 'tits and teeth'.

CHAPTER 3

Thinking about fifteenth-century music these days produced in Andrew an almost uncontrollable urge to re-acquaint himself with his find. He checked once again that Earl was still safely asleep, slid the blue plastic folder from beneath his lecture notes and gently withdrew its contents. Here it was: his Holy Grail, his Ark of the Covenant, but indisputably real. Academic disciplines usually proceeded slowly and carefully, yet this discovery would immediately redraw the musical map.

It was potentially the biggest early music discovery of the past fifty years: a thirty-four-part, anonymous motet written over a hundred and fifty years before Striggio's missing forty-part Mass or Tallis' equally grand *Spem in alium*. It was the obvious inspiration for the twenty-four-voice *Qui habitat* attributed to Josquin and the thirty-six-part *Deo Gratias* that had been assigned mistakenly to Ockeghem. The text was from Psalm Fifty-one – Psalm Fifty as Ockeghem would have known it from the Latin Vulgate Bible – *Miserere mei*, a text for Ash Wednesday. But something on this scale had to have been written for a very special occasion. Identifying the exact circumstances of its first performance would help him to determine who had written it; there was no attribution on the manuscript, nor was there any reference to it in any fifteenth-century source. All he knew for certain was that it was related in some way to Tours, France's capital in the fifteenth century, even though he had found the manuscript in Amiens. That much he had established from the accompanying letter written by Geoffroy Chiron, who was a *chambrier* at St Martin in Tours, the same abbey at which Ockeghem had been treasurer and singer.

The motet could have been written by any of the composers who were linked with the royal chapel – Antoine Busnois, Loyset Compère, or even a lesser composer like Jehan Fresnau. It could even be by Josquin, though he really hoped it wasn't; as the musical equivalent of Leonardo da Vinci or Michelangelo, Josquin's reputation needed no help at all. What Andrew really wanted was for it to have been written by Ockeghem, the figurative godfather to the younger generation of Josquin, Compère, De La Rue and countless other composers. And it definitely bore some Ockeghemian trademarks, though any of those could have been the result of influence or deliberate *hommage*. Such hope arose not merely from a despairing idealisation of the composer whom he loved above all others, but also from a rather more base inclination: the more important the composer, the greater the reflected glory. If he could prove it was by Ockeghem, Andrew's own success would be assured.

The manuscript never failed to raise his spirits. It was not the original, of course. That lay in the place he had found it, as the padding in the spine of the chapter records in the church library in Amiens Cathedral, where it had remained hidden from the world for five hundred years. He would have loved to have taken it, but provenance would have to be shown; it needed to stay where it had come to rest by a twist of fate, the details of which might never come to light.

Looking at the music now, Andrew was in a state of rapture, oblivious to the rude noises of Earl's snoring and the roar of the engines, as free of earthbound concerns as the plane that rose effortlessly through the mantle of cloud into a naked sky.

The copy in his blue folder was his latest transcription. He'd worked on it for five months, expanding it from three discrete parts to its thirty-four voices by following the instructions given in Latin. They told him that that each part was a canon whereby one part repeated the same line at a fixed rhythmic interval, a musical device understood by every child who has sung *Frère Jacques* and *London's Burning*. Just as such simple rounds can produce an infinite number of parts, so the three statements were designed to yield thirty-four parts: nine *discantus* and nine *contratenor* lines; eight each of *bassus* and *tenor*. The original singers would have been able to render their vocal part from the single iteration that appeared in the original manuscript, their part isolated from the others like a modern orchestra; modern singers, though, would expect the immediate visual geography of a score format which detailed the resultant parts, and it was this that Andrew would present to Emma Mitchell and her group.

Even with no modern edition, the manuscript was a valuable and exploitable historical artefact. His current thinking was concurrent articles in the *Journal of the American Musicological Society* and *Early Music*, and a shorter presentation in *The Musical Times*, together with a series of lectures at key institutions that he'd earmarked with a view to job placements. With Karen wanting to be closer to her mother in Florida and Andrew wanting to be closer to Europe, which he thought of as his cultural home, he'd already ruled out Stanford and Berkeley on the West Coast. Yale, Harvard and Princeton were top of his list, and Columbia and Duke would do at a pinch.

There was no doubting, though, that performances of the composition would enhance its reputation. Over the past thirty years, performers had brought fifteenth-century music into the musical mainstream on the concert stage and recordings. The music of Josquin and others was now regularly performed, a situation that would have left the original composers' heads spinning, and Andrew intended to reach the largest possible audience. In order to do that he needed a group with an understanding of concert-giving, recording and imaginative programming, which was where Emma

Mitchell and Beyond Compère came in. He had their recordings and used them in class. Everyone did. For one thing they were well-researched, well-presented, and brilliantly performed, but they also appealed to the younger audience. The early-music audience of the 1970s had grown old, but Beyond Compère had reached a new demographic and he wanted to tap into it. It was the final part of his plan.

But there was a problem, and it was a serious one: he couldn't get the parts to fit. However hard he tried, however many assumptions he made about copying errors, he could not get the four voices, let alone thirty-four, to sound anything other than simply wrong. Harmonies that could never have existed in the fifteenth century sprang from the page directly into his mind's eye revealing parallel fifths and octaves: simple contrapuntal errors that even a choirboy wouldn't have made. Cadences were displaced by one or two notes so that the expected resolution lagged behind in one part, or two parts leapt forward to arrive ahead of the others. The results were like the gridlock produced when traffic lights failed and cars piled around each other, with honking horns: chaos where there should have been order.

He'd tried everything. He could have sought advice, written to more senior colleagues – any of them, generous with their time and undoubtedly excited by his extraordinary revelation, would have helped him. Once they'd picked themselves up off the floor, that is. And therein lay Andrew's dilemma: he needed help because he couldn't work it out for himself, but ambition required that he keep it a secret. A discovery as big as this was his meal-ticket out of the Midwest, his free Round-the-World trip to every major university. There he would be feted and celebrated after delivering the same, well-worn lecture. It was his entrée into the Ivy League that had excluded him for so long, and he didn't want to blow it by having the news leak out. Much as he trusted these respected colleagues, he knew their adherence to the unwritten academic code of sharing knowledge and research.

So, working on his own, he'd made countless attempts at reconstructing the parts, the results of which, once they'd proven themselves unfit for purpose, he destroyed. Given the number of unsuccessful attempts, it was amazing the shredder still worked. He still hadn't solved the notational riddle and all he had to offer Emma Mitchell and her group was this: one of two un-performable editions.

Application and hypothesis had failed; maybe intuition was the way forward? Which is why he stared at the familiar fifteenth-century square shapes, trying to clear his mind and let the key to the puzzle come to him, waiting for inspiration to strike. He knew the music backwards as well as forwards, for he'd even tried notating it in reverse. That wasn't entirely an act of desperation; puns, acrostics, riddles, mazes and anagrams were frequent devices in the music and art of the period, and there was always the chance that the anonymous composer had employed a Leonardo-like cipher of mirror-writing. Perhaps the parts needed to go forwards *and* backwards, like the tenor parts in the Agnus Dei from Josquin's *Missa L'Homme Armé Super voces musicales* – but that didn't work either. Nothing did. So here he was, once more staring vacantly at the notation, hoping it would somehow expose itself through an act of veneration.

'Any good tunes?'

He jumped and instinctively covered the manuscript with his hands. Earl was awake and looking over his shoulder. Andrew's immediate thought was to put the music away. But that might draw attention to its importance and, in any event, he doubted very much that Earl, brass player that he was, could read fifteenth-century notation.

'Er, well, not tunes exactly. Fifteenth-century polyphony. "Lines" might be a better term.' He looked down and saw that the *discantus* part was clearly visible.

'Any good lines, then?' asked Earl, smiling slightly, and he started humming, a high, not unpleasant sound.

'Er, it's a C clef,' said Andrew, noticing a semitone where he should have sung a tone. 'It's not a bass clef, which is an F clef. So, you see this – ' Andrew pointed at the C clef at the beginning of the stave. 'That means this note is a C –' he traced the line with his finger along the stave – 'so this note –' he pointed to the one below it – 'is a B natural.'

Too late he realised he should have kept his mouth shut for, by dropping into teaching mode, he'd inadvertently encouraged Earl.

'Oh, okay,' said Earl casually, as if he'd been reminded of something he knew, and he started humming again.

Andrew was impressed. For one thing, the square notation didn't slow Earl down at all and he sang all the correct pitches. It was only the values that didn't work. Where, according to the laws of fifteenth-century notation, he should have altered the consecutive breves – so one was worth three beats and the following one only two – Earl had accorded both notes equal value. Andrew saw his way out: he'd point out the difficulty of reading this music and put him off.

'But, er, unfortunately, you're not altering the note values. This notation works differently; the notes aren't the value that they seem to have on the page. They alter according to the mensuration sign and the context –' *blind him with science*, he thought – 'so the same note can mean two different things. This breve here is worth three beats and this one here is worth only two.'

'That's a bit stupid, isn't it?' said Earl.

Brass players, thought Andrew. *Always literal.*

'I used to play some early stuff – Gabrieli and guys like that – on the sackbut.'

The sackbut, an antecedent of the trombone, was a sixteenth-century instrument, and this explained why Earl had some experience in the world of early music, and why he was unfazed by the square notes.

'You guys think too much. I think it should go like this.' Earl started to sing the notes according to modern notational rules.

It wasn't a bad sound that he made, thought Andrew, even if what he was singing was clearly wrong. Someone across the aisle stared at them and Andrew mouthed an apology.

'I think we're disturbing the other passengers,' he said.

'No class, eh?' Earl jabbed Andrew in the side with his elbow. 'I guess we'd better leave 'em in peace.' He leaned forward to retrieve the in-flight magazine and started flicking through it.

Despite the fact that it would have been historically impossible, Andrew was almost inclined to accept the sweating salesman's literal solution to the notational conundrum. For one thing, the resultant melody had balance and flow, and it sounded more convincing than any of Andrew's solutions. But it was absurd. How could a fat salesman from the Midwest have cracked the code when Andrew, with all his experience, had been so confounded?

He dismissed the thought and closed his eyes, as much as anything to indicate to Earl that the conversation was over. And now, as he had done so many times, he surrendered to a fantasy of a future in which his reputation was secure, a pristine world in which work and pleasure were inextricably entwined.

'And how did you come to discover the key to the puzzle?' asked the interviewer.

'Well,' he would say, turning to Camera Two with accustomed ease, 'for the benefit of the viewers I should just explain that pieces written at this time used a different system. I tried writing it out according to the rules that applied at the time, but it didn't work. Then I tried several variations. Composers of the time loved puzzles – anagrams, acrostics, hidden messages – like cryptic crosswords really – so I tried a few different approaches. None worked. But then I thought...'

The daydream collapsed as quickly as it had formed, the solution still out of reach.

All he had to do was crack the notational riddle and prove the authorship of the motet and then ... then he wouldn't have to suffer this kind of physical inconvenience. He'd have a big chair, in First Class, and the stewardesses would attend to his every need rather than treat him with the kind of sour contempt he'd suffered on this flight. In fact, he'd probably never travel in Coach again.

✦ ✦ ✦

At the stage door Emma was beset by a small clutch of eager concertgoers and obsessive fans. Peter, Susan and Claire were already patiently answering questions and offering appropriate encouragement. The tenors and basses were long gone, probably well into their second pint.

A man in his mid-fifties with a moustache like an overused toothbrush pushed towards her.

'Miss Mitchell,' he breathed, his voice tight, 'I have all your CDs. Could you sign them for me?'

She smiled. 'Of course.'

Here they all were, in chronological order. The first, *Beyond Compère* by Beyond Compère, the live recording of their first and only theatrical production, followed by the more refined but, to her mind, rather restrained and too-perfect studio version, issued on EMI. Then came the later releases: *Dufay Defined* and *Josquin Can*, jokey titles that belied the essential seriousness of the projects, but which helped in the current climate of falling CD sales and the dumbing-down of classical music. Both were adorned with stickers proclaiming the prizes that they had won – *Grand Prix du Disque, Diapason D'Or*. If all else failed, thought Emma, they were sure of a welcome in France.

'And when will your next disc be coming out, Miss Mitchell?' asked the unctuous man, beads of sweat popping on his bald head.

Emma bit her tongue. What she really wanted to do was challenge him for calling her *Miss* Mitchell. There was a condescending edge to the sycophancy and she resented being adored and patronised simultaneously. This wasn't a question of the fan lusting after her (she batted away the thought), but of regarding her with awe mixed with, well, disbelief: there were still some for whom the term 'female conductor' was an oxymoron.

She knew that sometimes she overreacted, that what she took for over-solicitousness was genuine concern, but the press in particular tended to focus on her gender rather than her relative youth: one rather pompous review in *The Times* had put the word 'conductor' in inverted commas, as if her role within the group didn't even qualify her for the title; and a small-scale publication for early music enthusiasts, from which she had expected a modicum of parochial sympathy, had once glided too swiftly from an observation on her gender to a criticism of her interpretation, thereby hinting that the two were interrelated. She had, in any case, given up even using the term 'conductor' and latched onto the idea of the *animateur*, a term that referenced her drama background and described her role far more accurately as the person who prepared, commented upon, interpreted and shaped the performances which she herself would introduce and present.

The fan was standing there, his wet mouth hanging open with anticipation, eager to hear the news about the next CD despite the fact that, with all the pre-publicity, he probably knew all about it anyway.

'Well, the next CD will be out very soon. It's Ockeghem year, as you know, and it'll be called *Ockeghem Gems*. Available in all good record stores,' she said. Her little joke was acknowledged with a keening laugh, which came just a little too early and a little bit too loudly. Her teeth on edge, she signed the accompanying booklet, then excused herself and moved over to two young students who were obviously eager to speak to her.

'Could you sign this for us?' asked one of them, tall, with glasses, the geeky type. Rather than a CD it was a score of *Nymphes des bois* that he proffered, a hand-written edition that he'd obviously made himself. In the top right-hand corner he'd written his name and the occasion for which he'd prepared the edition.

'Your own edition, I see?' said Emma. 'And for a concert you're giving tomorrow?'

He giggled slightly, a nervous sound. To announce his presence, his better-looking and clearly more-self-confident friend answered.

'Yeah. Gig at the University. A celebration of Ockeghem on his death-day,' he said. 'I'm Steven and this is Simon. I'm the conductor and he's the brains.'

'The two aren't mutually exclusive, you know.' Emma realised she'd responded automatically, and she blamed her tetchy correction on her previous encounter with the oleaginous fan. She could see from the looks on the students' faces that they thought she had taken offence, so she quickly added, 'Conductor and musicologist? It's a winning combination.'

She signed the score and, to break the awkward silence, expanded on her observation: early music, more than any other field of music, was built on the kind of partnerships of which Steven and Simon were an example. She herself relied a great deal on musicologists who specialised in fifteenth-century music: they were the experts who provided the group with transcriptions of the original manuscripts in modern notation, whilst her own research provided the social and historical background.

'The musicologists give us the black and white sketch, and we conductors just colour it in,' she said, repeating a line she'd used recently in a radio interview. The students beamed their understanding and told her proudly of the name of the group – JDP – from Josquin's initials. She reciprocated by telling them how the name of Beyond Compère had been a jokey, provisional name that had eventually stuck.

She much preferred talking like this than receiving empty adulation, but sometimes it was difficult to steer the right course between encouragement and advice. She spared Simon and Steven the stuff that increasingly took up her time: the contracts with promoters and record companies; the promotion of the group; the fund-raising; the Trustees' meetings; the finances. It made her tired just thinking about it all, and she knew that however much she warned them about the vicissitudes of touring – the lack of sleep, the late nights and early starts, the busy airports, the crummy hotel rooms, the exhausting repetition of it all – they would still come away with a false image of international glamour.

Her rise had been as rapid as it was unplanned and it had begun in theatre, quite different to the more obvious routes of singing and teaching that these two students were following. There was only so much advice she could offer, therefore, for her own progress towards the recognition she now enjoyed was so quirky and unintentional, so laden with good luck and serendipity, that there was no clear path for her to extrapolate that would in turn guide them to equivalent success.

Encouraging them to keep in touch, she gave them the contact details of her agent and walked back to the hotel past Newcastle's pubs and clubs accompanied by the occasional thud of a bass-line from an unrecognisable pop song. She would have liked Ollie to be there, and not just to provide a reassuring protection from imagined threats of late-night high spirits. As director of the group she spent her days switching between assumed roles – fairy godmother to some, wicked witch to others – a parade of conflicting identities that exhausted her and prompted a vague, enduring sense of doubt. When she admitted her worries to Ollie, he responded with typically blunt pragmatism, telling her to have a drink and forget about it – a solution he would now be pursuing in a pub somewhere with Allie. Absence really did make the heart grow fonder, Emma thought. Recently she and Ollie had been spending more time in their respective flats in London, as though trying to reproduce the same conditions of isolation that she now found herself regretting. Without the familiar work context, their differences tended to fester and, ironically, the relatively independent social lives they pursued on tour meant that their occasional arguments were more often resolved away from home where they were afforded the space and time to heal wounds and appease resentment.

Arriving at the hotel, Emma booked an alarm call and headed towards the bar. It was comically depressing, a windowless box situated in the heart of the building which, despite being on the second floor, felt as if it was in the basement. The dark wood, dim lighting and low ceiling seemed deliberately designed for illicit assignations, and made it feel oppressive and unwelcoming. The seating was pure 70s kitsch: orange cloth over Henry Moore-like rounded sofas and chairs. Peter, Susan and Claire looked miserable, but, as she neared them, Emma saw that the unflattering shadows on their faces and sunken eyes were the result of up-lighting.

'Well done tonight. A really good show, I thought,' she said. 'A drink?' She waved at their glasses.

'No, we're good,' said Susan, speaking for the others as she often did.

'We promised ourselves just the one,' said Peter, turning to Claire for confirmation. The latter nodded and Emma thought she caught a look of regret. Although a fully paid-up member of The Wet Set, Claire could on occasion fall spectacularly off the relatively teetotal wagon. On evenings like that she accepted drink after drink, each greeted with a qualification of 'Just the one'. Susan, the self-appointed leader of the 'sensible' arm of the group, could be controlling and needy in equal measures, and, though all of them could easily head off with the rest of the group, Claire could often be heard asking about the previous night's events and expressing her disappointment not to have been there. Still, with a short night like this ahead of them, Emma guessed that Claire would have chosen abstinence and that tomorrow her caution would be vindicated.

Emma ordered a glass of chardonnay for herself while Peter continued his account of a recent fling with a waiter, another in a line of brief encounters that had failed due to incompatible lifestyles. The conversation wound down at the same rate as the drinks in their glasses drained. None of them mentioned the evening's concert or the following day's trip to Tours, a pretence that suggested that here, in the gloom of a darkened bar, the conversation was a choice they had made and not a consequence of their nomadic existence. Emma insisted on paying for the drinks and they confirmed the time of their departure the following morning as they travelled up in the lift, mouthing a final, silent goodnight in the quiet corridor before retreating into their individual rooms.

Emma slept well that night and woke only once, visited by a repeating musical phrase that looped endlessly through her dream. It was the plangent, limping phrase from Josquin's *Nymphes des bois*:

'*Josquin, Brumel, Perchon, Compère…*'

CHAPTER 4

The Memoirs of Geoffroy Chiron: Livre I *ed. Francis Porter*

Frevier 6, 1524

I, *Geoffroy Chiron, Chambrier of St Martin at Tours, Chapelain to the Royal French Chapel, procurator to the late Johannes Ockeghem, loyal subject of François I, King of France, writing in the year of our Lord 1524, do hereby testify to the veracity of the events I here impart.*

It is time for someone to set down the events of the life of Johannes Ockeghem so that his memory may be honoured. Today, February 6th, 1524, is the twenty-seventh anniversary of his death. The provision for a composed Requiem Mass to be performed in St Martin in Tours no longer obtains, but I have spoken to the Bishop; prayers for his soul will be offered and a plainsong mass sung.

As I was fond of reminding Jehan, we met when I was a young choirboy at St Martin and our first conversation took place when I was but ten years old. He was, therefore, my guide from a very young age, and thenceforth throughout my career – first as clerk, then as procurator, then as chambrier; *always as friend. He acted as my example and the words of his famous chanson served me well:* Prenez sur moi vostre example *[Take me as your example]. He taught them all: Desprez, Compère, Brumel, Busnois. Others made their acquaintance with him at events organised by composers and choirmasters throughout the land, travelling from their hometowns specifically to sit at his feet to learn firsthand the techniques of composition that he had mastered.*

Today there are more people who have heard of Jehan Ockeghem through Desprez's composition than know Jehan's great works: the masses, the motets and the chansons. People should learn of the man and his music, and of his service to the Kings of France and the people of Tours. I will paint a new picture in words rather than through the medium of music.

Johannes Ockeghem was St Martin's most famous singer. His duties as Treasurer and Baron of Châteauneuf meant that he did not always attend services and, as choirboys, we always felt flattered when he was part of our choir. He was immediately recognisable, not simply because of the striking scarlet cloak that he wore (made, it was rumoured, from cloth given as a gift by Charles VII), or because of his stature (he was a tall man), or even because of his impressively deep bass voice. No: it was because of his spectacles. Only the very rich wore them and, impressionable children that we were, they were cause for comment. Pierre Laffroy maintained that they enhanced the mental faculty and had nothing to do with vision. Writing contained knowledge, he explained, which should proceed by the most direct route into the brain. The glasses aided the process and that, he concluded triumphantly, was why sometimes Ockeghem was seen without his spectacles, his nose pressed against the choir book. It was, argued Pierre, through being close to writing that true understanding could be achieved. Looking back now it's easy to see that this theory suited Pierre perfectly – he himself had poor eyesight and always had to stand directly in front of the choir lectern. Through his physical proximity to the music, he was, according to his argument, the choirboy with the deepest musical understanding, a theory that might have been more convincing had his reading been more accurate.

Maître Ockeghem (as we knew him then) was the only singer of whom we were not afraid. Never did he hit or berate us, pull on our hair to keep us in time, or kick us if we sang in the wrong mode as did the other chapelains. *Whenever he entered the room, the mood became serious and tranquil, for he had an air of calm that imposed decorum and order upon any situation. It was as if the phlegmatic humour that was so abundant in him was carried through the ether and enveloped us all. Under the choirmaster, behaviour in choir practices and the services was otherwise poor, we choirboys unruly, a cue that we took from some of the more rowdy* chapelains.

Although I knew him by sight, Jehan was not aware of me until that day he attended our class. It was there that we were taught the rudiments of music – the names of the musical intervals and the principles of discant – and we still wrote the solmisation symbols on our hands daily to remind ourselves of the notes of the gamut.

When Maître Ockeghem walked in that day you could have heard a stylus drop. We looked at each other, puzzled by his presence. We assumed that he had come to find Martin le Kent, our usual teacher (the Englishman whom none of us liked and whom we found difficult to understand) who had not yet arrived.

We must have looked confused, for Jehan laughed. His singing voice was attractive enough but his laugh exemplified his generosity of spirit: dark and rich, coming from deep inside his body, rumbling up from his stomach into a regular five-note pattern, repeated according to the level of his mirth.

'Good morning, boys,' he said in his perfect accent, with a twinkle in his eye. 'My name is Maître Ockeghem.' He smiled. 'And can you say that? Ockeghem?'

We couldn't, for none of us could produce that distinctive 'gh' noise that the Northerners make in their throat. In Tours we are proud of three things: that we are the capital city of the great nation of France; that our wine, made from vines which grow on the banks of the Loire, is the finest in the world; and that the way we speak is the purest and most perfect form of the French tongue. Thus everyone in Tours ignored the original pronunciation of Ockeghem and adapted it instead to the French tongue so it sounded 'Oh-ke-gan'.

'Don't worry if you can't,' he said. 'I really don't mind.' And from feeling that we had let him down we were suddenly forgiven; we all returned his warm smile. Jehan went on to explain that Monsieur le Kent was ill and that, as a favour, he had agreed on this occasion to conduct our lesson on writing musical notation. He asked the boy closest to him, Denis Laforgue, what we had been studying recently and how class usually began. With trembling voice, Laforgue told him that we always started by cleaning our cartellas *[blackboards] with a cloth, and that the last lesson had been on setting words to music.*

'Excellent,' boomed Maître Ockeghem. 'That, boys, is one of my favourite subjects. So let us do as...?'

He looked at Laforgue expectantly.

'Denis Laforgue, Maître Ockeghem.'

'... as Monsieur Laforgue suggests, and clean our cartellas.*'*

Addressing Laforgue as 'Monsieur' had pleased us all. We weren't used to such respect, and certainly would never have expected it from a luminary like Jehan Ockeghem. Some said that he was the most important man in Tours, more important even than the Bishop or the Mayor, by virtue of his connections to the King.

'And what, Monsieur Laforgue, do we do next?' asked Jehan.

Laforgue beamed at this new-found status. 'We write the clef, Maître Ockeghem,' he said, turning around to us all as if to imply that we, too, should show him the same deference.

'Ah, the clef. Yes, of course,' said Maître Ockeghem, 'though I expect we need to decide which clef?'

Laforgue's shoulders sank. He'd forgotten to inform Jehan that we usually wrote a C clef on the bottom line of the stave, the register with which we, as choirboys, were most familiar.

'And, Monsieur Laforgue,' said Jehan, seeing his distress, 'what clef do you like?' Laforgue's face brightened. 'The C clef, on the bottom line, Maître Ockeghem.'

'And so it shall be. Please, everybody. A C clef on the bottom line.'

We all picked up our chalk.

'Now,' said Ockeghem, 'let us write in some notes. I would like you all to write a breve on that same line. Ut: the home note.'

We duly wrote in the first note whilst Maître Ockeghem sat back in his chair, took off his glasses and closed his eyes. Then, quite slowly and deliberately, he proceeded to dictate the notes for us to write. This went on for several minutes and I noticed that some of my colleagues were struggling. Many had written the notes too large and found that they had run out of space. Because my preference was for joining notes together, not merely because it saved time but because I preferred the way it looked, I still had plenty of space left.

When we had reached the end of the exercise, Jehan opened his eyes, put his spectacles back on and surveyed a room of glum faces. We all felt that we had failed. He stood up and walked around the room, looking at what we had done. It must have been immediately obvious to him that the exercise he had set was well beyond our ability and, with customary graciousness, he took the blame upon himself by praising our efforts. The work he saw here today, he declared, could not be bettered by any of the monks who worked in the scriptorium of St Gatien, or even by the great Jehan Fouquet. He had seen some extraordinary manuscripts, he proclaimed, collections of music from foreign lands decorated in aquamarine and gold leaf, adorned with pictures of strange animals and freakish men, but never, never had he seen such clear and honest efforts. He had no idea, he added, that the boys who sang in the choir were such talented scribes.

When he got to my desk he stopped.

'And your name is…?' he asked.

'Geoffroy Chiron, Maître Ockeghem,' I replied.

'Chiron? Ah, the centaur,' he said, 'or should that be a foal?'

None of us knew what he meant and, seeing our incomprehension, he explained. Chiron was a centaur, half-man and half-horse, the half-brother of Zeus, who surrendered his immortality when the pain of a wound proved too great.

'Well, well,' he said, looking at my work. 'This really is excellent. You like ligatures, I see?'

'Yes, Maître Ockeghem.'

'We will have to keep an eye on you. You have a steady hand. And that is entirely appropriate, for the name Chiron comes from the Greek meaning "good with the hands". You also have a good musical understanding.'

He turned to the rest of the class.

'And that, boys, is what we must all aim for. We must not merely be singers: we must be musicians. We were put here on earth to comprehend the world and not merely to be agents of God's will, and we must understand music in the same way that we seek to understand God. And that is what young Monsieur Chiron has done here. He has not just written the notes: he has applied thought to the notes. Well done.'

As I look back now I can see that Jehan's praise was exaggerated in order to encourage me. He must have know that my use of ligatures was not conscious as he suggested, but merely an affectation like the loop of the letter 'g' or the flourish of a signature wherein the letters of the name itself become impossible to read. It was an *outward display with no real comprehension, but at the time I was so proud I could have burst.*

What Jehan actually saw that day was a steady hand matched by a steadfast nature; I was accurate and I was neat, the two essential qualities of the scribe. It would be ten more years before he saw evidence of my hand again, when his usual copier had left the city to travel to Bourges and he needed help with the transcription of a new mass.

It is to Jehan Ockeghem, then, that I owe my early career as a scribe, a skill which, though he was happy to encourage, he viewed as only a stepping-stone to greater things. I should not, he insisted gently on several occasions, become an artisan when I had a brain and wit better suited to high office. Thus it was as a scribe that I began my working life and, with him as my patron, I was introduced to men of high office in the city of Tours for whom I would perform simple tasks such as drafting documents and even personal correspondence.

I have wandered from the path again: Ostende mihi Domine viam tuam et deduc me in semita recta

 [Set me, O Lord, a law in thy way, and guide me in the right path].

This is about Jehan Ockeghem, as I must constantly remind myself. I am old now, the assured stroke of the quill that characterised my youth now subject to illness and an infirmity of age whereby my hand shakes and my fingers seize up, particularly in the cold, damp days of winter; sometimes it hurts to write at all and instead I am forced to turn my mind to contemplation. That is no bad thing for composition of any kind, as Jehan taught me. The process is one from thinking to writing, from designing in the mind to crafting on the page. Indeed that is my aim here: to set down the events as I witnessed them, to bring to my thoughts and to incidents the clarity of reflection, thence to refine them in the act of writing. And that, of course, is the same process as the one I developed through transcribing Jehan's compositions.

As I was saying, I developed my skills as a scribe over many years in the service of Jehan Ockeghem. He never made any musical sketches of any kind. To do so would have been contrary to his learning. Instead, he held the music in his mind and then would relate each part in turn, just as he had done on that occasion when I had first met him as a ten-year-old. This required much of me, for I had to mark down the notes immediately on the first hearing. Over time I developed a simpler method, assigning notes their own value within the tactus, *and not according to alteration as explained by Franco of Cologne. (If modesty would permit, I might suggest that unwittingly I anticipated the thinking of Gaffurius and Tinctoris, though I never had the patience or interest in the theory of music to pursue the idea.)*

Although under great pressure, I enjoyed those sessions together. We would work between Mass and Vespers on a Sunday, a day that Jehan loved because he could forget

the affairs of state and city and devote himself to God and to music. In the morning we would sing in the choir, where he and I were the basses, and then leave St Martin for his house across the river in St Cyr.

It was a pleasant walk with the shops closed for the Holy Day, quieter than the weekdays when the hawkers lined the Rue de la Scellerie. We would pass by the churches of St Hilaire, St Étienne and St Vincent, and the tall houses of the rich silk merchants, then turn north towards the river at the Cathedral of St Gatien, its bells signalling the end of Mass. There we would inevitably encounter clergy and noblemen leaving the Cathedral, and Jehan would stop to talk. Finally, we would cross the river just beyond the Château de Tours. He still maintained the residence accorded to the Treasurer of St Martin in Châteauneuf, though he preferred the calm of the north bank and the view it afforded him of the City of Tours.

'Sometimes,' he said, 'it is important to view the City as a whole, and that is only possible when you are far enough away from it.'

The house in St Cyr was small but cosy, and Christiane, his servant, would provide us with a wonderful meal before our afternoon's work. Jehan always sat behind me on a trestle using his cloak as a cushion. Having told me which line he wanted to start with, he would remove his spectacles, just as he had that day in class, and indicate the tactus with a light tap on my shoulder.

The first dictation was for the notes themselves, and the second for me to write in the words. Jehan never cared if I made a mistake. 'In my experience,' he said, 'singers are intelligent creatures. If they want to change a word, let them.' (How different from Desprez's attitude!)

Later, in my own home, I was usually able to correct my own errors simply by singing the music, for it possessed a logic and internal consistency like the canons of which Jehan was so fond. Even the more free-flowing lines that I loved so much revealed a design that escaped the ear at times. There would be one more stage of consultation and then a final correction – usually rhythmic changes, occasionally the addition of a ficta note that he knew would save argument in a rehearsal, perhaps the use of ligature to suggest to a singer the shape of the line – and then I created the final performance copy.

I would present it to Jehan and we would pour some of his favourite wine and make a toast to God, to the King, and to Tours, his beloved town. Finally we would raise a glass to Bacchus. By then Jehan would have relaxed enough to tell me the stories that I knew and loved so well: stories of his travels to the North; of his meetings with famous men; of the parties he had organised; of his troubled dealings with the chapter of St Martin; of meetings with Dufay (or Silenus, as he called him, Dufay being a man much given to drink); of Gilles Binchois, his teacher and advisor; and of singing in the choir at St Martin.

Though my memory of more recent events is less clear, I can accurately recall the old anecdotes, and the testament that I am writing will contain some of those tales. It would be a shame not to record them for whoever might read this.

Alas, I may not be able to revisit what I have written; this version may well be my last. If Jehan were still alive, I would offer a draft of my memoirs for his approval, though, through his natural modesty, he would doubtless remove many of my most sincere expressions of regard for him and insist upon the removal of any criticism of the likes of Desprez. And so what you will read will be but one man's view, subject to no revision or interpretation like a musical composition. No choir will ever sing this text and realise in sound the mental design contained herein; no one will guide my hand. It is my vision, and mine alone. As the psalmist says: Quia ipse Deus Deus noster in saeculum et in perpetuum ipse erit dux noster in morte. Amen

[For this God is our God for ever and ever: he will be our guide even unto death. Amen].

CHAPTER 5

Andrew Eiger bumped his battered suitcase up the metal steps of the bus and looked around: nowhere to sit. He grabbed the plastic strap hanging from the rail as the bus lurched through the slow-moving traffic past a succession of terminals. It looked like the Third World – or at least like his private image of the Third World, for he'd never visited any part of it. People were rushing in different directions, too much traffic honking and snorting its way to myriad destinations past double- and even triple-parked cars and buses, the sidewalks lined with hawkers, taxi drivers and hustlers.

Still, it was only a short trip from Terminal 4 to Terminal 7 at John F. Kennedy airport and he would have plenty of time to make a phone call home. Rather than the fond farewell with Karen that he'd envisaged, it had been a frantic parting, with him snatching his belongings from the trunk, late for check-in because they'd had to return to the house to pick up his forgotten luggage. John, strapped into his car seat, had sensed the gathering tension and started crying, then screaming when he was ignored. Andrew and Karen had begun one of their frequent arguments, which traced the same familiar course: she accused him of being unable to apply the necessary common sense to the simplest of organisational tasks, and he resented being treated as a child.

He was able to review the argument calmly now, his mood considerably more buoyant without Earl, the trombone-playing salesman, next to him. He knew there was more than an element of truth in Karen's criticism, though that never made it any easier to back down. His intellect could grasp the most abstruse arguments, be they mathematical, musical or philosophical, but even aged sixteen he lacked common social graces and, left to his own devices, was late for everything. He had expected that when he became an adult such inadequacies would become less important and, for a while, when Karen entered his life, they had. She managed the kinds of things at which he was so bad – organisation of his time and his basic needs. But all too soon he realised that what she once found endearing was becoming irksome and, after John's unexpected arrival, things had got much worse. When they had first moved to Ohio for Andrew to take up his first full university post, the plan had been that Karen would finish her training as a psychotherapist. Then, when the situation allowed, she would set herself up in practice and, some five years down the road, they would start a family. But Karen had become pregnant and Andrew suspected that his wife held him and his characteristic ineptitude responsible for the failure of a condom. When John was born, it was clear that Karen's training would have to be put on hold, and it was equally obvious that Andrew was not going to get a 'World's Best Dad' mug unless he bought it himself. As John grew from baby to toddler, once again Andrew found himself dealing with the minutiae of everyday life from which the ministrations of a capable woman had momentarily freed him – only now, in addition to looking after his own needs, he had to care for John as well. Bathing his son, changing nappies, preparing his food, even playing with him, didn't come naturally, and an exasperated Karen would frequently have to take over the tasks with which Andrew had been charged. Impatience, the constant companion of young parents, grew exponentially, manifest most obviously in the arguments that took place in the relative privacy of the bedroom at the end of another unrelenting day.

It wasn't John's fault, an understanding of which fortunately neither of the child's parents lost sight. The simple truth was that they had not foreseen the amount of time that a baby demanded. It didn't help that John was active and inquisitive, proclivities that revealed themselves to often disastrous effect once he'd learned how to crawl. The video machine was his first victim, rendered inoperative by a typically unrelenting investigation into its mysteries, followed shortly by the pedals of the piano and, once summer arrived, a collection of potted herbs. After the piano incident, Karen and Andrew had systematically raised everything four feet off the ground, which worked until John started to walk some three months before any of his peers, leaving his parents wondering if their strategy had inadvertently been taken by their precocious offspring as a challenge.

For all the frustrations caused by his dynamic curiosity, John was charming and loving, qualities which his father would have done well to cultivate. For, since the shattering discovery of the composition in Amiens, Andrew had become aware that, in his wife's eyes, his usual self-centeredness had spawned a dangerously selfish obsession that often excluded the rest of the family. As much as it was the focus of Andrew's attention, so it was the object of Karen's resentment, both cause and symbol of the constant crises of which their home life seemed to consist.

The significance of the trip to Tours was not lost on either of them on that fractious journey to the airport, their argument inevitable. Andrew was desperate to go; Karen was eager for him to leave. It was this guilty truth that neither was quite able to acknowledge and which made Karen volunteer to drive Andrew to the airport and him accept. She framed it as a financial decision – a cab would be an extravagance – but behind it lay an unspoken hope: that things could change; that the trip might make Andrew realise something about his behaviour; and that the break would do them both good.

Why he'd left his suitcase on the bed he didn't know, nor why he'd told Karen that he had put his suitcase in the car when he hadn't. Karen would probably describe it as a slip of the mind, which meant that, even if he hadn't consciously intended it, a part of him had. He was guilty either way; the onus was on him to call one last time before he headed to Tours. It wasn't just that he needed to express gratitude for the lift to the airport and apologise for what Karen would see as leaving her literally and metaphorically holding the baby whilst he swanned off to Europe for three days to talk, eat and drink with interesting people. He knew that when he returned in three days' time his wife would be tired and stressed after caring for John on her own and, tired and jetlagged as he would be, a phone call now might buy him some much-needed credit.

Of course, he also wanted to tell Karen that he might have cracked the notational puzzle. The nagging sense that Earl's naïve reading of the score might just work was now no longer possible to ignore. It made sense; the transition from the old to the new notation systems was not down to the theorists who explained it, but to the scribes who developed it. Obviously the Amiens example was one of the first such examples – yet another valuable feature of his extraordinary discovery. Without referring to the transcription – opening the file once more would doubtless have rekindled Earl's interest – Andrew sat for the remainder of the flight extrapolating the lines from memory and fitting them together in his head. He'd immediately been struck by the consistency of the solution. Earl's proposition, though lacking musicological reasoning, was nonetheless correct; and knowing too much had led Andrew up a blind alley. Not that he would credit Earl for his inadvertent perception, even to Karen. His was a fortuitous error, no more, like a child discovering that a round peg could occasionally fit into a square hole. No, this deserved a thorough academic explication, and it would get one, in a chapter entitled 'Notation in transition'. That would be the premise from which the solution flowed.

The call home had to wait until the flight was nearly boarding. Check-in had been fairly efficient, but it was a busy day at JFK and getting through security had taken more time than Andrew had expected. He found a payphone with a vacant power point close by, plugged in his laptop to charge the battery for the transatlantic journey ahead, and dialled home. Eight o'clock: John would be in bed. He realised his mistake as soon as Karen answered, slightly out of breath. It was seven o'clock in Ohio, slap bang in the middle of John's bath time. Karen was obviously on the cordless phone, John in the background, singing tunelessly.

'Karen,' said Andrew. 'I've just realised. It's seven there, isn't it? Bath time?'

'Yes. John. Put that down now. No. Don't splash mummy. Yes. Bath time. Is there a problem?'

'No. No problem. Thought I'd just ring to say hi. I'm at JFK.'

'Good,' she said absently. He could hear her reasoning with John, her voice muffled, the phone against her chest. He waited.

'Are you all right?' she asked again. She was probably fishing for an apology, he thought.

'I've cracked the code.'

'Sorry? John, Daddy's on the phone. Do you want to talk to him?'

Karen came back on the line. No, then.

'The code? Sorry?'

'The notational problem. You know. I couldn't get the motet to work. I'm pretty sure I've worked it out. I've got to check it, but it just seems right. D'you know what?' He chuckled to indicate that he was being rhetorical. 'It was simply a question of real note values. I'd been assuming alteration and imperfection, but it's in a later notational system. It's written in modern note values. Do you see?'

'No. No!'

Andrew wondered why Karen was so assertive about her ignorance and was about to embark on an explanation of medieval musical notation when he realised that she wasn't talking to him.

'John's just tipped water on the floor. Hold on,' she said. There was a clunk as she put down the phone, followed by the muffled sound of her crying out and John laughing. 'That's naughty. Mummy's wet now.' Her voice came more clearly down the line. 'He just dumped some water on my head. Didn't you? Didn't you? And now he's laughing because he thinks I look funny with a towel on my head. You're not helping, aren't you?'

'Well, I can't...'

'Not you, Andrew. Can't you tell I'm talking to John? I'm talking to you, aren't I, you cheeky boy.'

'Not a good time, is it?' he said hopefully.

Karen sighed. 'Look, Andrew, I'm very glad you've cracked it, even if I don't understand, but can we talk another time? You know how it is at bath time.'

He'd wanted to share the moment with her, to discuss the implications with someone who knew how important this was to him. Was she paying him back for the airport incident? Surely she shouldn't allow his barely sentient son to upstage this triumphant moment? Throwing him a rubber duck or a sponge would keep him occupied for the five minutes of Karen's time Andrew felt he deserved.

The announcement for boarding broke the silence between them and reminded him that he needed to secure his seat to prevent a repeat of the cramped conditions of the previous flight.

'I shouldn't have called at bath time,' he said, hoping his bald admission counted as an apology. 'I'll call you when I can. From France, but I don't know when that will be.'

'Fine. That would be better. And try to make it when I've got some time to talk, rather than at meals or bath times, OK?'

As a request it was reasonable enough, but he resented the world-weary tone and, rather than thank his wife for the lift to the airport, he offered a curt farewell. 'Love to John.'

He joined the line of people boarding the aircraft, most of them Brits with harsh accents. This being British Airways, the six-hour flight would provide his first of many authentic re-engagements with European exoticism. Momentarily now meant *for* a moment and not *in* a moment. A cigarette was a fag, the trunk of the car the boot, sidewalks would become pavements. His brief stopover at London's Heathrow would provide scant opportunity to use any of these substitutions, yet the amateur philologist in him – a string to every medieval musicologist's bow, he observed – thrilled to the mutability of language and entertained him as he stood in line. No, not in line. In a queue. And in another ten hours' time he'd be in France and it would all change again and *queue* would mean 'tail'.

'Welcome on board the British Airways flight, sir. Can I see your boarding pass, please?'

He registered the glottal on 'Airways', the sibilant 't', so different to the softer dental 'd' to which he was accustomed, and the general harshness of the open vowel sounds, the more so without the velvety, post-vocalic 'r' typical of Irish and American speakers.

'Over to the other side, then down to your right, sir.'

Directed away from the Club Class cabin, he recalled his reverie from the previous flight and, for once, felt none of the usual jealousy and bitterness towards the privileged few. Soon he would join them.

There was a spare seat between him and the young man in the window seat to whom he nodded a hello. He arranged his luggage in the overhead bin, stowed his bag at his feet and immediately withdrew his blue folder.

He began with the acid test: would the *discantus* and *tenor* parts fit together? If they didn't, he was back to square one. It was too easy: they fitted perfectly as he'd instinctively known they would. He heard the careful contrary motion between the flowing lines in perfect harmony. The second test was the canon within each part. The Latin instruction made immediate sense to him and, habitually paranoid as he was, he realised that it was fortuitously impenetrable to the average transatlantic tourist. *Canon ad breve.* It told the singers to sing the same phrase exactly one breve after the previous singer. He heard the parts setting off at fixed time intervals, like a staggered race. The long note values in the *bassus* made it easy to sing, but only professionals would be able to shape that line with the necessary grace to make it sound convincing. When all the parts joined in it would sound much more rich and complex than it looked here on the page. That was equally true for the *contratenor* part, which, in the manuscript, was provided no musical example of its own, only text: *Contratenor sequit bassus in diatesseron in canon ad breve.* It told the singer to sing the bass phrase a fourth higher and a breve later. Where the *bassus* would sing the first note to the value of a breve, the *contratenor* would sing the same note pitched a fourth higher. But there was a different mensuration sign for the *contratenor*, effectively a tempo marking which meant that the part would be sung at a faster speed than the basses. That principle would hold for the eight other *contratenor* singers as well, and the net effect would be that they would overtake their bass colleagues. The image of a race was, Andrew realised, quite appropriate and also explained why there were only eight *bassus* parts, yet nine *contratenor* parts. Otherwise the *contratenors* would be holding long notes waiting for their colleagues to catch up.

Andrew could imagine most of it. He heard the texture thickening like a musical stew from the lower, steady notes upwards. All his early attempts had produced loose, almost abstract lines for the basses, but now that he had correctly identified the note values, what had originally seemed a dull harmonic underpinning was revealed as a free expression of genuine melodic force. At first anticipating and then echoing the faster-moving *contratenor* line, the technical assurance of the complex canon was astonishing. Above these duelling parts the *tenor* part moved serenely in a sequence of slow-moving notes like a stretched-out plainchant tune, though not one that Andrew had thus far been able to identify. Above that, the more obviously decorative *discantus* parts chased after one another to produce bright cascades of running scales. The compositional design was astonishing and, more than ever, Andrew was convinced that this was the work of a composer at the top of his game.

It worked. It really did. It was everything he had expected it to be, and, *marvellously*, as someone like Tinctoris might have said, it all fitted together. It had everything, as far as Andrew could tell. The final test would be hearing it sung, of course, but it was already more than promising. The canon between the *contratenor* and *bassus* at the interval of the fourth was centre stage, the same interval as Ockeghem's chanson *Prenez sur moi* – though that didn't prove it was by Ockeghem. It could be another composer referring to that work, or an unrelated echo of the same musical device.

Yet why had this *Miserere mei* never been performed? A piece this large had to be a commission of some kind, which required advance planning and organisation. And the number of singers required for its performance far exceeded that of any one choral institution. Given the vocal ranges, it was doubtful that boys would have sung the *discantus* lines but, if they had, then they would have been singing at the very least three-to-a-part which would mean twenty-seven of them; no choir school at the time had more than eighteen. And without boys, it required thirty-two adults at a time when the largest choir numbered only twenty-four.

The motet had to have been written for a big state occasion. Louis XI's funeral in 1483? Impossible. The paranoid, ascetic King was buried without state ceremony. But maybe Ockeghem, as *premier chapelain* and Treasurer of St Martin at Tours, both direct royal appointments, had written it as a tribute to his patron? The only other possible occasion would have been one where several choirs gathered together, such as the event in Cambrai at which Compère's *Omnium bonorum plena* was first performed. Three choirs – those of the French and Burgundian courts, and of the

Cathedral at Cambrai – had joined forces to sing the new piece in which several of the singers were named.

Andrew knew he was missing something and that there were other musicologists who would have better hypotheses to offer. All of them would be in Tours. He'd perused the conference proceedings on the first flight, noted its usual ragbag of topics – a keynote paper which would summarise the state of Ockeghemian scholarship and doubtless add something more provocative, perhaps a new attribution. Or maybe something that tied Ockeghem more closely to Compère and Josquin, and once again raised the question of how much the older man had taught the younger? Then there were papers by other international scholars: on Ockeghem and musical puzzles; on Ockeghem and his links with churches in Paris; on Ockeghem and his relationship with Dufay (there were rumours that the meeting between the two of them in Cambrai in 1462 was not the only one); on Ockeghem and the liturgy; and two or three papers that would present the findings of the kind of archival research that would provide details of the composer's personal life. Andrew's hope was that some new piece of information would emerge which would make reference to the motet and even tie it to Ockeghem, a discovery the significance of which only he would fully appreciate.

Even without knowing the intended purpose of the piece, there was plenty to be going on with, the only possible problem being the very thing that made it so valuable: its uniqueness. Somewhere there might be another version of it, perhaps a better copy, clearer and more accurate, which would make his discovery a composer's sketch like the Bouchel composition scribbled in the back of a choir book in Cambrai in the 1450s. Andrew didn't want his scrappy version to be trumped by some later edition, and the longer he waited the more chance there was of such a catastrophe occurring.

The hand in which the manuscript was written had given him pause for thought. When he'd first begun to copy down the notes in the library in Amiens Cathedral, he'd noted the distinct characteristics of the writing. He'd realised immediately, and with some sadness, that it was not in Ockeghem's hand. Ockeghem's signature was steady and upright, the lettering like modern Gothic, composed of hard angles, no more so than the 'e' which had the appearance of a flag on a pole. The script of whoever had written the music and the *Miserere mei* text was considerably more rounded, yet more functional as well; any flourishes were kept to a minimum, as if there was no time to attend to careful calligraphy. Where the 'g' of Ockeghem's signature had a studied, neat swoop that ended with a horizontal serif, the tail of the scribe's 'g', like all the other writing, sloped diagonally from left to right and ended with a loop.

In fact, the scribe's work seemed almost amateurish, far from the carefully spaced layouts of something like the Chigi codex, the text only loosely aligned beneath the notes, often abbreviated. It even contained a misspelling. It was clearly a very first rough sketch, perhaps dictated, from which a more careful and considered copy would have been made. It was no performing copy either, for no group of singers gathered round a choir lectern, let alone one consisting of thirty-four voices, could have read from something that small.

'Would you like a drink from the bar, sir?'

Andrew had been oblivious to the pre-flight checks and take-off. Instinctively he hid the score.

'Oh. Er. Yes. Tomato juice, please.'

'Tomahto juice?' she confirmed.

'Tomahto juice, yes,' he replied, making the Ts slightly wetter than usual.

'Worcester sauce with that?' she asked, dropping a solitary ice cube into the clear plastic glass.

'Er, no thank you.' He took the proffered drink and snack. Sipping the thick juice, he heard the song in his head: 'You say tomayto and I say tomahto.' Pronunciation. That was another matter he needed to consider. How should Emma Mitchell's singers pronounce the text? If the piece had been written for Tours, then any final consonants of the Latin texts would only be pronounced at the end of a grammatical phrase. The sound would probably be more strongly nasalised than modern French, with words ending in '-em' sung as an [am] sound rather than [em]. In other words, *Iniquitatem* would come out *ih-nih-kee-tah-tam*, not *ih-nih-kwee-tah-tem*.

Andrew knew he was obsessed and once again recognised the symptoms: everything, even the seemingly trivial issue of fruit juice, came back to the motet. But he could allow himself a small pat on the back now, surely? Karen would sigh and roll her eyes if she were here – but she wasn't. The beauty of a flight like this was that he was on his own and could indulge himself. He was able to enjoy the airplane food at a leisurely pace unlike the fraught mealtimes at home or the slices of pizza he would hurriedly cram down in the staff canteen. He even had a glass of wine with the meal – French, from the Loire no less. Here, thirty-five thousand feet above the Atlantic, he felt cocooned and pampered.

Over the next four hours he worked on the score, fortified by three cups of coffee. The man in the window seat was curled up in a foetal ball with a blanket over his head and once the crew had dimmed the cabin lights there were few distractions. Andrew's overhead light and that of the spare seat next to him described his workspace: the pad of blank music manuscript paper on his seat-table and the original transcription on the spare seat to his right.

A single sheet of paper no bigger than a greeting card contained the entire original score, but he didn't have enough paper to provide a complete transcription. It reminded him what an extraordinary model of economy the original notation was, like a dried sponge that expanded to a disproportionate size when wet. But even with a few bars missing at the end, his makeshift edition would nevertheless be sufficient for the purposes of his meeting with Emma Mitchell. In any case, it was a valuable insurance policy: he didn't know how much he could trust her.

Now that he had cracked the notational key, the copying part of his task was mundane and mechanical. If he'd had a pair of scissors he could have cut up the individual rows of notes and slid them easily into place above or below the initial statements, like pushing pieces around on a chess board. As it was, his task was orderly and soothing. Occasionally he took a break and rewarded himself with a moment of aesthetic appreciation, noting an interesting clash of a semitone here, a quirky cross-rhythm there. And then the gathering storm as finally all thirty-four parts moved inevitably towards a huge cadence, the shortening notes giving the impression of acceleration, the harmony pushing the ear toward final tension and a fulfilling resolution.

After two hours he had filled thirty pages in his neat script. The relationship between the words and the notes gave him the greatest problems for which he blamed the scribe. Nevertheless he had a good enough working knowledge of word stress and vocal line to resolve instances where the relationship between music and text was either unclear or clumsy.

It was a rough first edit and, as far as it went, satisfactory. His finished version would be far more thorough, each editorial decision footnoted, each *ficta* suggestion carefully qualified, the final, massive score prefaced by a short history of its discovery and its place in fifteenth-century music. Perhaps there would be a foreword by one of the conference delegates, an expert in the field with whom he might collaborate in the future. He felt a quiet sense of reassurance as he stacked the pages. There wasn't sufficient space to lay it all out here and he looked forward to that moment, probably in his hotel room with the bed used as a drawing board.

He reclined his chair and switched off the reading lights to grab ten minutes of sleep. As if on his cue, the cabin lights came on and the noises from the galley announced the imminent arrival of what would pass for breakfast. His neighbour stirred and emerged blearily from a nest of blankets, yawning. Andrew stood up to allow him to join the scrum of people gathered around the restrooms at the back of the plane, and stretched both arms to loosen his shoulders. His writing hand was cramped and the palm felt stiff and sore where the metal lock in the overhead bin had pierced his skin. From the galley a freshly lipsticked stewardess pushed a trolley towards him, dispensing antiseptically wrapped breakfast-packs. Hurriedly he placed his various papers into the blue folder and pushed it into his briefcase. He was tired now, his eyes stinging from the recycled air and unnatural light, and he took off his glasses and rubbed his face while he calculated the time differences: eight o'clock in the UK, landing at around nine: two in the morning in Ohio. No wonder he felt like this. Jetlag didn't just refer to the effects of a broken body-clock, as he knew from his experience of flying once from London to New York on a day flight. Even then, when his body knew it was only eight in the evening, the ground beneath him had shifted unpredictably and he'd found himself gabbling, as if he'd stayed up all night; the low cabin pressure and oxygen-depleted air took their toll.

The food, a rubbery croissant and raspberry yoghurt, was difficult to digest and he tried to wash it down with a cup of rusty-looking tea. He always tried to eat and drink what the locals did. He really needed the caffeine fix of coffee but decided to keep the treat of *un grand café crème* for Tours. After all, once he got to France he'd experience a quantum leap in culinary know-how. He smiled. It hadn't always been like that: in the fifteenth century it was the other way round, and the French were jealous of English cookery.

He rested an arm on the brushed aluminium armrest, laid his head back on the flame-resistant, foam-filled chair, and sipped his Indian tea from his plastic cup. Closing his eyes, he saw notes he'd just transcribed moving slowly across the page from right to left, dancing on the inside of his eyelids. Simultaneously he heard the sound of high voices singing descending phrases, a logical, musical pursuit supported by the lower voices, their strict imitation more difficult to discern in the thicker register. He wasn't hearing or seeing the exact lines, yet here and there a familiar shape emerged, much as the sound of his fellow passengers' conversations offered up the occasionally distinct sentence. Wrapped in the sonorous bath of meaningless chatter from the other passengers and his imaginative re-creation of the *Miserere mei*, the reality of his surroundings and the fiction of the musical performance became increasingly blurred. Andrew Eiger fell into a deep, easeful sleep.

CHAPTER 6

The alarm went off at five forty-five and Emma snapped awake, knowing exactly where she was and what the day entailed. Despite the itinerant lifestyle, she never woke in an unfamiliar hotel room experiencing the momentary, thrilling panic of dislocation. Nor, unlike her other colleagues, had she ever been roused from a drunken slumber by The Call of Shame, as it was wryly known.

She flicked on the light and stowed her alarm clock and sleeping pills in a United Airlines travel bag she'd filched from a Business Class seat on a transatlantic flight. The tablets were from her avuncular doctor, a fan of the group who, when she had described her lifestyle – the early starts, the late nights, the jetlag – suggested she carry them in case of emergency. It was a sweet thought, a gift rather than medicine, and, with them as a guarantee, sleep always came easily. As yet, she'd never had to resort to them and now they were merely part of her routine in an alien hotel, a ten milligram Temazepam tablet placed by the side of her bed next to her alarm clock 'just in case'.

It was dark outside, the hotel quiet. She'd slept well, stirring in the night only when she'd heard the others come back. There was a vague memory of Allie's low bass rumble bidding someone goodnight – or had that been a dream? As she padded into the bathroom she saw that a note had been pushed under the door and her heart gave a little skip. She hoped it was a *billet doux* from Ollie, a response to the one she'd put one under his door saying that she missed him, signed with a jokey heart with an arrow through it. Such exchanges were part of a routine they'd established over three years of touring together, a touching, almost old-fashioned courtship. The heady days of teenager-ish infatuation had given way to a steady and relaxed mutual acceptance, which Emma took as evidence that she was finally in a mature relationship, one in which in the brain was as important an organ as the heart. The frenetic touring provided most of their excitement to which life at home was a quiet counterpoint. When she and Ollie treated themselves to an expensive meal out in London, she would find herself savouring it rather than loving it, and when they made love she was never as uninhibited and wanton as she had been with former lovers. When Ollie's ex-wife had broached the subject of divorce, Ollie and Emma had talked about living together, an idea they'd approached tentatively after yet another of his frequent moans about the torments of living in rented accommodation with no room to house all his books, CDs and extensive collection of comics. They had never taken that step and nowadays the subject never arose unless, as sometimes happened, it formed the focus of the group's dry humour, an expression of fondness for them as a couple, which made Emma blush and Ollie wade into the punch and counterpunch of teasing banter. They'd also briefly considered the subject of children, but both had agreed that Beyond Compère's current unpredictable success was rare in the world of professional music: it was the kind of wave few groups were fortunate enough to ride, and there would be time enough for Emma to engineer a sabbatical, perhaps leaving the group to fend for itself for six months in a few years' time. At Christmas lunch last year, her mother, who at Emma's age had already produced three children, had pointedly asked her daughter how old she was, as though she hadn't been present at her birth. Emma had patiently explained that things were different in the modern day, that more and more women were having children in their middle or even late thirties. 'You're not a lesbian, are you darling?' her mother had asked.

Now, looking in the mirror, Emma's early-morning inventory revealed lines around her eyes, a reminder that she'd turned thirty last year. Susan, the self-confessed Moisturising Queen, who'd spent many a student summer holiday working on the ground floor in Selfridges whilst staying at her rich father's *pied-à-terre* in Baker Street, had promised to act as Emma's personal shopper in Tours while she was otherwise detained delivering her lecture. The erstwhile perfume seller could speak knowledgably and at some length on the principles of layering, bliss points and anti-oxidants, a script that sounded as rehearsed and polished as her singing, and had developed in Emma an almost junkie-like dependence on Clarins toners and moisturisers. For all her expertise, though, Susan always had a slightly overdone appearance onstage, more mask than face, and Emma preferred her own minimal approach to make-up.

She packed her things, pulled on last night's clothes, then rang down to reception to check that the cabs were on their way. 'Aye, lass,' she was reassured in a warm, Geordie accent. In any other context she would object to being called a lass, but up here in the North East she sensed none of the patronising assumptions that she encountered in the South, only an affectionate concern. She picked up her luggage and scanned the room for anything she might have left behind, then stooped to pick up Ollie's note. It was a disappointingly short scribble: one large word and then a signature. Susan was emerging from her own room further down the corridor, immaculately made-up as always, her eyes, haloed in eyeliner, eye shadow and mascara, improbably bright for the time of day. They waved at each other, mindful of the 'Do Not Disturb' signs on various doors.

Emma glanced at the note.

Sam-boo-kah!*

Love you

O

X

She had no idea what Sam-boo-kah! meant, and the asterisk, which referenced a tightly written footnote at the bottom of the page telling her to pronounce the word 'in a Geordie accent', didn't help. She presumed that Ollie was talking about Sambuca, the clear Italian liqueur often served flaming with three coffee beans floating on the top. The reference to alcohol didn't surprise her; after rugby players, she reckoned that the hardest drinking culture was to be found amongst musicians, both ancient and modern. When she spoke to an audience she would often throw in stories of infringements of decorum at choral foundations, of which she had over the years collected extensive, humorous examples, most of them provided by academics willing to share their archival research. Thus she had a ready stock of stories about singers running off with money collected for parties, of drunkenness in church, or being paid in wine rather than cash. It seemed that fifteenth-century singers were just as likely to get drunk as their twentieth-century counterparts, and she would deliver these anecdotes to audiences with a raised eyebrow and a wry look upstage to the men of the group.

The exact details of how Ollie and the others had been drinking Sambuca would doubtless emerge. They'd visited Italy only two weeks before, and after the concert the tenors and basses had tried unsuccessfully to recreate a drink called a Zombie by layering several Italian liqueurs on top of each other. Maybe this was a continuation of that tradition?

The group were slowly assembling in the lobby, some talking animatedly, over-compensating for the early start, others moving carefully with sheepish grins, caught between residual inebriation and an emergent hangover. Of the men, only Craig looked awake, almost feverish, a radio clamped to his head, parroting information about the England cricket team's progress against New Zealand in the Second Test Match in Wellington to anyone interested. Emma hadn't really been aware that England played cricket in the winter until she'd travelled with Craig, whose sleep was disrupted more than most by his steadfast commitment to his beatified sport. In the summer months, he would scurry from rehearsals across the road to the local pub to watch a few overs, or stand looking gloomily up at the skies if rain threatened to disrupt a day's play. He approached Emma now, a stern expression on his face, and she thought for a moment he was about to tell her he'd lost his voice.

'Play delayed. New Zealand put themselves in. Not much happened yet, but they've brought Caddie back. He'll sort them out.'

'Oh. Thanks, Craig,' she said, despite understanding only the vaguest implication of his report, and he nodded like a soldier pleased to have delivered a message to his senior officer.

She found herself in a taxi with Allie, Ollie and Susan, which she knew would be awkward for them all. When Susan started asking her what she needed in the way of Clarins, Emma caught Allie rolling his eyes theatrically and Ollie responding with a grimace. The two basses had little time for Susan, thinking her shallow and superficial;

though the accusation was not entirely unfounded, Emma often found herself taking the other woman's side in both private and public, pointing to her abilities as a singer and her command of languages which far outstripped that of either of the basses. In fact, they delighted in their ignorance, an obvious enough defence for their affected laziness, and often giggled like overgrown schoolboys at words in foreign languages. Emma had some sympathy for Susan, who lurched from one amorous disaster to another and demonstrated a quite staggering capacity for self-delusion in the short time that her unsuccessful relationships lasted. The soprano had variously gone out with her car mechanic, the man who repaired her boiler and – much to the delight of Allie and Ollie who competed over suitably obscene puns – her plumber.

Emma and Susan chatted about eye creams and lipsticks and ignored the men's silent, resentful communication. They were taciturn at the best of times but now they seemed to emanate hostility. Perched in the back seat between Ollie and Susan, Ollie seemed to shrink from Emma, avoiding the flirtatious press of her knee on his thigh, gripping the overhead handle with both hands so that his body was angled away. She knew from experience that Ollie was at his most guarded early in the morning, sensitive to bright lights and loud noises or any extrovert behaviour, including his own. When Susan searched in her handbag for a lipstick, the colour of which she thought would suit her, Emma took advantage of the pause to enquire about the previous night.

'Short night, boys?' she asked, looking at both of them in turn.

'Short. And sweet,' said Ollie, speaking for both of them.

'Sambuca?' she quizzed, hoping one of them would elaborate.

They both laughed. 'Tell you later,' said Ollie, continuing to stare out the window. At least on the plane she and Ollie would be seated together and would be far enough away from the rest of the group for him to disclose the full story without having to worry about sparing Allie's blushes.

The budget wouldn't stretch to the expensive tickets that would take them directly from Newcastle to Paris, so the route was to take them via London. Flying these days had none of the glamour that had attracted Emma as a girl and which had caused her to announce confidently at the age of seven that she wanted to be a stewardess when she grew up. It was the faded picture which her mother kept as a bookmark that did it: a super-slim young woman in a pencil skirt walking down the aisle of an aircraft with one arm on her hip, the other holding a silver tray of martinis above her head, a mythical image of independence and sophistication that spoke of an earlier, more optimistic age. Flying these days was purely functional: time to grab some food and read the paper, or do some work.

By the time they'd boarded, a tapestry of overheard conversations had provided a rough outline of the previous night's events but Emma heard the full story about the Sambucas from Ollie on the first flight. Allie, Ollie and Charlie had gone to the pub straight after the concert and worked their way diligently through three pints each of Newcastle Brown. 'When in Rome...' was their motto, and, though they all thought the beer overrated, they shared the same unspoken concern that they would get called soft southern Jessies if they didn't drink the city's famous brew. They needn't have worried. The locals took to them, the more so when Allie, generous as ever, bought a large round. His instincts rarely failed him in such matters and he had picked a pub that regarded licensing laws as a fluid social experiment. Later, Marco and Craig had joined them after a quick pasta at an Italian restaurant around the corner. Having drunk a bottle of red wine between them, Marco had no intention of changing to beer and, when offered a drink by one of the group's new-found drinking partners, he'd panicked and blurted out the drink he would have ordered had he still been in the Italian restaurant.

'Sambuca?' he asked in a quavering tenor voice.

'Sam-boo-kah?' cried the Geordie. 'Sam-boo-kah? What the blazes is that?'

Marco quickly tried to change his order to something less obscure, but the Geordie was already asking the landlord if he had any 'Sam-boo-kah'. The word was picked up all around the pub and suddenly the singers were surrounded by a chorus of 'Sam-boo-kah' chanted in broad accents. After that Marco had little choice but to drink the seemingly endless pints of 'Newkie Brown' that came his way and they'd ended up getting to bed some time after two.

Now the late-nighters were sound asleep. Emma had no concerns about their performances later that day – they all had the constitution of oxes – but sleep would help, and she told Ollie to get forty winks while she checked through her papers for the day ahead.

The first flight arrived in London on time at 09.05. It was then a hop on the Tube to change terminals, followed by a wait of about an hour and a half. They'd all agreed that what they needed then was a fry-up: a good old-fashioned British breakfast, their due reward for an early start.

At Heathrow, Allie led The Breakfast Club (as Ollie insisted on calling it after a film that only he had seen) to his chosen restaurant. Over years of touring, Allie had sampled breakfasts in most airports and provided expert guidance to those who required it. Emma almost expected him to ask for his customary table. Reverently he intoned a mock grace – 'Praise the Lard' – before tucking into his cholesterol-laden plate as if he hadn't eaten for weeks. Emma would have been quite happy with a coffee and a croissant, as would Susan (who'd chosen the more healthy scrambled-eggs-and-smoked-salmon option, much to Allie's disgust), but there were times when individual preference was overridden by an unspoken demand for collective conformity.

Having been asked by the *Guardian* to write a piece on the touring life of musicians, Emma had recently read Freud's analysis on group psychology, hoping to find something with which to anchor her first paragraph. She'd been amused to discover there the contention that one of the characteristics of communal behaviour was that mental ability was reduced to the person of the lowest intelligence. Looking around the table now, it was difficult to say who could lay claim to the dubious prize, for each had different strengths. Allie and Ollie would have nominated Susan, though her skills as a linguist argued otherwise. Others might deem Allie's silence as evidence of ignorance, but his chosen reading was Nietzsche and T.S. Eliot and, had he not married so young, he would have done a Ph.D. on Auden. Neither of the tenors – Marco or Charlie – had gone to university, instead attending music college where they had respectively specialised in Italian madrigals and German lieder. Marco, born of an Italian mother, was bilingual and well versed in Renaissance architecture; Charlie was drawn to the Gothic cathedrals of Northern Europe. For both, travel represented a chance to indulge their passion and many a tour saw them organising cultural excursions for anyone who expressed an interest. Peter and Craig, the altos, had both studied music at Oxbridge colleges – Peter at King's College, Cambridge and Craig at Christ Church, Oxford – examples of perhaps the most common template for English choral singers. On the face of it, they were the most erudite, though Emma thought them in many ways the least motivated, as if the map laid out for them from the time they were choirboys – at Westminster Abbey and St Paul's respectively – had led to premature success and left them directionless after graduation. Certainly they contributed least in rehearsals to debates on the meaning of text and musical interpretation. Susan and Claire were chalk and cheese in many ways, Susan the glamour puss to Claire's plain appearance. They had been mistaken on more than one occasion for a lesbian couple, which made Susan blush and Claire angry. Claire, the oldest in the group, was happily married and the most domestically oriented of the group, mother to a boy of eleven and a girl of seven. At university she had studied biology and played for the hockey team, and her naturally competitive instincts were now exclusively channelled into her children. It was wise, the members of the group had learned, to ask after them; otherwise Claire could become morose and withdrawn, sometimes sitting on her own, looking at photos and crying. Given the opportunity, pictures would be produced, even photocopied school reports, and her mood would instantly brighten.

Emma felt that Freud should have focused more upon the ritualised social behaviour of eating and drinking. If there was any surrender of individual standards to the lowest group denominator then it was probably manifest in culinary expectations, here represented by Allie for whom food was, more often than not, merely an accompaniment to drink. He was chomping on a piece of fried bread loaded with mushrooms and tomato ketchup, gesturing to Claire, who was playing 'mother', to fill his mug with teak-coloured tea. Emma was struck by the contradiction: in twelve hours' time he would open that same mouth and out would come a resonant, rounded, controlled, intimate expression of faith that would combine with the voices of his fellow breakfasters and create a moment of sheer sonic beauty. And then, half an hour after the concert had ended, he'd have one of his trademark roll-ups in one hand and a glass of beer in the other. Touring life, thought Emma, was an endless roller-coaster of descents from the sublime to the ridiculous and back again, from the dull demands of travel to the realms of high art: one minute they were careering down an escalator to catch a flight, the next pondering the mindset of an arcane fifteenth-century composer; breakfast was egg and chips in England, and dinner would be chased down with fine champagne in France.

Allie was mopping his plate with a piece of toast when Marco arrived. The tenor had skipped breakfast on account of his hangover and now had considerably more colour in his cheeks and a smile on his face. He was waving a copy of *The Gramophone* above his head like a newspaper seller.

'Read all about it,' he cried.

'Feeling a bit better, then?' asked Charlie.

'Getting there,' his colleague replied.

'What's it like?' Susan asked eagerly. The soprano was intent on sharing her excitement with others who hadn't, like herself and Emma, already seen the review of the new album in galley proofs. 'Read it. Read it,' she instructed, clapping her hands.

Marco read the review out loud, occasionally interrupted by one-liners and the odd cheer when obvious praise was offered.

'He could have mentioned us by name.' Craig looked up from his cricket magazine.

'You know him?' asked Susan.

'Sang together at Oxford a few times. Nice guy. American.'

'Reviewers never mention singers.' Allie winked at Emma. 'Only conductors.'

Emma stood up and took a small bow to show that she'd taken no offence. 'I mentioned everyone by name, but they don't always print these things,' she said – but already the subject had moved on.

'What's his problem with new repertoire?' Marco asked, passing the magazine around the group so each of them could read the review. Porter had begun the piece by saying that there was no new music here, something that, out of context, sounded like a criticism of the group rather than an observation about music history.

'We should write a new piece,' said Marco.

'Yeah. Peter. You studied music,' said Ollie. 'Can't you knock out a quick mass in the style of Ockeghem? We'd clean up.'

The idea gathered momentum, with several suggestions of unlikely tunes upon which the mass could be based, The Bee Gees' *Staying Alive* being the clear winner. Emma remembered her meeting with Andrew that night. Might the young musicologist have made a real discovery? Repertoire was still coming to light in odd places, dropping out of neglected books in Tallinn, such as the recent 'new' motet by Dunstable, and not so long ago someone had found a manuscript of a composition by Tallis which had been used by a Renaissance plasterer to fill a hole in a wall. If Andrew Eiger had inadvertently stumbled across something like that, then she wanted herself and the group to be involved. But she was dreaming. In all likelihood, he probably only had some new pet theory about the structure of a *chanson*, something arcane that thrilled him but which was no more than a cosmetic detail to a modern audience. Musical archaeology was a laborious process with few Eureka moments.

'Oh, hang on,' said Marco. 'There's an interview. With Em.'

'Oh, don't read that out,' said Emma.

It was always embarrassing to see her life reduced to a few words, the struggle and hard work compressed into a single sentence, foresight attributed to her where the reality was a series of unplanned accidents and coincidences. Fortunately the bill arrived at that point, prompting the usual debates about who owed what.

Emma managed to retrieve the magazine from Marco and skimmed it as she and Ollie walked together to the gate. There were two pictures of her and one of the current group, a posed photograph with fixed smiles and polished shoes, far from the shambling image they presented that morning. The same gap between the public image and the private reality struck her again with the photos they had taken of her. Backlit in the bay window of her house, she looked unnecessarily earnest, more an intellectual than a performer. The cameraman had caught her leaning forward, a crease of worry etched into her forehead, the reason being that the interviewer had just spilled his tea rather than, as the image suggested, that she was struggling to explain something to someone less erudite than herself.

The history of the group and its development was dealt with in two paragraphs; ironic, she thought, because in many ways Beyond Compère's transition from stage play to concert group was the story of two romances. She had originally conceived the theatrical production with Paul, whom she thought of as her first 'serious' boyfriend. They were both post-graduates at Nottingham University; she had just begun an M.A. researching early Italian opera, whilst he was in the second year of his Ph.D. on Loyset Compère. The soundtrack of their life was fifteenth-century music and inevitably she came to learn a lot about the little-known French composer. That November they had set off in Paul's battered Citroën Dyane for a two-week journey around Northern France to visit the key towns of Compère's life: St Quentin, Douai, St Omer, Cambrai. While Paul scoured the archives, transcribing church records and searching for elusive leads, Emma wandered through the narrow, chilly streets. The townscape seemed to be perpetually blanketed in damp mist, and her own image of the composer emerged as if from the cold November fog itself. Each evening over dinner, Paul would share some new biographical detail and a new idea would form in Emma's imagination. On their final evening in St Quentin, she outlined her vision: a theatrical production which told the story of the composer, Loyset Compère, using a simple set, tableaux and commentary, with music by the singer-composer and his contemporaries. The style would be boldly eclectic, ranging from detailed re-enactments of events in musical history to surreal sequences that explained the past using modern references. Already she could see key scenes perfectly crystallised: Dufay hawking CDs on a market stall outside Cambrai Cathedral; the Pope as a disc jockey introducing Josquin in the Sistine Chapel; Compère, the priest with a girl in every town. It would, she declared, be the first early-music musical. Paul, an historian through and through, had little time for such theatrical conjecture, but, amused and impressed, he agreed to act as consultant. Over the next few months, she developed a script and workshopped it, before staging three performances at the university. Its immediate success encouraged her to take the company to the Edinburgh Festival Fringe for a short run, a heady three-week period during which her love-life crashed and burned.

In retrospect she realised that she had failed to heed the warning signs, enervated and distracted as she was by the demands of the show and the critical acclaim. She also realised that she'd lost interest in her own research and in academia generally, the more exciting path of 'directing real plays with real people in the real world' having opened up before her. That was the unfortunate line with which she had expressed her misgivings to Paul, whose sole aim was to be a scholar. From then on their dissimilarities seemed to inform every aspect of their lives, even the smallest details such as the different ways they peeled the potatoes or made the bed; every instance of disagreement amplified their incompatibility and presaged their separation.

As consultant, Paul's input was confined mainly to the development period, though that hadn't prevented him from expressing his opinions in rehearsals. He seemed to enjoy the interaction with the cast and his role as advisor, sitting in the stalls with his notebook, offering the occasional comment in a tone of long-suffering tolerance that suggested his personal vision was a more authentic version of the past. At times his observations were valuable, but increasingly his comments seemed to Emma to be self-serving, presented to display his knowledge, smacking of the same kind of pedantry that so dominated early-music performance at the time. And, given that the show consistently used contemporary reference and made obvious play on anachronism, such criticisms struck Emma as not just unhelpful but also unsupportive. At first he had dismissed the idea of accompanying the production to Edinburgh, so she was surprised when he announced that he wanted to come along. When, in the second week of its run, a West End impresario contacted her and requested a meeting, naturally she asked Paul to attend. He refused brusquely, saying that ambition was rather vulgar. Emma was confused. He'd often said that he wanted Compère to be recognised as a great composer and, given that few people had even heard of him, surely the opportunity to reach a larger audience was something he would want?

That evening, Emma was made an offer she couldn't refuse: the chance to stage *Beyond Compère* in London with a professional cast. Rather than accept immediately, she had explained that she needed to talk it over with the man with whom she had devised the show; she would give the impresario her answer tomorrow. But she'd already decided. Paul could call her ambitious if he wanted, but it was too good an opportunity to miss. She would, though, try to get his blessing.

Returning to the rented six-bedroom house that the cast had taken for the run, she was surprised to hear voices upstairs. The others had planned to see a comedy show that evening and it was still too early for them to be back. When she reached the top of the stairs, a bedroom door opened, that of one of the actresses, and out stepped Paul in his underwear, his clothes held in one hand, the other waving goodbye to the bedroom's occupant. He didn't even see Emma, who stood frozen on the penultimate step. When she walked into their bedroom he was feigning sleep.

There was nothing to be said. The quiet carping from the stalls, Paul's late-in-the-day decision to come to Edinburgh, finally made sense. Emma packed a few things in a bag and booked herself into a hotel. The next morning she rang the impresario and, three weeks later, was running auditions in London. Reluctantly, she had informed the amateurs that their involvement in the project was over and glimpsed for the first time the degree of single-mindedness that professional life entailed. Splitting up with Paul was more straightforward. Limply devoid of any moral authority, he soon abandoned a half-hearted demand of payment for his consultancy, though she continued to credit him in the programme, a recognition which she knew did no harm to his standing in academic circles. For the professional replacements she drew on London-based singers, both from opera and from the world of early music. A successful run at the Almeida in London led to performances in Hamburg, Paris and off-Broadway.

As director, Emma's control over the project was total, although she called upon the singers for advice on matters musical. Thus began a gradual shift towards a more collective mode of working which would characterise her work with the concert group, but when it came to matters of staging she dispensed with the democracy of musical co-operation and her say was final. The three opera singers and two actors had some experience in movement and were used to taking such instruction, but the remaining four – Ollie, Marco, Peter and Susan, the core of the future concert group – had no such experience and were worryingly stiff on stage, particularly the men. It was Emma who had to berate them for their stagecraft, direction that maintained a professional separation between them.

When the London run began, she regarded her cast as colleagues, though not necessarily as friends, and the trip to New York was to bring them only slightly closer together. The constant flow of celebrities and famous theatrical people who beat a path to Emma's door kept her further apart from her cast, so much so that she didn't know that Ollie had begun a trial separation from his wife. For herself, she was quite content to be single. She was free in the day to shop, sightsee and plan her next move without any encumbrance of personal commitment, and occasionally free in the evening to take in plays and musicals, the latter a medium which increasingly interested her.

Such independence also afforded her plenty of time to consider her past and plan her future, one in which she was certain theatre would play no part. There were many factors in her decision, yet crucial to it was the realisation that of all the aspects of production – staging, lighting, acting, writing, the music and its performance – it was music that surpassed everything else. It *excited* her emotionally and, as she'd abandoned her Ph.D., it provided an alternative intellectual outlet. Now she could indulge her interest in history and performance *and* travel the world. She was not blind to the rigours of touring and took advice from several people, but new possibilities had opened up before her and she was determined to embrace them. By then she had also developed an exaggerated contempt for actors – hardly a good basis for a life in theatre. It was no accident, she thought, that dressing rooms were ranged with mirrors, the actors' reflections multiplied in an endless celebration of self. Actors were constantly, unhealthily aware of how they appeared to other people, possessed of a narcissism which never seemed to switch off. Their voices at dinner were affected, their honeyed tones reflexive, rather than those of the singers' which were released from their physical constraints after the show – drinking, laughing and shouting – as a woman might loosen her corsets. They had experience of touring and knew how to do it; the singers were, quite simply, more fun to be with.

When the New York run ended, Emma invited Ollie, Marco, Peter and Susan to dinner at her flat and announced her intention to re-launch *Beyond Compère* as a concert group. She explained that, although she could not promise anything definite, she was confident that she could organise an American concert tour and that, in time, European bookings would come. The three opera singers were unsuitable, their voices too heavy for ensemble singing, and Emma needed four singers of similar ability and voice-type to each of them: respectively Soprano, Alto, Tenor and Bass.

Two weeks later, four singers were duly appointed, all of them known to one or more of the group and to Emma from their various recordings. The group was reborn; the new eight-voice Beyond Compère rehearsed two programmes and the first concert took place in a small church in Berkeley, California. All music was sung from memory, which allowed more theatrical elements to be incorporated into the conventional concert format. Movement, lighting, and singing from different parts of the building and in various combinations were distinctive novel features that would become the group's trademark. The approach demanded of the singers commitment and considerable private study, something which those who were used to the defined limits of session singing – where one turned up, read the music, and went away – found challenging. The US tour was a great success, the reception from West Coast to East Coast ecstatic, which only added to the almost narcotic rush they got from being in America. Ollie and Marco were the only ones who had toured the States before (with The Tallis Scholars and The Sixteen) but now they were part of a new group – founder-members, even – thus more involved and better rewarded, feted and honoured in this, the New World. Rave reviews were passed like trading cards amongst the group at breakfast and at airports, and Emma's confidence as a presenter grew. She kept her delivery fresh by pretending she was addressing the group that sat behind her, not the concertgoers in front. It both relaxed her and gave her material a lightness of touch that had audiences eating out of her hands.

Touring itself proved to be a very different kind of bonding exercise to the stage show. The shared experience of constant travel and daily uprooting to a new city brought them closer together, their individual exhaustion displaced into expressions of care and concern. Each of them saw tiredness only in others, their senses dulled by a constant flow of caffeine, alcohol and adrenalin. Exhausted as they often were, tempers were nonetheless kept and an addictive, wild-eyed enthusiasm for experience prevailed as if this was their first and last tour. Virtually every night there was a post-concert party of some kind, organised by local choirs eager to rub shoulders with the famous English singers: in Jackson, Mississippi, they ate cornbread and barbecued ribs washed down with beer and mint juleps; in Boston it was a keg of Sam Adams and lobster; in San Francisco, Sierra Nevada Pale Ale and sushi at a private house with glorious views of Alcatraz and the Golden Gate; and on the final night in New York the group itself hosted an impromptu party for an amateur choir in a suite that Allie had been assigned through the hotel's clerical error. Between the concerts, the parties and the travel, they managed to fit in seal-watching in Monterey, wine-tasting in Sonoma, a visit to Graceland, a trip to the Rock and Roll Hall of Fame in Cleveland, and a late-night helicopter ride over Manhattan.

It was then, reminded as he was of the starlit flight over New York in *Superman*, that Ollie had recited to Emma the whole of Lois Lane's monologue, 'Can you read my mind?', a gesture that hinted at the dawning of a new intimacy. Even in retrospect Ollie maintained that it was only the indiscriminate romance of touring that had inspired him, not any nascent desire, but the following night Emma had stayed up late talking with him about his marital problems, an event which for others at least was freighted with significance. Time might yet confirm the interpretation that Peter was eager to offer – that Emma and Ollie were meant for each other – but the protagonists themselves believed that it was only the persuasion of coincidence that lent these episodes a poetic lustre.

It was with unprecedented sorrow that the group parted company at Heathrow. The next dates in the diary were not until the summer, a run of concerts at various festivals in mainland Europe and Britain. Until then the singers would be working with other groups, either as session singers or as early-music specialists, and some – like Ollie, Allie and Peter – would be returning to their day-jobs as singers – at Westminster Cathedral, St Paul's, and Westminster Abbey respectively. The group knew, as they hugged and kissed each other in the artificial light of the baggage claim area of Terminal Four, that there would never be a tour quite like that again. Never would such a gruelling schedule be endured with such equanimity, nor would they be so willing to draw upon their own resources in the spirit of camaraderie to buoy up others when spirits threatened to sink them.

Over the next two years the group flourished, and a regular pattern of concerts and recording was established. Touring in Europe and Britain was, by virtue of its brevity, more circumscribed by the realities of individual professional and domestic life, and Beyond Compère's status as a second family was less keenly felt. The blueprint for most engagements was a hectic twenty-four hours of travel, drinking and eating, somewhere in the chaotic midst of which they would give a performance to an anonymous audience. If the American tour was responsible for fusing the different identities of nine people into a functioning social group, it was the following two years that revealed the fault lines of social organisation and more personal agendas, which had only been dimly sensed on that mythological tour. The Wet Set was soon established: Susan, Claire and Peter were the first to leave the post-concert celebrations, whatever form they took, and Emma was grateful for their sober example. Marco and Charlie assembled an inventory of cultural and historical landmarks, a partnership of shared interest for the daytime hours, and in the evenings they formed a triumvirate with Craig who otherwise kept himself to himself. Emma, depending on her mood and directorial duties, spent time with all of them, but the Allie/Ollie alliance, one forged in beer and emotional reserve, proved to be the most durable and the most problematic.

The two were almost an item, their behaviour on tour as well-matched as 'Aglio e Olio', Marco's nickname for the pair, appropriate enough given that *Spaghetti aglio e olio* was a late-night dish favoured by drunken men, and not to everyone's taste. After a concert they would emerge into the fresh air, lift their noses into the breeze and follow a scent that led them directly to the nearest watering hole. There they would order beer, the stronger the better, a beverage chosen in part for its prolier-than-thou image, then pass what remained of the evening in silent companionship. They could be garrulous at times, chatting with members of the audience or with other members of the group and, both family men, were talkative at home and adored by their children. Yet together they shared some unspoken understanding that rendered conversation inessential. Communication in rehearsals was likewise minimal. Agreed nuances of musical expression were implemented without discussion, a process that, to the lay person and even to their fellow singers, appeared telepathic. They shaped the musical lines in exactly the same fashion and anticipated each other's breathing, producing effortless, consentient phrasing. Allie was a Catholic ('Lapsed – there's no other kind,' he mournfully remarked once) and could not only translate the Latin texts, but also, to use the biblical phrase, understand them in his heart. Ollie channelled his colleague's religious response like a good method actor and learned from his example. Together they created a unique sound and provided a template for others to follow. When required – or if they felt it appropriate – they would ratchet up the dynamic of the whole group, creating a sense of an expectation fulfilled, rather than inappropriate individualism.

There was no emotional resonance and none of the personal detail to be found in the brief précis of the group's history provided in the article in *The Gramophone*. The story of the group was too clear, too glib, the random narrative twists and turns appearing predetermined rather than the result of chance. But for good luck, Emma might still be working on her Ph.D. in some library carrel, and America and Europe places she pondered visiting for a holiday if she ever got a job.

Reduced to virtual bullet points, her life seemed paradoxically empty and purposeful. 'Intelligent and determined', she had 'failed to complete her degree' and 'lived alone'. And, as if to compensate for her personal shortcomings, the rise of the group had been made to sound inevitable, the result of her 'obvious aspiration'. What reference she had made to ambition was in the context of the group and not herself. But maybe that was how the amateurs of the first production saw her? Perhaps the actors and opera singers whom she had 'let go' thought of her as a neurotic, loveless, pushy woman who, when she wasn't hogging the limelight, was plotting the next phase of her career. There were two sides to every story.

CHAPTER 7

The Memoirs of Geoffroy Chiron: Livre II *ed. Francis Porter*

Frevier 13, 1524

On a day like today I can be glad that travel has never been a part of my life. As I stood on the bridge this morning, watching the boys with their rods angled at the Loire, fishing for perch or carp, I traced my history in the skyline of Tours: from my birthplace east of the Cathedral of St Gatien towards the church of St Martin in the west where I served as a choirboy, chapelain *and* chambrier. *My entire life was contained within the single sweep of my gaze.*

My physician, Gillet Cossart, lives close by the Abbey of St Martin and, as I had all but finished the tincture he had given me, I decided to arrive unannounced. He comes highly recommended. He accompanied the King's troops in the Italian campaign [1486] where he met Compère (a brief meeting and one which left him slightly puzzled about the composer's reputation). It was on his travels that the surgeon developed new techniques for amputation. That, he told me, was work for a young man: cutting through bone and gristle requires a singularity of purpose closely allied to physical strength. His current occupation in the City of Tours was, he declared, more suited to a man of his age and temperament, and he was glad to have put away the larger of his surgeon's tools. Aside from the occasional accident, he had not been called upon to perform an amputation for some twenty years.

He was thus, by his own admission, not entirely qualified to deal with my condition. The quality of honesty is rare in a physician and led me to place my trust in him. He had some experience dealing with something similar in another patient whom, he explained with due severity and concern, he had been unable to save. Surgery was not an option, the stomach and its contents being so delicately and harmoniously arranged as to make any kind of invasion dangerous. I should expect the growth, already visible beneath the thin skin of my stomach, to increase over the coming months. The treatment he would offer would be twofold: accommodating the pain (which he told me would increase) and managing the worst of the symptoms. He would make poultices and tinctures for me, the one to be applied externally, the other to be ingested as and when required. His aim was to keep me as comfortable as he could. Thus far he had provided me only with a green liquid to be taken both before and after eating, and whenever the warning signs of vomiting came upon me. Its primary taste was of mint, though the heat that it produced in my mouth also suggested the presence of fermented liquor.

The Doctor was dismayed that I had finished the tincture and advised me that I should take less in future. It was, he said, the kind of medicine the effectiveness of which would diminish the more I took it. Suffer the symptoms, he said, and pay no heed to traditional mealtimes. Eating was important to maintain my constitution, but it would be better to eat small things at odd hours rather than one large meal at midday; I should follow the example of the cattle who graze, not the dog which eats everything all at once. Whilst on the subject of food, I explained to him that I was writing a Mémoire and asked him what I might eat to help me recall events of the past. Avoid red wine and garlic, he said, and take cumin and ginger in an infusion of hot water.

He asked about the pain and I told him how it was at its worst at night and that the burning and stabbing sensations faded away during the morning hours. He advised me to build bolsters so I slept sitting up rather than lying down, adding that the ginger for my memory would help my digestion. He promised to visit me next week and I welcomed this. I know that in this way he will increase his fee, but money is no longer my concern.

Being told that I was going to die did not surprise me and, in many ways, I welcomed it. God has already been generous to me in granting me more than my three-score-years-and-ten. Jehan was old and infirm when he died, and there were times when I believe he would have embraced death if it were offered to him. I am now four years older than when Jehan's soul departed his body, and I understand better the blasphemous urge to end one's existence voluntarily. At least I am able to anticipate my end and I am provided with the time necessary to put all my affairs in order and to make my peace with God and my fellow man.

I am a widower: my wife, Marie, died some ten years ago. I have a servant who prepares my meals and keeps my home clean and tidy. My only son, Jehan (named after Jehan Ockeghem, one of his godfathers) now lives in Amiens, but rarely do I see him. In his early life he acted as a clerc to the Royal Household, and now he has taken up a position as an advisor to the Duc de Picardie. He is married and blessed with three children, though I have only met the oldest, Pierre, who, I am proud to say, is a chantre in the Royal Chapel. My son has promised that he will visit soon and, as Amiens is only a six-day journey on horseback, I am hopeful that if my condition worsens there will still be time for him to visit me before I meet my God.

Even if my thoughts seem focused only on the past, it is not my intention to crawl towards death's embrace. I try to walk every day; I spend time writing this account; I regularly attend Mass – all things that I have achieved today. After my visit to the Doctor, I walked towards the Abbey of St Martin for Mass. Arriving early, I said my prayers and then walked in the beautiful cloisters, which afforded shade from the wintry sun and protection from the wind. It was here that I would walk from the schola cantorum [song school] as a choirboy whilst the older chapelains would cast a critical eye over our deportment.

Being a choirboy was an exciting opportunity, which made men of children. Jehan, who, like all singers and composers, was once a choirboy, thought that it was an unnatural life and held it responsible for the ambition of many composers, particularly Desprez. For me, looking back, it nevertheless remains a time I remember with fondness.

The past is my friend in a way that the present has ceased to be. The memories, stored for so long, have become as a room full of pictures and treasures, each one catching my eye and urging me to consider them. I remembered the occasion when I had a hiccupping fit that I thought would never end, and the tenorista, Claude Martin, had caused it to stop by jumping in front of me, his hood over his head and his arms extended like a giant bat. I remembered the snowstorm – unheard of in these regions – that blew snowdrifts into the walkways of the cloister so we had to take a detour to the south side of the square; and the celebrations for St Martin, the patron Saint of the city and its Abbey, whose feast day fell in November and which would require us to process, singing plainsong hymns, occasionally stopping to sing a Salve. That was always the most tiring day for us as boys, severely testing the limits of how long we could sing. Our throats would seize up and we would return to the choir school and put a stylus into our mouths, pretending to create enough space for us to be able to talk again.

I had corresponded with the Archbishop, Martin of Beaunes, and, after several letters and a small payment, it was agreed that Mass today would be dedicated to the sick of the Diocese, and that my name should head the list for whom intercession was sought. Additionally a Mass of my choosing would be sung by the chapelains of St Martin for which I would compensate them. I instructed them to sing Jehan's Missa Cuiusvis toni, which many think of as in the old style, but it holds special significance for me. Recently all the news is of composers whose music I have never heard – Clemens and Créquillon, Mouton and de Sermisy – music we do not hear now François I has moved the court to Paris. I am told by one singer, Charles de Saint Leu, that the new music is much richer and fuller, that they commonly use six, seven or even eight parts at a time, and that they have rediscovered the lower pitches of which Jehan was so fond. I had to smile when I was told that. If only they knew that Jehan had written in thirty-four parts.

The Missa Cuiusvis toni *is not a difficult mass so long as you remember one thing: which mode you are singing in. The design of the piece ensures that, from a single written example, the music can take three different forms in sound and, in this variety, Jehan grants to the singer a freedom of choice and an openness of purpose that is a true reflection of his generosity. For Jehan, music was for God and for all of His children.*

On the page, the Missa Cuiusvis toni *looks simple and, indeed, it makes no particular demands. The notes are not over-fractured, ensemble is easy to attain and it has become a favourite of many. It continues to be used not simply because it is found in the choirbooks, but also because, written to be sung in three modes, it can be made to fit in with any chants that surround it; thus it is fit for every day and every mood. As Boethius, following Aristotle, says: the modes are possessed of their own qualities in much the same way that the days of the week have their own smell. Of course, I could have asked for something more flamboyant for my intercession, like the* Missa de plus en plus, *which requires much rehearsal, a clear mind and great vocal fortitude and, though they may not have thanked me for my choice, the singers would certainly have appreciated the extra payment they would have received for the additional preparation.*

But my reasons for choosing the Missa Cuiusvis toni were personal and date back to the earliest days of my friendship with Jehan. I had been appointed sommelier de chapelle *[junior singer] some two years earlier, having served my apprenticeship as a choirboy and acquitted myself well. Though not possessed of the sweetest voice, I was quick with my studies, of sound memory, and was able to* cantare super librum *[improvise] with more certainty than many others. What I lacked in suavitude, I compensated for with application. When my voice broke, it was clear that I could no longer sing any of the high notes and so I developed the ability to sing* en fausset *[falsetto]. I had hoped that I could thus be part of the choir, but the* maître de chapelle *decided it would be better to have me sing the same part as some of the* chapelains. *Unfortunately the* chapelains – *or at least one of them, Pierre de Gilles – saw this as a challenge to his status. When he found himself standing next to me in a rehearsal and singing the same line, he stopped, waved his hand and confronted the* maître de chapelle.

He was outraged; this went against the natural order, he said, a boy singing a man's part. It was not fitting. It was a challenge to him, to the choir, to the hierarchy of heaven and earth, and to God himself. That, in itself, was sufficient argument with which none could disagree. But then he made a foolish assertion that was a direct challenge to the authority of the maître. *It was, asserted Pierre de Gilles, not something that would happen at Orléans. Orléans was the home town of the* maître *and it was rumoured that he had been passed over for appointment there.*

'Well, fuck off back to Orléans then!' was the maître's *blunt retort.*

Unfortunately for me, the result of this dispute – which was ultimately settled by a meeting of the chapter – was that I, a junior member, was made a sacrifice. Despite my innocence in the matter, I was required to leave the choir for a year until I reached the statutory age of sixteen. In that time I continued to sing at home or in the nave of the church where no one could hear me. It was there that I developed my adult voice. I taught myself by listening to the other singers, in particular Jehan Ockeghem who was recognised as the finest of them all. His voice could descend unnaturally low, but as it rose it maintained its shape and sound. He could sing in the range of the higher, contratenor voices without losing any of the distinct sweetness of his sound. My voice never had this higher register (other than by singing en fausset, *something I was not inclined to do lest the other* chapelains *remember my failed usurpation and take against me) and, when I was appointed* chapelain, *I stood next to Jehan Ockeghem himself and sang the same part. Pierre de Gilles never addressed me directly, which in many ways was a relief.*

Jehan was always kind to me, and encouraging. At that time, the choir was probably the finest in the land and hosted many other composers, amongst them Antoine Busnois. I learned much from Jehan, not simply through his understanding of the music, but from his example. His voice was always firm and clear and I watched the way he stood and breathed. Occasionally he would compliment me, not necessarily by direct observation but through acknowledging the choices I made. 'That was a good place to breathe,' he would say when I chose to break a phrase at a particular point. Or, 'This motet suits your voice.'

But the greatest compliment he paid me was when he asked me to help him with his new composition, the mass-setting that was to become Missa Cuiusvis toni. *I remember the occasion well. It was after Mass on the feast of St Michael and All Angels.*

'Geoffroy,' he said (he always called me by my first name), 'I remember that, as a young boy, you had an elegant hand. I wonder if you would be good enough to help me with some work I am doing? My usual scribe is unavailable.'

There was only one answer.

Thus the first composition upon which I worked with him was that very mass, the Missa Cuiusvis toni. *And that is why it holds the place it does in my heart. It was a piece that I came to know well, not just through singing it many times with Jehan himself at the Abbey of St Martin, but because I was there at the inception of the idea and responsible for its first realisation in written form. Jehan could have asked one of the monks who worked daily in the scriptorium to write out the music, yet he preferred to work with someone familiar with singing. He explained: St Gregory had not merely written down the chants when the Holy Spirit had dictated them to him, he had understood them too. In this – blasphemous as it might be, and with all due humility – it was I who was St Gregory. Jehan, of course, was the true Orpheus.*

Today the Mass was sung by four men whilst the choirboys sang the plainsong, and all the singers accomplished their task commendably. Seated in my stall, I was able to see and hear, yet as always, my awareness of the difficulties of their task made taking pleasure from their endeavours difficult. I reminded myself that we should not be bound by earthly matters, and instead, quite properly, I followed the direction of their praise: to God in heaven. If I might be permitted to comment, I would say that the endings of the Credo and the Kyrie were uncertain and, rather than a sense of finality, I experienced instead a feeling of loss, hardly a fitting ending for a statement of our faith in God. That would not have happened in our day when the choir was enlarged by new appointments made by Louis XI. Then, with more singers swelling our ranks, one would have heard a noise more suited to the expression of faith. Nor would the Mass have taken so long given our preference for faster speeds.

The plainsong was acceptable. Plainsong is the foundation, the rock upon which the education of choirboys is built. It must proceed from the heart and be controlled through breathing and a gentle movement of the body. The boys are not so good this year. There is a roughness of tone where there should be sweetness, a hesitancy of movement that cracks the line so one hears individual notes and isolated voices. Plainsong should flow like a river. The occasional inflections and decorations should be like the stones that lie on the river bed, making no disturbance to the progress of the water, but suggesting instead a design beneath the surface. One or two voices dominated where the aim is to sing praises to the Creator una voce [with one voice], as Shadrach, Meshach, and Abed'nego did when they were thrown into the fiery furnace. Only a practised eye like mine, weakened as it is by old age, could discern the occasional look between the boys when one voice threatened to drag the others back; only a trained ear like mine could hear a syllable applied to the wrong note.

Observing the jeune chapelain [the oldest boy] commanding the younger ones, I fell to thinking about Jehan's theory about the young Compère and the young Desprez. Jehan liked to study causes and, though he had no proof, he believed that their time as choirboys at St Quentin was the root of their unsteady relationship.

Loyset Compère was the older of the two by some five years and thus, when Josquin Desprez arrived from his home in Condé, Loyset would have been one of the senior boys with authority over Josquin. According to Jehan, as children they would have been much as they were as adults: Compère would have been innocent and unaware, blind to his own abilities, and unable to communicate with people, for he could not understand the emotions of others; Desprez, by contrast, was defined by his confrontations with others and, throughout his life, was prepared for a fight if he thought he had been in any way slighted. Such physicality was a family trait, or so it was said, for Desprez's father had been a violent man, which is why the young Josquin was cared for by his uncle and aunt.

I could quite easily imagine little Loys and little Jos meeting at St Quentin, the former already renowned and respected for having composed a piece that the choir performed occasionally, even though he was but thirteen years old, and little Jos, *ambitious even at the tender age of eight, immediately jealous. Put the unaware older boy in charge of the arrogant younger one, and conflict would be the consequence.*

For anyone else, the resentments of youth have been forgotten when they became men. But Desprez never forgot. And Desprez never forgave. I never saw Desprez smile, nor did I know the sound of his laugh. If I ask myself now to describe him, all I can summon are images of darkness and anger – those piercing small eyes, his shaded complexion, and the constant concentration expressed as a scowl. He was not a happy man. In contrast, Compère was always smiling, the expression of one who does not fully understand, like a child who does not comprehend the conversation of adults. And he laughed a lot as well, like the braying of a donkey. For all that, and for all his lack of social grace, he was a man full of joy and without guile.

Compère was to Desprez as Esau was to Jacob, the elder in possession of a birthright that the younger felt was rightfully his but which he could only gain through deception. And, even in later life, when Desprez had become the more celebrated of the two, he must have believed he had achieved fame by guile, not because of his own ability.

There was never to be a reconciliation between them. Undoubtedly Compère would have said to Desprez, had he been asked, the same words that Esau said to Jacob: et ille habeo ait plurima, frater, mi sint tua tibi [And he said: I have plenty, my brother, keep what is thine for thyself]. But even if Compère had said it, Desprez would never have been able to accept it for thereby he would have had to acknowledge to himself his own true nature. Such wilful blindness was similarly evident in the younger's opinion of the elder's music: Desprez believed that Compère was the better composer. It was an opinion that only Desprez held, one that he sustained throughout his life against the force of his own reputation. He formed that view as a child, when it was undoubtedly true, but to believe it as an adult was possible only for a man who could never admit he was wrong. Thus Desprez hated himself, and his anger turned into hatred of Compère, a man who remained happily oblivious.

Desprez was a great composer, perhaps even greater than Jehan, yet he himself never believed it. When he looked at Compère or heard his name, all he saw was an older, more celebrated figure. Yet Compère remained a child throughout his life, from his days as a choirboy to his elevated state as a composer. Little Jos? Well, he became a monster. A monster with talent.

CHAPTER 8

The deep, intense sleep that had overwhelmed him after breakfast was broken by the bump of the plane onto the tarmac. For a moment Andrew thought he was back at home, that perhaps he'd fallen out of bed or John had jumped on top of him. The announcement from the captain to remain seated until the seat belt signs had been turned off returned him to his prosaic surroundings; he was still on an aeroplane, the second of his three flights. His eyes were glued shut and his body felt too weary to have experienced real sleep. God, why had he done this? He could have broken the trip here in London, maybe stayed near the British Library, drunk a pint of beer and eaten fish and chips. Budget was the main reason, that and the argument he'd had with Karen when he'd announced that he would be attending the conference in Tours 'and might fit in a trip to Paris at the same time'.

It had come out the wrong way, as things always seemed to. What he should have said was that he would take advantage of flying all that way to do some research. A couple of days in the Bibliothèque Nationale might provide him with circumstantial evidence to prove authorship of the motet, and further biographical detail about Geoffroy Chiron whose letter accompanied it. If he'd framed his plan in terms vague enough to suggest his pursuit was a dull and necessary chore, holding little interest for him, then he might have stood a chance, but the veiled implication that he was hiding the real reason had raised Karen's suspicions. Almost immediately he'd found himself in the middle of one of their familiar rows with its well-visited themes: his selfishness, her sacrifices, and their shared responsibility for John. The subsequent price of his lack of forethought was forty-eight hours of the silent treatment, broken only by the occasional terse instruction and heavy sighs when he failed to fulfil simple domestic tasks. He had responded in kind, conducting a loud conversation with his travel agent. 'You're sure I can make that connection?' he'd asked, frowning and shaking his head. 'Well,' he added, sucking his teeth, 'I suppose it will have to be like that.' Now, halfway through his arduous journey, he felt a stab of pure hatred for his wife, which softened only slightly into angry jealousy as he thought of her sleeping soundly in their bed.

In the musty air of Heathrow's Terminal Four, he eased the stiffness out of his body with a gentle walk and followed the directions provided by the prim British

Airways ground staff to his gate. As his final destination was Paris, the indignities of immigration and customs were mercifully few; he'd face more at Charles de Gaulle airport.

To sit down would be to risk being overcome by sleep and missing his flight, so he bought a coffee and a chocolate bar then browsed the newsagents where he bought *The Times* and *The Gramophone*. Normally he wouldn't consider looking at such a magazine, but its cover promised an article on Ockeghem and, on further investigation, he found it contained an interview with Emma Mitchell of Beyond Compère. Given that he was meeting her later that day, it seemed propitious, yet when he reached the boarding area and saw Emma Mitchell sitting there, the coincidence was less easy to dismiss. For a split second he wondered, had she come to meet him? In his tired state he was unable to immediately accept the obvious explanation: that she and her group were simply on the same plane to the conference.

He was tempted to introduce himself, but reasoned that he was in no fit state. The ground had been shifting beneath his feet since he'd landed as if it was made from the same rubberised walkway as the travelators that had aided his journey across the terminal, and he was hardly at his best. His clothes were rumpled, his teeth un-brushed and his body limp with fatigue. He took a seat, set down his coffee, and picked up his purchases. *The Times* provided cover and, like a teenager hiding a pornographic magazine inside something more respectable, he opened up *The Gramophone* behind the newspaper. The real Emma Mitchell was sitting just twenty feet away with several other people, all of them dressed casually in jeans, jumpers and sweat-shirts. These must be the members of her group, and the photograph accompanying the interview provided the key: Susan Moore, Claire Slingsby, and Peter Merrill were sitting together, and Emma Mitchell herself was sitting next to a man whom the photo identified as Oliver Martin. Emma was smaller than Andrew had expected, *gamine* as the French would have it, with her short hair and elfin features. He saw her nudge Oliver Martin and point out something in her newspaper at which they both laughed. Andrew wondered if they were a couple. There was something about their body language that suggested they were, though he had no faith in his powers of observation and knew that he lacked a simple understanding of others' motivations and behaviour. Gossip and innuendo provided most people with an appreciation of the human condition rendered in complex hues of diverse colours, yet to Andrew the emotional world was sketched in black and white. Affairs between colleagues had usually run the entire course, from desperate secret assignations to bitter dénouement, before he found out. Rivalries and long-held resentments between academics that he read as hyperbole or irrelevant diversions turned out to be evidence of intense, immature, territorial skirmishes. And tensions in his own marriage always took him by surprise. He certainly couldn't assume, then, that Emma and Oliver Martin were a couple. In fact, the more he thought about it, the more he realised this was probably the kind of easy relationship that actors and performers usually enjoyed. It was all 'darling' this and 'darling' that, wasn't it? Perhaps this Oliver was actually gay or even bisexual? He wouldn't be surprised if they'd all slept with each other.

He scanned the interview. It began, predictably enough, with the announcement of the Ockeghem anniversary. Suddenly he was fully awake. This was the day! This was the day and he'd forgotten it! It was the travel of course, the jetlag and the resultant confusion of time. But, yes, it was February 6th, 1997, exactly five hundred years since the death of Johannes Ockeghem. Andrew felt as if he'd betrayed the composer; today, of all days, his first waking thought should have been for him. Ironically, obsession with Ockeghem was exactly what Karen had once bitterly accused him of, and now, here he was, on his own, free to enjoy the moment and he'd forgotten. It was as if one of his parents had died and he'd forgotten to commemorate the day. He reached for a further example with which to berate himself, but all he could come up with was forgetting his wedding anniversary, something he'd done twice in five years. He made a small embarrassed noise in his throat as he remembered Karen's reactions: the first time she'd been angry; the second, upset as she was, she had been unnervingly calm, as though she had expected it. He looked back at the article to push the thought away. There was little here that he didn't know. It traced the original theatrical production of *Beyond Compère*, the transition from a stage show to a concert-giving group, and the subsequent recordings. A CD of Ockeghem would be out next month, a review of which appeared elsewhere in the magazine.

Other than that, there was little of interest to Andrew beside Emma's assertion that she wouldn't necessarily devote her entire career to early music: she was still young and still developing as a musician. The only other thing that caught his eye was a constant refusal to call it '*her* group', a refrain to which the interviewer drew attention. *The* group, she said, was a collection of talented individuals, not a pack of which she was the leader. They certainly didn't need her on stage to conduct a *chanson*, for example. Her role, she emphasised, was very much as a programmer and researcher and, to use the term in the theatrical sense, director. Looking across at her now, her hand gently stroking Oliver's arm, she certainly didn't look autocratic.

He turned to the review.

Ockeghem Gems, Beyond Compère, cond. Emma Mitchell; 2 CDs EMI 3507, 121 minutes; *Prenez sur moi*, Kyrie and Agnus from *Missa Prolationum*, *Presque Transi*, *Ave maria*, *Petite camusette/S'elle m'amera*, *Intemerata Dei*, *Tant fuz gentement*, Kyrie and Agnus from *Missa cuiusvis toni*, *Resjouy toi, terre de France*, *Mort tu as navré de ton dart*, *Requiem*, Josquin des Pres, *Nymphes des bois*.

1997 marks the five-hundredth anniversary of the death of Johannes Ockeghem, the great Franco-Flemish composer and the *bon père* to the generation of Josquin, De La Rue, Compère and Brumel. Unlike recent debates about his younger colleague, Josquin des Pres (a composer whose name was used as a designer label, slapped on second-rate material by opportunistic publishers, thereby presenting serious problems for Josquin scholars) the Ockeghem canon is fixed and finite. There have been no new additions to the repertoire for a while now – no missing masterpieces reclaimed, no hidden treasures brought to light. And Ockeghem's music, because of this, has been much recorded; already this year we have seen three versions of his *Missa De plus en plus* (by The Tallis Scholars, The Orlando Consort and The Clerks Group – see Jan. 1997 pp.123–125). How, then, does a group successfully capture the old man? The answer is brilliantly given here. This is a living, breathing portrait of someone who was, by all accounts, revered and loved throughout his long life.

Following the now usual format of Beyond Compère's recordings, this double CD collection is in every respect elegantly designed. In addition to the thorough texts and translations provided in the beautiful 128-page booklet (the hardback covers of which house each CD), we are given incisive essays on the editions used (by Jaap van Benthem), a portrait of the composer himself complete with new biographical information (David Fallows), and a carefully argued presentation of the music by the indefatigable leader of the group, Emma Mitchell. It is she who is ultimately responsible for this musical portrait and, as she explains, the programme aims to give a sense of the man and his contribution to music history.

To that end, the first CD interleaves the more personal chansons (if any love song that works within the conventions of courtly love can be described as personal); the motets (amongst them a brilliant interpretation of *Intemerata Dei mater* that captures both its derivation from some of Ockeghem's own chansons and its more solemn, liturgical function); and movements from the *Missa Prolationum* and *Missa Cuiusvis toni*. These last demonstrate Ockeghem's ludic bent, a fascination with musical puzzles and their solutions that is manifest throughout his *oeuvre*. That theme is picked up and expanded with each disc's multimedia component. Place the CD in your computer and, while the music plays through the speakers, you can see the original notation and its modern translation side by side. This is not only a brilliant educational tool, but also great fun and I would strongly urge everyone to avail themselves of this feature.

We have come to expect from Mitchell's singers a dramatic flair which combines the benefits of the cool efficiency of the English choral tradition with an embrace of a more flamboyant continental sound, and both aspects are appropriately used throughout the recording with music sung mainly one-to-a-part. The recording quality is equal to the exceptionally high vocal standards and it too reflects something of the imagination shown in live performance (listen to *Prenez sur moi* where the stereo separation is dazzlingly extreme, a device which brilliantly illustrates the strict canon).

The second disc is a moving meditation upon death and loss. Central to the disc is Ockeghem's Requiem, the first extant polyphonic setting of the Requiem Mass (Dufay's, which pre-dates it, is lost to history), probably written for the funeral of Charles VII in 1461. Mitchell, perhaps sensing the inadequacy of that historical context to illustrate the music's emotional core, chooses to make it a requiem for three fifteenth-century composers – Binchois, Ockeghem and Josquin. The disc begins with Ockeghem's *Déploration* on the death of Binchois – *Mort tu as navré de ton dart* – and ends with Josquin's lament on the death of the Ockeghem himself, *Nymphes des bois,* and thereby reveals the development of the expressive potential in music across forty years (Binchois died in 1460). Mitchell and her group have brought Ockeghem to life in a musical essay about death: it is an essential addition to any musical collection. I must also urge the listener to explore the other fine discs that this group have produced, in particular the award-winning *Josquin Can.*

    Francis Porter

Francis Porter: it would be him. His name seemed to pop up everywhere like a bad penny, and one of the most irritating things was that he was a difficult person to dislike. They'd bumped into each other on several occasions at conferences over the years and Porter was always annoyingly pleasant, encouraging, witty and personable. He wouldn't be coming to Tours, not because he hadn't been invited, but because he was currently on sabbatical at the University of Sydney, a ridiculously glamorous venue where Andrew enviously imagined his rival adorned with Hawaiian Leis, the kind of incongruously geographical manifestations of success with which his career seemed to be forever garlanded. As if Porter's contribution to the world of musicology wasn't enough, he had also effortlessly entered the elite world of the English choral tradition, which was otherwise barred to anyone who was not a United Kingdom passport holder. Active at Yale as a singer and conductor, when at Oxford he had sung with several of the college choirs and got to know many of the same singers who appeared regularly in the line-ups of early-music groups like Beyond Compère. These days he provided performance editions and programme notes and regularly appeared in the 'Thanks to' section of CD liner notes. At least with Porter some thirteen thousand miles away, Andrew now stood a chance of being regarded as the resident expert on reception theory at the conference.

    Porter's review had reheated Andrew's old enmity. He resented the condescending tone of the review, deliberately repressing for a moment the obvious fact that a musicologist such as himself was hardly the average reader. He knew all the pieces well and understood the design of the programme with its montage of contrasting idioms and moods, the secular chansons alternating with the lengthier, intense sacred motets; he didn't need someone to point that out to him. There was no doubting the credentials of the authors of the notes for the disc – David Fallows knew everything there was to know about fifteenth-century music and Jaap van Benthem was a highly respected editor – but the suggestion of 'new biographical material' was disingenuous: nothing new about the life of Ockeghem had emerged in the past twenty years.

    What annoyed Andrew in particular, though, was the argument of the second disc which, it seemed to him, Porter had deliberately amplified so as to point the listener away from Ockeghem and towards the more expressive later generation, specifically to Josquin. That was typical, thought Andrew: Josquin again. It was like his Medieval and Renaissance music course. Here he was trying to champion Ockeghem, and all people wanted to talk about was Josquin. The first piece, *Mort tu as navré de ton dart*, was Ockeghem's lament on the death of Binchois. That was fine as far as it went; it was a piece that should be on the disc, not just because it was a great piece but because it showed Ockeghem's musical debt to Binchois. Then came Ockeghem's Requiem Mass. So far, so good. But then came a piece by Josquin, his *Nymphes des bois*, the lament on the death of Ockeghem. That damn piece! If it wasn't so beautiful, then maybe Ockeghem would be remembered in his own right and not because someone else wrote a piece about him. If Ockeghem year was going to be hijacked by Josquin, then Andrew might as well give up now.

He looked up from his magazine to see Emma and her group picking up their bags. The plane was boarding. In the light of *Ockeghem Gems,* his original plan looked misconceived. If Emma Mitchell could do this to Ockeghem, then maybe she wasn't to be trusted with the *Miserere mei*? She'd probably want him to prove that it was by Josquin. Perhaps he should offer the motet to someone else?

He finished his coffee and slid his magazine and paper into his briefcase, careful not to crease any of the pages of the transcription he'd made during the night. It was all there, carefully protected in its blue folder. For the third time in less than eighteen hours he handed his boarding pass to an attendant and stepped into an aluminium tube. The colour scheme was depressingly recognisable: antiseptic white with red-and-blue trim, the practised 'Welcome on board, sir' as stale as the recycled air. His spirits were low. Suddenly he felt tired and very alone, full of doubt, and he wished he'd apologised to Karen. He needed her.

It was the same tortuous progress to his seat that he'd experienced on the first flight, with each person trying to cram too much luggage into the overhead lockers. He sighed and then realised he was standing next to Emma Mitchell who was seated in an aisle seat. He looked down just as she looked up and she smiled slightly at him. Without intending to, his face registered recognition. Panicked, he held out his hand. 'Andrew Eiger. We're meeting later.'

She looked confused, then laughed. Her hand was small, the handshake quite definite, so much so that it hurt him. He remembered the lacerations in the palm of his hand, which was now throbbing slightly.

'Oh, yes,' she said, smiling. 'At the conference. I'm sorry. Of course. You're on the same flight then?'

'Yes.' It was all he could think to say. 'Um, later then? At the conference? Or after the concert, as we said?'

'Yes. After the concert. We'll all be going out for a meal, so do join us. The concert's in the Cathedral, but I'll see you at the conference, won't I?'

'Yes, I know,' he said. He hadn't meant to be so forceful or defensive and realised that for some reason he wanted to impress her. He was, much to his surprise, a little star-struck, or maybe just unprepared for a meeting that seemed to have begun without him knowing it.

'I'm looking forward to seeing what you have for us, by the way,' she said. 'It sounds very intriguing, whatever "it" is. Will you be talking about it at the conference?'

'Er, no. Just talking about the reception of Ockeghem's music at the end of the eighteenth and beginning of the nineteenth centuries. The usual stuff, you know? The way that people see Ockeghem as mathematically inclined – more of an intellectual than an artist. It's a myth we need to destroy.'

He'd clicked into academic mode, now more relaxed and in control. He wanted to know where Emma stood on Ockeghem and had deliberately thrown in the final line as a challenge. She made some small gesture to him, a flick of the finger towards the back of the aircraft. Was she suggesting they go to the back of the plane and talk about it? He looked in the direction she was pointing and realised that she was trying to tell him that the aisle was now clear and he was holding up his fellow passengers.

'Oh. Yes. See you later then,' he said, taking his cue and moving forward.

'Are you being picked up at the airport?' asked Emma quickly.

'No. Getting the train.'

'We might be able to give you a lift. The organisers are picking us up in a minibus. If there's room, you can come with us if you like?'

By now the pressure of people behind him had propelled him three rows forward and he nodded to her as he was herded towards the back of the plane. She seemed nice enough, he thought, even attractive. But, as a performer she was probably used to smiling for the camera and putting on her best face; he wasn't going to fall so easily for her charms and surrender control of the manuscript until he was certain he could trust her. Still, a lift to the conference would save him a lot of time and energy. It would be door-to-door and would avoid the complications of getting into Paris, onto a train, then from the train station at Tours to the conference. He was prepared to sit on the floor of the van if necessary.

He tucked his briefcase under the seat in front of him. He wanted his new transcription to be within sight at all times and didn't want to surrender it to the chaos of the overhead bins. In many ways this most recent result of his labours, an edition from which modern singers could easily perform, was surplus to requirements and it made him nervous. His guiding principle had been to cover his tracks with each new version, immediately consigning the earlier model to the shredder. Now three copies of the motet existed, which meant three times the possibility that someone else could stumble on his treasure. At his feet lay two and at home, in the safe-box bought from Staples expressly for the purpose, lay the first transcription he'd made in the library six months ago. The real manuscript, of course, still lay in the library in Amiens. He would destroy one of the copies in his briefcase when he got to Tours; he couldn't take the risk.

He closed his eyes and thought back to that glorious moment six months ago. He'd been alone at the time, conducting archival research, something he hadn't done since the first year of his Ph.D. when he'd spent a summer foraging through documents in the Bibliothèque Nationale, a comparatively simple pursuit in that it required of him only a working knowledge of modern French, his main realm of enquiry being microfiched reviews of concerts and the private papers of various eighteenth- and nineteenth-century musicologists. Last year's archival research in Amiens was considerably more difficult and demanded knowledge of Latin, medieval French, and a great deal of patience. It was prompted by intellectual fashion rather than a spirit of unquenchable historical enquiry. Several important discoveries had recently been made about the singer-composers of the fifteenth century, in particular work on Ockeghem, Busnois and, of course, Josquin, and primary research had made a comeback, replacing fashionable theorising that had for a while occupied centre stage. Andrew had little time for the arcane posturing of poststructuralism, which he deemed to be about as useful as sticking a model of Chartres Cathedral in a wind tunnel to test its aerodynamic properties. In his opinion, such theoretical agendas were shrill, repetitious, incomprehensible and ultimately self-defeating. If you were going to deconstruct music and make the author explode in a cloud of critical smoke, then what was there left to talk about? So he had welcomed the revival of first-hand research and decided that he should do some himself. The trouble was that he didn't know how to do it or where to begin.

That hole in his education raised the spectre of ridicule by his peers. He couldn't exactly go to, say, Leeman Perkins at Columbia and ask him how you got to read through the records of Chapter meetings at the Cathedral of St Gatien at Tours. Besides which, Perkins had already done it. And he couldn't ring up, say, Craig Wright at Yale and ask him on which shelf he could find the documents that described Dufay's order for wine, made when Ockeghem had stayed with him.

The second problem was choosing the focus of his enquiries. The obvious place was Tours, but he'd heard that a young French researcher had spent five years working on the archives there under the sponsorship of the Centre d'Études Supérieures de la Renaissance (Université François-Rabelais, Tours) – a typically long-winded and typically French soubriquet, thought Andrew. He had picked the composer Jean Mouton and spent his time in Amiens in much the same way as he'd submitted his vague application for research funding, ticking a series of boxes whilst framing a loose and hopeful description of his project's aims. That Amiens had no Ockeghemian connections was a good thing; it showed that he was moving beyond his narrow realm of specialisation. And focusing on a composer from a slightly later generation was a logical progression. He'd always liked Mouton's music and would base his research around the period when he had been master of the choirboys in 1500. Some three years after Ockeghem's death, he knew the immediate historical background and thus saved himself time and effort. And, he discovered, Amiens had good rail links to Paris, so, if the place turned out to be a dump, he could easily return to France's political and cultural capital.

And so, in September of 1996, Andrew had arrived at the Gare d'Amiens and headed directly to the Cathedral of Notre Dame in the centre of the city. It was a hot day so he hadn't wasted any time pondering the lopsided towers, the elaborately sculpted portals or the polychromatic façade, plunging instead into the interior's welcoming chill. He was early for his meeting with the archivist at the West Door and, although architecture was not his real interest, he'd sat down on a chair at the back of the building to take in its shape and proportions. It was a classic Gothic design – the Nave, the Crossing with the Transept, the Choir, and then the Apse, beyond it the Ambulatory – the ceiling sweeping high overhead, the eye guided there by the numerous columns that ranged towards the east end. Tourists were speaking in low voices, the sound of their steps bouncing off the stone floors up into the vaulted arena. To Andrew, such buildings always suggested spaceships, huge vehicles that would carry the faithful upwards to heaven, and in many ways that's exactly what they were, but the uncertainties of human faith were of no interest to him. The sentiments of aspiration and glorification expressed in the architecture, from the shape of the cross described by the Nave and Transept to its leaping vertical articulation, were secondary to his narrow enquiry: the music and its realisation. He didn't notice the intricate inlaid black-and-white tiling in the floor and the daunting maze traced at the centre of the Nave.

The librarian, an elderly stooped man, barrel-chested and wheezy, was right on time. He shook Andrew's hand, immediately launching into an enthusiastic and detailed description of the building. Andrew's heart sank. All he wanted to do was to get his hands on the Cathedral records and establish his own private, leisurely routine. The careful, loving narrative woven by the archivist held no interest for him, and he offered occasional grunts, not so much as an acknowledgement of the procession of interesting facts but more to indicate polite disinterest. The closer they got to the area where the choir would have sung, the more disappointed Andrew became. Instead of stories of the singers and composers, he was regaled with an account of the fire that had destroyed the first cathedral and the subsequent rebuilding in the thirteenth century. At one point, when the old man mentioned the archives, he looked up – but again it was only the historical context that was being sketched, in this case another fire that had destroyed Cathedral records in 1218. Fire, the archivist had said, chuckling: it's as if God was trying to tell us something. When he had finally suggested that his visitor might now want to see the Chapter records, Andrew quickly agreed, but he was further detained when his host, looking upward to the Rose Window in the South Transept, declared that no one should come to Amiens Cathedral without learning its most valuable lesson. There, in the intricate circular design of the stained glass, was a palimpsest of Egyptian, Greek, Roman and medieval European mythology. Described in the image of the wheel, an idea common to all of those cultures, were meditations on the universal themes of fate and fortune. One could not rely on anything, the old man intoned: life was a constant movement from success to failure and back again; what went around came around. Andrew mechanically traced the patterns that the old man outlined with his index finger whilst privately fuming at the delay in his schedule. His ears pricked up only when mention was made of Boethius, a major figure in medieval musical theory, before he realised that the archivist had begun a lengthy exposition on the role of Fortune in *The Consolation of Philosophy*. He switched off again. The old man must have finally sensed his impatience; quite suddenly he announced that he would not show the young musicologist the exterior of the South Transept, before adding that Andrew should not leave Amiens without studying it. There are two sides to every story, the librarian remarked cryptically, and what was shown in the Christian images within the Cathedral was challenged by the exterior design. Andrew nodded eagerly but he could tell from the barely disguised exasperated sigh that the old man had finally understood that Andrew had no interest in the superstitious and irrational medieval mind.

Amiens Cathedral maintained its own archive, unlike almost all other French *départements* where the task of storing valuable, historical documents was the province of regional government. Andrew was shown to a small room and was solemnly advised of the special dispensation that he had been granted, along with its associated responsibilities. At long last, he was left on his own to begin combing the annualised minutes of the Chapter meetings.

Over what remained of that day and the next, he patiently drew up a list of common abbreviations used for payments and quantities, but without a medieval French-English dictionary to hand he stumbled frequently. The handwriting, perhaps neat enough at the time, was haphazard, and for the first few hours all but indecipherable. The mystique of history that the ancient books initially offered soon faded. The white gloves that he was required to wear to protect the parchment became an annoying second skin, and the increasing carelessness with which he handled the heavy books told its own story of his dwindling commitment to the project. At first he obeyed the archivist's instructions and carefully turned over each page with both hands, but soon he began flipping them over as he would a reference book in a library, causing the books to creak and crack in protest like an arthritic great-uncle.

Only the hope of discovering a reference to Mouton, or perhaps the name of a composer who till now had no known associations with Amiens, sustained him in his dull hunt through the records. There were precious few of the former and none of the latter, and he was forced to conclude that the records held no valuable secrets. Having read several articles by other academics that cited amusing infringements of proper behaviour in church, he'd expected more. There was nothing new here, nothing that hadn't been more engagingly and wittily described in similar accounts of behaviour in the Sistine Chapel, and the Cathedrals of Notre Dame in Paris and Cambrai.

And so, on the third day, Andrew sought new diversions outside the archive to relieve himself from the repetitious tedium. The only part of the building that excited him was the Choir, where the lectern, around which the singers would have gathered, still stood. In his mind's eye he saw Mouton himself indicating the tempo of one of his compositions, a robed choir with arms draped around each other, the boys jostling for a view of the music. The archivist spotted Andrew deep in contemplation and came over and asked him if everything was all right. He replied rather too quickly that everything was fine; he was just taking a break. Guilt for abandoning his task was an unwelcome new sensation and he vowed to stay in the library for the whole of the afternoon rather than leaving around four as he had done the previous day.

His research had begun to feel like homework, something expected of him by others, rather than the vacation pursuit he had envisaged. Everyone else – the tourists, the shopkeepers, Karen and John at home – were out enjoying the sunshine whilst he was detained inside until he'd learned his lesson. Later that day, the archivist poked his head around the door of the library and asked hopefully whether Andrew had any questions. Andrew had looked up quickly. Every day the old man had offered to help and every day Andrew had nothing to ask. Panicked, he offered the only thing that had piqued his interest that morning, an inscription on the inside front cover of one of the bound books: 'Qui te furetur, cum Juda dampnificetur'.

Without a Latin dictionary, his translation was only approximate and, prompted by his own mood as much as anything, he had decided that it was a warning to the reader not to feel frustrated. He had thought that *furetur* derived from *furor*, meaning anger, and had assumed that anyone becoming annoyed or displeased with these records would be damned. *Furetur*, the old man explained, came from the Latin verb meaning 'to steal'. The inscription was a common curse written in books of all kinds in the medieval period, which, by virtue of their rarity and labour-intensive production, were very valuable. It was known as the Judas curse, added the old man; anyone stealing the book would be damned like the thief Judas Iscariot. There was nothing new under the sun, thought Andrew. As a child, he'd methodically written in all his books: 'If this book should ever roam, box its ears and send it home, to: Andrew Eiger'.

Encouraged by Andrew's question, the archivist lingered, clearly expecting a greater challenge than this simple translation until it became obvious that Andrew had nothing more to offer. Abruptly, he turned on his heel and left.

Chained once more to the dull archives, Andrew developed a new diversion that allowed him to remain at his desk in an attitude of work: an investigation into the construction of the books themselves. They were leather-bound and fitted with heavy metal clasps and locks, the keys kept on a special key ring with which he'd been entrusted. The leather of the binding was carefully hand-stitched, as regular as the machine stitching on his shoes and more secure, the covers and spines embossed with gold lettering which now, half a millennium later, had flaked off in places. The pages were made from vellum – prepared sheepskin; once they were soft and flexible but now they were stiff. The binding was fixed by some sort of resin, discoloured by age, and redundant given the strength of the stitching. Despite the solid construction, in some instances the cover had come loose, revealing a tongue of leather that folded over the lip of the spine into the space between it and the pages. Here Andrew could see the structure of the book itself, the dark, yellowed glue and the stitching that held all the pages together, and then the spine itself, an inner layer of vellum, which filled the empty space to provide reinforcement and lent the spine its fat, plush appearance. In some cases this extra padding had disappeared as though time had wasted its bulk, and those books fell open rather too easily. It got Andrew thinking. Vellum was a valuable material, and in the medieval period everything was recycled. Maybe the stuffing in the spine contained something mundane or even something interesting? Shopping lists, rough drafts of the chapter records, a love letter perhaps? And maybe such treasures had been discovered and removed by an historian who'd been here before?

When he was sure that the librarian had gone for lunch and he was entirely alone, he took the records for the year 1501 and prepared to unpick the spine. He didn't have to force anything. The glue was old and cracked and had lost its adhesive properties, so his task was like unwrapping a Christmas present. He simply opened the fold at the top and grasped the filling between thumb and forefinger to remove it. But it wouldn't budge; the glue might no longer hold the leather binding in place, but it still held the padding to the leather.

He thought no more of it and returned to his research. The next day, however, after two hours of reading the records for 1502, he tried the same thing with a different volume and managed to extract a folded piece of vellum from one of the bindings. It was disappointing. He'd seen it, or something like it, before. It was simply one of the pages from the chapter records sullied by the scribe, a large blob of ink and a hastily scribbled 'Merde. Merde!' over a half-completed page. Nevertheless, it was an encouraging human engagement with the past, and considerably more personal than anything he'd read thus far. Subsequently he went back over all the books he'd studied to see if he could find anything similar, and an hour later he'd discovered four similar folded sheets, further examples of nothing more exciting than scribal ineptitude.

Eventually he became almost as bored with his search as he was with the investigation into the records themselves. There wasn't even the satisfaction of developing a methodology. His early attempts had sometimes resulted in torn vellum, but, in a relatively short space of time, he'd become quite an expert. He had a feel for it now. He knew the right amount of pressure he could exert before the vellum would rip and had found that a small amount of saliva could sometimes loosen the glue. Thus his developing skills as an historical pickpocket became his real pursuit, rather than the quest for historical discovery, so much so that he found he'd extracted three folded pieces of vellum from three different books and, suddenly worried that he might put them back in the wrong places, almost forgot to consider their content. The first and second were the usual spoiled entries. The third was different: a letter. The writing was obviously not of the same hand as that of any of the scribes he'd viewed thus far, though it shared with it the same preference for loops on 'g's' and 'y's' in particular. He suspected that it was of the same era, a thought that was immediately confirmed by the careful dating at the top right hand of the page: *Tours, Martius 19, 1524*. Tours: Ockeghem's city, though Ockeghem had died twenty-seven years before the letter was written. It was addressed to *mon fils* – my son – and the author was a Geoffroy Chiron, a name that, at the time, meant nothing to Andrew. In floral, formal language, the father explained his poor state of health and expressed the hope that the son would be able to visit soon 'by the grace of the Lord, and of the Duke'. Some of the words were unclear and some smudged, quite different in style from the limited, recondite vocabulary of the chapter records, but one word stood out: *ung motect* – a motet.

The letter was smaller than the other pieces of vellum used for bindings, and two accompanying sheets, larger still, provided further padding and had ensured the letter's survival. These supplementary sheets had been folded over themselves, widthwise and several times, to fit into the spine and thus they revealed their secret to Andrew slowly and, in retrospect, almost teasingly. The first thing he did was to unfold the extra pages, which resembled a fan. When he had smoothed out the creases, it became apparent that he was dealing with only one piece of paper. The final fold was not quite in the middle of the page so that the overlap, which had made it appear from a cursory glance like two pages, actually consisted of the top and bottom of the same sheet. This single piece of paper was stuck together but two centimetres of handwritten Latin text were visible, and above that, two parallel horizontal lines.

He recognised them straightaway, the dimensions as familiar to him as a fragment of a ledger would be to an accountant or the symbols of a wiring diagram would be to an electrician: it was the bottom of a musical stave, and two fat, square breves confirmed it as fifteenth-century music notation. He looked up to check there was no one around then slowly placed the document flat on the desk, smoothing out the folds as best he could by running his hand gently from top to bottom and side to side. He knew that he had to be careful now. The ink itself might be sticking the page together and may well have bled from one side to the other. He peeled off his white gloves and laid them to one side; this would require a delicacy of touch that could only be achieved with bare fingertips. He wiped his hands on his trousers to remove any sweat, and then looked around him once more. He was alone.

He placed the folded sheet flat on the desk and pressed down with splayed fingers and thumbs to anchor it. Then he lifted his index fingers, brought their tips together and, with the lightest of pressure, gently inserted them between the folds. It was warm to the touch and much smoother than he'd expected, as though its resting place had kept it alive. Slowly, evenly, he separated his index fingers, moving them in opposite directions, caressing the stave beneath them. The top fold loosened from the bottom and, after about a minute of this insinuating movement, he had cleared about three millimetres to reveal almost a complete new line on which were traced two new note heads. As tempting as it was to examine them, he stuck to his immediate task and, with the same tender insistence, repeated the process. After ten minutes, he had succeeded in exposing three centimetres of writing. He dropped his head so that his eyes were level with the document and congratulated himself; none of the ink had bled through and he could clearly see a bass part in fifteenth-century white notation. He was tempted to push forward now with more urgency but, fearing that the vellum might tear, he endured the beautiful torment of his calculated probing.

He repeated the same movement several times, delicately easing apart the folds of the paper to ensure that no damage came to his treasure and, after twenty minutes, he had revealed a single sheet on which three musical parts were notated. The text was *Miserere mei* – Psalm 51 – the same words that had been set countless times by other composers, most famously by Allegri in the seventeenth century. It was immediately obvious that this manuscript was not a performing edition. It was tiny and whereas, in fifteenth-century choirbooks traditionally the voice-parts were separated, here the three, named parts were ranged on top of each other, like a modern score.

It was no forgery – why would a forger hide it here, after all? – and his faith in its authenticity grew with each small discovery. Here and there he found faint *ficta* markings, which seemed to have been added afterwards. It was a living document of compositional practice and, according to the letter that accompanied it, must have been in some way linked to Tours. It was clearly what music historians called an autograph: a working copy made by – or for – a composer; and as such, it was extremely rare.

Andrew stood up, crossed the room quietly and locked the door. He was about to slide the manuscript surreptitiously into his bag and then fill the spine with another piece of paper when it occurred to him that it was not only safer to leave it here, but wiser. Provenance would have to be shown, something that could only be done with a witness, and this was far too precious to share with anyone else. He would leave it here. Back home, in America, he would gather all the necessary corroboration and consider the perfect circumstances in which to reveal it. Now, though, he had to make a copy so that if someone else discovered it – he shuddered at the thought – he could claim to have found it first.

By then it was late afternoon. He had only one day left; the day after that he would fly home from Paris. And so he returned the motet carefully to its resting place and the following day, with more confidence, he retrieved his precious find. There was less time than he would have liked; the archivist had promised to visit him that afternoon to answer any remaining questions and collect the keys.

Geoffroy Chiron's accompanying letter, whatever its relevance, could wait; the music was the thing. Suppressing his desire to study the motet itself, he yielded to immediate needs, proceeding methodically and with a detachment that belied his excitement. Firstly, he measured the document. Although it was clearly not for inclusion in any collection, perhaps its dimensions and other identifying features would allow him to tie it to a time and a place. Just because Chiron had sent it from Tours didn't mean it had been composed there. Then he traced some of the handwriting and a few of the notes and their shapes; such details might match other fifteenth-century French sources.

Finally he began to make a copy of the document itself, being careful to maintain exactly the same layout as the original scribe. He discovered almost straightaway that it was not a three-part-piece. The Latin instruction in the bass part indicated a *contratenor* part; it was a four-part motet. On further investigation of the text he saw reference to a canon and realised just how much he'd underestimated the ambition of the composition: it was, unbelievably, a piece for thirty-four separate voices.

It was difficult to concentrate now, copying a cruel necessity when all he really wanted to do was yield to the seduction of the music. There should have been choirs of angels singing, not the dull task of reproduction, and he should be running in the streets shouting 'Eureka', spraying strangers with champagne. Instead he had to labour against the urgent ticking of the clock. It was like the nightmares he once had of sitting exams and being the only one in the examination room, looking down at a blank page, realising too late that he'd written nothing at all.

He checked and re-checked his transcription, stowed it safely in his bag and then placed the original manuscript back in the spine. The only task that remained was to present his research findings to the librarian, who arrived punctually at five o'clock. What he had to show was unimpressive – a few anecdotes about singers misbehaving, records of payments to Mouton for instruction of the choirboys, a half-completed chart of references to other known composers. He struggled to think of interesting questions to ask, if only to ensure future access to the archives, and the old man showed his disappointment all too clearly, muttering something under his breath about Americans with too much money. Andrew's breath caught in his throat. The archivist, after all, could stop him returning to the library and thus bar access to the manuscript. Charm was needed. Sweating, his heart thumping, he fulsomely thanked the old man for his patience and offered exaggerated assurances that he would make more progress the next time; although he had little to show on paper, he was now much more familiar with the archaic formal language as well as the handwriting of the scribes, and he was sure that any future trip would be a success. The archivist did not, at least, argue the point, and Andrew was sure that he would yet be allowed to return to claim his treasure.

Thinking he had been left alone, Andrew began gathering his things together and was surprised to see the old man still standing there. Had he, asked the archivist, taken a look at the South Transept? Andrew hadn't. He casually glossed over his omission by saying that he intended to do so now. The old man nodded and waited for him to leave.

Outside the sun was low in the sky. Shadows rested on the complex carvings of the portal and, above it, the tracery that surrounded the Rose Window. Andrew struggled to remember what the librarian had said, but all he could recall was something about Fortune. He looked up and picked out a parade of figures from pagan religions, most of them Egyptian. Here, next to the King, sat Anubis, the Egyptian God of the Dead, a jackal, and around the window danced figures of the zodiac. The images were certainly strange. The design seemed to suggest that within the church one was safe from secular influences, but outside darker forces were to be found. Casting his mind back to a course he'd taken on Shakespeare, Andrew remembered the wheel of fortune. What went up must come down was the essential lesson, here manifest in four stages of fortune represented in the quarters of the hour: *Sum sine regno; regnabo; regno; regnavi* – I am without a kingdom; I will reign; I reign; I have reigned. The archivist had been right, and how fitting it all was. Andrew had been without a Kingdom and now things were changing. I will reign, he thought.

He rang Karen to tell her of the discovery of the manuscript, cupping the mouthpiece close to his lips so that no one could hear him through the thin hotel walls. John was crying in the background and, rather than raise his voice, Andrew remained vague about the manuscript, merely telling Karen that he'd found something very important.

He got drunk that night, as deliberately and methodically as he had copied the manuscript. He didn't order a bottle of champagne as a French musicologist would have done, but began the evening with a Kir Royale and silently toasted his good fortune. A carafe of white wine accompanied his meal and he stopped off at a bar on the way home where the locals were watching a soccer match, and ordered a Rémy Martin.

'Santé, Andrew,' he mimed to the Ricard mirror over the bar, then stumbled to his hotel and slept solidly.

The following night saw him back home. John was delighted to see him, or at least delighted to see the cuddly toy he bore; Karen likewise gave him a surprisingly warm welcome, perhaps because the present of Duty Free scent was not only the one she liked, but also the perfume rather than the less expensive eau de toilette he'd intended to buy.

When John was asleep, he told his wife about the motet and proudly showed her the copy that he'd had laminated at a stationers in Amiens. This was the first time he'd been able to talk to anyone about it, and the release was exquisite. He outlined the future: the acclaim, the rewards, the recognition, the adulation. He couldn't get the words out quickly enough, each thought overlapping the previous one, a hectic succession of scenarios at the centre of which he stood, the modest, unassuming but deserving recipient of endowments and encomia. He described the material prospects that lay in store for him and Karen, the potential for promotion and self-promotion that the discovery afforded, and the impact it might have in his field of research. His body no longer realised that it was two in the morning back in Amiens where he'd started the day, the effects of latent jetlag manifest only in thirst and volubility, and, as he talked, he downed glass after glass of water.

As a psychology graduate, Karen was practised in the art of listening, yet she had to fight her instinct to instil in him a sense of proportion; even if he was exaggerating the manuscript's importance, it was their first night together in nearly two weeks and she didn't want to be negative.

Later, in bed, Andrew should have fallen straight to sleep, for he had now been awake nearly twenty-four hours. Instead he tossed and turned, made two trips to the bathroom to rid himself of the water that had seemed to act as fuel for his discourse earlier that evening, and found it impossible to discover a place in the bed that was cool enough. After an hour or so, Karen, who had been woken three times, mistook his restlessness for sexual frustration and asked if he wanted to make love.

'No,' he said quickly, and immediately regretted his response. He wasn't aware that he'd casually rejected his wife, distracted as he was by the thought of sex, which he now realised was something that he would have liked. What he'd meant was that his fidgeting had nothing to do with sexual frustration, not that he was disinterested. And it was a rare offer on Karen's part, for the injuries she sustained in childbirth and the sheer exhaustion of looking after a baby had cruelly combined to render their sex life all but non-existent.

Karen turned away from him angrily. Rather than try to explain himself and precipitate an argument that he knew he could never win, he lay in silence until he deduced from her breathing that she'd fallen asleep. Finally he turned onto his stomach and pressed his useless erection into the mattress, his thoughts firmly fixed on the motet.

CHAPTER 9

'Who's Radar?' asked Ollie, gesturing with his head to the back of the plane.

'Sorry?'

'Radar O'Reilly. From *M*A*S*H*?'

Ollie seemed to have spent most of his formative years watching television and reading comics, in contrast to Emma, who had learned the clarinet and sung in a madrigal group. Despite the fact she was poorly versed in popular culture, Ollie made few concessions to her ignorance, constantly comparing events and people to mythical counterparts, a prism of allusion that excluded others. Part of the reason that Ollie and Allie got on so well was that they shared a common frame of reference. The basses frequently talked of Marvel comic-book superheroes (Ollie even had a Spiderman duvet, though Emma had refused ever to sleep under it) and discussed films of which Emma had never heard, posters of which adorned Ollie's cramped flat. She felt jealous at times – his life seemed the richer for it, a magical, hyper-real world layered with significance and association – and when he had to spell out his similes there was frustration for both of them, as if he had to explain a joke to her.

The reference to Radar O'Reilly needed clarification if only because the immediate prospect of sharing a van with Andrew Eiger, even working with him, meant there was every possibility that Ollie's comparison to a fictional character might well be taken up by the group; he rarely stopped repeating a new nickname until others had adopted it.

'He was the geek in *M*A*S*H*,' said Ollie, raising an eyebrow in the way that he knew made her laugh. 'Henry Blake's secretary. You must know *M*A*S*H*?'

'Sitcom, right? American? Doctors and nurses?'

'Yeah, but set in the Korean war. Alan Alda was in it. You know Alan Alda, don't you?'

Emma wasn't entirely sure, but nodded. It was easier that way.

'Anyway,' continued Ollie, 'Radar O'Reilly. Slept with a teddy bear. Short. Round glasses. Squeaky voice. He looks like that guy you were talking to. Who was he, by the way?'

'He's the musicologist I told you about. The one who's got some project or other he wants to talk to me about after the concert? I'm not quite sure what it is he's got in mind, but I'll hear him out. He's giving a paper in the same session as me, this afternoon.'

Ollie grunted. He and Allie felt that the contribution of music historians should be limited to providing clear editions in modern notation; anything more than that was an unjustified incursion into the performer's private domain. A particular focus for their contempt was performance practice, the branch of music history that described the way in which the music was originally performed and which, on occasion, prescribed how modern performers should realise it today. For the basses, this was like being told how they should behave, a straitjacket of convention that interfered with their inalienable right to perform the music in whatever way they bloody well wanted. Emma could sympathise with that view. She wagered that the original performers claimed exactly the same kind of artistic licence, though her sympathy for Allie's and Ollie's position only went so far. Without academics, the basses wouldn't have a job, their parts being played by various 'bits of plumbing', as they dismissively described all medieval instruments.

She hoped that Andrew Eiger would prove to be more sensitive than their awkward first meeting had suggested. He hadn't acknowledged Ollie's presence, and seemed physically and socially graceless, a parody of an academic in his blazer-and-tie outfit and his owlish glasses. Ollie would give him short shrift, as he did most intellectuals, an attitude stemming in part from jealousy. Whenever Paul's name came up, as it sometimes did, Ollie stiffened. He felt her former lover had treated her badly and that she was over-generous in acknowledging his role in the genesis of the group. It was Ollie's view that Beyond Compère had only really begun when it was a touring group and that the stage show was a completely different entity. Doubtless he had placed Andrew Eiger in the same category as those musicologists, including Paul, who deigned to criticise performers for exercising musical intuition.

Most of Ollie's opinions were merely bluster. He was far from the cocksure man he appeared to some, and far more astute than he liked to let on. It was not a lack of A-levels that meant he hadn't gone to university, opting instead for the vocationally oriented route of music college, but, thought Emma, a consequence of his upbringing. His father was in the Navy; he was a disciplinarian who would always put practice ahead of theory and, according to Ollie, was proud of the fact that he was tone-deaf. His mother, meanwhile, taught music in a local infants' school, which meant there had always been a piano in the house and piles of printed music. It was as if Ollie had taken his cue from both of them; music college combined his mother's love of music with his father's pragmatism. Perhaps, at times, he resented the assumptions of others that he had missed out on something by not attending university, that somehow he hadn't allowed his mind to expand either through listening to jazz and dabbling in drugs in a basement flat, or pondering the nature of the universe in a philosophy seminar. Whatever the reasons – and Emma was still slowly stripping away the defensive layers – a lot of his bluff exterior sprang from a benign, protective instinct that she found attractive. Only occasionally was he arrogant, and even then he was able to catch himself in the middle of some rambling tirade and laugh at himself. It was not calculated on his part, or at least rarely so, though knowing that his attacks were a form of shyness made it easier for Emma to indulge his occasional childishness. She knew he was sometimes incapable of stopping it, much as he might want to, and even while he displayed the most clichéd traits of the Alpha male – brawn and raw emotion – he appeared to her as a young boy, out of his depth and uncertain.

Their relationship was now three years' old, and only last week they'd celebrated their anniversary. That was a rather grand term for what was, to all intents and purposes, a commemoration of the first time they had made love. Since then, they'd managed the transition from friends to lovers and negotiated the treacherous waters of an early relationship to the more settled realm of coupledom in full view of their colleagues. Peter, who always thought he had a special insight into people's true feelings, particularly when he deduced homosexual inclinations in heterosexual men, asserted that the writing had been on the wall for some time, pointing out the number of times they had sat next to each other in restaurants and how, out of all the women in the group, Ollie had chosen Emma with whom to discuss his marital problems. Looking back, Emma was less sure. She and Ollie had not been particularly close during the runs in London and New York and there were times when she had even wondered if their relationship was a direct result of the touring life, a convenient office romance. But the opposite could also have been true, she reasoned: as a theatre director her role as objective commentator had been clearly defined, and perhaps it was that distance that blinded her to the possibility of finding love amongst those over whom she exerted authority. Nevertheless, there were times when she felt that Beyond Compère was as much the consequence of her backstage romances as her relationships were the by-products of the group's well-documented history.

The plane had begun to rumble towards its take off point and the brakes gripped one final time before the pilot set the jets to full thrust and they were hurled down the runway. Ollie had already fallen asleep and Emma took out her papers and began to study them. It would be easier to work now than later on the bus, not least because then Ollie would be peering over her shoulder.

She was used to seeing her name in print, but it looked out of place here in the timetable of conference events. Where everyone else was identified in parentheses by their university, she was qualified by 'Beyond Compère' as if it were a place. The session at which she was speaking was entitled 'Ockeghemian promotion and reception', to be chaired by Daniel Huibert (Université de Nantes). Emma would speak first, followed by Andrew Eiger (Ohio State University) on the subject of eighteenth- and nineteenth-century reception of Ockeghem's work, something about which she had no knowledge and in which she had no real interest. Her image of Andrew was opaque, derived solely from their exchanges concerning the mooted project about which he was frustratingly vague. The brief meeting, with him hovering awkwardly in the aisle, had added nothing to her impression. In his correspondence he had hinted at new material, or at least she thought he had, but he was so guarded that it was sometimes difficult to work out exactly what he was saying. Still, she knew that some music departments in America had considerable private funding and, if it allowed her and the group to spend a few days in the Midwest working with students on interesting repertoire, then she was not going to turn down the offer. They'd talk about it later and, if it sounded promising, she would give the details to the British and American agents and let them sort it out.

The third speaker was Étienne Baraud (École Normale Supérieure), the title of his paper – 'Ock' j'aime; L'homme/le nom' – as baffling as the brief précis that accompanied it. Such a summary was known in academic circles as an abstract, and Emma thought that the term was singularly appropriate here.

It wouldn't be the first time that she had addressed an audience of musicologists. It would, however, be the first where the audience consisted of experts in such a specialised field and, were it not for the fact that many of them had helped her in the past, providing her with editions and advice, she would have found the prospect daunting. The thrust of her argument was simple: performers created their own images of composers, often based on little more than their experience of performing the music. This mystical communion with a distant historical figure was, she argued, a necessary human identification and, imaginary though it may be, it was a corollary to convincing interpretation. How, though, did the performer react when the real historical facts collided with their expectations?

Her lecture was entitled 'The Image of Ockeghem' and began with the famous painted miniature of Ockeghem dated thirty years after his death. No one could even agree on which person in the picture was Ockeghem. Was it the old man with the hood and spectacles? Given that Ockeghem received a gift of rich, red cloth from Charles VII, maybe Ockeghem was the man in scarlet behind him, a younger man?

When researching the original stage production of Beyond Compère, she had read many accounts of fifteenth-century composers that had brought them to life as characters. Here they were, flesh and blood, having arguments with the church officials, climbing their way up the greasy pole of advancement, securing generous annual payments called benefices from churches they would never visit. Emma thought it important that the singers were as enthused as her and thus she had once told Allie of Francesco Florio's report of Ockeghem written after a trip to Tours in the 1470s which had described the composer in hyperbolic terms: 'so pleasing is the beauty of his person, so noteworthy the sobriety of his speech and of his morals and of his grace. He alone of all singers is free from all vice and abounds in all virtues.' Allie's response had been to dismiss Ockeghem as a goody-goody, forcing Emma hastily to reassure him that the report was literally too good to be true. According to other contemporary accounts, Ockeghem was a fine bass and almost certainly up for a drink after the gig; Dufay, the other great composer of the age, had purchased Burgundian wine when Ockeghem stayed with him in Cambrai in 1464. That kept Allie happy. She wanted her singers to like the composer whose music they would be performing extensively that year, and providing a positive image was an important aid to meaningful musical expression.

Her paper proposed a more philosophical argument about a shared psychological DNA between twentieth-century singers and fifteenth-century singer-composers, using stories of drinking and debauchery to underline more base common characteristics. To illustrate her point – and entertain her audience – she would alternate anecdotes of singers misbehaving in the Sistine Chapel and Westminster Abbey, Notre Dame in Paris and the Duomo in Florence, Cambrai Cathedral and El Escorial in Madrid, though without providing the dates. And then she would reveal to her listeners that they took place in 1456, 1987, 1478, 1995, 1476 and 1992. For all the differences in harmonic language and compositional approach, for all the alienating, convoluted codes of social behaviour, and for all the constricting literary and musical conventions, at the end of the day these composers were as human as their modern interpreters.

She would then turn to the issue of historical speculation. She had a few scores to settle with some musicologists who had demanded of her total historical accuracy, and she still smarted from a review that had criticised her for making Compère more famous than Josquin. It was undoubtedly true that Josquin was more celebrated, but it was a necessary narrative device, a matter of perspective – and here she would cite Stoppard making Hamlet a bit player in *Rosencrantz and Guildenstern are Dead*. Of course the stage show was historically inaccurate: it was a fiction, not a documentary, and modern performance of ancient music was ineluctably condemned to conjecture until someone built a time machine. In Emma's view, there was as much chance that she would be proved right in the future as proved wrong and, with the amount of research in archives and religious institutions in France going on these days, there was every chance that stranger truths might yet be revealed.

As she read through her paper she underlined certain words, much as she might mark up a musical score. On the first page she wrote in red ink a reminder to stand properly and breathe freely: 'Lengthen spine!' This would relax her and help make the most of her height of five feet and three-quarters of an inch. She provided indications of the shape of the sentences and the contours of her argument, the same kind of reminder that a singer might make in their copy to indicate the direction of a musical phrase. She then added a few pause markings so the structure of her argument might be clearer to the listener, and also to leave space for the laughter that she anticipated. Occasionally she also used the standard abbreviated musical markings – *Accel* and *Rall* – to remind her to speed up or slow down her delivery. After all, giving a lecture was a performance.

There was little more that she could do now. Trying to second-guess the questions her paper might provoke was futile, so she closed her folder.

'A drink from the bar, madam?'

She asked for an orange juice and next to her Ollie struggled awake and ordered a coffee.

'Did you get your stuff done?' he asked.

'Just about. Not much more I can do really. Did you sleep?'

'A little. There's always the bus.'

Ollie and Emma had become a couple on the very same day that, had things taken the slightest of turns, they might have separated forever. Every time Emma looked back, she did so with the unsettling sensation that remembering might of itself reverse the outcome and send her spinning back to a vertiginous moment which had threatened the very existence of the group. Allie had subsequently apologised for his behaviour, but Ollie and Emma never discussed the matter. In turn, none of the group mentioned it either, and it became the only narrative which, by its very seriousness, was too delicate to take a place in the group's repertoire of shared reminiscence. Last year, on their second anniversary, Emma had felt the time had come to address history, but Ollie had urged her not to 'go there'. He was, he said, not prepared to risk an argument, though he didn't mind arguing about not arguing. Tempted as she was to make some comment about history repeating itself, Emma had surrendered to the more intimate purpose of the evening.

The roots of the crisis lay in the seemingly innocent issue of pronunciation. Emma felt that it was inconsistent to sing a French chanson with a French accent and then perform a Latin-texted motet by the same composer in an English accent, a view that she repeated in programme notes and interviews. Regional and historic variances were part of the same argument and, as a consequence, authentic pronunciation had become a further defining characteristic of Beyond Compère. To aid the singers, experts in the history of language provided phonetic transcriptions. Ironically though, modern scholars sometimes proved as unreliable as medieval scribes, which meant that questions about intention and execution arose regularly, disagreement staged between those who had some specialised knowledge and those who regarded the process as an annoying diversion to the real task of singing. In the arena of foreign languages it was Susan and Marco who had some claim to be consulted ahead of the others, and Allie and Ollie who were usually the object of any critique.

Things came to a head slowly. The group had been rehearsing for a concert the following week in Spain. That meant a day of rehearsals in a church in London, with the following day set aside for private study to memorise the music. Most of the repertoire was familiar and Emma had added a few new pieces, not simply because the resultant programme answered the specific brief of the Festival ('Spain and France'), but also because it kept everyone on their toes and expanded their repertoire. Motets and chansons by De La Rue and Agricola would interleave others by Peñalosa and Escobar to demonstrate the many links that existed between the two countries around 1500.

Emma asked Susan to demonstrate the basic vowel and consonantal sounds of Spanish, and Allie and Ollie scribbled in their copies, parodying the examples out loud to make the other laugh. Emma ignored their sniggering and, after they'd sung through one piece, asked Susan to comment on what she'd heard.

'The consonants were pretty good,' she said. 'People are stumbling on the "V", though. It should be a soft "B".'

'As in "Bagina",' observed Allie. Childish as it was, it made everyone laugh – even Susan who blushed through her make-up. Ollie, to signal his disdain for the whole exercise, laughed more than anyone else. Emma had learned that it was best to allow the basses to let off steam about such issues rather than chide them and, whatever Allie's intentions, it lightened the tension and the group worked contentedly till the mid-morning break.

Shortly after the rehearsal resumed, Emma felt that they were all slipping back into English pronunciation and asked Susan and Marco for their opinion. Marco, who preferred Italian vowels even when singing in English, didn't seem too concerned, but Susan went straight for it. 'It's the aah sound. That's typically English and it doesn't exist in Spanish. You should be singing ah, like in "hat", not aah as in "heart".'

She looked across at Ollie and Allie, as if they were the only culprits, and added, 'It's Allie, not Arlie.'

Emma tried to say something – anything – to break the sharp silence and prevent the response which she feared was coming, but Allie was too quick. 'So I should call you an ass and not an arse then?' he asked with mock innocence. If Susan had blinked, a tear would have rolled from her eye. Emma intervened quickly, announcing that they'd sing the final section one more time before the lunch-break.

Things settled down in the afternoon. Allie had apologised to Susan at lunchtime and everyone's false cheer promised a less eventful session. The basses worked harder on their vowels and Allie even asked Susan how to pronounce the words of a villancico they were learning.

'Billancico,' corrected Susan with an embarrassed smile.

The problem came when they rehearsed a piece they had already sung many times in previous concerts. Because the concert was recreating a performance at the Spanish court, the singers had to ignore the familiar sounds of French that they'd already learned and instead apply Spanish pronunciation. For Allie and Ollie this was going a step too far, putting the cart before the horse in privileging pedantry over performance. They blustered and argued, but Emma stood firm: it wouldn't be as difficult as they thought. They bridled at her attempt at reassurance; she could tell that they thought they were being patronised and, if they were going to be treated as children, they would act like them too. They sang the next run-through of the piece in a cheap imitation of a

Mexican *bandito*, a bright nasal sound with trilled 'r's', and succeeded in making each other laugh so much that they didn't notice how uncomfortable everyone else was.

When the piece came to an end, Emma spoke first, pre-empting any discussion.

'Right. Well, that was a waste of everyone's time. We'll now start from the top and I'll have to ask the basses whether this time they're going to take it seriously or not. If not, you can leave now; it's your choice.'

She hadn't meant to make the threat so clear, but when she turned to look at them both were staring at her, a challenge enough in itself, made worse by their satisfied smirking. She would meet their immature challenge. Whatever the validity of their arguments – and she could see precious little – over the years she had always treated them with respect and now they were showing her none. If they walked out she really didn't know what she would do. That, though, lay in the future and for now she awaited an answer.

Neither Allie nor Ollie had expected a showdown. To them it was a game, one that they could stop at any time. As they saw it, Emma had overreacted, leaving them no way out. A private apology, such as Allie had made to Susan, was one thing: to do so publicly was humiliation.

It was Ollie who responded first. He reached slowly into the back pocket of his jeans and drew something out. He placed an object on the back of his thumb and then flicked his thumb upwards. Nine pairs of eyes followed a coin as it spun upwards in an arc, hung in the air and then tumbled over itself, landing in his outstretched palm. He slapped it onto the back of his other hand and showed it to Allie, who nodded at Ollie.

'Yes. We'll sing it again,' said Ollie, and they picked up their copies and readied themselves.

The rest of the rehearsal was awkwardly tense. No one risked trying to lighten the mood with a quip, no one smiled. Emma felt suddenly weary and sad, weighed down by the responsibilities of musical and social leadership. The looks between the singers, the basis of the group's immaculate ensemble, were absent, heads awkwardly buried in copies. She knew that the others weren't angry with her; indeed, she believed she had spoken for them all, and was confident that she had made her stand on the unchallengeable grounds of professionalism. From the basses there was no visual communication at all, the leads she gave to them seemingly ignored, though she knew they were following her beat.

She made her move as soon as the rehearsal was over.

'I'd like to talk to both of you,' she said to Allie and Ollie before they had a chance to speak. 'Now, if you're free. Can we meet in the Star and Garter?' They nodded and she told them she'd join them in the pub soon. She wanted to give them time to talk to each other, to work out how – or if – they would climb down.

The rest of the group realised what was happening and passed no comment as they gathered their things together, instead talking about the next trip, and organising the sharing of lifts to the airport. Eventually Emma was left on her own and she sat down to give herself a moment to think. She liked both Allie and Ollie, valued their talents, their uncanny partnership; she didn't want to lose either of them. Ollie had been there right from the start and, although occasionally immature, he had proved a loyal and protective colleague. She realised that she felt particularly close to him; they were friends, she the woman in whom he would occasionally confide, he a vulnerable, sensitive man compromised by a sense of grievance that even he didn't fully understand. Like Ollie, Allie could be touchy and she didn't underestimate their fierce pride; she knew that self-justification might well already have cast her confrontation as an act of betrayal. The very real possibility existed that both might resign from the group and next week's concert for which they were rehearsing would have to be cancelled. Yet it was also obvious that she couldn't allow them to run the show, and that she would have to obtain from them assurances as to their attitude towards her and her authority.

She walked into the dimly lit pub and saw the two of them sitting at the back, halfway through their first pint. She delayed the showdown a moment longer by offering them a drink and insisting that she bought her own; she had no desire to be left at the table making small-talk with one of them while the other was up at the bar. As she sat down on the high-backed bench, they pulled their bar stools closer to the table; she sensed that they wanted her to talk first but, with no sign of an imminent apology, she launched into her speech: their actions were childish and disruptive at best, unprofessional at worst; they sought to undermine not only her, but the identity and ideology of the group, the very things which had made it a success; on a personal level, they had also upset their colleagues; it was not up to them to determine how rehearsals were run. This meant the decision they had to make was simple: they could either surrender themselves to the requirements of working as part of the group, or leave.

Only then did she let them know how important they were to her and the group. Having slapped their wrists, she could then speak from the heart, tell them how much she valued their abilities and their input, their company and their musical instincts, their camaraderie and concern for others – all the things, in fact, that had been missing that day.

Ollie and Allie sat in neutral silence throughout, occasionally sipping on their beer, looking her in the eye or contemplatively over her shoulder with no sign of shame or any indication of what they were thinking. When she'd finished, she sat back to let them speak. Neither said anything. Allie turned to Ollie, and Ollie met his colleague's gaze. Some exchange occurred, perhaps a faint smile or a flicker of the eyes, Emma couldn't be sure, and then Allie reached into his back pocket. He withdrew a coin, placed it carefully on his bent thumb, and tossed it into the air. Catching it in his palm, he held it out to Ollie who, with exaggerated slowness, appropriately matched by the low-pitch of his speaking voice, said 'Okay.'

Emma had no time to consider the consequences of her response, and only later would she realise just how beautifully poised the moment was. All she experienced at first was a lurch in her stomach as her challenge was met; the coin toss was either an instance of confrontational immaturity or an ironic commentary on earlier events: only her reaction would determine which. Perhaps it was the hint of a smile on Allie's face, or the gentle way Ollie had spoken and the slight suggestion of childlike remorse. Perhaps it was the studied seriousness with which Ollie placed the coin in front of her, a breviloquent memento of the day's events, or maybe just half a glass of chardonnay and a release of tension. Whatever it was, Emma understood that Allie and Ollie were admitting that she deserved an apology. By the time she could speak again, her stomach hurt from laughing and the tears were drying on her face. Recovering her poise for a moment, she was set off again by the sight of Allie silently wheezing, his face locked in an expression of pain, and Ollie lying on the floor where he had fallen from his stool.

From that day on, the basses turned from sceptical followers to committed disciples, defending Emma's vision of concert-as-theatre against singers like themselves who would have preferred the easier option of merely reproducing of the notes on the page. Allie, in particular, championed her cause, on one occasion savagely taking to task an arrogant young tenor who had railed against the difficulties of memorising music and movement, even questioning Emma's credentials as a conductor. Ollie, too, demonstrated his commitment to Emma, though more overtly: he and she had become lovers.

In the pub, once they'd recovered from their fits of laughter, Emma bought a round of drinks and the three of them stood and clinked glasses. The next round they did the same, and then Allie, on Emma's instructions, ordered food for them. It was a pub curry with raisins and coconut scattered on the top like a school-dinner garnish, and Emma ate hardly any. The rest of the evening was a blur, but she had apparently berated the barman for not having any jellied eels. She wasn't even sure what a jellied eel was.

They were the last to leave the pub, and Emma was incapable of getting herself home. Allie and Ollie agreed that they should get her a taxi, and then Allie suggested that Ollie should accompany her and put her to bed. Embarrassed that by now Emma had attached herself to him, and concerned for her safety, Ollie flagged down a black cab.

On the way back to Emma's flat in Balham, she tried to kiss him several times. Flattered as he was, a relationship with Emma hadn't really occurred to him before – and not just because, she being his employer, it represented a rather risky career move. He behaved like the perfect gentleman. In the kitchen he insisted that she drink water to prevent a hangover. She hit him, before sulkily obeying his advice. Then she threw up. She made it to the bathroom in time and was sober enough by then to want her privacy, but, later, after vomiting again, she'd asked Ollie to put her to bed. He took off her dress and put her under her duvet.

He woke quite early the next morning after about four hours' sleep during which the image of Emma in her underwear had flickered through his dreams. He had no hangover, possibly because he was still drunk, and he sat drinking tea until Emma staggered out of bed two hours later. Something rolled beneath his sternum as he heard her stepping uncertainly towards the kitchen. She was dressed in an oversize towelling gown, her hair uncombed, her skin horribly pale, her eyes dark. For all of her unkempt state, or perhaps because of it, she looked gorgeous.

Over coffee they pieced together the previous night's events, small details of which made her groan. When Ollie told her about her advances towards him she didn't so much blush as simply become less pale. They looked across the table at each other. Something had changed. Whatever their relationship had been, today it was different. Though they hadn't as yet even kissed, they now shared a new wordless intimacy.

They spent the rest of the day together. A trip to the supermarket to buy milk turned into a walk in the park, which turned into a fry-up at a café to help the hangover. In the afternoon they dozed together on the sofa and then, without saying anything, moved to the bedroom. They fell asleep after they made love and woke to find the day darkening. Over dinner in a small Portuguese restaurant, Emma determinedly drank mineral water.

Later, in bed, drifting off to sleep, Ollie kissed the back of her neck, and a buried sense of the person she reminded him of surfaced.

'You look like Audrey Hepurn.'

'Who's she?' asked Emma.

CHAPTER 10

The Memoirs of Geoffroy Chiron: Livre III *ed. Francis Porter*

Frevier 22, 1524

As a young man I wanted to compose music but, sadly, I was not blessed with such gifts; in the city where France's greatest composer lived, I contented myself with a life as a singer and an administrator. What training in the musical arts I received was taken at the feet of the great Johannes Ockeghem and not at the university. I am a maître, *but a* maître *in civil law, which befits my role as* chambrier *and* procurator *and, although I received payment throughout my life as a* chapelain *and understand fully the teachings of Boethius and Guido, I am not a* musicus *even though Jehan kindly introduced me as such to visiting dignitaries.*

Jehan believed strongly in the congregation of musicians. Unlike the silversmiths and other artisans, they had no guild through which they could serve an apprenticeship and receive training at the feet of other musici. *There were limited opportunities for the great composers to discuss their art. Jehan himself was indebted to the composer Binchois whom he commemorated in his fine motet* [Mort tu as navré de ton dart] *and it was a debt he intended to repay by offering advice and guidance to anyone who sought it. Composers, he said, were like seeds that were blown by the winds across borders. Communication between them was thus often more by musical than verbal means, scattered as they were across many lands. When one composer used another's chanson as the basis for a new composition, it was like a conversation they could not otherwise conduct given the distance that separated them.*

And thus, despite his dislike of travel, Jehan would often visit other towns and cities when singers and composers were gathered together in one place as part of the retinue of dukes and kings, or when a particular choirmaster or composer organised a celebration or commemoration. Many stories were told of these gatherings, most of them, according to Jehan, with only some basis in fact, exaggerated by the course of time and countless re-telling. He attended such meetings not only to offer his services to the younger composers, but also to make the acquaintance of the talent that our country nurtured, so that France's chapels might be filled with the finest musicians. And when he couldn't – as was the case when he was detained by a dispute with the widow, Jourdain, and prevented from travelling to Cambrai for the convention of the French Court Chapel, the choir of Cambrai Cathedral, and the Burgundian court chapel [1468], he was greatly sad. He was not the only one: drunk at one of the several parties, Guillaume Dufay, the composer who had done more for Cambrai's musical reputation than any other, announced that they should repeat the exercise, 'but this time with my friend Ockeghem'.

When Dufay wanted something done, there were plenty of people willing to realise his wishes. Jean Hémart, the newly-appointed master of the choirboys at Cambrai Cathedral (an ambitious young man) organised the event himself and so, two years later, the finest singers and composers in Christendom, including Jehan, gathered in Cambrai. Many had brought new chansons, some had simply brought local wine, and, over three days, old friendships were renewed and new acquaintances were made. The singing was of the highest standard and it afforded them all the opportunity for many serious (and not-so-serious) discussions about music.

The main event of this later gathering was the first performance of Compère's motet written in honour of the Virgin, the patron saint of singers [Omnium bonorum plena – 1470]. Its text featured the names of those who formed the choir. Top of the list was, of course, Dufay and, standing by his side, was Jehan, his good colleague, whom Dufay respected deeply and to whom he owed a debt of thanks (and not just for putting him to bed once). Then followed Antoine Busnois, the former master of the choirboys at St Martin, renowned in France and Burgundy, another of Jehan's loyal friends. Also present were Jehan du Sart, Firminus Caron, Georget de Brelles, Johannes Tinctoris, Josquin Desprez, Jean Courbet, Guillaume Faugues, Jean Molinet, and Hémart himself.

The rehearsal time was, as ever, too short and, though they all could read the manuscript and give a convincing version of it at sight, Jehan was of the opinion that the piece would have sounded much better had not so many of them been drunk the night before. A festive dinner followed the commemorative service and passed in suitably sober fashion, but afterwards it was to Dufay's own house that everyone retired for the party, which eclipsed all others before and since. Dufay, as Jehan put it, owed a debt to Orpheus but paid it to Bacchus, and thus, as at any celebration at the maître's house, the wine flowed freely. There are many stories about Dufay and, though I cannot swear to the veracity of them, it is surely no coincidence that all of them feature wine in one way or another. (Jehan once pointed me towards the lines of a beautiful chanson by the Cambrai composer, Adieu ces bons vins de Lannoys, *which* spoke of his regret at leaving behind the wine, women and people of his country. ('Take note of the order,' said Jehan with a smile, 'and remember that in a rondeau the refrain is sung thrice.')

Compère's motet had been warmly received by all present, praised by Dufay and Jehan, enjoyed by the singers and composers named therein. And, of course, it was the talk of the party. Dufay insisted that they sing it again and he sent Hémart to get the copy. Jehan, however, who knew Dufay better than Dufay knew himself, was convinced that the idea would soon be forgotten and told Hémart not to bother: walk a little way and then return, he told him. Jehan believed that sacred music should properly only be sung in church and not at a drunken party. More than this, he understood that the solemnity of the music would disturb the mood of celebration. Indeed, the party was noisy enough already. The neighbours complained about the shouting and singing, and some singers played haut instruments so loudly that someone commented that the noise would be heard as far away as Metz.

Johannes Tinctoris, usually a rather staid man given more to criticism than encouragement, had, it was reported, been particularly drunk. Afterwards it was rumoured that a high-ranking cleric (which everyone took to mean Dufay himself) had assured the young man that the strong taste of the local beer was the effect not of alcohol, but of medicinal herbs that were 'good for the digestion'. Whether born of inspiration or inebriation, Tinctoris locked all the doors and demonstrated a theory of mensural proportion by dancing, his right foot hitting the ground nine times whilst his left foot struck eight times.

The party was significant in one other respect: it was the first meeting between Jehan and Desprez. I say the first meeting between them for I am aware, nearly thirty years after Jehan's death, that a modern chronicler, wishing to add further to Desprez's reputation, might prefer to suggest that this was the first time that Ockeghem met Josquin (as the latter is familiarly called today). I consider that it was the day on which Desprez was fortunate enough first to make the acquaintance of the maître of Tours: Johannes Ockeghem. Time is the ultimate judge and I hope that in another thirty years the importance of Ockeghem to his pupils will be fully appreciated. What is certain is that this was the first time the two spoke to each other and not, as Desprez would have it, the earlier meeting in Cambrai when Jehan was absent. (I suspect that Desprez preferred his version, for it in no way referenced Compère and his motet.)

Jehan told me that throughout the rehearsals and the party he was aware of a young man whose piercing eyes did not leave Jehan himself, Dufay or Busnois. Those three maîtres were, of course, the very men who could ensure the progress of a young composer. And Desprez was a man for whom advancement meant everything. The proper course of action would have been to wait for an introduction, though it seemed to Jehan, from the way that the other singers ignored him, that Desprez was not a popular man and thus could not rely on such a courtesy. The obvious person to make *such an introduction was Compère, and, of course, therein lay the problem: Desprez could not allow the man that he saw as his rival to become a person to whom he was beholden. At the time Jehan had no knowledge of that context, and what he observed, aside from Desprez's dark glare, was that this was a man who did not enjoy life; in Jehan's eyes, that was a snub to the Creator. Whereas the others were quaffing wine and wrapping their arms around each other, playing instruments badly or singing raucously, Desprez sat in a corner on his own, wrapped in his cloak.*

Eventually he walked over to Jehan and introduced himself. Whatever the propriety of the situation, Jehan was not a haughty man and, by way of putting the young man at his ease, he asked him what he thought of the motet that they had just sung. The angry criticism that followed surprised Jehan: Desprez pronounced it old-fashioned, immature, backward-looking, unadventurous and fatuous. He said that he had written a far better motet, one which, like Compère's, referenced singers praising the Virgin, and that he would be prepared to dedicate it to Jehan. That put Jehan in a difficult position; to accept the dedication would be to endorse Desprez's composition and confer upon it a recognition that only years of service would normally merit. Yet, given the young man's clear self-confidence, Jehan knew that declining the dedication would condemn him to a long and probably tiresome argument. Jehan said that he would be happy to see the motet and then quietly left the party.

The next morning Jehan left Cambrai for Tours and he never saw Desprez's Illibata Dei virgo nutrix, *the text of which announced the ambitions of its young composer in an acrostic of his name. Ockeghem's doubts about Desprez concerned his behaviour as a man and, though he had yet to produce the fine music that he did in later years, perhaps if he had seen that example of his work he might have been prepared to recommend him to other patrons. What was clear to Jehan was that Desprez was a young man with much to learn.*

Shortly after that, Jehan was approached, as he often was, by a rich patron for advice on the appointment of a new singer. The request came from the Duke of Milan, Galeazzo Maria Sforza and Jehan had no hesitation in advancing Compère's cause; he immediately sent the Duke a copy of Omnium bonorum plena *together with a warm recommendation [1472]. By then Jehan and Compère had become good friends. They shared many common interests, amongst them a fascination with puzzles and mazes that were often displayed in their music. Where Jehan would challenge himself to create music that could be sung in any of the four modes or to address mensural issues, Compère would set himself different musical puzzles and then solve them. Compère's letters, Jehan told me, were fascinating and demanding, perfumed with puns and anagrams, acrostics and macaronic texts, the meaning of which would leave even Jehan baffled.*

In truth, I could not quite discern the qualities in Compère's music of which Jehan spoke though, as a mere cantor, *I deferred to the judgement of a* musicus. *The* confusion manifest in Compère's wordplay and the way that some of his compositions, beautiful as they were, eluded my understanding were also evident in my relationship with him. He was a good man, that was clear to all, possessed of no guile or bad faith, yet he lacked the graces which marked out a man like Jehan. There would never be a career for Compère as a representative of France, nor as a Treasurer. He was short in stature, wore a rough beard at most times, and his clothing always looked as if it belonged to somebody else, his cloak often hanging to one side. His hands were always busy with an intention difficult to divine – now touching his ear, now his eye, now his stomach. And his eyes likewise seemed to have their own life, never meeting anyone's gaze, instead roving across the ground from his feet then suddenly lifting into the sky as if he had heard something there. In conversation he would say something and become distracted by it, his speech suddenly halting and a look of fascination passing over his features. The undeniable correctness of his compositions bore no relation to the shifting deportment of the composer himself.

Although Compère lacked fluency in discourse with other people, Jehan was confident that the younger man would stay at the court in Milan for a long time and that he would take his service to the Duke – and to Jehan as well – seriously and diligently. He also had no doubt that Compère would benefit from the experience and expand his understanding of music through familiarity with the Italian style, and that he would honour his patron by providing him with compositions. And indeed, in his time of service at the court in Milan until the time that the Duke was murdered [1476], Compère wrote several mass settings, many motets and some wonderful chansons.

Though Jehan didn't know it at the time, Desprez's envy of Compère was profound and unreasoning, and Jehan's advancement of Compère to the Milanese court only added to that bitterness. Just as when they were at choir school together, Compère was one step ahead of him and Desprez felt that he had been unfairly overlooked. Yet the truth was that Desprez was not ready for the positions that he coveted; only in later life did his true talent [ingenium] emerge and, by then, his nature was cast as iron in the fire.

While Compère travelled to Milan, Desprez went instead to Aix to endure the heat of the south in the service of René d'Anjou [1474], and he should have had no complaint. He was not ready for Italy and Jehan believed that the politics alone would have seriously damaged the young man's future career. In time, Desprez would go to Milan to work for both Cardinal d'Ascanio Sforza, the brother of Galeazzo Maria Sforza, and then for Galeazzo Maria Sforza's son, the young Duke Gian Galeazzo Maria Sforza. It should have been enough for him, but somehow it was not. Somehow, nothing was ever enough – the masterpieces he wrote, the choirs that sang them, the money that he inherited, the money that he earned, the benefices that he accrued or the fame that he gained.

The problem, once again, was that when Desprez came to Milan, an oltremontani [one from across the mountains], his reputation did not precede him. Rather, he was *greeted with stories of Loyset Compère, the man who had been there before him. How many times would he have to agree with the opinions of the Italian noblemen that Compère was a great composer, and how often would he have to sing pieces by his older peer in the chapel or at feasts? Desprez saw Compère as the man who plagued his life, from the first notes he sang as a choirboy to his final days in the church of Notre Dame in Condé-sur-l'Éscaut, a position he gained by virtue of Compère's ministrations.*

I now know something of how Desprez felt. Many things change with death, amongst them reputation. Jehan belongs to an older generation, and Desprez has become the prime representative of the new. Since the death of Josquin Desprez, it is Josquin – and seemingly only Josquin – about whom people wish to talk.

Fifty years ago, any dignitary visiting Tours was greeted by a Noel that Jehan himself had composed. They all wanted to meet Magister Johannes Ockeghem and their attendance at service had less to do with saving their souls than hearing the voice of the most famous contrabassus *in France. No one then could have believed that those who had learned at his feet would ever eclipse their* bon père. *Perhaps Jehan should have worked on his reputation as hard as he worked for Tours and the King.*

I am still a respected figure in the town and, as such, invited to attend feasts and to grace civic functions; and I am, after all, the man who knew Johannes Ockeghem. Ockeghem, though, has now become merely the man who knew the great Josquin Desprez.

But we must trust in the Lord ultimately, not in the fleeting truths of fame and ambition. As the psalmist says:

Noli contendere cum malignis neque aemuleris facientes iniquitatem, quoniam sicut herba velociter conterentur et sicut holus viride arescent.

[Be not emulous of evildoers; nor envy them that work iniquity. For they shall shortly wither away as grass, and as the green herbs shall quickly fall.]

CHAPTER 11

'Where is he?' asked Marco for the third time.

Most of them had been sitting on the small coach for fifteen minutes and Marco was annoyed by what he regarded as an unnecessary interruption to the group's steady progress towards their final destination. Generally, the bus was a quiet space and singers travelling with the group for the first time were struck by the lack of ritual and rehearsed banter, the only clue to the homogeneity of purpose being the repeated seating assignment. In the single seats on the right-hand side of the bus sat Susan, Claire, and Peter. Marco had abandoned the seat now occupied by Peter on discovering that the wheel arch resulted in little room for his legs. He was now in one of the double seats and, immediately in front of him, the front seat had been reserved for Craig. Prone to travel sickness, this position provided him with a reassuring, unimpeded view of the horizon and the road ahead, with easy access to the driver should an emergency stop be necessary. Now Craig was standing outside the bus getting some fresh air and trying to find a report at the end of the first day's play of the Test Match in New Zealand, his shortwave radio pressed hard against his ear.

Allie and Charlie were in the back row, the traditional area for Bad Boys. With four seats to themselves, their comparative freedom of movement was offset by the discomfort of travelling at the rear where the bumps of the road and the pitching of the vehicle were exaggerated. It was from here that The Social Secretaries, as Charlie and Allie had been named by Ollie with a touch of bitterness that acknowledged his disappointment at not being one himself, would dispense provisions after an evening concert. Otherwise Allie remained silently committed to his book and Charlie, who seemed to be able to sleep anywhere, was shrouded by his coat that he'd draped over his head.

'Where's Em?' asked Marco redundantly. He and the others could see her standing just inside one of the exits to the circular Charles de Gaulle Terminal awaiting Andrew Eiger, who had been held up at immigration and had yet to retrieve his luggage. 'Who is this guy, anyway?' he added.

'Musicologist. American. Looks like Radar O'Reilly. Coming to the gig tonight and has some kind of project he wants to talk to Em about.' Ollie retreated back into his comic book.

Marco was still fractious from his hangover, the forty winks he had enjoyed on both flights succeeding only in making him short-tempered and impatient. To distract himself he pulled a red Michelin guide from his bag and flicked to the pages on Tours to revise the sites that he would visit later that day, but the thought of their destination reminded him once again of the irritating delay, and he went to talk to Emma.

'Is this guy coming, or what?' he asked her, more aggressively than he'd intended.

Emma could imagine the scene on the bus: people anxious to leave, keen to get to the hotel and familiarise themselves with the City.

'Are people getting twitchy?' she asked.

Marco had the good grace to look sheepish. 'Only me, really,' he admitted. 'But the bus driver doesn't look too happy,' he added hopefully. Emma waved to a man emerging from the customs hall with an old suitcase and a battered black briefcase. Andrew Eiger approached, nodded to her and, without acknowledging Marco's presence, muttered an apology and began to complain about the rigours of immigration.

'They're here,' said Marco flatly as he boarded the bus. Emma took her seat next to Ollie as Andrew levered himself into the only remaining place: the single seat over the wheel arch. Peter immediately felt the pressure of Andrew's knees in his back and turned around slightly to hint at the discomfort his new companion was causing, but Andrew was oblivious. To make matters worse, the musicologist was now banging on Peter's seat with the lid of his briefcase. Emma, witnessing the incident, worried that offering him a lift might have been the wrong decision. He hadn't so much as acknowledged the rest of the group when he'd boarded the bus or apologised for the delay, with the result that there had hardly been a rousing welcome for their new travelling companion.

Craig finally climbed into his seat.

'Score?' demanded a voice from behind Andrew.

'Sixty-eight for six,' replied Craig.

Goodness, thought Andrew; *6,846. That must have been some match.*

'Who got them?' inquired the voice.

'Three for Caddie, three for Goughie,' answered Craig.

'Who got the other 6,840?' asked Andrew.

'Sorry?' Craig looked puzzled.

'The other 6,840. Goals. You are talking about soccer, aren't you?'

'No,' said Craig in a manner that made Andrew think he had offended him. Maybe the score they were discussing was of an American Football game, the information designed to make him feel welcome? But Andrew knew too little about the subject to know who might be playing and didn't want to reveal his ignorance.

'Oh. Touchdowns, then. Who scored the other touchdowns?'

'They're talking about cricket, Andrew,' said Emma.

'Cricket?'

'Yes. Do you know anything about the sport?'

'No,' he admitted. Cricket! He thought that was a summer game played on grass, not something staged in the middle of winter. They must be hardy types, he thought. Embarrassed, he buried his head in his briefcase. He was still berating himself for having forgotten the significance of the day and now, on the road to Tours, he intended to honour the composer in a private act of homage by reading Guillaume Crétin's *Déploration*, a poem written on the death of Ockeghem. His copy fell open at a well-thumbed section: a rondeau in the middle of the poem ostensibly written by Chiron, a centaur from Greek mythology. It was an important section, to Andrew at least, because it added another layer of reference that tied the letter to the manuscript and offered a possible connection between the motet and Ockeghem himself. At first sight the passage was merely a standard medieval convention whereby a mythical figure, in this case Chiron, the centaur from Greek mythology knowledgeable in medicine, offered a homage. But Andrew now knew there was another Chiron, Geoffroy Chiron, friend to Ockeghem, which suggested that he might have stumbled across a more personal allusion. Three months ago Andrew had contacted a young French research student who was researching Ockeghem's life as the Treasurer of the Abbey of St Martin, and had received an early draft of an article in which the name had popped up. Geoffroy Chiron figured extensively, firstly as a singer in the choir of St Martin where he would undoubtedly have worked with the great man, next as Ockeghem's procurator, a sort of bailiff, and finally as *chambrier*, holder of the keys to the treasury. The composer had held the last position until old age had meant he could no longer fulfil his duties. Thus Chiron, in Crétin's poem, was a knowing nod to Ockeghem's colleague and good friend. It was the real person who, in the poem, regretted that Ockeghem had not lived to the age of one hundred, and he who mourned the loss of a 'bon chantre tant saige' – a wise and good singer.

Surprisingly, the student had overlooked the reference and Andrew could easily have pointed it out to him. He would have been credited in a footnote ('I am indebted to Andrew Eiger for drawing my attention to this') but he wanted to keep it to himself. It would be another in a series of small discoveries for his book, another significant piece of the jigsaw puzzle: not absolute proof, but telling nonetheless. There was more in the poem as well, a reference to a thirty-six part motet. Could this be the thirty-four part motet that Andrew had discovered? Might the references to Chiron and this mythical motet be two pieces of circumstantial evidence that would convince his colleagues that Ockeghem was the composer of the *Miserere mei*?

Emma called everyone to attention. Books were laid in laps, heads turned, and Charlie stirred beneath his coat and shifted onto his other side.

'Just to let you know what's happening for the rest of the day. Tours is about a hundred and fifty miles from here, so we're looking at nearly three hours on the bus. Hopefully we won't have to stop for a pee-break because…' She looked at her watch – 'it's now midday, local time, and – sorry to be selfish – my paper is at four. The rehearsal'll be at five and you may have to begin it on your own. I'll get there as quick as I can. The gig's at eight-thirty, so there'll be time to get a cuppa after the rehearsal. Sorry it's so rushed, but you know how it is. The hotel's in the centre, not far from the Cathedral – *Hotel de l'Univers* – and we're booked into a restaurant after the gig: *Les Tuffeaux.* Apparently it's one of the best. And I meant what I said last night: the champagne's on me.' Murmurs of gratitude crescendoed to a stifled cheer, and a hand emerged from beneath Charlie's coat and waved.

'Oh, and this is Andrew Eiger, by the way,' continued Emma. 'He's a musicologist from Ohio, a specialist on Ockeghem, so ask him any questions you like about the composer. He's going to the conference too. I thought he might appreciate the lift – door to door and all that – and he's got a project that he wants to discuss with us later. After the concert.'

Hellos and nods of greeting were addressed to Andrew, who responded with a shy wave. Now he was actually in their presence rather than seeing them across the departure lounge or in a photo, they seemed much more impressive: confident, assured, adult. And they all looked relaxed. He, however, was having trouble with his limbs. The rounded wheel arch was forcing his legs into his chest and his briefcase banged into his face each time the van rolled over one of the traffic-control strips that studded the airport's perimeter.

Emma leaned towards him solicitously. He shifted in his seat and the briefcase fell on the floor. As he stooped to reach it, he banged heads with Emma, who was trying to pick it up. He thought she was trying to tell him something in private, this being the only place in the cramped confines of the bus suitable for such an exchange. But Emma thought that maybe Andrew had got stuck and couldn't move. They stayed like that for a moment in an attitude of mutual supplication.

'Er, your knees are digging into Peter's back,' Emma said in a low voice. 'It's really uncomfortable for him. Could you move slightly?'

'Oh. Sorry,' he stage-whispered back. Facing forwards, he found that the only way he could avoid pressing his legs into the seat in front was to sit sideways, like a nineteenth-century Victorian woman on horseback, and now he found himself facing Emma and Oliver. To make it clear that he was not trying to engage them in conversation, he shut his eyes, then felt something brush against his thigh. He looked up to see one of the singers stepping over his legs to get to the front of the bus.

'He's entertaining, I'll give him that,' said Ollie quietly to Emma.

'Don't,' she said, a smile in her voice.

Charlie had abandoned his slumber, emerging stunned and blinking like an animal coming out of hibernation, and he joined Marco in his double seat at the front of the bus.

'Va bene?' said Marco, making room for his colleague and looking up from his Michelin guide.

'What're we going to visit, then?' croaked Charlie.

'I just checked out the restaurant Em mentioned. Doesn't tell us much, I'm afraid, but it's certainly close to the Cathedral. We don't have to make a special visit to St Gatien seeing as we're singing in it, but maybe we should visit the Basilique St Martin? It's where Ockeghem worked, after all.'

Hearing the name of the composer, Andrew turned towards the conversation.

'Used to work there,' he corrected. 'The real Basilica of St Martin was destroyed in the sixteenth century. Nothing's left of where Ockeghem worked apart from the remains of two towers.'

'Spoilsport,' said Marco.

'Well, it wasn't me who did it. It was the Huguenots,' snapped Andrew, tiredness rendering him even more incapable than usual of discerning anything other than a literal meaning.

'Marco's just joking, Andrew,' said Emma, laying her hand lightly on his wrist. 'Have you got a map there, Marco? Perhaps Andrew could show me where the conference centre is?'

When he was conducting his research in Paris, Andrew had visited Tours regularly, a simple-enough round-trip by train, and he was familiar with the topography of the city. Taking the map from Marco, he unfolded it and traced the outline of medieval Tours, a simple east-west orientation, as opposed to the north-south direction of the modern city. To the west lay the Abbey of St Martin, where Ockeghem had worked and lived, and to the east lay the Cathedral of St Gatien. In the fifteenth century the two landmarks had been linked by main roads which still existed today: the Grande Rue – now the Rue du Commerce – and the Rue de la Scellerie. To the west, close by St Gatien, lay the Chateau de Tours, a fortress that had housed the retinue of the Valois Kings. The Centre d'Études Supérieures de la Renaissance lay fittingly adjacent to the site of the original St Martin and the current Basilica. Everything was within walking distance.

'Did Ockeghem not work at the Cathedral then?' Charlie asked Andrew. With his love of history, the tenor was slightly disappointed to learn that the venue for the concert was not the actual place where Ockeghem had sung.

'Well, he *probably* did,' said Andrew, trying to appear more knowledgeable than he was about the subject. 'Busnois certainly worked there. Famously he was involved in a fight, or at least he beat someone up.'

Marco and Charlie laughed, and Peter turned in his seat to smile at Andrew, a gesture that indicated the previous awkwardness was forgiven.

'But you have to remember that this is a small town, really,' Andrew continued, 'or at least there are only a few people who can sing well. And, given that Ockeghem's one of the best around, you have to think that he might have sung now and then at the Cathedral.'

'He needed the money, like we all do,' said Charlie.

'Oh, I doubt that. I read through his will once and it's clear that he was a rich man. He wouldn't have moonlighted in the Cathedral for the money, but I assume there must have been big occasions which he attended, and he might have sung at them as well.'

Andrew was aware that he'd engaged his audience and was pleased. He guessed that, over the years, they must all have sung in religious, choral institutions and their fascination arose from a recognition of the same loose arrangements between the members of one church that still obtained today.

He pressed on. 'He was, after all, much more than a musician. Very much the older statesman, in fact. He served the various Kings of France – Charles VII, Louis XI, Charles VIII – and the position of Treasurer wasn't just a benefice: it was a real job. Like you have, in addition to your singing.'

He was immediately aware that he had said something inappropriate. The small encouraging nods had stopped, the phatic ums and ahs suddenly ceased. Without knowing it, he'd insulted all of them by suggesting that singing was an idle, amateur pursuit that needed to be supplemented by some other form of income, that what they did was not a 'real' job. Emma felt Ollie stir next to her and pre-empted the full force of his annoyance by explaining to Andrew the full context of his unintentional insult. It was an assumption often made by rich sponsors and donors to singers at post-concert receptions, voiced in condescending tones of well-intentioned sympathy in a world wherein artistic endeavour was subordinate to market forces. At such moments the assumption of amateurism reminded the singers that, even in the twentieth century, art existed only because of suffrage, and the monetary status of the questioner often underlined their reliance on patronage.

'We're all pros, you know,' she said. 'Everyone here makes their living entirely by performing.'

'Of course, of course,' Andrew said quickly. 'I didn't mean to … I know you're all professionals who sing all the time…' He looked around the bus anxiously, aware that he'd lost some of the credibility he had briefly enjoyed.

'I'm tired,' he mumbled into his lap by way of apology.

Charlie and Marco had returned to the Michelin guide and Emma, in an attempt to interrupt the awkward silence, asked them if there was anything else worth viewing.

'The Place Plumereau is meant to be quite interesting. If you like inauthentic medieval things, that is,' said Charlie. 'It's an area in the City which they've tried to make as much like medieval Tours as they can – tall, half-gabled houses, that kind of stuff. Full of bars as well, so Allie should be happy.'

'Well, if it's got booze, then we can get authentically pissed,' said Ollie.

'And it would be authentic to throw up the next morning,' added Charlie, though, as he said it, he worried that he might thereby encourage Craig's travel sickness.

Andrew laughed with the others, keen to rejoin the group conversation and to demonstrate that he too understood the particular resonance of the word 'authenticity', which was one of the watchwords of early-music debates.

Suddenly Susan screamed, 'Eiffel Tower! Eiffel Tower!'

Everyone followed her pointing finger. Somehow neither arriving at Charles de Gaulle airport nor driving around the Boulevard Péripherique had quite convinced the travellers that they were in France, or certainly not in the way that the vista across the urban landscape now did. The sight of Sacré-Coeur and, beyond it, the arrogant Eiffel Tower, was proof that they were indeed in the modern capital of France, and finally on their way to its former political centre. Each of them – even Allie, who maintained an air of disinterest as though ashamed to display any enthusiasm – experienced the nostalgic sense of excitement they'd felt as children on holiday when the sea finally came into view.

Emma clutched Ollie's hand and he squeezed back. They smiled at each other and she angled herself away from Andrew Eiger's twisted frame to discourage any earnest discussions about anything fifteenth century that would disturb her mood. She snuggled into Ollie's body for warmth and comfort and closed her eyes.

Ollie lifted his arm and put it proprietarily around her, a gesture that he hoped sent a message to the American musicologist. The possessive urge sprang not from any sense of rivalry for Emma's affections – the guy was a wimp and not Emma's type – but from a developing resentment of the call on her time and attention that the planned collaboration had already entailed. He had no idea what the mooted project was, nor had he spoken to Emma about it, which meant that it was either so vague as to be not worth talking about or a private residency for Emma alone which would thus not involve Ollie and the others. It would not be the first time. Only recently Emma had turned down an overture from her old university to teach there for a term, a commitment which, had she accepted, would have meant Beyond Compère could not have worked for at least a month. And there had been enough informal overtures from academics in America for Ollie to know that a post awaited her, should she express any interest. If Emma moved overseas the group really would be over. And it would probably be the end of them as a couple.

In the fifteenth century, the 130-mile journey from Paris to Tours was a three-day journey on horseback over level ground through the forests of central France with overnight stops at hospices or monasteries. A more scenic and more comfortable, if slower, route would have been three days by horse-drawn wagon south to Orleans and thence to Tours by river barge, a leisurely week-long trip along the Loire. The minibus sped along the Autoroute du Sud, the A10, from the new capital of France to the old one, a predictable band of tarmac the vibrations from which eventually lulled all of the passengers to sleep.

When they pulled up in front of the *Hotel de l'Univers*, a grand edifice built in the nineteenth century to accommodate travellers arriving at the new train station, Andrew was still asleep and it took both Peter shaking him and Emma calling his name to rouse him. His glasses had slipped to the end of his nose and he was blinking, an image which reminded Emma of Mole in *The Wind in the Willows*. He fell rather than walked out of the bus, his briefcase clamped under his arm.

By the time he had re-arranged his clothes, the others were in the hotel lobby collecting their keys. Evidently Andrew had no plan and seemed to have decided that his fate lay in Emma's hands.

'What shall I do?' he asked.

She knew Andrew was staying at a smaller hotel near St Martin and, not being required to be at the conference till four, she wanted the time to herself to get a bath and to freshen up.

'Well, it's up to you,' she replied, bouncing the question back. 'Personally, I would check in to my hotel room.'

'I'll go and check into my hotel room,' he echoed, taking her suggestion as an instruction. 'What then?'

He looked sad and forlorn standing there, a lost little boy, but she could see her precious time slipping away. How did his wife put up with him?

'I don't know,' she said, hearing the slight irritation in her voice. 'Register at the conference?'

'Yes,' he said, nodding as though she might not have heard him. 'Where am I?'

In the end Emma had to take him into the lobby to find a street map, at which point Andrew seemed to snap back to full consciousness. He would, he said, prefer to get something to eat and maybe a coffee to waken him. He also needed to find a pharmacy; he'd hurt his hand on the flight the previous day and had some kind of infection. He opened his clenched right hand gingerly to reveal two holes that looked as if they'd been punched into the palm of his hand with a hammer and nail, as though he was trying to create his very own stigmata. From the smallest wound oozed a fresh trail of blood and what looked like pus, the sight of which made Emma gasp. The second seemed at least to have closed over, but it was swollen and looked as if something had burrowed beneath the skin and was now trying to get out. Grateful that Andrew had not shaken her hand, she urged him to find a *pharmacie* ('They're much better than in the UK or the US,' she commented) and, lest he had decided in the interim that their new friendship warranted physical contact, she stepped back and waved goodbye.

CHAPTER 12

Emma's hotel room was accessed through a small, redundant annex that would keep the noise of the echoey corridor to a minimum. The tall, heavy door opened to reveal a large double bed, an ancient wardrobe, and French windows with a small balcony. She stepped out into the cold, clear air and shielded her eyes against the sun that cast deep shadows across the pavement. Here, three floors above the broad tree-lined streets, she could glimpse through the leaves and branches various shops and banks, and off to her left she could see the *beaux arts*-style Hôtel de Ville.

Below her, Marco and Charlie emerged from the hotel, consulted a map, and then headed off, presumably in the direction of St Martin. She had little time to herself and quickly unpacked, a familiar and comforting routine in an otherwise pressurised day. She hung her peacock-blue dress on a hanger and draped the coral-pink silk scarf that she thought went so well with it around the neckline. This was her lecture outfit, a careful balance of sobriety and flamboyance that fitted the tone of her paper. Checking that the net curtains over the windows were drawn, she stepped out of her clothes. The bathroom was warm, the radiator set to its highest level, and she surveyed the toiletries laid out on the shelf over the basin. This was always the acid test for her; the state of the mattress and the number of hangers were important, but it was the freebies that really mattered. She was impressed. At first sight she thought the selection was random until she realised that careful thought lay behind each choice: the hand-soap and the soap on the bidet were Roger & Gallet – lavender, which reminded her of her grandma; the bath gel – which she tipped into the running bathwater – and the shampoo were from a local manufacturer; and the bath soap was a chunky Provençale-style, olive-coloured cube. That gave the hotel a five-star rating in her book and she regretted they weren't staying there two nights so she could use it all.

It took her half an hour to bathe and dress and she left the hotel with only twenty minutes to find the conference. The concierge didn't know the exact location but he provided her with rough directions that took her along the main shopping street. She would have loved to have stopped at the various clothes shops which promised the relaxed elegance that French women seemed to effect so effortlessly. She didn't have the height or the sinuous grace of the mannequins or the photographic models in the shop windows, but she was happy to dream. The patisserie and wine shops taken for granted by the French provoked within her a guileless enthusiasm and, when she turned off the main Rue Nationale and towards the conference venue down a road empty of shops and people, she had to suppress an urge to skip. This was her first time in Tours and, in the fading light, the cobbles and soft grey stone of the smaller streets felt familiar, reminding her of similar wanderings through the towns of northern France where the idea for Beyond Compère had first formed.

The Centre d'Études Supérieures de la Renaissance looked like a dilapidated house. In front of the large eighteenth-century building was a gravel courtyard. There, huddled around an incongruous, rusting Renault 4, were a gaggle of smokers sporting the regulation academic uniform of jacket, tie and plastic name-tag. She knew some of them and recognised others but pre-empted any conversation by heading straight for the main door with her head down. Inside the house it felt cramped, an unlikely venue for an international conference, but the delegates were hand-picked, the numbers small. To her right was a small office with a long table attended by two women and a man to whom she introduced herself.

'Ah, oui, Mademoiselle Mitchell. Nous avons votre carte d'identité et un petit pacquet pour vous.'

She took the badge and, not wanting to make any holes in her dress with the safety pin, held it in her hand. In the envelope she found a running order of the conference, together with fliers for publishing houses, and a local map. She was asking the administrator where the lecture theatre was when the musicologist assigned to chair the session, Daniel Huibert, interrupted.

'Emma Mitchell!' he said, an announcement for the benefit of anyone within hailing distance. He grabbed her by the shoulders and kissed her enthusiastically on both cheeks. He was olive-skinned, effortlessly handsome and impossibly French, even down to the faint whiff of garlic and the almost manicured stubble that had scraped Emma's cheek and left it tingling. Or maybe that was her blushing, she thought, resisting the temptation to put her hand to her face in a pre-Raphaelite pose of innocence. His suit was beautifully cut, as was his dark hair, and the slight dimples in his chin and fine lines around his bright eyes completed the picture of a successful and confident man. Emma was surprised to find herself checking his right hand, where a band of gold confirmed his marital status, and even more surprised to find that she felt slightly disappointed. Thankfully, he seemed not to have noticed this last look, speaking quickly to one of the women behind the desk whilst he held Emma's upper arm and steered her gently away from the table.

'Zis way,' he said. 'And your flight was all right? From London to Paris, yes?' The accent seemed slightly overdone, even with his nod towards the English pronunciation of Paris.

'Yes,' she said as they walked beneath the fluorescent lights along a carpeted corridor. 'Everything's okay. A long journey, though. We had to come from Newcastle.'

Daniel sighed sympathetically and Emma suppressed a smile; Newcastle didn't figure much in the field of Renaissance studies, and certainly not in French renaissance musical studies, and she guessed he had no idea where the city was. He pushed open a double door to their left and guided her into a lecture theatre. Like the rest of the Centre d'Études, its original design as a private house was striking and, aside from the projector and screen, little attempt had been made to disguise the room's former use for family dining.

Andrew Eiger was seated at a table facing her, his hand wrapped in something white which, as she approached, she realised was a bandage.

'Ah, Monsieur Eiger. Enchanté. Je suis Daniel Huibert, résident de séance. Votre voyage s'est il bien passé? Et votre main? Vous vous êtes blessé?' asked Daniel, pointing to Andrew's bandaged hand. Why he had chosen to address her in English, and Andrew in French, Emma wasn't sure, though she guessed he was testing Andrew, a touch of Gallic competition over the only female in the room. Andrew was unperturbed and explained in perfect French that he had hurt his hand and a local pharmacy had helped him.

'It's fine,' he added in English to Emma.

'So you have met before?' asked Daniel, observing the exchange. Emma explained how they'd given Andrew a lift, whilst Andrew buried his head in his papers and began taking notes, almost as though Emma was issuing him with dictation.

Daniel was confirming the order of events when, right on cue, the third speaker, Étienne Baraud, dressed in a white linen shirt despite it being winter, ambled towards them, placing sheaves of paper at the ends of each row. He introduced himself in a strong accent and gave them copies of his handouts which were headed by a picture of a tree, the signs of Gents' and Ladies' toilets, an image of a Moebius strip and an optical diagram. Emma was glad she would be at the rehearsal when his paper began.

She had sent an advance copy of their new Ockeghem CD to Daniel and it was playing as the room slowly filled with the delegates, amongst whom she spotted several familiar faces. She exchanged a wave or a smile with some as she flipped through her lecture one last time. Daniel was deep in conversation with the final speaker and had placed her on his right where, seated next to Andrew, she observed the American, head down, writing out numbers and letters like a private game of *Countdown*.

'How is it?' she asked, nodding towards his hand. 'What did they say?'

Andrew looked up, pushing his glasses back onto the bridge of his nose.

'Oh. Not bad.' He waved his bandaged hand and twiddled his fingers, then winced and rested it on the table, palm upwards, fingers curled protectively over his palm. 'They gave me strong painkillers and antibiotics and wrapped it in a dressing. They told me to keep it dry and said I should let the air get to it tonight. Oh, and I should really get a tetanus shot and maybe a rabies one as well, but I told them I'd injured myself on an aeroplane, not been bitten by a bat.'

Emma laughed. She hadn't expected wit from him, let alone droll humour.

'By the way,' she said, 'I have to leave halfway through your paper to get to our rehearsal, so I think it might be better if I left before you begin? Otherwise people might think I'm walking out on you. I could get Daniel to explain that. I'd love to read the paper though, so perhaps you could let me have a copy?'

Andrew didn't mind at all. It was only the meeting tonight that really mattered and, in any case, he was currently distracted by his new calculations. The numbers and the letters on the sheet of A4 in front of him were beginning to take shape remarkably quickly.

He'd only told Emma part of what had occurred between leaving her at her hotel and meeting her again here. After the pharmacy and rather than checking in to his hotel, he'd picked up a baguette and grabbed a quick espresso in a café, then he'd registered at the Centre d'Études. One of the staff had wheeled his luggage away to an office, and behind him the conference attendees had spilled out into the hall from the early-afternoon session. The smokers were first, heading straight for the front door to pollute the fresh air – a few Brits, a couple of Americans and a hefty Dutch contingent that Andrew knew only by reputation. The rest had gathered around a table where coffee was set out, and Andrew had slunk behind a portable notice-board. He wanted to hear a few of the papers and get a sense of the direction in which the critical wind was blowing before he spoke to anyone.

When he was sure he wouldn't be seen, he quit his temporary shelter and moved towards the lecture theatre. Expecting it to be empty, he pushed hard on the door and sent a tall, bespectacled man reeling backwards. He apologised, but the lanky academic shook his head and told him there was no need. Besides, he added, looking at Andrew's bandaged hand, he was the injured party.

'Dirk Schut,' the man had announced, holding out his hand, and then he laughed. 'But of course, you cannot shake hands. *Domkop!* Me. I'm the fool. Not you.' He had quickly stooped to look at Andrew's name-tag. 'Eiger. Ohio! Excellent. That's … twenty-one and twenty-two makes forty-three … and then fourteen and eight is … twenty-two and twenty-one! Wonderful symmetry! Congratulations!'

Andrew, who had witnessed his fair share of intellectual eccentricity, had no idea what the man was talking about. What were these numbers and what did they have to do with him?

I'm sorry, I get excited by names,' explained Dirk. 'It's a new area of research for me and I've got one of those brains, you know. I'm not mad, don't worry. I'm giving a paper on it tomorrow.'

A bell rang dimly in the recesses of Andrew's brain. From his conference schedule he remembered that someone was talking about numerology. He didn't know much about it other than the fact that *gematria*, as it was known, came from the Hebrew belief that each letter had a numerical value that lent to each word a particular property. He had never dabbled in the study himself, content to share a general disdain for a subject that, to many people's minds, failed basic tests of consistency. For a start, there was the alphabet you used and the numbers to which they equated; some systems leapt in units of ten after the letter K had been reached. And any biblical text had been translated from Aramaic, Hebrew or Greek into Latin and thence to modern languages, each transition subject to the translator's poetic and stylistic bent.

He had a vague memory that Schut was using numerology as a methodological tool to establish the real spelling of Ockeghem's name, a perennial conundrum recast in an interesting new light, though it was, in his view, a dull and ultimately redundant exercise. Ockeghem was particularly rich in variations – Obeghem, Ockeghem, Oquagan, Okegem – in all forty-nine different spellings and still counting, the consequence of local pronunciation and mis-transcriptions in a predominantly oral culture where the spelling of a name was relatively unimportant.

He wanted to sit down and get his lecture in order, but the Dutchman was not to be deterred. He pulled out a notebook from his pocket and a small piece of paper with yellowed edges.

'I call it my crib sheet,' he said, showing Andrew a list of the letters of the alphabet, next to which were numbers.

'So you see, it's a very simple principle. Each letter has a number value, except I and J, and U and V – they're the same. So, A is one, B is two, and so on. So: the cipher of Eiger – that's lovely. E – five; I – nine; G – seven; E – again, five; R – seventeen. And you can see the symmetry already. The first three letters add up to twenty-one and the last two add up to twenty-two. It's not perfect, but it's pretty good. But this is why I got excited; you get a mirror image with the cipher of Ohio.'

He jotted something down in his notebook and showed it to Andrew:

```
E   I   G   E   R      O   H   I   O
5   9   7   5   17     14  8   9   14
  \___/    \___/         \___/   \___/
   21       22            22      21
```

'Do you see?' he said triumphantly. 'Twenty-one and twenty-two are perfectly mirrored in your name. It's beautiful!'

Andrew adopted the standard academic defensive stance when confronted with a new idea: impressed, but sceptical. His name, after all, was not Eiger Ohio and the significant design seemed to be the result of inspired coincidence and Dirk's quirky methodology. That was the problem with this numerology stuff, he'd always thought; it seemed somehow random, a case of throwing numbers up into the air and seeing what patterns could be found when they fell. It was different with music, where arithmetic was often the conscious basis for aesthetic form; when Dufay was commissioned to write a piece for the consecration of Brunelleschi's famous dome in 1436, he had clearly used the proportions of Florence Cathedral as the guide for the musical plan. Complex mathematical schemes certainly informed medieval music, but numerology and ciphers of composers' names were considerably more conjectural.

'I give you my handout,' said Dirk, digging into a large canvas shopping bag and withdrawing a sheaf of papers. 'You can have a look at it and we must talk tomorrow.'

It amounted to four pages of A4, stapled together, covered in a confusion of numbers and letters, pictures and diagrams. Running down the sides of the first page were two alphabets, one English and one Latin, and their mooted numerical equivalents.

'Seventy,' said Dirk as he headed for the door.

'Sorry?'

'Seventy. It's the value of "Goodbye",' said the Dutchman over his shoulder as the door closed behind him.

For all his doubts, Andrew's interest had been piqued. The numerology angle was one he hadn't considered. Might the value of Ockeghem's name somehow tie the motet to the composer?

Using Schut's handout as a reference for the numerical equivalences, Andrew had spent the next fifteen minutes pondering the various spellings of Ockeghem's name, and that was how Emma and the director of the conference had found him, doodling with letters and numbers. He'd not met Daniel Huibert before and the Frenchman struck him as too good-looking to be an academic, someone who'd probably got where he was through a mixture of good fortune and charm, the latter being very much in evidence whenever he addressed Emma. Clearly she was the star turn and, as a woman, was of particular interest.

Daniel was now delivering his prelude to the assembled delegates, his agenda, Andrew felt, crudely evident by announcing the panellists in reverse order to maximise the anticipation of presenting a 'proper' musician into their academic midst. Étienne Baraud, the third speaker, was obviously some kind of post-structuralist acolyte, with a background in semiotics and arcane French psychoanalysis. It was a school of critical thought which Andrew believed had no place in medieval studies; whenever he came across references to Lacan or Derrida in footnotes, he expected that the accompanying text would be full of woolly prose, obscure puns and sweeping generalisations. He wondered if he, like Emma, could leave before the paper.

Daniel, after a sly dig at the barren cultural wasteland of the American Midwest, traced Andrew's brief career. He mentioned the title of his Ph.D. and described him as young – an epithet that was either laudatory or condescending, Andrew couldn't decide which. The pause that followed was entirely for dramatic effect and showed scant respect for Andrew and his fellow French panellist. Daniel sighed, glanced almost coyly at Emma, and then looked up at his audience.

'Emma Mitchell,' he began, and for an instant Andrew wondered if he was going to leave it there, as if merely the mention of Emma's name was charged with such mystical significance that no further clarification was necessary. Then Daniel, who had introduced the first two panellists in English, lapsed into French, but no ordinary French. This was the language of Mallarmé and Baudelaire: Emma was not only talented, she was also responsible for embracing the fifteenth century and delivering it to the wider audience without, at any point, betraying the essence of the music or compromising the key values of truth to history and intellectual rigour – the key themes, he noted severely, of this very conference. As he bestowed upon Emma each section of his encomium, he looked down at her and then out to his audience with an expression that suggested that they, as mere academics, could never hope to emulate her contribution. He said she was beautiful, immediately qualifying his description as a reference to her contribution to early-music performance, before likening her success to a flower bursting from the fecund soil of England's intellectual tradition. Judging from the looks on some of the delegates' faces, Andrew was not the only one who, when Daniel uttered the phrase 'de bon goût', wondered if the chairman of the session was commending Emma for her good taste or, as seemed more likely given the slight flush in the Frenchman's cheeks, thought her 'tasty'. Unaware of the awkwardness that was spreading through the audience, there followed an extended, overtly sexual metaphor about intellectual probing that led to a cul-de-sac, which left Daniel – mercifully, as far as Andrew was concerned – lost for words. As if emerging from an erotic daydream, Daniel picked up his notes, read the title of Emma's paper and abruptly reminded the audience that the concert that night would be at 20.30 (Andrew always had problem with the European twenty-four hour clock and momentarily thought that meant ten-thirty), and that no one – no one, he repeated – should miss it. And with that, like a game show contestant, he applauded his own speech. The delegates had no choice but join in, though Andrew noted that a few people leant over to colleagues and made what he assumed were caustic asides under the convenient cover of the clapping.

Throughout, Emma suffered Daniel's inflated tribute with an embarrassed smile and the occasional laconic glance at her audience to distance herself from the laboured eulogy and to mask her concern about the consequent expectations. She found herself reminded of the fawning fan who had pressed her for her signature the previous night in Newcastle. The Chairman's lubricious turn as Master of Ceremonies seemed designed to ignite desire in the male delegates and, once again, Emma's gender had been artificially and artlessly foregrounded, thus drawing attention away from her real abilities. Academics and performers, it seemed, were separated in much the same way as men and women were, the latter adored and venerated. There were some, she thought to herself bleakly, for whom the best paper she could deliver would be one where she remained silent and looked pretty.

'I thank Daniel,' she began, ad-libbing, and not entirely certain where or how far she was going, 'for that … for that flattery. We are in France, of course, so I can only say that, as a woman, such praise is, well, *de rigueur*.' There was a polite laugh from the audience.

'But we're here to talk about Ockeghem, a man of course, and a man of the cloth who did not consort with women. I expect that he would have had less favourable words to say about an Eve like myself, and in many ways, of course, condemnation of women is simply the reverse side of praise; both, in different ways, treat women as an object. I would just ask you to set aside any claims I might have to being a performer – and indeed set aside my gender – and invite you to consider what I have to say to you today with the same detachment that you would accord a fellow-academic. That would be true flattery.'

She hadn't meant to be so cutting and was surprised at her own eloquence. When she'd started talking she thought she would just précis her paper and apologise for reading it, but, once she'd begun, her anger had gathered and focused. The sentences had unrolled rhythmically, guided by some internal logic that found its way only rarely into her speech, and by the time she'd reached her conclusion Daniel was clearing his throat and busying himself with his papers.

Anne Frewing and Jenny Riddsdale, both of Emma's age, were in the front row, the one a tough New Yorker and the other a blunt Yorkshirewoman. Emma had shared bottles of chardonnay with them at a conference two years before and set the world to rights, a moment of sisterhood in a male-dominated arena that had ended with Jenny asking, 'When shall we three meet again?' Emma very much hoped it would be later so she could ask them if they thought she should apologise, but, judging from their broad smiles and folded arms, she could tell they approved.

Andrew, meanwhile, had lost interest. Almost as soon as Daniel had begun his over-the-top introduction, a diagram on Dirk Schut's handout had leapt out at him, a macaronic version of Ockeghem's name that combined the Latin with the accepted French variant: Johannes Ockeghem. An academic in the 1930s had suggested that the composer had deliberately adopted this spelling so as to render its numerological equivalent more symmetrical, more – to use a word better suited to both music and the medieval period – harmonious.

Beneath the letters Schut had traced out the respective values:

J	O	H	A	N	N	E	S		O	C	K	E	G	H	E	M
9	14	8	1	13	13	5	18 = 81		14	3	10	5	7	8	5	12 = 64

Whether or not the proposal was valid, the resultant values of the names struck Andrew as somehow elegant. What was it about them? Eighty-one? Sixty-four? And then he realised they were perfect squares. The value of Johannes was 81; 9x9: the value of Ockeghem was 64; 8x8. For a moment he was pleased with himself, but almost immediately his pleasure gave way to disappointment. All he'd discovered was that the numbers were squares, which proved nothing in itself; it was merely an observation, something he might raise at the end of Schut's paper to pick him out from the crowd, but no more. 'Do you think there's anything significant in the fact that they're both squares?' he would ask, and there would be a murmur amongst the other delegates as they considered this small *aperçu*. 9 and 9; 8 and 8. And then Andrew had felt his body go hot and just as suddenly cold again; a shiver had ripped through him as if he'd been wired to the mains. 9 and 9, and 8 and 8? That was the very layout of the parts in the thirty-four-part *Miserere mei*: nine *discantus* parts; nine *contratenor* parts; eight *tenor* parts; eight *bassus* parts. 9 and 9, and 8 and 8?

My God, he thought, *that's it! It has to be!*

The motet was by Ockeghem; his signature was here in the arrangement of the voice parts. Andrew looked up. In front of him was an audience of Ockeghem scholars, all of them listening to Emma talking, which, because the blood was pumping so loudly in his ears, he could no longer hear. He should stand up right now and tell them! Tell them all! He'd interrupt Emma and, as an apology, announce that Beyond Compère would be giving the first performance of Ockeghem's *Miserere mei*, a thirty-four-part motet, sometime in the near future. *Look*, he would say: *here's the proof*: the circumstantial evidence of Chiron and his letter; the stylistic similarities including the use of the canon at a fourth; and the numerological solution that was staring him in the face. And what better place and time to announce it? Here, in Tours, Ockeghem's home town, on the five-hundredth anniversary of his death, in front of the group of people who would immediately appreciate the true impact of his discovery?

Except that he would do no such thing, despite the ecstasy bubbling through his body. It was too precious, too perfect, too personal for him to share with anyone. And, of course, the glory would be his and on his terms. It would have to wait.

Inspired, he began searching for further symmetries, just as Schut had with the Eiger/Ohio example. His own paper was no longer important, and Emma's, which now and then raised the odd laugh, had become merely background noise. He stared at Schut's diagram for a while then wrote it out again on a blank piece of paper. It was an approach he had taken to the notational code, staring blankly at the symbols, hoping that somehow their meaning might speak to him. Idly he began pairing numbers, and adding them together. After a few minutes, he'd revealed further symmetries:

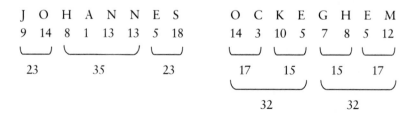

Could he find these numerical values inscribed in the piece itself? He needed to look at his most recent transcription and the original copy, both of which lay tantalisingly close at hand in his briefcase. Might there be, say, twenty-three breves of music and thirty-five breves of rest? Or might the values of Ockeghem's surname, so beautifully balanced in the numerical reduction, be somehow located in the values of the notes? Sixty-four, after all, was the cube of four and maybe the number four had some special significance in the piece? Of course. There were four basic parts and the time signature was in four!

He couldn't take it all in; he needed more time. However, he was now convinced that the idea that Ockeghem had deliberately changed his name was a sound one. The symmetry of the numerical values was just too – well, as Schut had put it, just too beautiful. When he got home he would read more about numerology and *gematria* and track down references to number games of which, like wordplay, the medieval mind was so fond. There was a lot of work ahead, which delighted him; it meant another chapter at least. His book was going to be a large one.

He set aside his papers just as Emma finished her talk and the chairman invited questions. The first was from a young Ph.D. student whom Andrew identified as the one who had sent him the draft article that mentioned Chiron. The Frenchman suggested Emma might want to revise her opinion about Ockeghem. His research showed that the composer was not quite the saint described by Francesco Florio in 1477, and that he had constantly quarrelled with the Chapter at St Martin. Emma, slipping effortlessly into the constrained language of academia, thanked him for his observation and, in the interests of reciprocity, imparted two quick anecdotes about the clergy at two English cathedrals who had recently shown themselves to be just as self-serving and uncharitable as anyone in the medieval period. The audience had laughed and, with perfect timing, she offered to provide the appropriate references should he require them.

The second question was from Anne Frewing, who all but swaggered to her feet and addressed her question not so much to Emma as to the other delegates. Did Emma feel, as she did, that the study of a man who was a priest and who thus 'knew' no woman, yet who chose to write about them in chansons or in motets, had anything to offer women in the twentieth century?

Emma smiled. She knew that Anne was feeding her a line, one that she could run with or ignore.

'Thanks for that, Anne,' she said with no enthusiasm in her voice, a dry delivery that raised a small laugh. 'Well, obviously, when we're dealing with sacred Catholic music and with traditions of courtly love we're up to our elbows in patriarchy, and I do sometime feel patriarchal pressure in fifteenth-century music. It's by men and performed by men, as choirboys or as adults, an entirely male-dominated world in which women don't get a look-in. So I'm really glad that women sing this music now, and not just because they're patently better than boys.

'As for Ockeghem himself?' She paused and squinted, as if seeing the composer in her mind's eye. 'I guess Ockeghem seems to me like one of the good guys, a *bon père* as Molinet would have it, more like a grandfather than a father. In fact –' she smiled – 'now I come to think about it, exactly like my grandfather: an old man who sat in his armchair doing cryptic crosswords. Ockeghem liked puzzles too, so, yes, I think of Ockeghem as a grandfather. Someone, then, who has divested himself – or *absolved* himself – of power. Not a politician at all.

'And that may be a fantasy, but then that's history and that's early-music performance. We hope to discover the truth, but we have to admit that there's a healthy dose of fantasy involved.

'I'm not sure that answers your question, Anne. This sense of a composer is important for me – for all of us, I think – and we all know that it's fictional. But then it's fictional in the way that history is fictional. We'll never know.' And Emma looked at her audience and shrugged, a gesture that acted as a cue for applause.

Daniel stood and thanked Emma, though with more subdued enthusiasm than he had introduced her. Emma placed her script back into her bag and, as she leant down, she saw Andrew with a lunatic grin pasted over his face, his eyes wide, his bandaged hand resting on a piece of paper covered in letters and numbers, the other hand raised, giving her the thumbs-up.

He really should get some sleep, she thought.

CHAPTER 13

The Memoirs of Geoffroy Chiron: Livre IV *ed. Francis Porter*

Martius 2, 1524

The greatest changes to our city occurred during the reign of Louis XI. The new King's hope was that Tours would become the symbol of a stronger France, renowned throughout Christianity for its culture and devotion and, just a year after his coronation [1462], he proclaimed Tours the capital of France and made his home there. The townsfolk welcomed the news for it meant increased fame and wealth for the city. The constant comings and goings of visitors and the court meant that a sol could be added to a barrel of wine, a livre tournois to a fine cloak lined with rabbit fur, and that employment was guaranteed for the craftsman of the city. Soon we had goldsmiths coming from the south and tailors from the north. Houses were built across the Loire on the north bank, and St Cyr, where Jehan lived, soon became a recognised part of Tours. Where French was once the only language spoken in the streets, now Italian, German and Spanish were heard. And the look of the town changed also, for Louis had hundreds of mulberry trees planted to encourage the production of silk. Many traders came from Lyon [1470] and they built new, higher houses along the Rue de la Scellerie.

As was well known, Louis had quarrelled with his father, Charles le Victorieux, and been banished. He had received protection at the court of Philippe le Bon, Duke of Burgundy, where he had plenty of time to plan his strategy. There he had come to know and love the music sung in the court chapel and at the various feasts. The premier chapelain at that time was Robert Morton, an Englishman, and Louis, seduced by the glory that was conferred upon Philippe, took it upon himself to learn something about music. His ambition was not merely to be King of France but to build a choir that could rival his current host's, for at the time Philip employed some of the finest musicians. Gilles Binchois, the great composer for whom Jehan would come to write his beautiful Déploration, had retired to Soignies and Louis asked Morton if Binchois would be likely to forgo the pleasures of an idle life and accompany him to Tours. Binchois graciously declined the offer and added that the finest composer in the land already worked for the Royal Court: Johannes Ockeghem.

Jehan knew nothing of this and it was with more than a sense of foreboding that he met the new king shortly after the coronation in Reims. Having observed many like himself advance only to be cut down, he knew well that he might be replaced as Treasurer of St Martin by a favourite of the new king. Thus he was pleased to discover that his place as treasurer was assured, and that his responsibilities to the court and to St Martin would, if anything, increase; Louis's first instruction was to find new and better singers for a larger choir so that its fame should reach Burgundy.

When Jehan took Holy Orders, he did so with Louis's encouragement and blessing, for Louis was a devout man and, like Jehan, dressed austerely. His clothing was usually grey or brown and of basic cloth, and he often wore a strange grey felt hat (it was not for personal reasons that he had invited the silk traders to Tours). Jehan likewise had little interest in fine clothing, and throughout his life could only be persuaded to wear garments fitting to the occasion if he were provided with them. Only when it would have been rude not to display the gift would he set aside his usual sober clothing in favour of convention. It was Louis who gave him a fine scarlet robe lined with rabbit fur so that, when Jehan appeared in an official capacity, he did not look like a mere citizen. Such modesty was complemented by a generosity of spirit. At New Year Jehan's éstrennes [gifts] to shopkeepers, servants and patrons exceeded all expectations, and, when he died, he left all his possessions and wealth to the church.

And there were further commonalities of spirit between the King and his favourite composer: Jehan preferred his smaller house in Saint Cyr to the grandeur of the Treasurer's home, and Louis lived in the smaller Château of Plessis-les-Tours rather than the Château d'Amboise. Although he had the former enlarged, it was to accommodate his retinue and not for reasons of ostentation. When the choir of St Martin paid one of its regular visits we were afforded the occasional glimpse of the living quarters and, where I expected to see wooden beds with soft materials, instead I saw straw beds and sparse decoration. Where tapestries might have provided colour and softness, the stone walls echoed, and the floors were hard and unforgiving on our feet after the long walk, with music the only concession towards indulgence of any kind.

With the exception of an outbreak of the plague [1472], all was calm during the early years of Louis's reign. The King would occasionally visit the city, his arrival heralded by haut instruments, but generally the townsfolk conducted their lives with no interruption. Jehan was occupied with his various duties as Treasurer, disputes with the clergy being his daily bread. Slowly and surely, I ascended the ranks to become procurator, working alongside Jehan in his office as Treasurer, administering the responsibilities of receiving payments in the form of local taxation, and pursuing monies that were not forthcoming. When Jehan was absent, away on business in nearby towns or detained by the King, I was entrusted with the keys to the Treasury. Now and then dignitaries from other cities and countries would visit, occasions for which the organisation of grand galas held in the Hôtel de Ville fell entirely to me. Sometimes Jehan would compose a piece, which I would transcribe, and we would be as we once were: he the maître and I his pupil. And, of course, Jehan and I still sang together in the choir of St Martin. The seasons came and went, with the feasts that marked the passage of the year respected and honoured, and signalled by the tolling of the bells.

It all changed when Louis fell ill in Forges [1479]. From then until his death four years later, the King suffered a series of strokes and his modest, predictable tastes turned from the sober to the bizarre. He began to wear increasingly refined and colourful clothing – scarlet, crimson and blue silks and satins trimmed with fine marten's fur – and, as if to complement this, the walls of the Château were adorned with paintings and tapestries. Where once there had been modesty, now there was affectation; where humility had dwelt, now was found vanity. Worldliness was not the cause – Louis was still a devout man – but the conviction of his beliefs had become an uncontrollable appetite as his love of God turned to fear.

Louis made Saint-Jean du Plessis, the small chapel in his Château, a collegiate church and Mass was now sung every day. He confessed his sins every week and, always a collector of relics, now sought them out in the hope that they might effect in him a cure. He brought the ring of Saint Zenobius from Florence and the blood of hard-shelled animals from Cape Verde. He even summoned St Francis of Paola and built for him a cave wherein the famed hermit from Calabria devoted his prayers for the King's life. For this, as for other services, Louis paid excessively, his largesse increasing the nearer he came to death. Yet his illnesses continued and he was increasingly drawn to charlatans and soothsayers for whom guile counted as knowledge.

Rather than face death and his maker with the kind of quiet acceptance I have observed in Jehan and others, Louis frantically sought solace wherever he could find it, the logic of which was never explained. The most astonishing addition to the household was a menagerie of fantastic animals: elk and reindeer from Denmark – relatives, one supposed, of deer but much larger and possessed of antlers and fur designed for the cold climates of the far north rather than the temperate climes of Tours; dogs of all kinds – greyhounds from England, bull mastiffs from Spain, spaniels from Brittany, and shaggy dogs from Valencia; and horses of various breeds. The last were at least kept in stables, but all the others, including a jackal, were kept in the Château where they were free to roam. God only knows what kind of mongrel bastards this array produced. The smell of the animals was obvious to us all when we entered the Château, hardly surprising given their fear, snatched as they had been from their homelands. Often the baying of dogs was louder than the choir and Jehan instructed us to sing out, whatever the meaning of the words. Better, he said, to drown out the din and, in any case, Louis, his shrunken figure just visible above the desk of his stall, was by this time rather deaf.

Louis now trusted animals more than men and soon set about removing his closest advisers. All around him he saw scheming where there was none and he banished many barons. It was as though he feared that the plotting against his father in which he had indulged himself as a youth was now being visited upon him. Phillipe Commines, one of the King's closest advisors, warned Jehan to be careful and Commines himself was dismissed shortly thereafter. It was testament to Jehan's ability to read other people as one would a book that he was never estranged from Louis.

Jehan advised me that he spoke to Louis exactly as he always had done. If Louis said something that made no sense, Jehan would tell him so; if he suggested that someone undeserving should be banished, Jehan would disagree with him. Truth was his guide, Jehan said, and in that way Louis could never doubt his sincerity. Yet it was a dangerous time for him and others close to the King, and he had to tread carefully and observe all the proper hierarchies of the court and behaviour fitting to them.

In these last years of Louis's life, Jehan's conversations with the King were limited mainly to matters theological. There was, though, one administrative matter in which Jehan attempted to intercede, namely the addition of Desprez to the Royal chapel. On the death of Le bon roi René [René d'Anjou – 1480], the duchy of Anjou became the property of France. René had built a fine chapel and employed some great singers and composers, notably Desprez, and, seeing an opportunity for the further expansion of the choir at St Martin, Jehan suggested to Louis that the best members of René's choir should come to Tours. Jehan had seen several of Desprez's compositions and was impressed; he was undoubtedly a man blessed with ability and had much to offer God, France and the King. Although Desprez was a difficult and troubled man, Jehan believed that he might yet be redeemed.

Louis, though, had other ideas. Many of the finest relics in the land were in the Sainte-Chapelle in Paris, brought there from Constantinople by Louis IX, and the King believed that any power they might possess could be enhanced by the properties of music. Rather than bring the singers to Tours, he instructed that they be sent to the Sainte-Chapelle.

Desprez wrote to Jehan from his new home in Paris. He thanked him for his intervention – though, with typical lack of grace, said he would much prefer to have been in Tours. Despite this minor inconvenience, he wanted to write a piece for Louis. It was a fitting gesture; a composition is often given to a new patron in the hope of future service. But Jehan was not blind to the game of advancement that Desprez was playing. With Louis's death there would be many changes. The Dauphin was but a boy and, when he succeeded his father, though he was unlikely to interfere with the smooth running of St Martin, Jehan's tenure as premier chapelain was by no means guaranteed. Jehan was an old man and, if the new King preferred someone closer to his age, then the post of premier chapelain might become available. If Josquin was close to the Dauphin's volatile father, then the son might well repay the debt.

Desprez asked Jehan to advise him on the text. Generally such a piece would be a hymn of praise, but Desprez had heard many rumours of Louis's strange behaviour, his illness and his obsession with death. Louis saw false messages where there were none and often spoke of codes and riddles hidden in documents and Desprez was right to seek advice; the choice of text for the composition would have to be made with great care. The answer, Jehan believed, was to be found in Louis's recent commission from Jean Bourdichon which was displayed throughout the Château Plessis-les-Tours: fifty glorious scrolls borne by angels, which, through the artist's skill, seemed real. And upon those scrolls were the words of Psalm 88 [Psalm 89]: Misericordias Domini in aeternum cantabo; in generatione et generatione adnuntiabo veritatem tuam in ore meo. Quia dixisti sempiterna misericordia aedificabitur; caelos fundabis et veritas tua in eis. [The mercies of the Lord I will sing for ever. I will shew forth thy truth with my mouth to generation and generation. For thou hast said: Mercy shall be built up for ever in the heavens: thy truth shall be prepared in them.]

Jehan had played his part as honestly as ever, for the King had discussed with him what might be the most suitable text, but at that time it was a secret known only to the King, Bourdichon and Jehan.

Thus Jehan, who always saw himself as a guardian to younger composers, wrote to Desprez and told him to compose a piece upon the words Misericordias Domini in aeternum cantabo. When he had completed it, Desprez should send it to Jehan who would arrange for it to be presented with due ceremony to Le Roi Louis XI. Knowing of Desprez's ambition and impatience, Jehan was more forceful than he would normally be. He impressed upon Desprez the importance of secrecy and made him aware that, without Jehan's introduction, the King would, in all likelihood, view a composition which quoted the very text that he had privately instructed to decorate his fortified Château as a sign of conspiracy. A man who already divined faces in clouds and designs in shadows would regard an unannounced composition using those words not as coincidence, but as evidence of a plot against his life. In this Jehan was trying to protect not only Desprez but also Bourdichon and other members of the retinue. And Jehan himself.

Desprez, as ever, listened to no one and, when he had completed the composition, sent it directly to Louis. Mercifully he also sent a letter to Jehan telling him what he had done, which allowed Jehan to prepare his defence. It was the only time that Jehan told a lie to Louis and it pained him greatly.

Ultimately Lady Fortuna smiled upon Jehan and upon Desprez, for Louis suffered yet another stroke and his memory failed him. Jehan was able to convince the King that Louis himself had asked Jehan to compose a piece using the same text that decorated the walls of his Château, and that Jehan – too busy with the affairs of St Martin and the daily services at Plessis-les-Tours – had asked one of Louis's new servants, the famed Josquin Desprez, to complete the task.

Jehan then explained the design to Louis, inventing his arguments as he went. After a lengthy exposition, he came to the final line: In te, Domine, speravi; non confundar in aeternum. Amen. [In thee, O Lord, do I put my trust: let me never be put to confusion. Amen.]

This, Jehan explained, was Desprez imagining Louis's prayer to God.

'I don't like it,' said Louis immediately. 'You write something for me.'

Louis was devout, Louis loved God, but Louis was afraid of death and did not want to be reminded of it too often. He had done many things in his life for which he might yet pay the price, and the suggestion of eternal damnation was like an open sore.

And so it fell to Jehan to compose a motet for the dying King, his five-voice Intemerata Dei Mater, a hymn to the Virgin which alluded only in the vaguest way to judgement in calling for safe deliverance through the intercession of angels, thereby recalling the figures that Bourdichon had painted.

It was, though, more than a composition for a dying King: Jehan was the same age as Louis and aware of his own mortality. This was a very personal expression, from the text itself, which referred to the dangers of living in exile, to quotations from his own chansons. It was a tapestry of the emotions and events of his life and, at the time, I was quite sure that it would be Jehan's last composition. And so it would have been had not Compère, over a decade later, asked Jehan to write a new piece.

Jehan returned Desprez's unperformed composition and explained what had happened. He assumed that Desprez was furious, for he heard nothing from him for several years, during which time the younger composer left Sainte-Chapelle and travelled to Hungary and Italy. Thus Desprez never learned how dangerous his actions had been, and Jehan never told him. It was fortunate that Louis's memory was clouded, for otherwise Desprez could have been accused of being a spy, for which the penalty was torture and execution. And, of course, his torturers would have gleaned information that may have led them back to Jehan.

It was not the first time that Desprez's singular wilfulness and desire for advancement had led himself and others into danger. Ultimately it was his ability as a musician that granted him safe passage through this life and, I am certain, will assure his fame after death. He will, though, have faced a sterner judgement in the next world.

As I look back now, an explanation that I had not seen previously emerges, one which suggests a reason for Desprez's later behaviour concerning Jehan's great thirty-four voice motet. Desprez, far away in Paris, witnessed none of the intricate details of Jehan's dealings with the King, and, in the absence of such explanation, he may well have formed the facile, false belief that it was because of the actions of Johannes Ockeghem that his own composition was never performed. Perhaps Desprez vowed *then to have his revenge against the older composer, not knowing that, through Jehan's intervention, he had actually been saved from pain and death.*

In this, as in so many other ways, Desprez was deceived by his very nature, for he would never seek or heed the arguments of others. In his isolation he would have remained convinced of the veracity of his opinion. As Thomas Aquinas says, the scribes and Pharisees were deceived in their understanding of our Lord Jesus Christ by their own malevolence; in the same way, Desprez was undone by his withdrawal from other men. He should have consorted more with others, for the truth is to be found in a group of men with shared goodwill and will never be discovered in the counsel of a single man who argues with himself.

Dominus mihi auxiliator et ego despiciam odientes me. Melius est sperare in Domino quam sperare in homine. Melius est sperare in Domino quam sperare in principibus.

[The Lord is my helper: and I will look over my enemies. It is good to confide in the Lord, rather than to have confidence in man. It is good to trust in the Lord, rather than to trust in princes.]

Your access to Cambridge University Press EBooks is provided by: *University of Florida at Tallahassee*	April 12th 2015 *Andrew Eiger.* You are now *signed out*

CHAPTER 14

Emma emerged into the courtyard of the conference centre. She thought her paper had gone well. No one had fallen asleep, nor had anyone leapt to their feet and challenged her. She knew that many were being polite, that they felt that her real contribution was this evening's concert rather than the afternoon's performance for which she would get no reviews. It was gone now, into the ether, and she felt the same relief she often experienced after a concert, when she would reward herself with a glass of wine. There was no time for that now, though; with the Basilica of St Martin just round the corner, she wanted to pay homage to the place where Ockeghem had sung all those years ago.

The modern basilica – modern, at least, by Ockeghem's standards – had been built at the end of the nineteenth century over the site of the original tomb of St Martin. The orientation of the new edifice was, in imitation of the new city itself, south-to-north rather than west-to-east. Gone was the elongated Nave, and in its place stood an eccentric confection of a cuboid base, neo-Byzantine decorations, and a strange neo-Classical dome atop which St Martin himself was perilously perched. Doubtless Marco and Charlie could explain to her its particular nineteenth-century charm, but it struck Emma as a rather random design, more fitting to the south of France than to a city famous for its association with the Valois Kings.

All that remained of the old building were two towers, which had marked the extremities of the former church: the one part of the North Transept and the other flanking the main West Door. Both had been renamed, as the Tour de Charlemagne and the Tour de l'Horloge respectively, giving the impression that they were self-contained edifices that had served different functions, the divorce from their original purpose total. Standing with the Tour de Charlemagne to her right, Emma looked along the Rue des Halles towards the remaining bell tower. The outlines of the original pillars were inlaid in the tarmac and she tried to imagine the columns rising into the darkening sky. The Altar would have been to her left and she would have been standing in the Transept. The scale of the building was immense, somehow more impressive in her imagination that it would be if it still existed, and the collegiate church could easily have housed everything that her vision encompassed – the road, all of the shops and the houses. It was impossible, in rush hour with cars and pedestrians hurrying to their destinations, to ignore the mundane and conjure the sublime. Where tapestries illustrating the life of St Martin might have hung, she discovered instead bright advertisements for washing powder; where a stained-glass window would have described the temptation of Christ, a sign for 'Galettes et Gauffres' shuddered into neon life.

As the sun began to sink beyond a grey slate roof Emma abandoned her efforts to commune with the past. She couldn't understand why the city had been so keen to destroy the remains of the old church and not restore it. A board at the foot of the Charlemagne tower showed a nineteenth-century engraving of the church as it was originally: four solid square towers topped with pyramidal saddlebacks, and spidery flying-buttresses running along the length of the building. A slightly earlier picture showed St Martin after its semi-destruction by the Huguenots in the eighteenth century and the subsequent adoption of the ruins as stables during the time of the Revolution. It was like a cut-through, three-dimensional model that allowed the viewer to see both the exterior and interior of a machine, the two remaining towers linked by a run of pillars and shattered arches. The authorities seemed to have fallen in love with a particularly Romantic image of history, one where ruins were invested with their own quality, and dilapidation celebrated as a melancholic reminder of the inevitable passage of time. Beauty was revealed in the destruction of perfection: *we are not like these people*, it said, *and here is a reminder of that defining difference.* The inadvertent consequence of this ideology was that the town planners had been allowed to run a new thoroughfare right through the old church.

It wasn't merely the desecration of an historic building that offended Emma, but the distorting reverence that such thinking bestowed upon what remained, as if somehow that was more valuable than reconstruction. Music history was quite different: rather than venerating the intrinsic beauty of a manuscript, its economy and its function – all essentially abstract qualities – modern performers restored the music to life by setting aside qualms of historical accuracy in the pursuit of a living engagement with history.

She turned and walked towards St Gatien and the rehearsal, a route that led her along the Rue Scellerie with its half-timbered fifteenth-century houses – tall three-storey homes for the richer tradesmen. Tours, it seemed, was more proud of its old dwellings than its churches.

It was quieter here, easier to imagine the medieval town, and Emma wondered if Ockeghem had walked this very street, perhaps on his way to visit his friend, Antoine Busnois, who sang in St Gatien. Old maps and books, eighteenth-century furniture and paintings displayed in the windows of specialist shops invited her to stop and browse but she couldn't spare the time. In any case, she had no interest in antiques and she didn't know anything about antiquarian books, although her eye was caught by a shop selling old coins. Trays of mainly silver-coloured pieces were laid out in the window, each of them carefully packaged in a plastic holder inside which a handwritten note provided key details. There were quarters and old silver-dollars from 1930s America, even old British coins like the half-crown her father had found one day in his sock drawer and given to her. She saw a rack of older items – perhaps Renaissance, she thought, before rejecting the idea; if so they'd be in a museum, along with anything else more than a hundred years old.

Then she realised she was wrong; the trays held coins from the era she knew so well. Here they were, the Valois Kings, their names and dates respectfully stencilled in small writing: Charles VII (1422–1461) who appointed Ockeghem as Treasurer of St Martin; Louis XI (1461–1483), the Spider, the paranoid one; Charles VIII (1483–1498), the Affable, a weak name which made him sound like a nonentity; Louis XII (1498–1515) who cared little for music but who at least had the good sense to bring Leonardo da Vinci to France; and François I (1515–1547) who employed Mouton and De Sermisy, and during whose reign Josquin and Compère had died.

Emma was no collector, her only instance of deliberate acquisition being a cheap, weekly publication called *The World's Great Composers* to which she subscribed as a child, yet something drew her inside. It was dark, and a woman of about sixty was sitting at a small table, writing with a fine-nibbed fountain-pen on a slip of blue cardboard. To Emma's left was a shelf of large catalogues, and the walls were covered with engravings and oil paintings of Tours in years past.

'Bonjour, mademoiselle,' said the woman. 'Puis-je vous aider?'

Emma asked her about the coins she'd seen in the window. How much would one cost from, say, the reign of Louis XI? The woman stood up and walked over to the window and withdrew a tray.

'Nossing 'ere from Louis onze,' she said, 'mais, zis one, from Charles Huit, c'est un *Karolus*. Ça, c'est trois cent francs.'

Three hundred francs: thirty pounds. Thirty pounds for a coin? It was a lot, but then it was a piece of history that one could own. Emma had seen music manuscripts from the period, even handled them, and the excitement of touching something five hundred years old surprised her now as it had before. She would never own a document that old. Perhaps she would one day own a piece of pottery from the fifteenth century, or an old painting, but that would be expensive and something she could only justify in her dotage.

On one side of the coin she could discern a heraldic cross and a single *fleur-de-lys*. The lettering around the outside was worn away but she could pick out some Latin: *Rex* was clearly visible, the rest illegible.

'*Karolus Francorum Rex*,' said the shopkeeper. Emma nodded to indicate that she understood, then turned the coin over. On that side there was a large *R* and on top of it a crown. The lettering here was clearer and she read it out loud: '*Sit Nomen Domini Benedictum*.' She recognised *Dni* as a contraction of *Domini*, the genitive of *Dominum*.

'Blessed is the name of the Lord,' she said.

'Oui.' The woman seemed impressed. 'Vous parlez Latin?'

'Très peu, comme mon français. Can I buy it?' asked Emma, as if her nationality might in some way exclude her from the right to purchase a piece of French history.

'Bien sûr,' said the woman.

Emma proffered her credit card and asked if the woman could wrap the coin. It was a present, she explained, not for herself. The woman looked around, lifting up papers and books, searching randomly for something to wrap it in, then stopped and held up a finger. She opened a drawer and took out a small velvet box. It was, she apologised, the best she could do and, as Emma was a worthy recipient of the coin, she would not charge her for the box.

Emma thanked her. It was a present for Ollie. They often bought each other gifts, even if it sometimes felt as if they did it for the sake of it. She preferred it when it was like this, an impulse-buy, and one made from the heart. She wasn't entirely sure that Ollie would share her fascination with history, but sometimes giving someone a present was an expression of oneself, and she hoped he would appreciate it.

It was only two hours since Emma had last seen the members of the group; while she had been working, they had been shopping. Susan had busied herself in the Galeries Lafayette and discovered 'a fabulous little bathroom shop that had some lovely smellies'. Claire and Peter had trailed behind her and the former was rather bashfully boasting a bright pink scarf that Susan had picked out for her. 'You're spring-flowing-into-summer, darling, and this colour is you,' mocked Peter privately to Emma. Peter himself had bought a vibrant striped scarf, a French take on the English college variety – 'École non-normale,' he joked – and Marco and Charlie had visited St Martin, which they pronounced boring. Craig had struck off on his own carrying his radio, searching for the best reception in order to check the cricket score later, and had ended up in a brasserie near the station where he'd had steak frites. Meanwhile, Allie had discovered the *Académie de la Bière* near to St Gatien where he had 'conducted some research' whilst Ollie had headed straight for the comic-book shops in search of *bandes dessinés*.

'How did it go?' Ollie asked her.

'Oh. Not bad. No one heckled or asked any difficult questions. How about you?'

'I got a couple of things. You wouldn't be interested,' he said, holding up a small plastic carrier bag.

'I got you a present,' she said, retrieving the small box from her handbag.

'Oh, thanks.' Ollie lifted the lid. 'Nice,' he said, but without any real enthusiasm. 'What is it? I mean, I know it's a coin, but you'll have to explain.'

'It's from the reign of Charles the Eighth, 1483 to 1498. I thought you might like it. It's a *Karolus* – Latin for Charles – and it seemed appropriate on a day like today.'

Ockeghem died one year before Charles died, so I just thought that there was a chance that Ockeghem himself might have used the coin. You could keep it in your wallet.'

'What, and use it?'

She smiled. She realised her explanation had made her purchase sound dull, quite different to her own excitement. For her, the coin was history, as if the emotions and sentiments of a town and its inhabitants were somehow contained in the thin sliver of metal. She'd thought Ollie would understand, or at least pretend to.

Marco approached them. 'Sorry,' he said, sensing he was interrupting a private moment. 'The lighting guy needs to talk to you, Em. His name's François. Over there.' He pointed to a man in his forties wearing jeans and an expensive woollen jumper.

'Look what Emma gave me,' said Ollie. His effort to express enthusiasm was strained and sounded false, but at least he was trying, Emma thought.

'It's a coin,' he explained, and she left the two singers staring stupidly at the present as if, in so doing, it might yield its mysteries.

Emma had at one time considered calling the new group *Chiaroscuro* to signal her interest in the dramatic potential of light and shade, and to announce a new direction in the staging of early-music concerts. Just because the original composers didn't notate dynamics, tempo variations, articulation, and phrasing didn't mean that the original composers hadn't wanted the singers to exploit such means of musical expression. And, by the same token, it seemed to her simply perverse not to use the resources of a theatre or the architectural potential of a church to enhance the emotional force of the music and supplement the concert experience. Removed from its original liturgical context as sacred music was, she believed that lighting and staging provided authentic compensation for the religious theatre that was otherwise lost. When the music was originally performed, those closest to the ritual – the priests and choir – would have witnessed candles, censers, and complex choreography; and to those at the back of the church – the townsfolk – such proofs of faith would have wafted towards them in the semi-dark, like a half-heard radio play, which encouraged – in the words of the *Magnificat* – the imagination of their hearts. Ripping this music from its original context and clothing it in the anachronistic attire of nineteenth-century concert conventions was as spurious as the city's desecration of the original St Martin of Tours. Such po-faced seriousness alienated some audiences and prevented the music and drama speaking to them of the ineffable.

Emma exploited whatever dramatic effects were available in each new venue, even if, at times, the possibilities afforded them were few, or the local helpers' commitment overzealous. On two occasions, careful advance planning had not prevented the concert from descending into farce, misadventures which had since become part of the group's mythology.

In Poland, a local film director, with access to various machines and keen to impress upon Emma his understanding of her vision, swamped the stage and the audience in choking oil smoke. The basses, closest to the source, began to cough first, closely followed by the tenors, and the carefully tuned *a cappella* rendition had sounded more like *musique concrète* than Renaissance polyphony. To clear the fog, which by now obscured the performers from the audience's view, the director had switched the wind machine to its highest setting, blowing away not only the smoke but also part of Susan's outfit. Fortunately it was only a small shawl, but it wrapped itself around her head and her desperate struggle to remove it had made both Allie and Ollie laugh out loud.

In the interval, the festival director had apologised for the behaviour of his overeager staff and Emma had been assured that the second half would proceed without incident. In one sense at least it did: it took place without any lighting at all, the crew having taken umbrage and left, taking all the fuses with them. That night, Emma finally won over the remaining doubters in the group who preferred to use copies rather than memorise the music. Without sufficient light to read the music, the concert would otherwise have been abandoned and, as if to confirm her aesthetic vision, during the last piece a sunset burst through stained-glass windows and flooded the interior of the church with a chromatic fantasy of red, green, orange and blue.

The second incident occurred in a small Italian village. It was a small, almost private festival, run by one man with limited finances and immense enthusiasm, and what he failed to provide in the way of a fee he made up for in hospitality. The group arrived at the village around noon and were taken to a small hotel where they were the only residents. Lunch was served *al fresco* on crude wooden tables in the shade of the trees: a display of beautiful, rustic dishes. Course followed course and wine was freely dispensed from rough pottery carafes; any attempt to moderate intake was dismissed with the assurance of *la sosta*, the Italian word for siesta. After lunch, everyone duly retired to his or her basic room for two hours of sleep. The church, which could only be reached by a small path that wound its way languidly through olive trees, seated about eighty people, but that night Emma reckoned it held nearer a hundred and fifty, most of them standing. The lighting board was manned by three twenty-year-old lads who talked loudly and waved their hands at each other. Despite their excessive animation, the lighting states were moody and imaginative, with lights placed on the floor to cast abstract shadows on ceilings, and red and purple gels throwing rich whorls of colour onto the white walls.

All went well during the first half, the boys on the lighting desk adopting a simple code: brighter for the secular pieces, darker for the sacred pieces. In the second half, though, they began to orchestrate the lights, responding to the words of the mass (Josquin's *Missa Pange Lingua*) that, as Catholics, they knew so well.

The Kyrie was a simple affair, the three movements complemented by the subtlest of changes. During the Gloria, though, there was a hint of what was to come. As Charlie intoned the incipit – *Gloria in Excelsis Deo* – darkness descended, save for a single low light at the back of the church. Just as people were beginning to wonder if it was a power cut, all the lights came on at full brilliance for the polyphony. Believing the confused reaction of the audience to be appreciation of their creativity, the boys began to experiment with bolder gestures.

Allie had the best view of all of them and his version of events, honed by repetition, possessed an unadorned simplicity that lent his version the solemnity of a received truth. With laborious deliberateness, he would explain that one of the boys had raised a fader for the gels as the other had lowered the control for the low-level lighting, and the third had played the master control. They looked, he would say, as if they were piloting an aircraft. An aircraft that was crashing.

It was their programmatic interpretation of the Credo text that hastened the final debacle. When the singers reached the words *visibilium et invisibilium* – seen and unseen – the lighting rapidly alternated full lighting with total darkness; *lumen de lumine* – light from light – was greeted by a single floodlight pointed directly at the audience, an assault against which many defended themselves by holding up their arms like Saul struck down on the way to Damascus. In the boys' hands, illumination now became a virtual weapon to turn upon the faithful as a judgemental reminder of original sin; when the words *Et resurrexit* – and he rose again – were sung, the three of them, as one, raised every fader on the small lighting board at the same moment. Already hot from overuse, the light at the back of the stage, which had cooled for a moment, burst into life and blew up. The crack made everyone, including the singers, jump, yet, true to the maxim that the show must go on, they ploughed onward. A chain reaction was well underway, though, and two other lights popped like gunfire. It was, as Charlie said later, like the 1512 Overture, the polyphony now accompanied by the sound of exploding bulbs. It was unclear quite who shouted fire and started a mad stampede for the exit. The singers, led by Allie and calm to the last, left the stage, followed by the promoter, and they exited by a door behind the altar. After half an hour, Beyond Compère once again took to the stage and completed the programme by candlelight, much to the relief of the traumatised audience.

After that Emma's policy was to make contact with a local lighting designer directly and well in advance, charging them with lighting three different locations to which they could always add a fourth with no lighting rig at all. There was no need for the singers to see the music, the only requirement being that they could see each other. Certain pieces worked particularly well with the singers out of sight, inviting the audience to consider the architecture which some of the music deliberately echoed in mathematical or metaphorical design. And the various movements of the Catholic mass, where the expression was one of praise, glory or supplication, were much easier to appreciate without the immediate presence of the singers to distract them.

Here in the Cathedral of St Gatien in Tours, the first position would be the traditional concert address with the singers facing the audience. It rendered the listeners a congregation, fittingly liturgical for the sacred motets with which the concert would begin. For a short sequence of mass movements, they would move behind the audience to be out of sight, and Emma would surrender the architecture to François's artistry. The third location was vetoed almost immediately by the singers – a place high up in the Triforium, the area at the top of the Nave, with no protective rail and a dusty, vertiginous walk to get there, which no one, not even Allie, had been inclined to try. François, who had spent some time rigging lights up there, was disappointed, though by no means surprised.

In the second half they would repeat the running-order of the second CD of *Ockeghem Gems*, beginning and ending with the two laments: the first Ockeghem's on the death of Binchois, and, for the final piece, Josquin's lament on the death of Ockeghem. These would be sung from the very centre of the audience in an isolated pool of light, almost like a cage within which the singers would face each other. It would make the audience witnesses to private grief, the darkness around them a contrast to a tightly defined, secretive space, a *mise en scène* designed to evoke in the audience a feeling of voyeuristic embarrassment. With the music sung so close to them, the listeners would benefit from a more immediate acoustic like that of a small hall, the lofty cathedral forgotten and the details of the more intricate polyphony more clearly etched. The Requiem Mass, though, would fully exploit the large space of the church with the different sections sung from various locations, and the audience vaguely aware of figures moving around them in the candlelight.

With so much to do, the rehearsal was inevitably too short and the long day began to catch up with the group. François usually worked for the Grand Théatre de Tours, and he was the calm hub to which Emma returned again and again, grateful to devolve some of her responsibility to someone else. Despite his prior communications with her, he remained aloof, casting his hazel eyes levelly over each arrangement with an air of tranquil satisfaction. Aside from the occasional squint of disapproval followed by a soft, monosyllabic instruction to his workers, he seemed quite disengaged, as if he'd been placed there as an advertisement for cashmere jumpers rather than to oversee a project. Yet he listened carefully to anything Emma said and paused at the end of her sentences to allow time for any revision or further explanation she might want to give: a Zen-like approach that at first had her filling the silence with apologies and expressions of thanks but which, as she became attuned to his habit, she came to enjoy and appreciate. When she told François that she wanted the plume of light within which the laments were to be sung to be as contained as possible, with no spill onto the audience themselves, Marco, who'd witnessed the exchange, was confused by

François's unstirring response, and leapt in with the offer of translation. Emma shook her head. François uttered two brief instructions into his walkie-talkie, and the soft pool of light magically transformed into a brilliant, rigid column.

'He's gooooood,' said Marco.

With the lighting arrangements complete, Emma and the others turned to the music and the acoustics. Their thorough rehearsals in London had prepared them well, but the music always had to change to accommodate the buildings in which it was sung. And, as well as the basic choreography, the singers always wanted to address particular musical moments. Susan wanted to sing a piece because of the high notes it contained to assure herself that the notes were 'there'; Ollie wanted to tackle a change of tempo; Craig needed to remind himself of the words he kept forgetting; and everyone – having spent the last few hours surrounded by French speakers – felt they could improve on their pronunciation. The unfamiliar building presented other problems: some of the faster tempi didn't work in the larger space, the acoustic was more favourable for the lower register, presenting issues of balance between the voices, and, in some parts of the Cathedral, it proved difficult to hear each other. And, of course, the anxiety of the evening's performance and more personal neuroses inevitably needed to find some sort of an outlet. There was truth in the adage that a good final rehearsal meant a poor concert for, if nerves didn't manifest themselves in the rehearsal, they might instead return during the performance. When things went badly in rehearsals, when stress and irritation showed, Emma was always privately pleased. Aside from it being a sign that nerves would ultimately be contained, it reminded everyone that the only people who could help them in the performance were each other.

After an hour, everyone was satisfied. Emma told them all to enjoy the concert and to get some rest if they could.

'I know that if Ockeghem were here, he'd love it. Just do it for him,' she said. 'You're his singers tonight.'

CHAPTER 15

The Memoirs of Geoffroy Chiron: Livre V *ed. Francis Porter*

Martius 13, 1524

Jehan was not born in Tours, but he lived nearly all of his life here. He once explained that, like its famous wines, he did not travel well, and he was grateful that, as Treasurer of St Martin and Baron of Châteauneuf, he never needed to seek employment outside of his adopted country. His friend Dufay travelled to Italy, but ultimately even he acknowledged the importance of his homeland by returning to the same city where he had served as a choirboy: Cambrai. That same road to Italy was a familiar one to the younger composers – Compère, Desprez, De La Rue and others, all of who learned their trade in the Cathedrals and churches of the North. Jehan had much sympathy for them and, whenever he could, he endeavoured to bring them back to their own country.

After the death of Louis XI, Jehan navigated the difficult straits between the funeral of an old monarch and the coronation of the new. A young man when he came to the throne, Charles VIII was different to his father in every way. Nevertheless he showed himself to be a shrewd judge of men and, like Louis before him, appointed Jehan as an advisor and premier chapelain. *Thus entrusted, Jehan immediately began recruiting new singers and composers so that the glory of God and France would once more shine forth from the Royal Chapel.*

The two composers whom Jehan most wanted to invite to Tours were Compère and Desprez. I cannot be sure, but I believe that even then he hoped to make peace between them, not that Compère was even aware of the enmity that his younger colleague felt for him. Desprez was at this time working in Milan for Cardinal D'Ascanio Sforza, his fame and reputation assured, and Jehan did not think that he would be interested. And, of course, there had been no communication since Desprez's composition for Louis XI had been rejected by the dying King. So Jehan first wrote to Compère. As fortune would have it, Compère had recently returned to France after working in Milan. Now forty years old, his thoughts were turning to the issue of where he might spend his last years, and soon he was ordained as chapelain to the royal chapel [1485].

And then, quite unexpectedly, Jehan received a letter from Desprez requesting a meeting. Desprez would be travelling to Paris and he wanted to discuss several matters; if it pleased Jehan, he would bring with him some compositions. Jehan, generous as ever, invited him to stay in the official Treasurer's residence. He also informed the younger man that he would honour him with a small party to which he would invite the singers of St Gatien and St Martin so they could meet the famous composer and learn of life in Italy. A letter came back saying that Desprez was greatly moved and that he looked forward to the event.

I had never met Desprez before, but Jehan's descriptions had to a degree prepared me for his lack of grace. My first sight of him was across the great chapter house of St Martin where the official reception was held. He was being talked to by a pair of singers from St Gatien. His skin was dark, more like a native of Italy than France, and his small black eyes flicked around the room rather than engaging with his two young admirers. They seemed uneasy, drinking quickly and nervously, a sign that their conversation was awkward. Indeed, Desprez's contribution was but two words and he never once drank from the goblet that he gripped in his hand. It was clear that the singers were in awe of him, and equally clear that Desprez had only contempt for them. He was looking around the room for someone more important, or perhaps more interesting, and his eyes settled on me. He saw my caputium [hood of a gown], noted my status as a Doctor of Law, and held my gaze for a moment. It was as if he was weighing up whether I was worth talking to or not. His decision made, he broke eye contact and continued his search.

Later that evening Jehan introduced me. There was no acknowledgement of our earlier visual exchange, and Desprez gave me a curt nod. Jehan was always extremely adept in such situations, able to relax people through his natural grace and gentle indiscretions, telling harmless stories about famous men. Yet even talking to Jehan, the most important person in the room, Desprez still continued to study the other guests, perhaps hoping that the King himself might enter. I tried to start a conversation by asking Desprez about Milan, but he volunteered nothing, as if to do so would be an act of charity. The only way I could provoke a response was to frame questions in such a way that they required only a one-word answer. It was no good saying, 'I gather that Milan is the richer city, that the women are fairer and the streets better kept.' I had to break it down into smaller sections, asking if the city was bigger ('No'), if the women were fairer ('No'), and if the streets were better kept ('No'). Even when Jehan asked Desprez about his own music, the younger man's distrust hampered natural discourse and the conversation limped along like a crippled dog.

The Chapter had provided funds for the party and the spread of food and drink was impressive. Laid out on a table in the centre of the room were breads, Parma tarts, fish from the Loire, chaudun de porc and two jallayes of wine. The real party, though, was to be held, as always, later in the evening, when we could divest ourselves of our gowns and, with them, our better behaviour. The magister puerorum of St Gatien, Nicolas Avalle, hosted the festivities in his own home and another jallaye of wine awaited us, bought at a special rate by Jehan with money collected by the singers themselves. This would be the chance for Desprez to entertain us with stories of intrigue and Italian politics; to offer us tales of the famous painters and sculptors who worked in Milan, Rome, Florence, Venice and Ferrara; to show us some of his new compositions and tell us of the new musical styles he had encountered across the mountains. It would also be a chance for the younger singers to present him with their own compositions or merely to ask for advice, in much the same way that Desprez had approached Jehan thirty years earlier in Cambrai. But Desprez was not Jehan. As we sat in Nicolas's house, sipping wine and talking amongst ourselves, I could see Jehan becoming more and more agitated. I asked him what troubled him.

'He's not here. And I would wager that he's not coming. Did he say anything to you?' he asked.

I admitted that Desprez hadn't and volunteered to go back to St Martin to see if he had got lost or, as we both suspected, had gone back to his room. Jehan thanked me for my kindness and instead sent one of the junior members of the chapel to run to St Martin and see if there was any light in Desprez's chamber. If there was, he was to knock and discover the composer's intentions. The young singer returned soon after. Desprez was in his chamber and had retired for the night, complaining that the food had disagreed with him.

That was the closest I ever saw Jehan come to losing his dignity and composure. He held his face in an attitude of restraint as he struggled to hide his feelings about the arrogant guest.

The following day, as we walked together to his office at the Treasury to meet Desprez, Jehan told me quite how angry he had been. I knew already that he viewed the recent custom of payment for composing a dangerous new path. The result of this new respect for the maker of compositions was fame and fortune. They were sought out by rich patrons, pampered and courted in foreign countries with no friends or close colleagues to curb their excesses. Jehan believed in the old ways, in the informal confraternity of singers and composers, like the guilds of workmen. It was the duty, he said, of any maître to guide his pupils. Music was a shared experience that could not be achieved merely by instruction; it was a living art, and one in which a sense of the family of man and the spirit of community was essential. Any refusal to partake in that spirit of community was an affront to God and to man. More than that, such hospitality required that one repay the kindnesses shown by attending any event hosted in one's honour, however lowly. Jehan told me stories of the generosity of Dufay and Binchois to those beneath their station and, although he was far too modest to offer his own behaviour as an example, I knew it to be equally true of him. Some of them, he said, left behind not just their friends and families when they travelled, but also their good manners; and Desprez had yet to find them again.

Desprez was waiting for us. He offered no thanks for the previous evening or apology for his absence, instead saying that, before continuing his journey (he was going to St Omer where he was to have discussions at the church of Notre Dame) he wanted to meet the King, Charles VIII. It was with a small smile that Jehan informed him that the King was busy.

This displeased Desprez and his sombre face became darker still, as if a thundercloud had appeared in an already overcast sky. For a moment it seemed that he wanted to say something, but he remained silent. Then he spoke the longest sentence I had heard him utter on that visit: would it please the new King to receive a chanson in honour of Margaret of Austria to whom he was betrothed? Jehan told me later that he wanted to respond with one word: no. Instead, he explained to Desprez that the music had already been decided. In his capacity as premier chapelain, Jehan had instructed someone else to write a chanson: Compère.

It is difficult for me to describe the effect that this new information had on Desprez. Even the mention of the name Loyset Compère inspired in Desprez the blackest of moods and now I feared that he would strike Jehan, his countenance was so fierce. However, once more he maintained his composure and excused himself to pack his few belongings. Desprez was more splenetic than usual that day and, rather than leaving behind him inspiration and guidance for the younger singers, and the memory of a wild party, he merely confirmed his reputation as a difficult and self-centred man. Ingenium [talent] some say: rudeness, say I.

Josquin returned to Milan and the employ of Duke Gian Galeazzo Sforza, and soon after that he joined the Papal Choir as a singer in the Pope's private chapel: the Cappella Sistina [1489]. I hoped he would stay there.

Music, such a central part of Jehan's life, was now secondary to his responsibilities as Baron de Châteauneuf and Treasurer of St Martin, and, when time permitted, he felt that his worship of the Lord could better be expressed through his dedication to pastoral care and attendance at services. It was not that he stopped composing – sometimes I could see that faraway look in his eyes and knew he was writing in his mind – but he had no time for the careful labour of dictation and revision that I so much enjoyed.

Thus I was surprised when, early in the new year with the frantic collection of Christmastide payments behind us, he approached me one day after Vespers and asked if I would be willing to help him with a new composition. It was, he explained, a piece on a scale that he had never written before: a motet, but for thirty-four different parts.

This was the grandest of all of his plans and on a scale that I could not imagine; I couldn't say no. Surely, I asked in my excitement, there were not thirty-four different notes that could be sung at the same time?

'You are right, of course,' he replied, 'though a note that will ascend is different to a note that will descend.' I had failed to appreciate this nuance, for a singer indicates with his voice not just the note that he has left, but where the next will be. Distracted as I was by the possible design of such a composition, I had forgotten to ask him for what occasion the piece was being written. He enlightened me anyway. The Cathedral of Saint Quentin where Compère had trained as a choirboy (and where he would spend his final years) had granted Compère a benefice. Keen to secure his services, the Chapter had acceded to his request for a convocation of singers. With due deference to the man who had supported him in the past, Compère wrote to Jehan and invited him to attend. The company would be good, the music excellent, and there would be a great party to rival those of the past. And, if Jehan so desired, he could write something.

Compère's letter was dated Genvier 1, 1490, the significance of which did not escape Jehan. In the tradition of éstrennes [New Year's gifts], the invitation was Compère's present to Jehan, and a unique one at that: no one else would write a new piece for the occasion. Compère had included a guest list, and Jehan, astute as ever, noted that the names were ordered according to their voice type. It was not just a list of those whom Jehan had helped over the years: it was an appeal to write specifically for their voices. At the top were those who sang en fausset: De La Rue, Japart, Mouton, and others. Then the middle voices: Desprez, Faugues, Molinet, Van Ghizeghem, and Caron. Finally, the basses: Jehan, Morton, myself and others. There were over thirty singers, enough to make a huge sound, but Jehan's mind was not thinking in terms of volume alone; his plan was more intricate. He wanted each voice – each person – to have their own identity. This would be an historic gathering of the finest composers in the land, a great testament to France. And Jehan was aware, even though he never talked about it, that this might be the last time he would see many of these colleagues. It would be a gathering essentially in his honour and he was determined to attend. And thus he began to compose again.

As ever, the text came first. He had chosen Psalm 50 [51]: Miserere mei, Deus, secundum misericordiam tuam, iuxta multitudinem miserationum tuarum dele iniquitates meas. *[Have mercy on me, O God, according to thy great mercy. And according to the multitude of thy tender mercies blot out my iniquity.]*

At the time I believed it was the prayer of an old man looking back on his life, a personal reparation, fittingly for a singer, taken from the Psalms of David. Yet a text for Ash Wednesday seemed a strange choice for an event which was to be, essentially, a celebration. Its expression of the desire to settle the scores of the past, to tally the good deeds with the bad acts and to obtain forgiveness was hardly appropriate for the bacchanalian excesses that would surely follow.

I decided to ask Jehan why he had chosen that passage. He smiled. It was, he said, a text that had struck him for a number of reasons. Firstly, of course, it was likely to be his last composition and so it was appropriate that he should ask God, in his great mercy, for release from the burden of his sins. And, as a psalm, it was also a hymn of praise to God, the Creator of all things.

His true concern though, was with the role that music played in worship and the way in which (as he explained it) the new generation of composers had forgotten their education and the true function of music. Quoting a passage from Aristotle's Eighth Book of Politics, he argued that music has the power to make you happy, but that you should not have too much of it. Music today, he believed, rather than serving a divine purpose, had become instead the mistress of those who shared the base desire for human recognition and the accumulation of wealth.

This sin of cupidity was no better exemplified than in Desprez, and the motet would be Jehan's warning to him: Desprez and those like him should be encouraged to pass on their knowledge to others, just as Jehan had learned from his masters. Jehan believed the younger composers had been isolated from the country in which their talents had been first developed for too long. Now they were older, it was time to set aside their concerns for personal wealth and advancement and return to their homeland to repay their debt by instructing the new sons of France. Jehan's motet would be a motet for singers, sung by singers, and, through the act of singing, they would come to understand their responsibilities.

It was not until after Easter that we began working on the motet and, when it was completed, the picture I had in my mind of singing Jehan's piece was no longer clear and the likelihood that it might ever be performed no longer so certain. Desprez had intervened.

CHAPTER 16

A combination of inefficiency and economy had landed Andrew Eiger in the *Hôtel Des Lices*. He'd only got round to booking his room the previous week and that at Karen's prompting, and hadn't expected much from the meagre description. As he knew from his stay in Amiens, two stars in a French hotel promised little other than a bed and possibly a wardrobe. Nevertheless, he'd hoped that his window might afford a view of something more interesting than a concrete wall and an overflow pipe that dripped water onto a grate some twenty feet below.

An indentation in the pink bedspread the size of a large animal betokened a saggy mattress, and the tubular pillow which, had he not been so tired might have appealed to his francophilia, held out the prospect of a stiff neck the following morning. The wallpaper was floral and peeling, a consequence of damp, and even without testing it, he knew the phone system would require him to ring out via an unattended reception.

He opened his briefcase and took out his laptop and charger. He spun the combination lock partly from habit and partly to prevent him retrieving the blue folder and laying out his new transcription as he'd been waiting to do since the long flight from New York. There were more pressing needs, a shower and shave amongst them. He opened his small case and took out his toilet bag, then quickly stripped off his clothes. As he pulled his arm through the sleeve of his shirt he caught his bandaged hand on the cuff and flinched. The pain was duller now, a gentle humming throb rather than a sharp stab. He popped another antibiotic and a painkiller from their respective blister packs and, cupping his left hand beneath the bathroom tap, washed them down with warm water. When he'd delivered his paper (received, he felt, with rather too polite applause), he'd felt all right, even awake, but during the final, tortured, self-congratulatory lecture given by the third speaker, he'd begun to wonder if it was the various pharmaceuticals that were making him feel nauseous. It occurred to him that he might have eaten something that hadn't agreed with him, but then he hadn't eaten anything in the previous four hours – which, on reflection, was probably not the wisest course of action. The pharmacist had told him to take the pills with food, but there were just too many things to do: not just the shower and shave, but also the promised call to Karen. That might have to wait. He would ring her after the concert and the meal that followed it. He'd feel better then.

He assembled the travel adaptor and inserted the plug of his laptop charger into it – no easy task with his bandaged right hand – and then looked around for a socket. There was none, or at least none visible. High up in the corner of the room was a small television set, but its power cable threaded through the window and trailed out of sight. The bedside light was nailed to the wall and controlled by a thin cord that swung from the ceiling. Finding no obvious power outlets, Andrew wandered into the bathroom. There, above the sink, was a rectangular light fitting with an inbuilt shaver socket. He tugged at the light switch and it came off in his hand. Still, the light was now on, which meant there was a source of electricity. Encouraged, he placed his laptop outside the bathroom door and trailed the power cord over the sink and up to the shaver point. With his good hand, he pressed the plug into the housing. The next thing he knew, he was sitting on the toilet in darkness. There was a smell of burning: smoked fish mingled with the sharp odour of charred human flesh. Why was he sitting on the toilet? His left hand hurt and he realised his fingers were still gripping the plug, but much more tightly than before. He willed them to open and release their hold, but they wouldn't obey. He realised, finally, that he'd had an electric shock and been flung across the room; the darkness was the result of the lights fusing. Out in the corridor he could hear the voices of guests, a rapid confusion of French that he couldn't make out, and then a voice sounding like that of the unfriendly burly proprietor who'd checked him in. His voice was deeper than the others and also more annoyed; the guests' voices sounded meek in comparison. There was a knock on the door: a loud accusing rap. Andrew slunk further back on the toilet. He wasn't going to answer, naked as he was, and be humiliated. Besides, it was the hotel's fault, not his. The knocking began again, more insistent, then stopped, and Andrew clearly heard the word 'Merde' before the proprietor clumped away down the corridor. Various noises followed: halting questions from the guests, grudging reassurance from the man, then the sound of a chair being dragged along the corridor before a series of unidentified clicks and thumps ensued.

The light in the bedroom came on and Andrew blinked. From the socket in which he'd tried to insert his adaptor wafted a thin wisp of smoke and the light fitting itself looked dead. He studied his left hand, still grasping the charger. Finally his fingers obeyed his brain's instruction and he was able to release his grip. As he uncurled his fingers, he noticed that the tips were black. He licked them and tasted something bitter, like cloves. All was quiet in the corridor now and he padded carefully into the bedroom and placed his laptop on his briefcase.

Back in the bathroom, he was about to switch on the shower before he remembered the pharmacist's advice to keep his bandaged hand dry. He looked around for something with which to protect it. A shower-cap would have done the trick, but there was no shampoo in the bathroom, let alone anything as exotic as free polythene head protection. The small waste bin hadn't been emptied; he foraged inside and discovered a small plastic bag emblazoned with the words 'Supermarché Foch', which he wrapped around his hand.

The smell of burning had been replaced by a smell of mould, the source of which was visible on the ceiling of the plastic cubicle into which he now crammed his body. The water dribbled from the shower rose, initially subjecting his exhausted body to a freezing baptism then, without warning, becoming a scalding deluge. The drain swallowed, burped, and then regurgitated a foul-smelling cocktail of soap, scum, human hair and a suspiciously dark liquid over his bare feet. Within the cramped shower stall there was no escape from the irruptions of an antiquated water system, and little room to soap himself. With his wounded hand wrapped in the plastic bag and his eyes stinging with soap, he switched off the water and lathered himself from head to toe before once again surrendering to a schizophrenic ablution. It woke him up, or at least kept him awake, and he dried himself as best he could with a thin brittle sheet before filling the cracked basin with brackish water and shaving.

Feeling clean and relatively fresh again, he turned his attention to the motet. He had little time to himself to correct his unfinished first draft, but his main priority was to destroy his earlier version for which the hotel, ascetic in every other respect, had provided two packets of matches in two ashtrays. Still dripping with water, he placed the paper in the sink and tried to set light to it. The damp air of the bathroom prevented the paper from catching, so he cracked open the window to let the steam escape. Turning back he saw that the fresh air had fed the flames, and black burning paper whirled above his head. He tried to close the window to stop the source of this new encouragement, but it had jammed and, with only one good hand, he could not apply enough pressure to close it.

By the time the fire had burned out, he was covered in small, charred remnants of manuscript paper, and, to wash off the debris, he once again stepped inside the shower stall. The small towel was already completely saturated and he tried to flick off what water he could with his polythene-covered hand then stood naked in the freezing bedroom to dry.

Laid out on the bed, the sheer physical size of the new transcription conveyed something of the grandeur of the piece. It was now on a scale more appropriate to a nineteenth-century symphonic score than to the intimacy of fifteenth-century polyphony. The thirty-four parts were ranged from top to bottom on three sheets of paper and ten of these vertical ranks were laid side by side describing the first fifty bars of the motet. The first page was to his left, beneath the bolster pillow, and the others were logically arranged so that, with a sweep of his head, he could read from beginning to end. Beneath him lay a gigantic musical map upon which his eye could wander, and within which he could appreciate the design and structure as a hill-walker might some natural vista.

He was awed by its imaginative scope and he marvelled at the boldness of applying the small-scale techniques of fifteenth-century counterpoint to such a large canvas. He felt almost unworthy of bringing this musical treasure to the attention of the world, but quickly reasoned away his hesitation: somebody had to do it, and it might as well be him. The recent discovery of its numerological symbolism lent the motet a new mystical significance. This was a physical embodiment of the composer himself: Johannes Ockeghem: eighty-one and sixty-four – the products of nine-times-nine and eight-times-eight. With all the parts now transcribed, Andrew could contemplate the intricacies of the counterpoint; the percussive patter of the smaller notes in the *discantus* part against the sustained sonorities of the lower two voices; the sway of tension and release; and the characteristic, meandering contemplativeness so typical of Ockeghem's style.

Andrew's meditation was not the calm, methodological approach of music analysis, but an indulgent wallow in the familiar and novel features of the motet, a rare gratification of the senses that he rarely enjoyed when listening to music. These days he was all too often distracted by an imperfection of tuning, the inappropriateness of style, or by the intrusion of a performer's ego. Here, however, the black-and-white transcription conveyed a pristine perfection that performance could never attain and, once again, he began to doubt the wisdom of offering it to Beyond Compère. He could, after all, experience something approaching transfiguration merely by reading the score, a pursuit that afforded him the added benefit of being able to appreciate the small details and the larger context simultaneously. His current range of vision granted him a moveable perspective that the muddy mundanity of choral rehearsal could never offer and, additionally, he could excise at any moment a phrase from an earlier section and contrast it with a later one. He was freed from the linearity of performance, presented here with an omniscient view, a position of privilege from which he could discern the secrets which, over the past twenty-four hours, he had magically revealed.

At first he thought he was experiencing some kind of aesthetic overload, that the sensation of dizziness was a consequence of his enhanced state of musical mastery; it must be his acute sensitivity that caused the notes to swirl inside his head like snowflakes in a globe and vibrate before his eyes. But when he found himself face down over the bed with an unexpected view of blistered lino, he knew that he had fainted. In falling, he had crushed his testicles and the thick ache in his groin presaged a deeper and more excruciating agony. It would, though, prevent him surrendering to sleep – which, now he was prostrate, was all he wanted to do. He was fairly certain that he hadn't actually lost consciousness but had merely lost his balance, presumably through fatigue; and his senses that, until recently, had been attuned only to looking and imagining now began to return. He was aware of the thrum of blood in his ears and the coldness of his hands and feet. He was still totally naked, pressed down on the harsh paper that, until a moment ago, he had been ogling in all its virgin glory.

Slowly he pushed himself up off the bed to consider the damage. His groin ached but that would pass. He was more worried about the fate of the transcription, at least four pages of which had been smudged. Laid out like this, he could clearly see the outline of his body, like an incomplete watermark: his very own Turin Shroud. The dim display of the digital clock read 7.29. He had to get dressed and get to the concert, but first he gathered the papers together, dabbing those that bore any traces of water with the pink bedspread before placing the transcription in his briefcase. Finally, he removed the plastic bag from his bandaged hand. Despite its protective shield, water had seeped beneath the plastic. His palm, the very area he was meant to keep dry, was saturated. His left hand didn't look much better. The fingertips, despite having scrubbed them with his sodden towel, were still blackened and he could flex them, but only slowly. He could also feel an unpleasant sensation not dissimilar to pins and needles, but this felt as if someone was actually inserting steel points into his fingertips. Perhaps another painkiller might help? He punched one from the blister pack and dry-swallowed it. There was no time for anything as luxurious as water now.

✦ ✦ ✦

When they had finished their rehearsal, the group was shown to the place which would serve as their Green Room: the Cathedral's former Library, a small chamber reached by crossing the cloister and walking up a spiral staircase to the Ambulatory and through the Scriptorium. Marco and Charlie were delighted at this privileged access ('It only costs five francs in the daytime,' said Allie to puncture their puppyish enthusiasm), and kept up a running commentary on gargoyles, guttering and Gothicism as they made their way to the room. Susan and Claire, seeing only an echoey stone room with upright, wooden chairs, were predictably sniffy about the makeshift solution and announced that they would change in the hotel.

It was only a short walk and Emma let Ollie guide her through the streets, happy to trust his better sense of direction. She was hungry but, with the concert soon and dinner planned for later, she decided to ignore it. Had she not had a bath earlier, she would have whiled away the time soaking in warm, soapy water, and a sudden wave of tiredness made her worry that she might fall asleep if she lay on her bed as she had planned.

Ahead of them lay the light-filled, nineteenth-century railway station. It reminded her of the Musée D'Orsay. In fact, hadn't Marco read something out about it being by the same architect? Was that, she wondered, today? Heathrow, and before that Newcastle? Thinking about the relentless schedule reminded her that she deserved a holiday and, had she known how attractive Tours was, she'd have suggested that she and Ollie stay another twenty-four hours, sitting in cafés and watching France go by. She loved the mornings in particular, the air of optimism, everyone out buying baguettes, kissing each other on both cheeks, smiling.

'Shall we have a coffee?' she asked.

'Sure, but there's something you have to see first,' said Ollie, steering her towards a small shop. Everything was closed and they were leaving far too early the next morning for her to buy anything. Emma was too tired to argue.

'It's got your name on it,' said Ollie by way of explanation and, with a gesture of triumph, pointed to the sign above the door. 'Emma,' it read, soft pink on pastel blue: a hat shop.

'I thought you might want to have a look. I've never seen you in a hat, of course, but it looked like your kind of place.'

In fact, Emma owned only one hat – dark blue with a stepped-up crown that she wore only to friends' weddings of which, over the past three years, there had been several. She'd never been particularly interested in hats; she'd always regarded them as overpriced and prissy with no redeeming functionality. Here though, with her eyes shielded against the streetlights to afford her a better view, splashes of bright orange and dazzling blue against a matt black background, they looked like sculpture. Unfussily displayed on wire frames, they struck her as luxury objects, indubitably French in design, and suddenly she wanted one.

'I love the orange one,' she said, pointing to a wide-brimmed straw hat. Ollie mumbled his agreement then stooped to tie his shoelace. She guessed he was bored, that he'd been more interested in the name of the shop than its contents, yet as she turned, she realised he was holding something, a package he had retrieved from his bag that, for some reason, he had brought to the rehearsal. Now she understood why; the package was a cardboard hat-box, which he opened to reveal a mound of soft white tissue paper.

'Have a look,' he said.

It was a wide-brimmed straw hat like the one in the window, but black with a thin white stripe around the crown.

'I thought the lack of colour might give you more opportunities to wear it,' he explained, concerned that the choice was the right one.

'I love it,' she said – but was it the right size? She turned to the shop window, which acted as a mirror, and placed it gently on her head. The fit was perfect and she adjusted it so the brim came level with her eyes. She could tilt her head down and her gaze would be hidden, or lift her chin and view the world with appropriate hauteur. Ollie was standing next to her and in the reflection she could see him smiling, reaching his arm around her shoulder to pull her close.

'It's absolutely lovely, but you shouldn't have spent all that money. It must have cost a fortune. It certainly makes my coin look rather inadequate.'

His reflection in the window shrugged: the coy, embarrassed look of a young boy.

'I just liked the look of it,' he said. 'Very *Breakfast at Tiffany's*, don't you think?'

Emma didn't admit that she'd never actually seen the film. Ollie often compared her to Audrey Hepburn – though, more tomboyish than the actress and with no chance of ever having a body as slim as that, she sometimes wondered if she could ever fulfil his idealised image.

'Of course,' added Ollie, 'that would make me George Peppard. Oh, and it makes you a high-class hooker and me a gigolo.'

She flinched. It was one of Ollie's typically clumsy comments, which over the years she'd come to believe derived from a simple fear of commitment bequeathed to him by his divorce. In the past she'd tried to explain something of the hurt he caused her, but that succeeded only in making him withdraw further into himself, annoyed and seemingly threatened by a sense that he was being studied, that perhaps someone might understand him better than he did himself. She turned away from him, back to her reflection in the window. She saw herself holding the brim of her hat in both hands, Ollie by her side, something stiff about his body now, and the yellow street lights adding a sepia halo around them.

'Coffee then?' asked Ollie briskly, putting the box back in his bag. 'There's a nice brasserie at the end of the road.'

The waiters fussed around them and offered them a table in the window, saying that Emma, dressed so elegantly, would attract more customers. Ollie, unable to follow the details of the conversation, smiled his approval and contented himself with his role of Knight to Emma's Belle Dame, even pulling her chair out from the table. Emma looked at the window in which she and Ollie were reflected. It offered a portrait of a contented couple, their drinks multiplied relentlessly in the etched mirrors of the brasserie. And then, as the waiter's body disturbed the light, in the distance the lambent interior of the railway station flickered into life like a nineteenth-century theatrical trick. The images of romance and travel melted into each other and it was possible to believe in the endurance of love.

After the concert the question with which Emma was repeatedly assailed was: 'What happened to the encore?' When she and the singers had discussed the matter at the London rehearsals, they had agreed that an encore was inappropriate to the design of the programme and the occasion. Now, in Tours, she patiently explained their reasons, pointing out that the design of the second half, as was clearly indicated and explained in the programme, deliberately framed Ockeghem's Requiem Mass with two laments to which the only due response was silence. Returning to the stage with some brash encore otherwise cheapened the memory of a man who had died five hundred years ago to the very day. It would have been like striking up a chorus of 'Roll out the Barrel' as the coffin left the church. When the fourth person had challenged her, she'd been tempted to offer Allie's more facetious answer: no encore meant more time for drinking.

She was introduced to the Mayor by one of his advisors in a way that suggested that it was she who had sought the meeting, but the dignitary turned out to be a fan of the group and apologised to her for the lack of reference within the town to its famous son. He would, he assured her, be asking for a statue of Jean Ockeghem to be erected in one of Tours' famous *jardins*.

Generally the singers preferred to leave the meeting-and-greeting to Emma and would head back to the dressing room to shake out the tension and plan the evening ahead, but on this occasion the welcome from the audience had been so warm (and the dressing room was so cold) that stopping to chat was no hardship. Marco and Charlie were talking to two young British musicologists, who had provided editions for the Dufay recording; Susan, Claire and Peter were speaking to locals. Even Allie, who was usually propping up a bar somewhere as the final applause died, was engaged in an earnest discussion with an intense American musicologist.

Emma hadn't spoken to Andrew Eiger since delivering her paper and she spotted him at the back of the Cathedral. He was standing at the West Door, his head tilted back and his mouth open, gazing upwards towards the ceiling.

'Ça va?' said Emma, noting the dark rings around his eyes. She hoped he'd managed to get some sleep.

'Oh, fine,' he said, as he returned her gaze and tried to focus.

'I'm going to be tied up a bit here,' she explained. 'There are always people to talk to after the concert, but I'll send you off with the singers and join you very soon. It's a different restaurant. A brasserie, not *Les Tuffeaux*. They cancelled on us.'

Les Tuffeaux, the restaurant into which the organiser of both conference and concert had booked the group at Emma's request, had rung to say that they couldn't stay open that evening. The chef was ill and one of their waitresses hadn't turned up, an excuse sounding as if it were cover for a secret romance between the absentees. Emma had taken the call only ten minutes prior to the start of the concert, with the sounds of the singers warming up, nervously clearing their throats and talking just that little bit too loudly, making conversation difficult. It was Ollie who'd come up with the solution: the brasserie at which he and Emma had their drink and where, it turned out, Craig had taken his lunch; given its proximity to the railway station, it was bound to be open.

She felt someone touch her arm: Ollie's familiar presumption.

'We're off now,' he said. 'See you there?'

Looking around, Emma saw that the singers were drifting away to change.

'Well done, guys,' she called. 'Great gig. Marco. Susan. Can you smooth things over with the brasserie? I got the impression they were keeping the kitchen open especially for us, and I'm going to be another fifteen minutes or so. Order three bottles of champagne – it's my treat.' Turning to Ollie, she said, 'Can you look after Andrew for me? Take him to the brasserie and I'll meet you as soon as I can?'

'Sure.' Ollie nodded to Andrew in confirmation. 'But I promised I'd have a snifter at the Académie de la Bière round the corner with Allie. They've got Oerbier,' he added, as if citing an exotic beer explained all.

'Well, can you take Andrew with you?' She registered the pause before Ollie agreed to her request, and she hoped Andrew hadn't. Clearly Ollie regarded the musicologist as a social encumbrance.

'I'll meet you here in five,' said Ollie to Andrew, and then – an afterthought which surprised Emma – kissed her on the lips.

◆ ◆ ◆

'It's a beer academy,' said Oliver Martin to Andrew, holding open the door of a bar from which rushed a gust of warm, malty air, 'so I hope you like beer.'

Andrew didn't. He'd always found it too gassy and bitter, a drink for those of limited palette and etiquette, a beverage you were supposed to drink out of a bottle in a macho display of nonconformism. His preference was for wine, usually white, ideally from this very region, the Loire valley – perhaps a light Vouvray or a flinty Pouilly-Fumé. Anyway, he wasn't going to be drinking tonight. He had been warned against it by the pharmacist and, despite Andrew's protestations in French that he was perfectly capable of understanding the contraindications himself, the shopkeeper had proceeded to mime vomiting and dizziness before, as a pantomimic finale, falling to the floor.

Allie – as Andrew had been told to call the taller of the two men – was first to the bar and was perusing the ranks of bottles in the various fridges that lined the rear wall, a cigarette in his hand that looked suspiciously like a joint. Above their heads were racks of glasses of different shapes and sizes, some of them displaying the name of the beer for which they had been specifically designed. Andrew knew from his visits to Belgium that there were many varieties, but he hadn't till then appreciated how many there were.

'What happened to the hand?' Ollie asked.

'Um, I caught it on a lock. Yesterday. Or was it today? Sorry. I'm a bit blurry. It's got infected.'

'Not that one. The other one. Gangrene?'

Andrew looked at his left hand. He'd almost forgotten about it. The pain had gone and his fingers now moved freely, but his fingertips were still blackened. 'Electric shock.'

Ollie pursed his lips, impressed. 'You live dangerously.'

'What do you want to drink?' Allie asked Andrew.

'Mineral water, please. Sparkling.'

'Yeah, right. But what do you want to *drink*?' The expectation that he would be drinking something alcoholic and probably beer was obvious, even to Andrew, and he didn't want to start off on the wrong foot.

'I'm, er, not really meant to be drinking. Because of the hand. Antibiotics and painkillers. They both react with alcohol, I'm told. So something light.'

Allie looked at Ollie. For both of them, 'Light beer' or, as it was spelled in America, 'Lite Beer' was an oxymoron, a desecration of the brewing process, which Allie, as a home brewer, regarded as a sacred ritual. Ollie, already resentful that his post-concert routine was compromised by Andrew's presence, offered a misleading summary of beer colour and strength, a prank that he and Allie had played on others in a more generous spirit than now.

'I'm having an Oerbier, and Allie's having a Westmalle Dubbel. They're both dark. And strong. But the rule of thumb,' lied Ollie, 'is that the lighter the colour, the lower the alcohol percentage. So maybe a Duvel? Interesting glass as well.'

Andrew nodded and Allie ordered the drinks, each of which was served in a distinctively shaped glass, poured delicately by a barman who, as if all beer drinkers were made from the same mould, save for the bald head and absence of a cigarette, looked almost exactly like Allie. The bass handed Andrew a tulip-shaped glass, its bulb holding a light, fizzing beer, the ballooning neck filled with a thick, craggy cloud of foam.

'Cheers,' said Ollie.

'Santé,' responded Andrew.

'Up yours,' said Allie.

The two singers considered their beer in silence, sipping occasionally and reading the details on the beer bottles. Andrew, in an effort to share their interest, picked up his bottle and turned it slowly in the dim light, confirming the details of the tastes he was now experiencing. Having read all the informative blurb, and still stuck for something to say, he began to peruse the incidental details and realised that his Duvel was eight-and-a-half percent by volume. That made it a high-alcohol beer, not the light variety he had sought, and a quick calculation told him that if he finished it he would have drunk the equivalent of a very large glass of wine.

'Not a bad gig,' said Allie to no one in particular, blowing out a thin stream of smoke towards the ceiling. Ollie nodded. Andrew wondered if this was his cue to critique the concert. His reservations about the performance were the same as those he had about the recent recording, as they inevitably would be, given that the second half was an exact replica of the second disc. He didn't like the suggestive chronology, which, to him, pointed the listener beyond Ockeghem's death, inviting them to contemplate the composer's heritage rather than his music. Still, he reasoned, he might as well start with some kind of compliment.

'Good low notes,' he offered.

Ollie, keeping his eyes on Andrew, flicked his head towards Allie to indicate the direction in which the praise should be directed. Allie neither moved nor spoke.

'Nice low notes,' Andrew ventured again, thinking that perhaps Allie hadn't heard him the first time.

Allie made a noise that Andrew felt rather than heard, a dismal rumble like a heavy table being dragged across a stone floor.

Andrew had been impressed by the viscous lines traced by Allie and Ollie in the *Missa Fors seulement* and *Intemerata Dei mater*. These singers were singing exactly the same low lines that Ockeghem would have sung, though he doubted the composer would have belittled the experience so easily by slipping into the nearest pub afterwards.

He couldn't leave it there, he knew. His comments were inadequate, but the only thing he could think about was the structure of the second half. He ploughed on. 'A shame to end with Josquin, don't you think?'

Ollie looked up sharply. 'So you didn't read your programme either, then?'

Andrew was confused. Was there something in the programme notes that suggested that *Nymphes des bois* was not by Josquin? That made no sense.

'It said quite clearly that there wasn't going to be an encore,' said Ollie, a touch of exasperation in his voice. Allie drained the remains of dark beer, stubbed out his roll-up and looked at his watch.

'Better join the others,' he said to Ollie. Ollie downed his drink in one short gulp and put his empty glass next to Allie's on the counter. They were both now looking at Andrew who had thus far taken only two sips.

'Better neck that,' said Ollie.

'I didn't mean the encore,' stuttered Andrew, trying to continue the argument and give himself time. 'I just feel that a concert of Ockeghem's music should end with Ockeghem's music, not Josquin's.'

'Yeah, but it's Josquin's music about Ockeghem, isn't it?' retorted Ollie. 'And it means the concert's all about Ockeghem the man, and not just Ockeghem's music.'

Andrew realised that Ollie had a point. Perhaps his own response was too, well, too musicological, too positivist even, a narrow appreciation of what was seen on the page and heard by the ears, not experienced in the heart.

'We're keeping the others waiting. Swallow your medicine and let's go,' said Allie. Andrew had no choice but to drink it down.

'So,' Allie said to Andrew, pushing open the door to reveal St Gatien floodlit against a matt-black sky, 'we're going to be working together?'

The cold night air slapped Andrew full in the face and he realised suddenly that he was drunk. As the door swung back on its hinges, he instinctively held out his bandaged hand to catch it. The pain shot from the centre of his palm along his forearm and into his funny bone.

'Yeeees,' he yelped, straining to keep up with the two singers as they strode towards the brasserie.

CHAPTER 17

As Emma walked through the front door, the champagne corks were theatrically popped by three waiters and the *Maître D'* rushed towards her. The *femme au chapeau*, as they greeted her, was ushered to the table, her place reserved on the red banquette next to Ollie and opposite Allie.

'He's a tosser,' Ollie had hissed, referring to Andrew. It explained why the American musicologist was seated so far away, being looked after by Susan, Peter and Claire.

At first, conversation amongst the group was directed towards the centre of the table, a communal celebration of what they had been through together over the past two days. Marco was called upon to rule on a dispute about the design of the brasserie, suggesting that it was *fin de siècle* with elements of *art nouveau*. He pointed to the ornate flowing lines in the posters and paintings, dated some of them, and made reference to the Impressionists and Toulouse Lautrec, before Charlie cut him off by calling him a smart-arse.

With their champagne glasses filled, everyone rose to toast Ockeghem. The brasserie with its the unfussy yet distinctively French menu was more suited to their post-concert revelry than the stuffy *Les Tuffeaux* would have been, which, lest anyone had any doubts, Allie had pronounced 'too pink'.

With the formalities over and the starters served – garlicky escargots, salade niçoise, and creamy fish soup – more intimate discussions started. Emma heard Marco, Charlie and Craig arguing about the pronunciation of 'Degas', while Allie and Ollie talked about the merits of Alsatian beers. Susan, who had angled her chair towards Andrew, was interrogating the musicologist, relaying each detail of his personal and professional life to the table at large, as if conducting an interview.

'Where exactly is Ohio?' Emma heard her say, and for a moment Andrew looked as if he wasn't entirely sure.

'He doesn't look that comfortable,' she commented to Ollie, who grudgingly lifted his eyes from his beer before throwing a few more croutons into his fish soup.

Indeed Andrew wasn't very comfortable. Walking in the fresh air from the Académie de la Bière, with the two basses ahead of him, he'd felt as if he was fighting his way through jungle undergrowth. His legs were heavy, he felt feverish and his hand throbbed. As soon as he'd reached the brasserie, he had sought out the nearest bathroom, convinced that he was going to vomit. The mirror confirmed his physical deterioration, his skin slick with sweat, heavy circles of tiredness beneath his eyes. He poked at his cheek with a finger, exploring a puffiness that he had never seen before, wondering vaguely if it presaged some rare disease.

He had splashed cold water on his face and returned to the table to discover that a place had been reserved for him between the two sopranos, the one heavily made-up and flirtatiously attentive, the other brusque and continually, inexplicably annoyed at something. Ollie and Allie, his recent drinking companions, were as far away from him as possible, something he was sure was no accident and which he regretted only because it also meant he wouldn't be able to talk to Emma. Clearly he would have to suffer the meal before he could get down to business.

He had intended to drink only water and had ordered a bottle of Badoit, but it had arrived just as Emma walked through the door and, in that moment of confusion, it was placed at the other end of the table where Allie and Ollie had made a joke of it, pushing it back and forth towards each other, an unwanted object that threatened their attempts to get drunk. Glasses of champagne had been poured for everyone and, knowing it would have been inappropriate not to, Andrew had joined in. He had sipped it as slowly as he could, but a new game had started which required them all to stand and toast various random suggestions – Emma's hat, Peter's scarf, Allie's dog – and the bottle of water, despite several requests, had remained stubbornly at the other end of the table.

He was confident that he wasn't going to be sick, at least. When the waiters brought bread to the table he had started on it straightaway and almost immediately his complaining stomach had been quelled. The pharmacist was right: he should have taken his antibiotics and painkillers with food. Something seemed to be interfering with his hearing, which might explain why he had lost his balance in his hotel room and fallen over. The excited chatter of his dinner companions washed over him and then receded into the distance like waves on a seashore, an acoustic effect which made him feel slightly seasick. But there was no denying the more immediate attention of Susan, the soprano, who had kept up an unstinting barrage of questions for the past half hour or so in a shrill voice that sliced through his head like cheese wire through a mature brie. There was seemingly no chance to interrupt and ask her a question, something that would at least afford him a moment to glaze over and adopt a pose of interest behind which he could figuratively breathe again. Finally he saw his opportunity: the waiters began serving the entrées – bleeding steaks, grilled freshwater fish and coq au vin – and, as Susan leaned back to allow the waiter to place a large bowl of crisp thin frites in the middle of the table, Andrew addressed his question loudly towards his other neighbours hoping to include them and break his hitherto singular exchange. With the broadest, most encouraging smile he could muster, he raised his voice over the hubbub, which, as each member of the group took their first mouthfuls of food almost as one, suddenly dropped.

'What's Lillet?'

He immediately realised that he had unwittingly committed some form of social faux pas. Glasses parked themselves in midair, faces freeze-froze, hands reaching across the table for a piece of bread stalled, and forks failed to find their targets, hovering inches away from open mouths.

Andrew was the only one who moved, giving a darting, despairing survey of his fellow diners. It was Emma who rescued him. Following the original direction of his gaze she discovered the source of his question: a mirror in the corner with the word 'Lillet' etched on it.

'Garçon,' she called to the waiter. 'Qu'est ce que c'est "Lillet"?'

'You can't ask that!' screeched Peter, burying his head in his napkin. The others laughed nervously, glad that the embarrassing silence had been broken.

'Un Lillet? C'est un apéritif. Désirez-vous un Lillet? Rouge ou blanc?'

'A Lillet,' explained Emma to Andrew across the table, 'is an aperitif in this country, and a tampon in the UK. I don't think you have the brand over there. Grow up, boys,' she added, looking at no one in particular.

'I told you he was a tosser,' Ollie whispered.

A waiter then presented Andrew with a glass of the cocktail which, with due ceremony which felt to him like penance, he drank.

Champagne, they all agreed, got you drunk quicker than anything else: it was the bubbles. It also woke you up and, given the day they'd had, none of them deserved to be awake, let alone like this: eyes bright, faces shining.

The table was strewn with various glasses and bottles, not just the champagne flutes with which they had begun the meal. Badoit and Evian, token gestures towards good health and sobriety, were lined up between various local red and white wines, some of which Allie had insisted on buying to prove his point that in a blind tasting none of them could tell which was the most expensive. In this he had been confounded by Andrew, whose palate had been able to discern not only the grape, but also the region. When the musicologist then successfully ranked them in order of value, Allie declared that from now on he should consider himself the group's *sommelier*.

For the first time that evening, Andrew felt that he belonged. He was tempted to announce that he would be honoured to accept the duty as long as it was used in its twentieth-century meaning – as a wine waiter – but not if they meant it in its medieval sense – as a clerk responsible for the maintenance of all the household items. Instead he suppressed his dry observation and congratulated himself on his social awareness, settling instead for what he hoped they would read as a shy smile. Nevertheless, he couldn't resist telling Susan that he wouldn't carry their bags for them. The duties of a *sommelier*, he explained, included the organisation of the baggage for long journeys and, indeed, some of the singers at St Martin during Ockeghem's era were designated as *sommeliers*.

'How fascinating!' she exclaimed, though he was relieved that, as she turned towards the others to tell them, they had their backs turned, focused on Craig who had lined up the table's cruet sets and was demonstrating a theory about cricket. In a group situation like this, with no divide between the private and the public, anything he said to Susan would be repeated and amplified. He was beginning to understand the rules of social intercourse and he wouldn't, as he had earlier, be so quick to speak. Already an aside to Susan about Loire wines had landed him in the middle of the wine-tasting, just at the point where he'd hoped he would be able to spend the rest of the evening drinking coffee. Still, he seemed to have discovered a second, or perhaps third, wind. He'd taken more painkillers and antibiotics, and the pain in his hand had once again faded. He did a rough calculation in his head: midnight here, six o'clock in Ohio. He'd left home at three o'clock the previous day and had about two hours' sleep, maximum. It didn't make any sense; he was beginning to feel better and starting to enjoy himself.

It was after the desserts were finished – crème brulées and îles flottantes, cheese and another bottle of red wine for the basses – that the stories began. His ignorance about the word 'Lillet', a linguistic confusion for which he now seemed to have been forgiven, had prompted a discussion about puns, and Andrew was pleased to note that modern singers seemed to share the same kind of fascination with wordplay that their fifteenth-century counterparts had.

'Hey, it's like the Julian St John story,' said Craig. 'You know, the Utrecht incident, with the telephone?'

Around the table people nodded and smiled; only Marco shook his head.

'You weren't there?' exclaimed Craig. 'But you must have heard it, surely?'

'No,' said Marco. 'I was on that Gabrieli trip to Rome. The one where all the luggage went missing?'

Craig, who sensed that Marco might himself be about to launch into an anecdote of his own, cut him off. 'You'll love it,' he said, and all other conversations petered out as chairs were pushed back and people turned expectantly towards the alto.

For Andrew's benefit, Craig began with a brief portrait of Julian St John, a singer known to most of them from other contexts, but whose sole appearance with Beyond Compère had been notable more for the amount of complaining he had done about having to learn the music from memory than for any musical or social contribution. Marco, it seemed, held him in particular contempt; he still hadn't forgiven Julian St John for his characteristically xenophobic dismissal of pasta as 'wop food'. While others, for whom eating and drinking was the primary perk of touring, scoured the town for good restaurants and bars, St John would eat cheaply with provisions bought from supermarkets or even brought with him in his luggage, and never, ever bought anyone a drink. Such myopic disinterest was similarly manifest in a general snobbery about people, colleagues included, for which he made no apology, his frequently voiced ambition being to quit the world of music and enter the world of high finance. Other than ambition, he lacked any relevant experience but nevertheless kitted himself out with what he considered to be the essential tools of the business: high-end gadgets.

'He turned up at Heathrow carrying this new laptop. It was huge,' said Craig.

'About the size of a breeze block. And about as heavy,' added Allie.

'And he had a mobile phone – and this was in the days when only a few people had them. So he's playing with his phone in the departure lounge and on the plane. The stewardess told him to switch it off and he got all uppity. And then it was the laptop on the plane. You know what he's like – he just kept showing stuff to people. Spreadsheets and things like that.

'Anyway, we get to Amsterdam and we get picked up and drive to Utrecht. It's one of those late-night gigs so there's time for lunch and we all arrange to go out to find something to eat, and Allie and Ollie go and do their thing.'

('Bert's Beerhouse,' said Allie.

'The first time I came across Oerbier,' said Ollie.)

'So we come down to the lobby to meet up for satay and frites or whatever,' continued Craig, 'and he's in reception waving his phone around above his head, like he's trying to get a signal. And he looks really annoyed. So we ask him if he wants to come along and he says "I've got better things to do".'

Marco and the others laughed at Craig's perfect impersonation of St John's plummy accent. Andrew thought for a moment that that the story had ended, but Craig hadn't finished.

'Off we go, and he obviously decides to go and buy his lunch at a supermarket, and after a while he works out that there's something wrong with the phone. In fact, what he hadn't done was tell them he was going out of the country – it was his first time with the phone overseas – and so they hadn't lifted the block on it. So he's furious with the phone company and wants to sort it out. Of course, to do that he'll have to ring back to the UK and you know how much hotels charge for that. But he thinks, sod it, I'll get the money back off them, 'cos he's the complaining type, you know. So he rings the UK. And that doesn't work.'

Craig, a natural story-teller, was into his stride now.

'So by now he's furious with the hotel as well. He reckons it must be their fault. They haven't switched his phone on, he guesses, so he comes down now to give the guy at reception an earful, just as we get back.'

'And us,' added Allie. Ollie shook his head in agreement.

'You too, right,' acknowledged Craig.

'And the towel. Don't forget the towel,' yelled Susan, laughing.

'Oh, the towel, yeah.' Craig nodded. 'He'd decided that he wants to get a shower, so he'd stripped off. He'd been wandering around in his towel, shouting at the walls, and worked himself up into a right frenzy. And when he comes down to reception, he's only got this skimpy towel wrapped round him.'

'No muscles,' added Susan, wrinkling her nose.

'And he starts shouting at the guy: "Why doesn't my phone work?" – "I've never been treated like this." – "What kind of hotel are you running?" That sort of thing. And the guy's just looking at him. So St John says, "Do you even speak English?" "Of course, sir," the guy says, "we all speak English in Holland." And he's right, of course, 'cos they've got British telly and they watch it all the time, and they all speak it really well.'

'Better than me,' said Allie.

'So – and this is it right – so St John says, "How do I ring abroad?"'

Craig paused and looked around him, checking that everyone was ready for the punch line.

'And this guy, the guy at reception, absolutely straight-faced, says, "You don't have to ring a broad, sir; you can simply go to the red-light district."'

All of them, even those who had witnessed it first-hand or had heard the story before, began to laugh. Marco, despite Craig's indication that the punch line was coming, had to spit a mouthful of water back into his glass. The basses too were laughing, Allie despairingly trying to tell Ollie that the red-light district in Utrecht was appropriately called *Hardbollen straat*, an observation that would have added something to the anecdote. It was taken up and passed around the table as something for them all to share, a suitable coda to Craig's story.

Andrew joined in the laughter. A thought struck him: maybe this was how the parties were, the ones described in the chansons and in various historical accounts, stories of meetings between Dufay and Binchois, Ockeghem and Busnois? Composers like that, having sung solemn Mass, would have loosened their tongues with wine provided by the authorities and told tall tales, outdoing each other with recollections of abandoned behaviour in foreign cities, perhaps exaggerating slightly, adding small details here for the benefit of those, like himself, who hadn't heard the story before. The singers here, even those who had clearly heard the stories that others were telling, welcomed the excuse that he, as an entirely fresh audience, provided. What he had witnessed this evening was surely not dissimilar to the oral traditions of the medieval period? Poetry would have been handed down from one generation to another, subtly altered to accommodate the company in which it was told, perhaps like this as a traditional part of a feast.

And here he was, a *musicus* amongst *cantores*, but were these *cantores* as ignorant as the theorists implied in their condescending descriptions that likened them to drunks unable to find their way home? Certainly they liked a drink, but most of them were graduates – witty, intelligent, insightful and undoubtedly talented. He felt at home here, but how did they see him? Did they think he was like this St John character, socially awkward with poor communication skills?

Charlie was lying on his back on the red banquette, alternately closing one eye and then the other, trying to make sense of the *trompe l'oeil* paintings on the ceiling.

'You'd think they'd look better from here, but they don't,' he muttered.

Allie pointed to the list of wines hand-painted on the walls: Chinon, Vouvray, Laurent-Perrier, Montlouis, Anjou. 'I'll have one of them, one of them, one of them, one of them...'

Peter repeated the mantra, pointing to the young waiters in turn until Claire physically wrestled him into silence, though not before he screamed 'rape' in mock horror.

'Des cafés?' enquired the head waiter.

'Coffees, anyone?' said Susan. A chorus of 'me' and *'café crème'* and *'au lait'* followed before Claire took the situation in hand and, like a schoolmistress, demanded a show of hands. The only other occupants of the brasserie now were a table of suited businessmen drinking Cognac and a young British couple arguing.

'Sambuca,' Marco shouted to the waiter and a volley of approximate Geordie accents ensued. Andrew was surprised but pleased; he had thought that the music for the evening was over.

'Who's going to play?' he asked Susan.

'Sorry?'

'The Sambuca. Who's going to play it?'

'It's a drink,' she said, looking askance at the musicologist.

Andrew knew Sambuca only as a medieval harp. So it was a drink as well? Clearly, if he was to fraternise with singers, he would have to devote some time to researching arcane alcoholic beverages. The table was cleared of the paper tablecloth: a sensible precaution, Marco pointed out, given the imminent arrival of the flaming *digestifs*.

Emma had kept an eye on Andrew during the meal. He'd chatted happily with Susan and sometimes eavesdropped quite unselfconsciously on others' conversations. Now, though, he seemed to be flagging. Craig was trying to explain how cricket was played.

'These are like your catchers,' he said, gesturing to a semi-circle of silver salt and pepper pots. 'We call them slips.'

'Slips?' Andrew said.

'Slips. It's like in baseball. When you have one catcher, we have five or six.'

'And they're all behind the batter?'

'Batsman. But these two are called gullies.'

'Girlies?'

'Gullies.'

'And the thrower's where?'

'The bowler. He's here. He bowls it. Oh, look,' said Craig, aware of Emma coming towards them, 'it's too complicated to explain. Come to a match. Actually, read a book.'

'How's it going down here?' she asked, one hand on Peter's back and an arm around Susan's shoulder.

'Wonderful, and thanks again for the champagne,' said Susan. 'Scrummy.'

'Yeah, thanks,' added Peter.

'Cheers, Em,' said Craig, obviously grateful to have been interrupted.

'Andrew, we must talk. Is now a good time?' asked Emma.

'Er, yes, of course. Do you want to go somewhere?'

'No. Here's fine.'

Andrew hadn't expected that his meeting with Emma would be so public. He looked around the brasserie. The businessmen were too smart to be academics and, even if they were spies, were unlikely to be on his trail. The young couple were distracted by their quarrelling and hardly likely to overhear, and the waiters hardly posed a threat. But, after six months of total secrecy, it felt strange to be here, on the precipice, about to announce to strangers a discovery that he had guarded all this time. He'd dismissed his earlier concerns about Emma and the group; he liked her – and them – and, after all, only he knew where to find the original. He'd come this far and knew he needed to take a terrifying leap. He could feel fear and excitement, a fluttering of ecstasy in his chest.

The strange thing was, he didn't know *how* to tell them. His frequent daydreams featured more formal presentations: he'd written and re-written the introduction to his book several times and provided the occasional modest preface to collections of essays in his honour; he had delivered keynote speeches at conferences devoted to reappraisals of fifteenth-century compositional practice, had wittily and modestly responded to excitable interviewers with self-effacing humour in brightly lit television studios in London and New York, and told pre-rehearsed anecdotes in French from cavernous sound-proofed radio stations. He had even mentally drafted his acceptance speech of the award of the Chevalier de l'Ordre des Arts et des Lettres here in Tours, which he was sure the government would ultimately award him for services to France. Such temporary assurances had sustained him when keeping such a monumental secret had tested his self-restraint, but for some reason he'd never imagined the moment that was upon him now.

Emma had pulled up a chair to his left and was looking at him expectantly. Susan was to his right and next to her was Claire who, after spending most of the meal finding problems with her food, was now smiling blearily across a glass of white wine. Surrounded by women, he suddenly needed Karen.

He took a big breath.

'I've found a new piece of music. By Ockeghem.'

He waited for the applause, but none came.

'It's a secret,' he said.

'Oh, goody. I love secrets,' said Susan, clapping her hands together.

'No. Really. You mustn't tell anybody. It's *really* important.'

'I'm sure we can all keep this a secret, Andrew,' said Emma gently. 'Go on.'

'Well,' he said, deliberately breathing slowly, 'it's a big piece. A *really* big piece. And it's definitely by him: Ockeghem. There's no question. And I've cracked the notational puzzle, all of this only recently. And it looks like a *really* good piece. I reckon it's a late work, probably the last thing he wrote. But there's no mention of it anywhere, which is really extraordinary in itself. Oh, and it's also an autograph sketch. Written by an amateur, not a scribe. Maybe by his best friend. It's amazing really.'

He felt deflated. This was not the fluent rendition of which he was capable, the carefully wrought, controlled discourse he had anticipated. The despairing inarticulateness of his description, with detail haphazardly piled on detail, each phrase underlined by the flailing repetition of the word 'really', a word he always crossed out when he came across it in student essays, had him suddenly doubting the importance of his discovery and the musical merits of the motet. With each frantic qualification, he heard himself undermining the composition's historical importance rather than testifying to its existence with academic certainty.

Emma was smiling, though he couldn't tell if it was reassurance or benign tolerance. 'That's great, Andrew, but tell us about the piece and where we come in. I assume you wouldn't be telling us if you didn't want us involved?'

'Of course, of course.' He gulped some water, then took another, deeper breath. 'I want you to give the first performance. I don't know where that would be, or how that would happen, and I need your advice on that. Also, you're big news these days and the natural inheritors of the fifteenth-century choral tradition, and ... and...' He'd lost his train of thought.

'The piece itself?' Emma prompted. Sensing the change of mood, Marco and Charlie had both now turned towards their end of the table.

'It's a *Miserere mei*. Psalm fifty-one. But it's in thirty-four parts.'

Charlie whistled, a sound like a firework streaking across the sky. 'Big piece then.'

'A *very* big piece. Scored for eight basses, eight tenors, nine countertenors and nine *discantus* parts. There's a numerological reason for the scoring: the design encodes Ockeghem's name. So, a big piece, and well before anyone else did anything like it. Canonic, of course. Intricate. Typical Ockeghem in many ways. It's probably the biggest musical discovery of the past fifty years. Maybe even a hundred.'

'And do you have it here?' asked Emma.

'Not the original, obviously, but a transcription. You can see it if you want?'

Emma very much wanted to see it. Her expectation of an offer of workshops or maybe a residency in the USA with her delivering a couple of lectures felt like a feeble joke now and she was glad she hadn't dismissed Andrew as she'd been inclined to when he'd first written to her. His proposal made her and the group partners in a major musical discovery. Her mind was racing. It would be an obvious piece for a Prom and, beyond that, the kind of large-scale work which would introduce Beyond Compère to the larger stages of the world: The Met in New York, Sydney Opera House, the Konzerthaus in Berlin, the Vienna Musikverein – the kinds of places at which an early-music ensemble would never otherwise perform. She told herself to calm down; she would need more than Andrew's say-so. The manuscript would have to be checked and authenticated, authorship proven beyond doubt. She didn't want to be famous for participating in the biggest hoax since the Hitler diaries, and, though that seemed unlikely given Andrew's guilelessness, she couldn't rule out wily ambition. The piece itself would have to be worth performing, but surely it must be? Thirty-four parts? By Ockeghem? That was a story in itself, whatever its aesthetic value.

Andrew pulled the transcription from his case and showed it to her – careful, Emma noted, to display it rather than let anyone else touch it. Its imaginative scope and sheer physical size was immediately obvious.

'Can we lay it out on the table?' Emma asked. Andrew looked doubtful, but already Charlie and Marco were creating space, collecting glasses and sweeping away the debris. Andrew started laying out the sheets in order. Suddenly he yelped with concern. The waiter had arrived bearing a tray of glasses filled with flaming clear-liquid drinks: the Sambucas. Emma took charge.

'Fire up that end of the table.' She pointed to Allie and Ollie who were debating whether it was possible to drink Sambuca while it was still alight. 'Music down this end. And ne'er the twain shall meet.'

Reassured by Emma's improvised safety curtain, Andrew arranged the manuscript as he had done earlier in the hotel. Craig, Marco and Claire left their seats and came around the table to give themselves a better view. Now Andrew was flanked by the singers and he hoped they couldn't discern, as he could, the shadowy indentation of his body in the crumpled pages.

'So here it is,' he said, holding his hands wide. 'You can see how it works. It begins with the *bassus* parts and the *discantus* and then soon – remarkably soon actually – the other parts enter. The tenor part works like *Missa Prolationum* – same notes, different mensuration – so you're singing slightly faster than the bass parts and, of course, at a fourth above.'

Other than Allie and Ollie who were deliberately ignoring the presentation, sitting in silence drinking their Sambucas and coffee, everyone was grouped around the manuscript. Marco and Charlie began humming their part in canon.

'It's interesting that he doesn't use alteration and imperfection. He's using some kind of mid-way notation system, so you read it as if it's modern notation. I finally cracked that riddle.' Andrew waited for the praise that he was sure was due. Marco and Charlie, ignorant of the rules to which Andrew was referring and not caring, exchanged a look of bemusement before returning to their rendition.

'Where did you find it?' asked Susan who, rather distractingly, had pressed her body against Andrew and was looking over his shoulder. The question delivered a rush of hot air disturbingly close to his ear.

'Er, well, as I say, it's a secret, but let's just say somewhere in Northern France. I would tell you, but...' He shrugged, a gesture which he hoped explained his predicament and, in so doing, rubbed against Susan's breasts which were nestling against his back. Was she trying to lead him on? Was this an attempt at seduction, the first promise of erotic adventure that he had heard success brought? Would Susan, and others like her, be beating a path to his hotel door in the near future?

'The original's safe,' he continued, 'but I have to confirm a couple of details before I reveal it. That's why it's a secret. I'd like its first performance to coincide with its announcement to the academic world.'

'So you want us, as a group, on our own, to perform it then? Not a collaboration with anyone else?' Emma was looking directly at Andrew. This, he understood, was a form of contract, each term outlined slowly and firmly, direct eye-contact the unspoken, binding handshake.

'Yes,' he said, trying to match her deliberateness. 'Of course, you'd need to get more singers, but you can do that?'

'Oh, we all know other singers and we can certainly expand the group, but is it realistic for the first performance to be the first time anyone hears about it? For one thing, the promoter would need to know what it was before they agreed to the concert. And the way to maximise publicity would be to announce it to the world in press releases and the like. After all, at least thirty-four people are going to know about it when they rehearse it.'

Andrew had given no thought to the people who would be involved in organising a concert – the promoters, the back-room staff – or to the buyers of tickets: the audience. His imagination had been guided by stories of epoch-making first performances. The history of music tended to gloss over the prior processes, such preparations, condensing the composing of the piece, its rehearsal and administrative prelude into the singular glorious moment of its first night. Stravinsky's *Rite of Spring* apparently provoked a riot, but did that really happen? Stravinsky had written many other challenging pieces before that one. And the first performance of Handel's *Messiah* apparently had King George II leaping to his feet, so impressed was he by the Hallelujah chorus. Or was the monarch simply stretching his legs after sitting down for nearly two hours? Such mythical events were products of a falsely retrospective historical view which

Andrew, in his excitement, had embraced; Emma, it was obvious, had considerably more experience and he would do well to heed it.

'Well, obviously we'd have to let many other people know in advance,' he said to Emma, hoping his peremptory response masked his naïveté, 'but what I mean is that you would be the group who would perform it first.'

'We'll need to talk about this properly,' said Emma. There was no humour in her voice; this was serious. 'I'm very excited. Who else knows? Which other musicologists, I mean?'

'None, actually,' said Andrew. He caught a look of surprise on Emma's face. 'I made a decision early on that I needed to be absolutely sure about a lot of things before I told anyone. You really are the first people to know.'

He offered the last observation, both flattering and defensive, in an appeal for complicity. He implied that he had maintained secrecy until he was certain of the manuscript's authenticity, partly out of respect for their professional standing; to have approached them any earlier would otherwise have compromised them. This rapid revision of his motives cast his actions as a gift: this was their opportunity to be an important chapter in the story of a major musical event.

'What's this bit? I recognise this,' said Marco, and he hummed a three-note phrase.

'Yeah, I do too,' agreed Charlie. 'It's the opening phrase of *Prenez sur moi*, isn't it?'

Marco sang the same phrase but now with the French words of Ockeghem's three-part chanson, a text that invited the other singers and the listener to follow his example.

Andrew realised immediately its significance. Here, in the motet, the phrase occurred on the word *mei*, the dative form of the personal pronoun meaning 'to me'. He could barely excuse himself for not noticing it, even if it was hidden in the middle of the texture almost like a *leitmotif* rather than, as was the convention, being part of the opening statement. *This is my piece*, Ockeghem was saying, *and here is my signature*. Andrew had spotted the use of the canon at the fourth, the interval used in *Prenez sur moi*, but failed to notice this specific musical quotation. What else had he missed? Setting aside his immediate excitement at this new proof with a reflex that he had developed over the last twenty-four hours, he claimed the insight as his own.

'Yes, *Prenez sur moi*. You spotted it. Well done,' he said to the tenors, his praise delivered in a tone of weary superciliousness that he habitually adopted when speaking to his students.

'Hurry up please, it's time. Hurry up please, it's time,' said Allie, relaying the brasserie's request to pay up and leave.

'Any last Sambucas?' asked Ollie, prompting another chorus of 'Sam-boo-kah'.

Allie and Ollie were well in their cups now, Emma noted, Allie's eyelids almost at half-mast, Ollie's eyes unnaturally lucent as if he'd picked up some new scent. There was no stopping them now and it would be unwise to, Ollie in particular likely to bridle at any suggestion that he wasn't in control.

'It's a really interesting project,' she said to Andrew, 'but we need to talk about it more. Can I keep this?' She pointed to the manuscript. 'I assume you've got a copy of the original somewhere?'

'Yes, of course. I wrote this out especially for you on the way over,' he lied. 'It's only rough, but I'll do a proper edition and send it to you when I get home.'

'You mean you worked on this last night on the plane? Did you get any sleep at all?'

'Not really,' Andrew admitted.

It was extraordinary that he was still standing and explained to Emma why he looked so terrible. 'You should get some sleep,' she said. 'Get back to the hotel and we'll settle things up here.'

'A hundred and twenty francs each,' shouted Allie as if on cue. 'More if you had Sambucas. They're twelve francs each.'

Andrew was suddenly exhausted. Ahead of him lay sleep, even if it was in a sagging single bed. With people clustered around him he'd begun to feel hot and claustrophobic, the lights were too bright and, as he turned, all he saw were Susan's shiny red lips before the room started to spin. He sat down quickly and groped in his briefcase for his wallet, as voices swirled around him.

'That's the right amount. You get back to your hotel. Are you all right on your own?' It was Emma.

He would be fine, said Andrew; he just needed sleep. He picked up his briefcase and said goodbye. Several members of the group waved and Susan pecked him on the cheek and, as the waiter unlocked the front door for him, he heard that strange chant again – 'Sam-boo-kah! Sam-boo-kah!' – followed by screams.

CHAPTER 18

The Memoirs of Geoffroy Chiron: Livre VI *ed. Francis Porter*

Martius 17, 1524

The pain is much worse now. I have not slept at all this night, the bells that tolled the hour my only company. The tincture Cosset gave me for the pain has no effect and I will summon him to my bed when daylight comes. I have not eaten for three days yet I have no hunger, my stomach tender and swollen like that of a pregnant woman. I do not know why God has chosen to punish me in this way and my only hope is that my affliction upon this earth is weighed against my time in Purgatory. I pray to God and to Jesus Christ, my only saviour, and to the Blessed Virgin Mary, that my suffering is brief. I have touched the bones of St Martin; I have given generously to the Church and to the poor; I have served God in His Temple throughout my life. I trust in the Lord's judgement and today I will make my full and final confession before God.

Circumdederunt me funes mortis et torrentes diabuli terruerunt me. Funes inferi circumdederunt me; praevenerunt me laquei mortis. In tribulatione mea invocabo Dominum et ad Deum meum clamabo exaudiet de templo suo vocem meam; et clamor meus ante faciem eius veniet in aures eius. *[The sorrows of death surrounded me and the torrents of iniquity troubled me. The sorrows of hell encompassed me; and the snares of death prevented me. In my affliction I called upon the Lord, and I cried to my God; and he heard my voice from his holy temple: and my cry before him came into his ears.]*

Easter fell early in the year that Jehan composed his Miserere mei *[1491]. Spring, he said, was a creative time in nature where the symbol of our risen Lord was manifest in the growth of plants and trees, a sign of hope and optimism; it was the autumn and winter months, the time for preserving and storing the fruits of the summer, when we transcribed the music. As the scripture says:* Omnia tempus habent et suis spatiis transeunt universa sub caelo *[All things have their season, and in their times all things pass under heaven].*

As always, I was not involved in the earliest stages of Jehan's composition. It was most frustrating. What have you been doing, I would ask him. Composing, he would reply. That, I knew, consisted of him sitting in a room on his own, thinking.

How, I asked, hoping he might ask for my help, could he keep all that music in his head? How could he test it, rearrange it, hear it? I had asked such questions about his masses and motets many times before and he had always answered them by saying that it was like the jugglers at the Place Foire le Roi: he needed to study the musical ideas as they tumbled over each other in the aether. I could only marvel at his great abilities, like those of Orpheus himself.

When finally spring had turned into summer then faded into autumn, he asked if I could come to his house. Knowing that the motet would be written in thirty-four parts, I brought plenty of vellum with me; I even stopped at the scriptorium in St Gatien and begged for extra supplies. He laughed when he saw me carrying such a heavy burden.

'You won't need all that,' he said. 'One sheet of vellum will be enough.'

I thought that he meant that we were only to work on one part at a time, and perhaps in time I would need another thirty-three. Realising this, he smiled.

'It is a canon,' he said. 'And a canon takes up very little room.'

Thereupon he described the design. The bassus *part would be the model for the* tenor *part, and the* contratenor *and* discantus *parts would be canons independent of each other. He explained that it was his commentary on the old style of composition which, for too long, had privileged the* tenor *over the other parts, as a consequence of which* tenor *singers considered themselves more important than other members in the choir. He sat back in his chair and I took up my stylus. The piece was to be in* tempus imperfectum *with minor prolation, at a slightly slower speed than was customary because, with all those parts, the ear would not otherwise be able to discern the details.*

When we had completed the bassus *part, he dictated the Latin instructions that would instruct the other basses and the tenors how to extract their parts from that single example.*

'So now, Geoffroy, we have written sixteen parts. That didn't take long! And can you tell me, how many mensura *we have written? I would like to get some sense of the scale of the piece.'*

I added up the units of mensura. *There were ninety-two.*

'Ah, ninety-two. A good number, don't you think?'

I mumbled something. Whatever his purpose, I assumed it was beyond my understanding.

'Oh, and Geoffroy. Eight parts for the basses and eight for the tenors? What do you get if you multiply them?'

I knew that, as Treasurer, he was knowledgeable about arithmetic and had no need of my help to produce the answer of sixty-four. And, because he had asked the question idly, as if something new was occurring to him, I offered no answer.

'Sixty-four,' he said. 'Sixty-four. Ninety-two. Good numbers. Familiar numbers, don't you think?'

I nodded. They were familiar, but I couldn't work out why. I understood from his prompting that there must be some deeper significance, and I searched my memory. Psalm 64 [65]: Tibi silens laus Deus in Sion et tibi reddetur votum. Exaudi orationem donec ad te omnis caro veniat *[A hymn, O God, becometh thee in Sion: and a vow shall be paid to thee in Jerusalem. O hear my prayer: all flesh shall come to thee.]? No. Psalm 92 [93]:* Deus ultionum, Domine Deus ultionum ostendere. Elevare qui iudicas terram redde vicissitudinem superbis *[The Lord is the God to whom revenge belongeth: the God of revenge hath acted freely. Lift up thyself, thou that judgest the earth: render a reward to the proud.]? No. Certainly, as the cube of four, sixty-four possessed a symmetry, but ninety-two did not possess similar properties. I was confused and beginning to feel rather foolish. Jehan's smile, affectionate as it was, was also beginning to annoy me. Then he gently chastised me.*

'Geoffroy Chiron. Geoffroy Chiron. Did you never as a choirboy work out the numerical value of your name? Did you never work out the cipher and did you never call each other numbers? I know you did, for I heard boys doing it all the time.'

I understood. The value of my name was ninety-two and sixty-four: ninety-two for Geoffroy and sixty-four for Chiron. I could not find the words to thank him, humbled as I was, and he smiled at me, pleased by my delight.

Then he explained that he had been inspired by further correspondences and had decided to celebrate it in musical form. His initials, J and O, had values of nine and fourteen respectively. 'Multiply those by four and you have the number ninety-two, the same as your first name.' His name, Johannes Ockeghem, had values of eighty-one and sixty-four. Therefore there would be eight bassus *parts and eight* tenor *parts which, when multiplied, created the number sixty-four, the value of his and my last names. And there would be nine* contratenor *parts and nine* discantus *parts which, similarly treated, gave the value of eighty-one, the value of his first name. 'I won't even need to sign the manuscript!' he declared triumphantly.*

It did not take long to complete the task. There it lay, a rough outline of a composition in thirty-four parts, yet upon the page were shown only three. It was like one of the illuminated pages by Jean Bourdichon or Jean Fouquet, not in its surface beauty but in the way that, through its density, it contained detail and beauty in miniature that could keep one occupied for hours. And as I copied it out later that evening, I began to appreciate its subtleties and discover the balance and design that Jehan had been working on all those months, an order and harmony in each of the parts and of the whole. More than ever, I was anxious to hear it.

Jehan wrote to Compère to tell him that he had completed the composition. It would obviously be some time before the performance could be organised. With so many singers involved, all in different cities and towns across the lands, it would be difficult to find a date on which all could attend, and Compère was not born to administer; he could barely take care of himself.

Nevertheless, Compère wrote back immediately and assured Jehan that he would begin planning. He was still in the employ of the King, Charles VIII, who had turned his back on Tours and was travelling around the country to raise money for future wars [1491], a pursuit that required Compère to accompany him as a demonstration of the artistic aspirations of France. This frustrating, wandering lifestyle was a further threat to the planning and the performance at St Quentin, yet Compère assured Jehan that it would take place.

And, indeed, confirmation of his good intentions arrived in the form of a letter from Perchon, the famous composer, who wrote to his former teacher saying that he looked forward to seeing him at 'the event that Compère is organising'. At that time everything seemed possible and I was happy for Jehan. He was now an old man and increasingly it was me who bore the burden of his duties to St Martin.

In the autumn of that year, we had a surprise visitor: Josquin Desprez. He had been granted two months' leave from the Sistine Chapel in Rome to obtain benefices in various churches in Northern France. When Compère had been granted his benefice at the church of St Quentin, he had done so on the understanding that he brought with him experience and commitment, of which hosting the performance of Jehan's piece was a demonstration. Yet Desprez's attitude to the benefices offered by churches in the North can be summed up in one word: money. St Omer, Bourges, Amiens and Chartres were amongst his destinations, though he concentrated on towns in the region of his birth: St Ghislain, Cambrai, Douai and Tournai.

Although Desprez was not pursuing benefices in Tours, he made the city his first stop. He seemed different. He still bore a fierce, dark countenance, yet his speech was more controlled, his anger tempered.

Jehan invited me to dinner and assured me that Desprez would, on this occasion at least, acknowledge my presence. Though I did not look forward to it, the meal passed agreeably enough. Desprez was older, and with age had come a less choleric humour, though I still did not trust him. He was clearly dissatisfied with life in Rome and complained of the politics and the favouritism, the heat and the Italians themselves. He was, at least, speaking honestly.

Jehan and he discussed music. Desprez had brought some of his recent compositions and Jehan was genuine in his admiration. Perhaps it was the wine, perhaps it was the genuine desire to forgive the differences of the past but, for whatever reason, Jehan, in answering Desprez's casual enquiry about whether he had composed anything recently, told him of his Miserere mei. *Desprez immediately became animated, saying that he too had considered writing a larger piece, that he was interested in six-part composition and that we should not be bound by tradition and limit our expectations. Jehan did not show him the sketch, but described its construction which Desprez said excited him. And when and where would it be performed, he asked? Jehan explained that Compère was organising the event to which Desprez would obviously be invited. At the very mention of Compère's name, it was as if he was possessed by a demon. Desprez's brow thrust forward, his lips curled and his eyes turned black. But suddenly, in an instant, he became the relaxed, charming man that he had been earlier that evening. Was Jehan sure, he asked, that Compère was capable of organising this event? Could he, Desprez, perhaps help in any way? Jehan thanked him, and assured him that Compère was capable of making the necessary arrangements and neither of us thought any more of it.*

Months passed and Jehan and Compère continued to correspond, though nothing further was mentioned of the plans for the performance. It was I, rather than Jehan, who was the more anxious about the fate of his composition. I urged him to contact Compère; the King still planned to invade Italy, and thus Compère, still part of the Royal retinue, was detained. Jehan, though, was not so easily seduced as I was by a glorious vision of the first performance.

After many requests, finally Jehan broached the subject in a letter. Compère's reply came as a shock. Desprez had written to Compère some time ago – not long after Desprez's visit to Tours – and informed him that, in consultation with Jehan, Desprez had now taken on the responsibility of arranging the performance of Jehan's grand motet. Desprez said that the church where he had recently obtained a benefice, St Géry in Cambrai, was better located – those invited would find it far easier to travel there, and the larger town would have no difficulty in offering hospitality to such numbers – and that Jehan had agreed. But the deception went deeper. Desprez also maintained that he had visited Jehan at Jehan's request, thereby implying that Desprez was favoured by France's oldest composer. Not only was this lie designed to advance Desprez's reputation, it was an obvious attempt to suggest that Desprez was a closer friend to Jehan than Compère.

I was very angry. I railed against Desprez's treachery and accused him of many sins, chief amongst them jealousy. I suspected then – and voiced as much to Jehan – that there was more here than Desprez's foolish rivalry with Compère. Desprez was now a recognised figure, renowned throughout Europe, with no need of Jehan's support. What I feared – and what time would eventually prove – was that Desprez's hunger for fame and renown had grown to the point where he felt threatened by every other composer and composition. And Jehan's thirty-four-part motet was no exception. Josquin Desprez's fame had risen as Jehan's had declined, but Desprez feared that the wheel might turn once more and that the name of Jehan Ockeghem would eclipse that of Josquin Desprez.

Jehan, as ever, chose to find a more charitable explanation. Had I not pointed out on several occasions that Compère was unable to organise the simplest event? Perhaps Desprez, knowing this and aware of Compère's duties to the King, had chosen to take the responsibility upon himself rather than let the opportunity slip away?

At my insistence, Jehan wrote to Desprez to discover the truth. There was no reply. Once again, Jehan wrote. Again, no reply. And then, quite by chance, two incidents occurred that confirmed my suspicions.

Firstly, Jehan was visited by Johannes Tinctoris who was travelling back to Italy from Nivelles. Many younger composers came to pay their respects to a man who they knew could not live much longer and, in the case of Tinctoris, I think the real reason that he was there was to apologise. He now described as 'youthful errors' the things that he had written about Jehan in his Proportionale musices *and elsewhere, and Jehan, in an act that he described as 'the gift of age', forgave him.*

I was unable to attend their final meeting, but I know that the two men talked for some time. Privately I gave thanks. (I'm sure the fault is mine, but I have never been able to understand the fascination of music theory and have always preferred its practice.) The subject turned to that of composers, and Tinctoris mentioned that the clergy at St Géry in Cambrai were annoyed with Desprez. It was something to do, he said, with Desprez promising to visit them at least once a year – a promise which, hiding behind the skirts of the Pope, he had already broken and which he did not intend to honour. Tinctoris had heard the story from a singer at the Cathedral of Notre Dame in Cambrai and could not confirm all the details. The theorist did not know of its significance to Jehan; if Desprez's commitment to St Géry was negligible, then clearly there would be no performance of Jehan's Miserere mei.

A second visit confirmed Tinctoris' story. A young singer arrived to replace Jehan as a bass. Like me, he had trained as a choirboy and then been appointed as petit vicaire *at Notre Dame in Cambrai. He, too, had heard stories of the of the clergy's dissatisfaction with Desprez, though his version had Desprez cursing the clergy behind their backs and other dreadful elaborations that I cannot repeat here. I also learned that, when Desprez had visited the clergy of St Géry only months earlier in order to increase the modest income that they had offered, he had said he came there with Jehan's own blessing. He claimed he had met Jehan a week earlier (that much at least was true), and that Jehan had said that, if they granted Desprez a benefice, Jehan would write a piece for St Géry to commemorate the event. Thus Desprez had obtained his position through outright deception using the promise of Jehan's* Miserere mei *as part of his recommendation.*

Or at least that was the way I saw it. And I still do.

Jehan remained charitable. He was very guarded about stories that he could not verify. He reminded me how the reports of parties held in Dufay's house somehow became rowdier and more drunken with each year that passed. People sometimes chose to turn away from the truth, he said, for in so doing they made their lives on earth more tolerable. Nevertheless, it was clear, even to him, that Desprez deceived as easily as he breathed. And it was now obvious that the Miserere mei *would not be performed, at least in Cambrai.*

Yet still I hoped.

CHAPTER 19

The walk in the fresh, still air through the streets of Tours was as effective as a strong cup of espresso in restoring Andrew's sobriety. His hand had started to throb again, the effectiveness of the painkillers once again diminishing, but he felt relaxed, the tensions of all the travelling and the demands of the past twenty-four hours draining from him, his limbs languid and heavy. A bell tolled twice somewhere in the distance, perhaps from the Tour de l'Horloge. Two o'clock. The first lecture began the following morning at nine: a short night. It didn't matter; there would be plenty of time to catch up on sleep. His meeting with Emma and Beyond Compère had convinced him that he'd made the right choice. Emma was capable, that much was clear, and she'd cut straight to the point: much more careful planning was required. But for now he would sleep.

He was relieved that he had finally told someone about the manuscript. It seemed more real now, and surrendering the transcription to their care had been surprisingly painless – a good sign, he thought. He had a feeling of liberation, the foretaste of an assured future in which all the editions of the motet and the commentaries upon it would be seen to issue from his trustworthy ownership. If he'd known that it would be like this he might have loosened his grip earlier, and he wondered if keeping the motet so secret had been wise. Karen certainly thought it was a mistake. On several occasions she'd chided him and urged him to share his discovery with others. Ultimately though, he knew that the intellectual territorialism of which she indirectly accused him was part of academia itself: unattractive, perhaps, but pragmatic. He had only followed the example of others who, presented with the same opportunity, would have set aside ethical qualms and pursued selfish ambition with the same obsessive zeal that he had. Till now he had made no great breakthroughs, had never found a missing biographical clue or solved some compositional riddle; nor had he casually floated an hypothesis which had rocked the academic community and earned him respect and recognition. And so, he reasoned, he'd needed to make the most of his good fortune; he was unlikely to get another chance.

His room was cold and he closed the bathroom window. He had promised to call Karen. Six hours' time difference. No: seven. Seven hours' time difference from France, he thought, congratulating himself, and it's now two o'clock. That's nine o'clock in the morning and Karen will be in the house, possibly on her own if it's a nursery day for John. Ringing from a hotel would be expensive, but that hardly mattered now. He got through first time.

'Hello?'

'Karen?'

'Andrew,' she replied, a statement rather than a greeting.

'It's by him!' he shouted. 'By Ockeghem. I worked it out today. Numerology. It's definitely his name – it's a cipher. You give each letter and number and then add them up and then… And it quotes from his chanson, as well. On the word "me". He's literally signed it.' Unable to celebrate the most recent solution to the riddle of authorship in the brasserie, one provided *gratis* by Beyond Compère's tenors, the words had spewed out of him only to be met by a chastening reprimand.

'No, John,' Karen said gently. 'He's trying to pour a drink on the floor. Aren't you?'

So John wasn't at nursery?

'We're both fine, by the way,' she added. 'You've done it again.'

'Sorry?'

'Rung at a bad time, Andrew.'

Maybe he'd got the time wrong, he thought, for why else would they be having breakfast this late?

'What's the time there?' he asked, checking his watch once again.

'Seven.'

'Seven? You're up early.' Karen was a great believer in set times for meals, a discipline which she believed was beneficial to John. Breakfast in their house was regularly at eight. Andrew took her silence to be reproof of his own careless relationship with schedules and routines – yet another site of domestic conflict – and her eventual, neutral response was sarcastic in its brevity.

'It's evening here.'

Evening? But there were seven hours between them, so it was morning.

'Evening? Really? But seven hours…? Are you sure?'

Yes, Andrew, I'm sure. It's evening. And it's the middle of the night there, right?'

The tone was one she reserved for him, a modulated version of the patient, reasoning delivery she adopted with John, yet stripped of all warmth, an address which provoked in him the same childish selfishness of which he was accused. He'd got the time difference right but somehow, in his tiredness, confused the direction: America was seven hours behind, not ahead.

'I'm tired,' he said sulkily.

'Yes, well that makes two of us then,' said Karen. John was in the background banging something on the plastic table of his high chair.

'John, put that down now. Thank you.' There was a pause, then Karen came back on the line. 'So the paper went well?'

It was, Andrew felt, a cruelly casual enquiry. He'd told her he had no concerns about his talk, or at least he'd never expressed any worries – which amounted to the same thing, but surely she'd remembered his meeting with Emma? He was tempted to echo her indifference with a noncommittal response and it was with some coldness that he commenced, but, as his report unfolded, he found himself becoming more and more excited by an almost hallucinatory description of the evening's progress. He couldn't contain his admiration and affection for the members of the group: Emma, their leader; Claire, who at first had seemed so hostile, yet was merely intense; Marco and Charlie, the cultured Oxbridge tenors with a genuine interest in history; Craig – how he could tell a story; Allie and Ollie, great guys when it came down to it; Peter, the camp one; and Susan, the glamorous one who, though he said it himself, seemed to have a thing for him. He was right to have given them the transcription; it was safe in their hands. Karen was right: he should have done it sooner. But she would still need to keep it a secret from others until a number of other things were in place.

'Sorry, Andrew. I didn't hear all of that. John managed to tip his food on the floor and I had to clear it up. So you had a nice evening then?'

'How much did you hear?' he asked suspiciously.

'Oh, stuff about the lovely people you're been hanging out with. Enough to get a picture.'

He couldn't tell if Karen was annoyed and, if so, about what exactly. He could understand that she might resent him enjoying himself, but the socialising was, after all, part and parcel of the important business of commissioning the group. Two could play at that game.

'How are you two?' he asked, hoping that he matched her level of disinterest.

'We're fine. Aren't we, John?'

Exhaustion nudged Andrew, his arm holding the phone to his head suddenly heavy. The two of them were fine: they were together. He was on his own, and, as suddenly as he had been overcome with elation, now futility possessed him. He needed sleep.

'I probably won't ring again. Before I come home, I mean. The conference lasts a couple more days, but nothing significant is going to happen here. And I'll get a cab back from the airport.'

'Sure. Whatever,' said Karen.

'OK then.'

'OK.'

'Say bye-bye to John for me.'

'Daddy says bye-bye.'

He put the phone in its cradle and lay on the bed, still fully clothed. He turned onto his side and curled into a ball, drawing his hands together and touching them under his chin as if praying. The last thing he saw before he closed his eyes was the white bandage on his right hand, the blackened fingers of his left; his past and his future melted away and the glorious amnesia of a dreamless sleep overtook him.

✦ ✦ ✦

Leaving your spouse was a decision that should be made angrily out of slighted passion, but Karen was depressingly calm as she considered her actions and gently resigned to the consequences. If Andrew had told her that he'd just slept with the woman with whom he seemed suddenly to be smitten – Susan was her name, she thought – Karen might have doubted herself, but the idea of Andrew conducting an affair was faintly comical and she actually laughed. As her sister had cruelly pointed out in the early days of their relationship, Andrew's level of attraction to the opposite sex was minimal. And, if the opportunity of casual sex ever presented itself to her husband, Karen would be the first to know; he would seek her permission. Whatever interest he had in this singer, it came a long way second to his infatuation with the manuscript. *That* was his real mistress and Karen had indulged his obsession for too long.

He was consumed by the damn thing, all his thoughts and actions traceable back to that single sheet which she had still not even seen. In fact, now she thought about it, no one had seen it. Did it even exist, or was it a fictional Holy Grail, a product of a bitter sense of inferiority, a fantasy that fulfilled his every desire, both valuable historical artefact and the solution to his aspiration for advancement? She dismissed the thought. It was only her hesitation talking, not a genuine theory. This was the last, guilty bid to justify her hitherto meek tolerance of his behaviour. He was not delusional. Obsessed, perhaps. Or was he possessed? Was the manuscript cursed, a buried treasure upon which a spell had been cast? *Pull yourself together*, she told herself. It was the gravity of her decision that was making her seek fanciful last-minute explanations. Ascribing to the manuscript a mystical power made Andrew the victim of a demonic force, but Karen was not going to indulge a theory of medieval voodoo to excuse her husband's obvious selfishness. Nevertheless, it gave her an idea. Their marriage was, for the moment, over and the role of the manuscript in its demise needed to be illustrated.

After putting John to bed, she rang her mother and asked if she and John could come and stay for a week. John had a cold, she said. Some Florida sunshine would do him good and, with Andrew away at a conference, they might as well be there as here at home. Without asking why the plan was so last-minute, an omission which suggested that her mother suspected the real reason for the visit, she replied that she'd be delighted to see them both. Before going back upstairs to haul the cases and some summer clothes down from the loft, Karen went into the study where Andrew spent so much time. The code for the safe was 1497, Ockeghem's death year, and she retrieved the original copy of the manuscript, the exemplar from which all of his working editions had been made. The transcriptions had all suffered the same fate, shredded in the overused machine which she now unplugged and carried into the kitchen, the customary place where she and her husband left notes for each other.

The gesture, she reasoned, was entirely symbolic; she would never destroy the original, whatever its role in hers or others' lives, and she knew it still lay safely in Amiens. Besides which, he had a copy with him, so no real harm would be done. She did, though, want him to be brought up short, to realise the full force of her fury, to fear, just for a moment, that his behaviour had pushed her so close to insanity that she had committed a criminal act of historical vandalism.

She plugged in the machine, placed the paper in its waiting jaws, and switched it on. It angrily chewed the manuscript, pulling it into the tray beneath. When only two inches of the paper remained, she switched off the machine, leaving just the heading showing: *Miserere mei*. It might not be as savagely resonant as burning a book, but a message like that, she reasoned, could not be misunderstood, even by him.

✦ ✦ ✦

'Get that thing off the bed,' shouted Ollie. 'Don't you know that it's bad luck to put a hat on a bed?'

'What's the sentence? Seven years?'

'No, that's breaking mirrors.'

Emma picked up the hat and placed it on her head. The woman who stared back at her from the mirror had the brim elegantly tilted, hiding one of her eyes, her hand placed coquettishly on her hip.

'What do you think?' She turned to Ollie. 'Alluring?'

He looked up slowly from his magazine. 'Yeah. But don't leave it on the bed. Seriously. It's bad luck.'

She wasn't entirely sure why Ollie was still in her room. There were only five hours to go till the bus picked them up and he was obviously tired, and more than a little drunk. In similar circumstances, they would have gone to their separate rooms knowing that the following morning would soon be upon them, but he had followed her to her room suggesting she might need help restoring Andrew's sodden transcription. She was surprised, if only because he had shown such little interest in the manuscript in the brasserie, he and Allie sitting at the other end of the table, all but ignoring Andrew's presentation. And, walking back towards the hotel, as she had chatted excitedly about the discovery, Ollie had ignored the gentle interrogatory lift of her speech, her gentle invitation to discuss the good news. Her sentences had hung unanswered in mid-air, making her discourse sound self-absorbed, less a conversation than a monologue. Still, it was Ollie who'd rescued the manuscript from its fiery end. As Craig had made his way back to his seat, he'd banged the table just as Allie was reaching for the tray of flaming Sambucas. The glasses had toppled, spilling blue fire across Andrew's copy. Ollie had acted swiftly, slapping his hands down and smothering the flames. As he explained later, it was a trick they used to do as kids – covering their hands with lighter fuel, setting light to it, then extinguishing it with a loud clap. The only damage done was that the paper was now soaked in sticky, white liqueur, something which could be remedied by air-drying it overnight.

Now that it was laid out on the desk, Emma could study it more carefully. With Andrew scrutinising her earlier, she'd measured her reactions, keen to impress upon him the realities of promoting a concert. Now she was free to imagine that future – the premieres, the recording, perhaps even a television documentary?

That Andrew had entrusted Beyond Compère with this musical pleasure meant a further validation of her and the group, which was why Ollie's reaction was so strange. Her boyfriend was dismissive of academics, childishly so at times, but this was music. Perhaps, though, he was as self-conscious as she had been publicly, and now, in the privacy of her hotel room, he could share the excitement?

'It's amazing,' she said, studying the opening bars. 'It's one enormous crescendo at the beginning, but then you begin to get those moody exchanges between the parts.'

She looked towards Ollie but he said nothing. He was lying on the bed, flicking through the *Canal Plus* guide, a pose of studied concentration.

'You don't seem that interested in the motet,' she said. Again no response. 'I'm really excited by it and I thought you would be too.'

'Yeah, but it's late,' he said, 'and we shouldn't really get into it.'

It was tempting to take the comment at face value. Perhaps Ollie meant that it was too late to be talking about aesthetics or work: that, at the end of a long day and after a pleasant meal, they should both go to bed. But there was no sign of that. She feared that what he meant by 'getting into it' was an argument and she assumed she had done something wrong. Whatever it was, it seemed that it was also her responsibility to discern that grievance and, just as inevitably, to apologise.

'We should go to bed. We're both tired. And a little drunk.'

'Drunk,' he said, looking up quickly. 'I'm not drunk. Are you? Is that why you're so excited about this thing? I can hold my booze.'

It was a ridiculous claim, his anger a crude attempt to deflect her away from the dubious allegations that it was she who was drunk and that he was sober. She hadn't counted his drinks, but she knew he'd had at least a bottle of wine, and then there was the champagne and the Sambucas, plus the beer he'd had before the meal had even begun. But he was canny enough to have conceded that he'd drunk a lot; the issue was one of how one handled it, something which he claimed he was always able to do, and something which, in amorous, teasing moments, he reminded her she couldn't, a reference to the night when they had become lovers.

'I'm just trying to work out why you're acting like this,' she said. She hoped that Ollie would hear in her weary delivery the love and concern she felt for him, but she saw his body stiffen. He held the magazine page vertically between thumb and forefinger. She could tell that he had found in her delivery evidence of the condescension for which he'd been searching – he the subject of anthropological enquiry, Emma the cultured commentator.

He let go of the page and it flopped down. 'Acting like what?' He cocked his head to one side.

Emma looked at him, trying to keep her face as neutral as possible. 'Distant. Bored. I know you don't share my fascination with the history and all that, or sometimes with the music, but I wouldn't mind a little understanding of how I might feel?'

He laughed, a short exhalation of breath as if he'd just remembered a joke. 'Is what I said funny?' asked Emma.

'No,' said Ollie. 'Not in itself. It just sounded funny.'

'What, to say that I might want my lover to understand me?'

'Lover?' he said, looking up. 'God, I know we're in France, but that's a little melodramatic.'

'OK. Let me put it this way.' She was angry now, frustrated and hurt by the denial, the hostility, the attempt to divert the conversation towards a petty discussion of the status of their relationship and what they should call each other. The argument was going to happen, come what may. She just wanted to get it over with. 'I might want a little empathy from someone who I'm going out with. Is that prosaic enough for you?'

'Perfectly prosaic,' replied Ollie coldly, turning another page in a magazine that he had begun to read from the beginning again.

Emma lifted a page of the wet manuscript paper from the table. It stuck to the desk and she eased her fingers beneath it to release it. Behind her she heard Ollie turning another page of the magazine. She walked across the room to her empty suitcase; she had to pack before the morning, so she placed it on the floor and began looking around the room. Her toilet bag was in the bathroom, but she could pack her other possessions now and began to fold the clothes that hung in the wardrobe. The regular movements helped calm her.

'Look, I don't know what I've done, all right? Whatever it was, I'm sorry. But I'd like to pack and go to bed now. Is it Andrew Eiger? Is that the problem?'

'He's a tosser.'

'Yes, I know that's what you think. You've said it more than once. And I don't think he's the greatest thing on God's earth and I think it's pretty dumb – not to say stupidly ambitious – to make a discovery like this and not talk to colleagues about it, but we've got to work with him if we want to perform this piece.'

'Well,' said Ollie, closing the magazine and looking up at her, 'we don't have to work with him.'

Emma was confused. There was no way to perform the piece without Andrew Eiger's involvement. In effect, he now owned the Ockeghem manuscript. Suddenly she understood what Ollie was trying to say.

'You mean we shouldn't accept the project?'

'Exactly.'

'We have to,' she said, making no attempt to hide her surprise. 'It's the most exciting thing that's happened in fifteenth-century music in our lifetime. And I'm not going to miss that.'

'So you've made the decision, and that's it?'

'Yes. I have.'

'And it doesn't matter what anyone else thinks?'

Emma could sense the drift of his argument, a gentle insinuation of himself as representative of the group, isolating her as surely as if his hands were on her shoulders and he were pushing her away from the other singers.

'It's my group,' she said calmly.

'My group,' he sneered. 'You should hear yourself sometimes.'

'Well, it *is* my group, and it's mine to take in any direction I want. That's not to say I would drag people where they don't want to go. Yes, it matters what other people think, but most of them seemed as interested as I was. It was only you and Allie who sat on your own ignoring it.'

'And how will they feel when they're just a face in a crowd?' he asked. 'Have you ever conducted forty people?'

'Thirty-four, actually.'

'Have you ever conducted thirty-four people?'

'No. Have you ever sung this piece?'

'No. But I know I can.'

'So you think I can't conduct it? Is that what this is about?'

Her conducting had never been an issue before, and her selfless acknowledgement that the singers often didn't need someone to conduct them was now being turned against her as a criticism of inadequacy. She felt something expanding just below her ribcage like a faded sensation of an earlier injury. Her throat was tight and she tried to swallow, her mouth dry. She was determined not to cry. She knew that, if she did, it would in some way fulfil Ollie's purpose. There was something too casual about his position on the bed, as if he had planned his attack. And now, as she looked at him idly reclining, she realised that it was a bid for freedom from her. She tried one last time to argue her case, even whilst knowing that it was incidental.

'You know,' she began, 'it's not much I'm asking of you here. Why are we arguing? I don't think it's much to hope that you might show some enthusiasm. After all, I try to share your interests. It just seems to me sometimes that you just want to contradict everything I do.'

Ollie looked up, the faintest of smiles on his face. 'So we're incompatible?'

The dull ache had sunk down to her belly. Exhaustion was forcing her into the ground, pulling at her legs and her face which suddenly felt slack and unresponsive. She had her concert shoes in her hand. She knew that, whatever she said, the outcome would be the same.

'I don't think we're incompatible. Do you?' She was surprised by the calmness in her voice. 'Are you saying we're splitting up?'

Ollie stood up and for a moment she thought he was going to come over, put his arms around her and reassure her. That it had all been a silly test and she had passed with flying colours. That he respected her. That they would be together. That he loved her. But she knew it was the question he'd been waiting for her to ask.

He reached into his back pocket and pulled something out. It was the small coin Emma had bought for him. He rested it on his thumb and flipped it into the air. She lost track of it against the silvered mirror but traced the path by watching Ollie follow the spinning coin through the air, tumbling over itself then reaching its zenith before falling into his waiting palm. He turned his hand over and placed it on the back of his other and, without looking at it, showed it to her.

'Yes,' he said. He walked to the door and opened it. Even then she thought he might turn, wrinkle an eyebrow and smile. But he left and she stood on her own, her shoes dangling from her hand above the empty suitcase.

◆ ◆ ◆

In the end, it happened just as the old man had imagined it, a nightmare in which the books that he so carefully tended were raped by fire. The archivist had pointed out many times to the Cathedral authorities that the *Salle d'archives* was one of the last parts of the building to be re-wired. Electricity, he believed, was a twentieth-century luxury that was incompatible with old books, particularly ones as rare and valuable as those held in Amiens Cathedral. History had delivered its lesson in the thirteenth century and the Clerk of Works was foolish not to heed it; hadn't fires destroyed the records that described the very construction of the Cathedral?

The University of Columbia in New York had received a major grant to digitally map Amiens Cathedral and upload the data onto a website, a project that the archivist had strongly resisted. What was the point of contriving a reproduction of a living, sacred structure for the benefit of sedentary atheists in America when the true heart of Christian worship still beat in the original edifice? Knowing that the cathedral rose a hundred and forty-four Roman feet into the air, equivalent to the height of heaven of a hundred and forty-four cubits described in *Revelations*, meant nothing unless you stood inside the building itself, craning your neck, and were awed by the reality. And to learn that the width of the Nave was the same as that of the Ark in Genesis counted for little; people needed to *experience* such facts as an act of historical imagination to appreciate fully the enormity of Noah's labour. The faithful should come and stand within the largest interior space of any Gothic cathedral, not download data.

His protests were ignored and, when the young students arrived with their theodolites and laptops, their strange cameras and measuring devices, he'd left them to it. They were in the *Salle d'archives* each morning with their coffee and, at the end of each day, he would make a careful check, picking up cups as he went and placing them in the rubbish bins. He disconnected their laptops that cost the diocese heaven knows how much in electricity and replaced any books that they might casually have browsed and then abandoned.

He blamed himself for not being thorough enough. The fire department report noted that a laptop had been left plugged into the mains. It was never made clear whether the battery itself had set alight or its heat had caused the book on which it rested to ignite, but the image was all too clear in his head: on the spine of one of the chapter records a crystalline smear of old glue had melted and a bright, liquid bubble had formed like a bead of plasma on an open wound. And then, in an instant – 'in a flash, in the twinkling of an eye' as Paul had it in Corinthians – a lick of flame had leapt into the air.

He was grateful the fire crew arrived so quickly. In a matter of minutes the entire archive would have been destroyed. When he drew up the inventory, it soon became apparent that it was mainly the chapter records from the fourteenth and fifteenth centuries that had been lost and, as fate would have it, the American musicologist had spent some time copying sections from those just last year. He would not have a complete account, but it gave the old man some comfort to know that important information might yet be salvaged. He would write to the American straightaway and ask him to send details of his research.

✦ ✦ ✦

Emma stood for several minutes, looking blankly at the bedspread where Ollie had lain, unable to focus her eyes or her thoughts. She tried to make sense of what had happened, replaying the argument in her mind, trying to find a logic in the callous gesture. Had he planned it like this, deliberately rehearsed the final moment of confrontation? She didn't know that he was capable of such cynicism, her gift thrown back in her face, a warped reminder of the day they had become lovers. For a while she was unaware of what she was looking at – the folder he had left behind, the one which held his music. On it, in Allie's spidery handwriting, was a parodic, adolescent comment on their relationship: a heart with an arrow through it, his initials, OM, answered by hers, EM. For the first time she was struck by the coincidence of their final initials; her own initials would have remained the same if they'd married. And at that moment of banal comprehension, she began to cry.

Tears fell onto her belongings as she packed quickly, throwing things into, and sometimes at, her case. As she busied herself in the bathroom with an abbreviated version of her usual night-time ministrations, fractured moments of dialogue played in her head. Lying in bed, rigidly awake, still hearing the unwelcome tortured soundtrack, she knew that sleep would not come. She switched the light on and looked at the small white sleeping pill that lay by her bedside and tried to envisage the face of her congenial doctor, but Ollie's face, set, determined, swam into view. She picked up the tablet, swallowed it down with fizzy mineral water and lay back down. Half an hour later she was still awake. Switching the light on again, she rang reception to place an alarm call, then took another tablet. Ten more minutes passed. She was hot and had thought it was her despair and anger, but she realised the room was stifling. As she padded across the room to turn it down, she could feel a heaviness in her limbs, her muscles limp and rubbery, and when she lay down it was as if she were lying in a warm bath.

She dreamed of full-length curtains that smouldered and then puffed into flame. She tried to beat out the fire but the heat was too fierce. Suddenly all that remained were charred curtain rings swinging from a blackened rail and sun was streaming through a sooty window, a bleached landscape beyond. And then the sun became an electric light shining in her eyes. Claire was bending over her, shaking her by the shoulder and trying to wake her, the phone ringing uselessly. At first Emma couldn't grasp what was happening or where she was. She was aware only of how floppy her body felt and the sense that something dreadful had happened. Only when Claire started hurriedly putting her few remaining belongings in her case did Emma realise that she'd overslept and a brittle memory of the previous evening locked into place like a door swinging wide on its hinges. She threw cold water on her face, brushed her teeth and dressed quickly.

'Aren't you going to bring that?' asked Claire, looking towards the desk where the hat that Ollie had bought lay.

Emma hesitated for a moment. 'No.'

When she stepped onto the bus, she was greeted with a quiet 'morning' and reassurances that they hadn't been waiting long. Ollie was seated on the back row staring out of the window. Everyone knew.

It was only when they reached the outskirts of Paris that she remembered the Ockeghem manuscript.

'Did you put the manuscript in my luggage?' she asked Claire.

'Where was it?' asked Claire.

'On the desk.'

'Under the hat?'

Emma rang the hotel from her mobile phone and the desk clerk assured her he would get housekeeping to check the room. When she rang back half an hour later she was told that they had found a hat and could send it on to her. The papers? They had found no papers.

No matter: Andrew Eiger had a copy at home. It would be embarrassing to let him know she'd lost it within a few hours of him surrendering it to her care, but nothing more serious than that. The fifteenth century and Tours were a long way away and Emma had more important things on her mind.

◆ ◆ ◆

Andrew took a cab home from the airport. After three days of academic skirmishing, he'd been glad to climb aboard a mercifully empty plane, order a lunchtime drink and flick through the various handouts and notes he'd accrued. Everything he'd learned at the conference had added to his certainty of Ockeghem's authorship of the manuscript. Papers which investigated his musical style, small hitherto unknown biographical details including further information on Geoffroy Chiron who, it seemed, was a friend to Ockeghem as well as a colleague, and other circumstantial details left little doubt that Ockeghem's *Miserere mei* was Andrew's ticket to a starry future.

Karen and John were out when he arrived home, perhaps at the supermarket buying dinner. A note on the kitchen table would doubtless tell him when he could expect them. There was something different about the house and at first he put it down to the fact that he'd been away for a few days. It was undoubtedly tidier than usual, but it wasn't usually his presence that added to the domestic chaos but John's toys, which he managed to scatter everywhere, each room stamped with his presence with plastic bricks and toy cars. Karen had obviously been hard at work, preparing for Andrew's homecoming. He should have got her a present, but it was too late now.

The shredder stood on the table, a piece of paper protruding from it. He presumed that it had been broken, probably by John, and that Karen had placed it there in the hope that he could somehow draw on an innate male reserve and mend it. He'd buy another; he could afford it. He picked up the note.

'I'm at my mother's,' it began – reason enough for concern – but Andrew read on blithely, failing to recognise the drift of Karen's message. Only when he reached the part about there being 'many reasons' for her action did he begin to understand the stillness in the house. And when his eyes skated over the remaining words, desperately seeking purchase in any hint of their imminent return, he began to realise that the focus of his wife's resentment and criticism was here, destroyed in the shredder, the title still visible like a swimmer treading water, struggling to resist the forces that pulled it downward to the depths:

Miserere mei, Deus.

Have mercy on me, O God.

Only when the letter from the archivist in Amiens arrived four days later and he learned that the original manuscript had been destroyed would Andrew understand the true meaning of those words.

CHAPTER 20

The Memoirs of Geoffroy Chiron: Livre VII *ed. Francis Porter*

Martius 19, 1524

It will not be long now. I have reached the final chapter of the life of Johannes Ockeghem and my own end draws near. My son has assured me that he will arrive soon and I trust that the Lord will deliver him to me:

In te, Domine, speravi, non confundar in æternum: in iustitia tua libera me, et eripe me.

[In thee, O Lord, have I hoped, let me never be confounded: deliver me in thy justice.]

Jehan was not well. For someone of such great age (the second oldest man in Tours) he was a man of great physical fortitude, but his mental faculties were not strong. Already he had relinquished much of the daily control of the Treasury to me, though he would still spend at least two hours each day signing the necessary documents, attending meetings, and dictating letters at St Martin. And, of course, he still sang in the choir, his voice not as loud as it used to be, though just as steady and assured.

He had always possessed an extraordinary memory. All singers could, of course, recite the psalms and the chants by heart, and he had no need of missals or tonaries. Jehan, though, could also recite poetry, and had intimate knowledge of the writings of Aquinas, Aristotle, Guido and Boethius, and many of the ancients. His house was furnished with several books, yet he never consulted them; he could remember all the information contained therein. The signs of his decline, he admitted to me, were obvious to him well before they became apparent to others; he would forget people's names and where he had put things; he would walk into a room and forget why he had gone there. I suggested to him that this was common and that often I experienced exactly the same thing. He agreed that perhaps his examples described the natural infirmity of age, though he ventured that forgetting a whole day was perhaps not so common. He was also concerned that, although when asked he could still recite, say, Psalm 119 in its entirety, he could not necessarily remember that Psalm 119 was the longest psalm. And in order to begin the recitation of the psalm someone had to provide him with the first line. He knew that he had lost the ability to retrieve objects from his memorial store, though, once he located them, he knew them as if they were old friends.

We talked for a while on the subject of memory – of the writings on the subject by Aquinas and Tully, St Augustine and Albertus Magnus – and it was apparent to me that Jehan's intellect was as sound as it had ever been. Yet his fear was that without memory he would lack prudence: a cardinal virtue. I could not argue with that for, as Cicero tells us, memory, together with intellect and foresight, are essential to morality. Instead I tried to encourage his waning spirit by telling him of his fame and renown; whatever happened to his memory, his reputation would prevail.

'I don't want to be remembered,' he said. 'I just want to remember.'

Only one year later, not only could he not remember the importance of memory, he could not remember us having the conversation. It was as if his memory had been destroyed, wiped clean like the cartella *he now carried with him upon which he would write things in case he forgot.*

In choir his voice was still acceptable, though he could no longer remember the order of the service so he would look surprised when someone began singing the Pater Noster *or the* Alleluia. *I would angle myself towards him and mouth the opening words, but even if he began to sing the psalm (and he would never forget the words once he started), he would be unaware that it was being sung antiphonally, so when we were meant to remain silent, he would still be singing.*

The last service he sang at St Martin was a sad occasion. The Mass was in honour of St Martin himself and the polyphonic setting was Jehan's own: the Missa De plus en plus. *It is, of all of his masses, the most difficult for the basses, demanding great vocal agility across a wide compass. But that morning he sang it as if he was a young man once again. The low notes were firm and secure, the high notes clear and loud, and his face shone as the disciples' when they were filled with the Holy Spirit. My own voice was not so secure but, like the angels, Jehan guided me until, as we processed out of the church, it was my turn to lead him. When we reached the vestry, he turned to me.*

'That mass was a marvellous composition,' he said. 'Who wrote it?'

He was never aware that he had been retired from the choir; I simply stopped coming to his house to take him to St Martin. Instead Christine, his housekeeper, would bring him to mass where we could occasionally hear him singing in his stallum, *a distracting, strong voice to those who did not know him, but a joyful sound to those of us who did.*

I would still visit him and he would recognise me, though he never knew why I was there. I would entertain him by reading from any of the books on his shelf and, if I looked up, I could see him speaking the words quietly to himself, perfectly in time with my delivery. A tall man, he developed a stoop like a hunchback and his hair began to thin. Yet during those sorrowful times I still maintained my hope that the Miserere mei *might yet be performed. In fact, I felt that it might restore him to health, that hearing this music for the first time might somehow reach into his brain and his heart and repair his damaged memory. To that end I wrote to Compère and asked him to help, but there was nothing he could do. His service to Charles VIII left him far away in Italy and, when he visited us in the last year of Jehan's life, I had to warn him of the deterioration. When Compère entered Jehan looked at him as he would upon a stranger. Compère sat with Jehan a long time, talking about music in the hope that something would rouse the ailing man from his waking sleep, until he left the room in tears. And then, only then, did I accept that Johannes Ockeghem's* Miserere mei *would never be performed.*

And as that year passed, so Jehan's memory failed to the point where he was unable to clothe himself and eat; now Christine had to care for him through the day and the night. Finally his mind forgot how to make the heart beat and the lungs breathe and, on a cold February day in 1497, he was taken by angels to heaven, there to meet with Dufay, Binchois, Busnois, and the Valois Kings whom he had served so loyally.

The Miserere mei *was never performed and thus the true portrait of Jehan's talent was never painted. It would be some time before Jehan Molinet would write his lament on the death of Johannes Ockeghem, and even longer before Desprez would set it to music, but the great poet Guillaume Crétin was swift to honour him in his* Déploration, *the long poem in which he acknowledged my friendship with the great composer.*

Twenty-nine years have since passed and during that time I have frequently gazed upon the motet, possibly Jehan's greatest achievement. His will dictated that all his wealth and possessions be given to the church, and thus all that remains are his compositions and the example he set by the manner in which he lived his life. His music lives on, but for how long I do not know.

Domine labia mea aperies et os meum adnuntiabit laudem tuam. Non enim vis ut victimam feriam nec holocaustum tibi placet. [*O Lord, thou wilt open my lips: and my mouth shall declare thy praise. For if thou hadst desired sacrifice, I would indeed have given it: with burnt offerings thou wilt not be delighted.*]

I will leave this humble account here in Tours. I am sure that the only reader it will ever have is its writer. I have, though, enjoyed honouring my dear friend and it is clear that this memoir has no purpose beyond that. My will is in order and rests here with my papers of tenure. As legal documents they will be respected, but I cannot be sure of the fate of anything else. Thus I will send Jehan's Miserere mei *to my son in Amiens for safekeeping. These past thirty years, it has served as a constant reminder of true friendship. It is my most treasured possession and a part of history and it is my hope that it might yet have some purpose after my death. It was to remain a secret until its presentation before the singers and thus no one has seen it. As I look upon it now, I can only hope that somehow it will yet be heard. I fear, though, that new compositions are more attractive to younger men, and that the works of Johannes Ockeghem will not see service other than in Tours in the coming years.*

Any achievements I may count are in the field of my labour for the Church and for God, as a singer and a clerk. All life has a purpose, all creation a design, and all our days upon this earth are but as nought when we are faced with death. The ways of men are understood only by God, and it is into His hand that I commend my spirit.

Miserere mei, Deus, secundum misericordiam tuam, iuxta multitudinem miserationum tuarum dele iniquitates meas. Amen. [Have mercy on me, O God, according to thy great mercy. And according to the multitude of thy tender mercies blot out my iniquity. Amen.]

	April 12th 2015
Your access to Cambridge University Press EBooks is provided by: *University of Florida at Tallahassee*	***Andrew Eiger.*** You are now ***signed out***

CHAPTER 21

Tallahassee, Florida, April 12th 2015

Andrew hears Emma's arrival before he sees her. At first he thinks that the hesitant applause is the patter of thick raindrops on foliage, the herald of another intense tropical downpour, but plastic glasses and plates of oozing finger foods are guiltily abandoned, an incongruous reaction to something so familiar, and the sound focuses and crescendos to greet the international conductor and singers of Beyond Compère. They have entered through the wide double-doors of The Modesty Room, the usual venue for post-concert receptions like this, and they acknowledge the whispers and nods of those nervously trying to be noticed by the honoured guests.

Emma Mitchell and her singers look out of place here in the Floridian setting, their clothes redolently English against the backdrop of white wood, pastel shades and louver-windows. It's a long-standing joke on campus that the room had been appropriately named, that rather than commemorating Rose Modesty, the charity-inclined wife of the local property developer whose flamboyant appearance belied her husband's parsimony, it more accurately described an exercise of cut-rate educational charity in the form of knock-off surplus from golf-course condos. Andrew had initially shared the opinion when, some years previously, he himself had been welcomed to the Music Faculty in this very same space, and had been disappointed that the university did not echo the educational traditions of the Ivy League. Those older American institutions, modelled on Oxbridge colleges, favoured manicured lawns and fussily tended gardens, soft stone that spoke in quiet tones of tradition, an idiom suggestive of history, more appropriate décor than that of the mail-order design of The Modesty Room. But over the years, as climate and age have tempered his aspirations, Andrew has come to enjoy the appropriateness of the mise-en-scène to an air-conditioned lifestyle that protects them from the eighty-degree heat, and now he deems naive his youthful preference for dense curtaining, dark wood and oil paintings whose encrusted patina celebrate time itself.

Beneath the ceiling fans, the staff and students mingle with sponsors of the concert series – older men wearing sports-jacket-and-tie combos, their wives in long dresses and diamanté in deference to the seriousness of the concert they have just attended. Emma looks much as she did then, Andrew thinks, perhaps less animated, her hair worn long rather than the short bob he remembers, assured and seemingly confident amidst the enthusiastic assault of concertgoers. Tonight's performance has been impressively polished, not surprising given that the group has been together for the better part of twenty years, and, when the head of the department had disingenuously delivered, as if *ad lib,* a line he had prepared just for the occasion – that Beyond Compère really were beyond compare – Andrew had readily agreed without mentioning that he had seen the group once before, many years ago in France.

He isn't sure if Emma will recognise or even remember him, and knows that, if they speak, she is bound to ask him about the motet. Yet, even after all these years, he isn't entirely sure how he will respond. He wonders, not for the first time, if he might leave and thus spare them both the embarrassment. It is, after all, only his professional responsibilities that have forced him here in the first place; as a senior member of the music faculty it's politic to attend all the events in their short concert series whether or not the music is of interest, and, though he has left the fifteenth century behind, he understands that, because of his former life as an early-music specialist, his absence might wrongly be read as a snub. It had not been his idea to invite Beyond Compère to Tallahassee but the brainchild of one of his younger, more ambitious, tenure-tracked colleagues who, even now, is steering Emma proprietorially around the room, nodding to colleagues as he goes.

Andrew watches as one of his students approaches Emma. There's something gauche about the enquiry, an air of presumption that suggests the student believes himself interesting enough to warrant her attention, combined with a nervy impatience at her response. Whatever it is that Emma's saying, it's not enough. The student is a singer himself who has recently submitted an excellent essay to Andrew marred only slightly by his tendency to elevate personal opinion to the level of fact. The essay's faults notwithstanding, it had prompted Andrew to ask the student if he was considering graduate studies? Yes, came the confident reply, but in England, where he could sing. Doubtless the student's earnest conversation with Emma is designed to elicit advice and garner likely contacts, an ardent exercise in social networking disguised as flattering enquiry, an approach which Andrew can tell isn't going particularly well. Emma is clicking a fingernail against her empty plastic glass and her eyes flick impatiently over the post-concert buffet. Someone less intense than the student would pick up on the signs and graciously invite her not to be detained. Andrew smiles at the scene, remembering his own restless desire for advancement which must have been so obvious to Emma even then. Clearly the student isn't doing much to help his own cause, and Andrew knows he can both moderate the young man's edgy aspiration and testify to the student's more genuine abilities. Thus it's out of altruism, and to spare Emma from any more social awkwardness, that he finally decides to intervene and re-introduce himself.

He pauses at the punch bowl to pour fresh glasses, both a pretext for his interruption and to deny her a reason for abandoning the conversation too quickly. As he approaches her, he realises that the student has already left.

'Not very exciting, I'm afraid,' Andrew says, indicating the brittle raw vegetables, carved cubes of cheese, and lemon curd pastries. From the guilty look on Emma's face he can tell she has been thinking the same thing.

'And the punch has no alcohol in it and tastes weird,' he adds. 'Your glass was empty.'

He hands her the fresh glass and Emma smiles, a smaller, more relaxed and genuine expression than the exaggerated, formal stage smile she'd been wearing all evening.

'That's very kind of you. Thank you.'

'My pleasure. I'm sorry we can't offer you something more appropriate at the end of the concert – beer and wine – but it's like many campuses: dry, by order of the university charter. I expect you get that a lot in America. Cheers.'

'Cheers.'

Rather than the clear tink of glass there's a disappointing tap of plastic, an ironic confirmation of the lustreless hospitality. Neither acknowledges it at first but, when they taste the pink punch, a strange blend of unidentifiable tropical fruits overlaid with a sweet soapiness, they catch each other's eye and simultaneously register its synthetic awfulness. Emma tries to restrain her laugh, which only makes it worse, and she has to dribble the liquid back into the glass rather than choke. Fortunately Andrew has swallowed his but, in keeping with the secrecy of their shared disdain, he tries to stifle his amusement and snorts instead. They both look around them quickly to see if their adolescent ill grace has been noticed by anyone, then laugh again out of relief.

'It's worse than I thought,' says Andrew. 'I really shouldn't have brought you an extra glass of it. Sorry.'

'Don't worry. We haven't been introduced. I'm Emma Mitchell.' She holds out a slim hand.

'Andrew. Andrew Eiger.'

'Andrew ... Andrew Eiger!'

She remembers him and he's grateful that he won't have to spend the next five minutes trying unsuccessfully to revive faded memories.

'Of course. Andrew Eiger. I'm so sorry. I should have recognised you. 'Ninety-seven: Ockeghem year. The concert in St Gatien. The conference in Tours. How silly of me. You look well.'

'You too.'

He had thought so earlier, viewing her from across the room, but now he discerns the effects of age: the face slightly fuller, facial lines, perhaps a few extra pounds around the waist – but she still manifests a sense of contained energy possessed by some short people, the suggestion that a lot has been put into a small space. Andrew knows he hasn't changed much and that, in some ways, he looks younger. He's always had a boyish face, and over the years it's become leaner, his haircut no longer so obviously of his parents' generation. He still looks like his fifteen-year-old photo on the music faculty website and the only recent change is a smattering of grey hairs at the temples which, he is assured, makes him look distinguished.

'So…' Emma raises her eyebrows. 'What have you been up to? I didn't even know you'd moved to Florida. Should I thank you for organising the concert?'

'No, no. That was my colleague whom you were talking to earlier. I moved here about ten years ago, from Ohio, and got tenure about eight years ago, so they can't sack me. I'm fairly settled. Now.'

He feels no embarrassment as once he might have done. He has deliberately hinted that his personal life has had its complications, an invitation for Emma to enquire further if she chooses. He notes a slight softening around her eyes, which makes him wonder if her understanding derives from similar experience.

'How about you? Everything going well?'

'Oh, yes, things are going fine,' she says brightly, a programmed response. Then, slightly less upbeat, 'On the road again which is "The Touring Life" as we call it.'

He isn't clear to whom the 'we' refers. The group presumably, but is she referencing her partner? Andrew can't remember his name and, from his reading of the concert programme, he'd guessed that Emma's boyfriend is now her ex.

'You sound like you've had enough of touring?'

Emma looks up quickly and, to hide her sudden movement, takes a sip from her glass. 'God, that really is awful.' She puts the glass on the table and pushes it away. For a moment Andrew wonders if her outburst is directed at the drink or if she's affronted by his assumption of familiarity. Whatever happened all those years ago, they really only spent twelve hours together – almost a one-night stand, he thinks suddenly – not enough time to warrant such intimate interrogation only five minutes after meeting again.

'Sorry,' she continues, as if she might have read his mind. 'The touring life? It's tough: on to Memphis tomorrow, New York the next day. A lot of travel and, yes, it's tiring.'

Andrew nods sympathetically. There was no defence in her answer and revealing her immediate plans accords with his feeling that, despite the debacle of the Ockeghem motet, the past is nonetheless meaningful to them both.

He can understand the disappointments of travel. Even from the little of it that he observed, it wasn't a lifestyle he envied. Once he had seen it as glamorous, an index of success and recognition, but he's come to realise that soon it would become a wearing and repetitive necessity, a false promise like that of glossy advertisements.

Emma leans closer towards him, an intimacy that surprises him but which nevertheless feels appropriate. 'I'm actually giving it up. This is our last American tour. My singers know and my agent, but it's not official, so don't tell anyone.'

'Of course not. Gosh. Giving it up. To do what?'

'To direct. Theatre. Sondheim in the first instance. A production of *Follies*, which I love. Not just the music and the lyrics, but the themes – age, memory, missed opportunity, desire.'

It's one of the few musicals he knows, recommended by a student who insisted that it was the equal of opera, and he admires its subtle examination of nostalgia and the self-deceiving nature of reminiscence.

'Over the years I've consistently turned down some pretty good offers simply because I was enjoying what I was doing,' Emma is saying, 'but it feels like the right time now. The travel's not all it was – too much airport security, too much hanging around – and we're old hat now. And old. Time to stand aside and let the young ones have their chance. It's the way of things.'

When he had met the group back in 1997, it was they who had been the up-and-coming group, the ones to whom everyone, including him, wanted to hitch their wagon, and he senses that behind her resignation lies a regret with which she has still to come to terms.

'How about you?' she asks. 'Still working on Ockeghem? Have you written anything I might have missed?'

'Well, funnily enough, rather like you, I gave him up,' Andrew admits. 'Shortly after we met, in fact. I left behind fifteenth-century music and turned to other things.'

His decision had perhaps been precipitate, certainly an emotional reaction to the destruction of the motet and the failure of his marriage, but he has had no regrets in turning his back on late-medieval music. Even then he was aware that he was not by inclination an historian, and that his interest was in the abstract qualities of Ockeghem's music, something which was echoed much more clearly and deliberately in the twentieth century. The music of Paul Hindemith is his new area of specialisation, coupled with more radical and recent mathematical approaches to music analysis. As one colleague had commented in an arcane witticism that perfectly summed up the esotericism of his chosen pursuits, Andrew had 'swapped isorhythms for algorithms'. For an instant Andrew contemplates trying out the line on Emma, who undoubtedly would know isorhythm as a term from medieval music, but he chooses not to risk alienating her by referring to a mathematical procedure of which she is happily ignorant. He smiles at the way he's avoided the social awkwardness. The old Andrew would not have been so self-aware; he would have blundered onward trying to demonstrate just how funny the joke was.

'I wrote to you, back then, after the ... the mess up with the motet,' says Emma. 'I wrote to apologise. I didn't get a reply. Not that I deserved one.'

Andrew smiles. There it is. Finally it's out in the open.

'No. You deserved a reply and I'm sorry I didn't get back to you. I'm the one who should apologise. My life was a bit of a disaster then. My wife left me and, well, I had a lot on my mind, and the fate of the motet wasn't that important suddenly.'

'I'm sorry,' Emma says, 'about your wife, I mean. Did you patch things up?'

'No. I'm afraid not. But things are fine now. She lives a couple of hours away. It was one of the reasons I moved here, so I could see my son, John. Ten years ago, as I said. Things are fine now. He's off to MIT to study engineering. You're looking at a very proud father.'

'Congratulations! That's excellent. So he's not a musician then?'

'Oh, no. I wouldn't allow that.' Andrew laughs. 'He has to keep me in my dotage.'

Emma frowns, as if remembering something. 'Funny, that. I split up with my partner around about the same time as you did. Ollie. Do you remember him? The baritone in the group? We had a filthy argument and … I still don't know. But we split up. Perhaps it was the motet? Maybe it was cursed.'

There's a theatrical exaggeration to the final word at which they both laugh, but the theory that the manuscript might have been hexed was one Andrew had seriously entertained. Then, sitting at the kitchen table, the shreds of his past and the emptiness of his future laid out before him, he had believed that the book curse he had encountered in the library was not merely a medieval superstition and that he was being punished for his transgressions. Eventually he had rejected that idea and, in the intervening years, his slow appreciation of human nature and his own selfishness had led him to a more rational conclusion.

'I'm sorry about your relationship,' he says. 'I suppose that explains why he's not singing in the group anymore?'

'Yes. You can't work together after something like that. Most of the people you met are still here.' Emma scans the room and, as she identifies the various members, images of the meal that night, at the brasserie in Tours, stir in Andrew's mind. Yes, it was a brasserie – lots of drinking, and him showing them the motet and... He can't recall much of it now.

'...and Allie and Susan are now a couple – no one saw that coming, I can tell you – but that's the nature of the touring life. Allie was married with two kids, and then he and Susan became an item. Another broken marriage.'

'Have you not met anyone else? I mean, an attractive woman like yourself...?'

There's no coy modesty, no acknowledgement of flattery. Emma is still possessed of a directness that Andrew remembers more clearly than many of the events of the past:

'No. No time for relationships. It's difficult to find a partner when you're away as much as we are. And I suppose I'm a bit driven as well. There's still time though.' She picks up her drink and then puts it down again.

'I'd be happy to take you somewhere if you'd like a real drink,' Andrew says. 'This isn't a pass. Don't worry,' he adds quickly, seeing concern clouding Emma's eyes. 'I have a partner. But it's nice catching up like this. And that punch really is disgusting.'

He isn't really expecting Emma to take up his offer and he feels sorry for her. From her comment about there being time left to find a partner he has inferred that she wanted children and, in her mid-forties, it might be too late now. For all the mundanity, for all its predictability and regularity in which a failed marriage stands alone as a feature in an otherwise ordinary life, Emma's existence, with all its awards and attendant renown, has entailed a cost that Andrew has not had to pay.

'You're right,' she says, 'the punch really is dreadful. And I would like a drink and to carry on chatting, but it's Memphis tomorrow, and I really need my sleep these days. It's a two-flight day. You know what they say about the South: if you die and go to heaven, it's via Atlanta.'

It's a practised line from a travel guide, or perhaps one learned at a reception like this, something that Emma has probably rehearsed and delivered automatically on countless occasions to charm concert promoters. Andrew regrets the falsely formal note in the midst of their personal confessions, a signal of a distance between them. His offer of a drink had been a genuine one and he knows that she has misread his intentions. Furthermore his hasty announcement of his own relationship has sounded condescending, even smug.

'Of course, of course. I quite understand,' he says. 'You must be tired with all this travel. If you want me to create a diversion for you so you can make an exit, I'm happy to shout "fire".'

He delivers the last line with a straight face and for a split second Emma takes him seriously, before catching the deadpan tone. He sees her hesitate, something like shock registering, then he remembers that she knows nothing of the role of fire in the archives at Amiens and how it all ended.

She smiles. 'That's really kind of you, but I'm used to making a more graceful exit.'

At that moment Allie, the bass of the group, approaches, nods a neutral apology for interrupting and touches Emma on the shoulder.

'We're off,' he says in a deep voice. 'I've organised lifts if you want.'

'Thanks, Allie. I'll just be a couple of minutes.'

Allie nods again, walks back to one of the sopranos – Susan, Andrew assumes – and puts a hand familiarly in the small of her back.

'I didn't introduce you. You probably won't see him again,' says Emma, placing her plate on the table next to the untouched punch.

He waves away her apology. 'Of course. And I may not see you again, but I must say it's been great to catch up.'

He holds out his hand but Emma doesn't take it.

'Likewise. It's been great to see you again,' she says. 'I must just ask you, though…'

Andrew knew she couldn't leave till she had asked the question, and here it was. But the question isn't about the motet.

'The Chiron manuscript. What did you think of it?'

The Chiron manuscript – a memoir by Ockeghem's friend, Geoffroy Chiron – has recently been discovered, a document of immense historical importance. It was as if someone had stumbled across a diary belonging to Christopher Columbus's First Mate, or unearthed an account by one of Leonardo's pupils of his master's rivalry with Michelangelo. Andrew has heard of it, of course. It was impossible to avoid, making the front page of the *New York Times* and the cover of *Time*, the subject of a BBC/PBS mini-series, and *the* buzz-word within musicology, mentioned in Emma's programme notes that evening.

'I'm ashamed to say that I haven't actually read it,' he says quietly. 'I know, I know. I should. But…'

'You really did leave the fifteenth century behind, didn't you?'

'Well…'

'Do you know,' says Emma, 'I sort of regret reading it. I mean, I think it's got a lot to do with why I'm turning my back on it all.'

'Go on,' he says.

'It's Josquin. I used to love him. Well, love his music anyway. You can't fail to love his music, unlike some of the others who are a bit more difficult. *Everyone* loves Josquin. But when I read the Chiron manuscript and found out what a jerk he was, I began to dislike his music. I suppose it's a bit like Wagner; it's difficult to separate the man from his music, and I guess that's true for Josquin now.'

Andrew has heard the same argument and there's a noticeably cooler response to Josquin in his classes than there used to be. The idea that Josquin was a bad man and not quite the man people once thought has quickly coloured his musical reputation.

'I suppose you're right,' he says. 'I should read the Chiron memoirs.'

'You should. I mean, it's fascinating, and there's lots about Tours and Ockeghem. I can't *believe* you haven't read it.'

Andrew holds up his hands defensively. 'I know. Look, I promise I'll read it. I'll listen to *Nymphes des bois* – your recording, of course – and read it. I really will. Maybe even tonight when I get home. Online.'

'You must read it. You really *must*.'

'Well, you should get going, I suppose,' Andrew says, holding out his hand, and this time Emma takes it.

'It's been great meeting again.'

'The honour is all mine,' he replies with the same straight-faced irony. She grins, but then immediately her look flicks away, still preoccupied by the subject which he thought was closed.

'And, of course, the other reason you should read the Chiron manuscript is that it's all about the motet,' she muses. Hesitantly she outlines the conundrum, each step of logic offered to Andrew tentatively and in the hope of confirmation. 'I guess there must be other references to the motet, and that's why you knew it existed? And you took your cue from that and decided to "compose" the motet that you showed us?'

Andrew remains silent.

'I suppose what I'm saying is...' She pauses and draws breath, a silent beat in which the fear of causing offence can be heard. 'The motet never existed. Right? Your version was an inspired guess and therefore it was a fake?'

'Well,' says Andrew solemnly, abstrusely serious, with the same flat, ironic delivery, 'you must understand that it was a long time ago.'

He looks over the crowd of people – the chattering students in their shorts, freeloading on the miniature desserts; men tinkling their car-keys cueing their wives to depart; the singers with their suit-carriers smiling their way out of the room and into the humid, spring air.

'I'm not really sure I remember.'

✦ ✦ ✦

The table lamp in the hall is on, the house silent. Andrew pads across the living room and checks that there's no light showing beneath the bedroom door; Tanya must be asleep. On the breakfast bar her bags are laid out, the homework she has marked that evening while he was at the concert neatly stacked; her iPod and car keys sit to one side ready for the drive to school in the morning. Andrew wonders if he might watch a little television, perhaps wind down after the concert, just forget the Chiron manuscript entirely. Driving home, fulfilling his promise to Emma had seemed like a good idea – sitting down in front of the computer, reading about the fifteenth century again, music from that period that he hasn't listened to for years playing in the background and dragging him back to those dizzy days in Tours. The coincidence of the loss of the motet and the breakdown of his marriage with the decision to turn his back on early-music history was one that Karen had expressed doubts about at the time. She'd urged him to keep some continuity in his life, warned him that otherwise he might be storing up issues that would return to haunt him in later life. He'd been grateful, if only because she thereby demonstrated that she still cared for him, but over the past few years he's come to the view that her advice was tainted by guilt. She may not have blamed herself for the break-up of their marriage, but she didn't want to be responsible for an act of professional suicide. But the truth, something which occasionally he still finds difficult to believe, is that he's genuinely at ease with life now, even happy – yet he can't deny that seeing Emma has stirred up old feelings, a sense of what might have been.

He takes a beer from the fridge; it will wash away the taste of that awful punch. Beer. Didn't he drink with those two basses that night? Something strong? He wonders if they would approve of what he's drinking now, a pale ale that a friend introduced him to and which Tanya now regularly buys for him at the supermarket.

He wanders over to the bureau in the living room where he keeps his CDs. Most of them are at the office. The ones he keeps at home are oddities that have little bearing on work – presents people have bought for him, some of Tanya's CDs, early music. He has three of Beyond Compère's albums, the most recent bought in 1997: *Ockeghem Gems*. He hasn't even opened it; it's still in its cellophane. He peels away the clear wrapping, twists the lid of his beer and wanders into John's old room. It's warmer in here, the aircon switched off to save electricity, and he leaves the door open to allow a breath of artificial air to waft from the living room. As a toddler his son had been fascinated by flying, and these days it's the construction of airplanes which inspires him. On one wall of the bedroom there are technical drawings of wing structures and fuselages which reveal the skeletons beneath the glossy airline liveries, and on the other posters of bands, reminders of his son's taste in music, the sounds of which occasionally thump through the closed door. In a corner, piled into a plastic box, are circuit boards, routers and cables, an abandoned laptop and a collection of monitors, old and new. Computers are John's other passion and over the years he has dismantled and rebuilt several. The one on the table, an old style desktop with a chunky monitor, is designed for optimum web-browsing, impervious to viruses and adverts, pop-ups and unwanted cross-scripting, a model John bequeathed his father when he headed off to college. There is no concession to design and Andrew appreciates its functionality, that and its retro styling.

He jiggles the mouse and the screen flickers alive, bright in the darkened room: John in his school graduation outfit, an arm around his girlfriend, smiling in the sunshine. Andrew has the same picture in his office, a reminder to his students that he's a father himself and that he's there to offer help and guidance if they want it. John is wearing sunglasses, his mortarboard tilted backwards on his head, an image that suggests the carefree spirit Andrew would like his son to be. He wants him to enjoy his life, to enjoy college, but MIT is as competitive as it gets. Will John and his girlfriend still be together when they graduate, as they have pledged to be? Love at that age is fragile, experimental, and Andrew worries; most romances die when two people are apart for any time and Massachusetts is a long way away.

He opens the CD and consults the track listing, chooses the correct disk and places it in the CD tray. He flips through the booklet, past the sleeve notes, the texts and translations, stops at a picture of the group. Here they are as he knew them. The picture is in black-and-white, and grainy like his memories. Consulting the rubric, he scans the characters. On the far left the two basses are laughing at something, a counsel of two. The tenors, next to them, look slightly puzzled as if they've been excluded from the joke and, beyond them, Emma is positioned dead centre, looking serious. Andrew is inclined to read the downturned mouth as mournful but he knows he's reading too much into the image. Next to her, the two sopranos are almost comically different, one grumpy and sour, the other inviting the viewer to look at her, flirtatious, a look almost parodied by the tall alto next to her. Finally there's the one Andrew remembers trying to teach him the laws of cricket. The photo was taken in winter, the singers bundled up against the cold in dark coats and scarves, the sun low and bright in a cloudless sky, a gothic church the backdrop. To Andrew the fractured discourse of looks is significant, the writing on the wall. Perhaps Emma herself has studied this picture and discovered, in the physical separation of her and her boyfriend, a warning that should have been heeded.

The opening chord of *Nymphes des bois* swells slightly and the room is filled with the clean, bright sound of human voices. Immediately Andrew focuses on the tenor line: *Requiem.* He types his log-in details on the University page and scans his emails while the lament unfolds. A couple of late essay submissions, a round-robin about that evening's concert, notice of a conference in Albuquerque. Nothing from Emma. He's surprised that he thought there might be, but he had imagined her sitting in her dull hotel room and firing up her laptop, searching out his email address on the web and sending a quick greeting. She'd seemed weary, not just road-tired, but some deeper malaise, and he wonders if she's romantically involved. He and Tanya are settled now and, though she keeps her old condo, it's pretty clear to everyone that she lives here.

He picks up his beer. The bottle is wet, beads of perspiration forming in the warmth of the room. He'll have a look at the manuscript and, when he's finished this last drink, go to bed. He types 'Chiron manuscript' into the search page and up come 684,972 hits. Top of the list is the free online version, and beneath it an article on it by Francis Porter published in the *Journal of the American Musicological Society*. He hovers his mouse over it and a miniature version of the introduction appears. He skims the text. Porter describes the 'painful paradox' of the Chiron memoir; its extraordinary value as a first-hand account of the musical life of the fifteenth century brings with it the terrible shock of deprivation when one learns that Ockeghem composed a great thirty-four part motet. Might it yet, muses the writer, come to light? If only he knew, thinks Andrew.

He reads and re-reads Porter's final sentence: 'We're forced to admit that, whilst truth to history is a worthy aspiration, historical truth remains forever unattainable.' It's a telling phrase, thinks Andrew, haunting and human. Five years ago he met his erstwhile nemesis at a conference. Both of them were attending a publisher's drinks party and Porter had made a point of asking Andrew why he hadn't written anything about late-medieval music recently, the only person other than Emma to ask that question in eighteen years. As it had been this evening, Andrew's answer was vague, but Porter hadn't let it go, insisting that he liked a lot of Andrew's thesis and that, even now, he should consider publishing it. They'd ended up having dinner together and Porter had told Andrew that his wife had left him; this was a man in need of a friend and he seemed to have few. Andrew offered up his own experience in the hope that Frank, as he insisted on being called, might discover there a vision of his own future, careful to avoid reference to Tanya whom he'd then been dating for two months, lest it made his colleague feel any more wretched. He assured Frank that things could turn around very quickly and they'd ended up exchanging email addresses, even corresponding for a little while before the demands of their own lives had intervened. Only a month ago, Andrew had received an email from Frank telling him that he was engaged.

There are several news items about the Chiron Manuscript, the most recent prompted by rumours of a movie. Andrew wonders who will play Ockeghem. It would have to be someone old, he thinks, or would Hollywood airbrush out that significant detail and cast the biggest star? And what about Josquin? Who would play him? This is no good; he doesn't know the names of the movie stars as Tanya does, and he's only delaying the inevitable. One click of a mouse is all it takes. He picks up his beer. In the background he hears the music. It's the moment in the lament when the poet calls upon other composers to pay their tributes. Josquin sets it as a stepwise descent, halting, like the heavy tread of mourners carrying a coffin: 'Josquin, Perchon, Brumel, Compère'. Then the exhortation to cry heavy tears, the final refrain that tells them they have lost their good father. Andrew sits back slowly in his chair; there's no doubting the beauty of the music, profoundly simple and direct, as if Josquin has distilled grief into musical form. No wonder his students wanted to hear it again: no wonder the piece is so loved. Why did he ever dislike it? It wasn't through hatred for Josquin or the music, nor, he finally admits, because of love of Ockeghem or his reputation.

He's never sat like this and allowed the music to speak to him; he was always talking over it, scowling, explaining, telling his students what they should be feeling rather than letting them discover things for themselves.

Andrew starts to read:

Your access to Cambridge University Press EBooks is provided by: *University of Florida at Tallahassee*	April 12th 2015 You are *signed in* as: *Andrew Eiger*

<u>The Memoirs of Geoffroy Chiron: Prologue</u> *ed. Francis Porter*

Frevier 6 1524

Josquin was a prick. Everybody thought so...

THE END

FACT AND FICTION

Several readers of early drafts of the novel have asked where the reality ends and the fantasy begins. Briefly, Geoffroy Chiron and all the named composers in the (fictional) Chiron memoir are real historical figures, though we know very little about their personalities other than a few clues offered by unreliable anecdotes. The sections set in 1997 feature real events – the conference at Tours, for example – but are peopled by entirely fictional characters. Any likeness to real people is coincidental and certainly not intentional; *Time Will Tell* is a work of fiction and not a *roman à clef*.

All of the compositions mentioned in the book – with the obvious exception of Ockeghem's *Miserere* – are available on CD. For more, please go to www.facebook.com/timewilltellnovel.

ACKNOWLEDGEMENTS

Andrew Eiger is not my common experience of musicologists, who have always been immensely generous with their time and willing to share their research. Fellow performers have likewise inspired me on and offstage, and they will know better than anyone else how daunting it is to 'step out' from the chorus. I owe a great deal of thanks, then, to the following musicologists, performers and friends – not always distinct categories – who have read the manuscript in various forms, and offered invaluable criticism and encouragement: Alan Colhoun, Sally Dunkley, David Fallows, John Frankish, Pat Frankish, Susan Hitch, Stephen Jeffries, Daniel Leech-Wilkinson, Robert Macdonald, Dominic Moore, Cecilia Osmond, Helen Paterson, Dudley Phillips, Paolo Ramacciotti, Jane Rose, Anne Stone, and Jaap van Benthem. Thanks also to Christian Benoit and Mark Dobell for advice on French and Latin respectively. Special notes of thanks to Ruth Massey for her practised eye and generosity (every writer should have a Ruth Massey); to Charlie for her advice on marketing; and to John for his brilliant designs and unwavering support. I am also very grateful to Kamaljit Sood and everyone at Thames River Press for their hard work.

And last, but not least, I dedicate this book to the person who first heard this tale, Tessa Bonner, without whom...

CPSIA information can be obtained at www.ICGtesting.com
Printed in the USA
BVOW072059120912

299891BV00001B/13/P